SHIPS OF WAR
MURKY WATERS
BOOK ONE

BRADLEY JOHN

SHIPS OF WAR — MURKY WATERS

COPYRIGHT © BRADLEY JOHN TATNELL 2018 – 2024
PUBLISHED BY HISTORIUM PRESS 2024

THE FIRST BOOK IN THE SHIPS OF WAR SERIES.

THE AUTHOR BRADLEY JOHN TATNELL* (BRADLEY JOHN) ASSERTS THE MORAL RIGHT TO BE IDENTIFIED AS THE AUTHOR OF THIS WORK.

ALL RIGHTS RESERVED. NO PART OF THIS PUBLICATION MAY BE REPRODUCED, STORED IN A RETRIEVAL SYSTEM, OR TRANSMITTED IN ANY FORM OR BY ANY MEANS, ELECTRONIC, MECHANICAL, PHOTOCOPYING, RECORDING OR OTHERWISE, WITHOUT THE PRIOR PERMISSION OF THE AUTHOR.

HARDCOVER ISBN 978-1-962465-55-7
PAPERBACK ISBN 978-1-962465-56-4
EBOOK ISBN 978-1-962465-57-1

HISTORIUM PRESS

This book is dedicated to

ISOBEL CLARE

(My Dear Mother)

"Heavily spiced with action... an unbridled and no-holds-barred adventure story that is very much in the illustrious rip-roaring style of the 'Hornblower' books of the great C.S. Forester..."

THE HISTORICAL FICTION COMPANY

CONTENTS

INTRODUCTION

    GLOSSARY   8

    PROLOGUE   21

BOOK ONE – MURKY WATERS

I	Portsmouth — 1791	29
II	The Admiralty	34
III	The Board Room	40
IV	Inn All Haste	57
V	Agamemnon	64
VI	Crispin Inn	73
VII	Chatham Dockyard	83
VIII	Four Bell	94
IX	The Lion	113
X	On the Tide	130
XI	Ortac	153
XII	Ortac Games	169
XIII	Twenty!	181
XIV	Joys of Port	201

XV	Pass the Cheese	217
XVI	Cheese and a Dirty Rat	225
XVII	Court Martial	256
XVIII	Reckoning	270
XIX	Pompee	289
XX	Brading Harbour	310
XXI	La Vénus	341
XXII	La Solitaire	364
XXIII	Vive la France	401
XXIV	To Our Utmost	424
	Epilogue: Of the Chevalier...	450
	About the Author	460
	Acknowledgements	462

1 Revolutionary France 1789–94

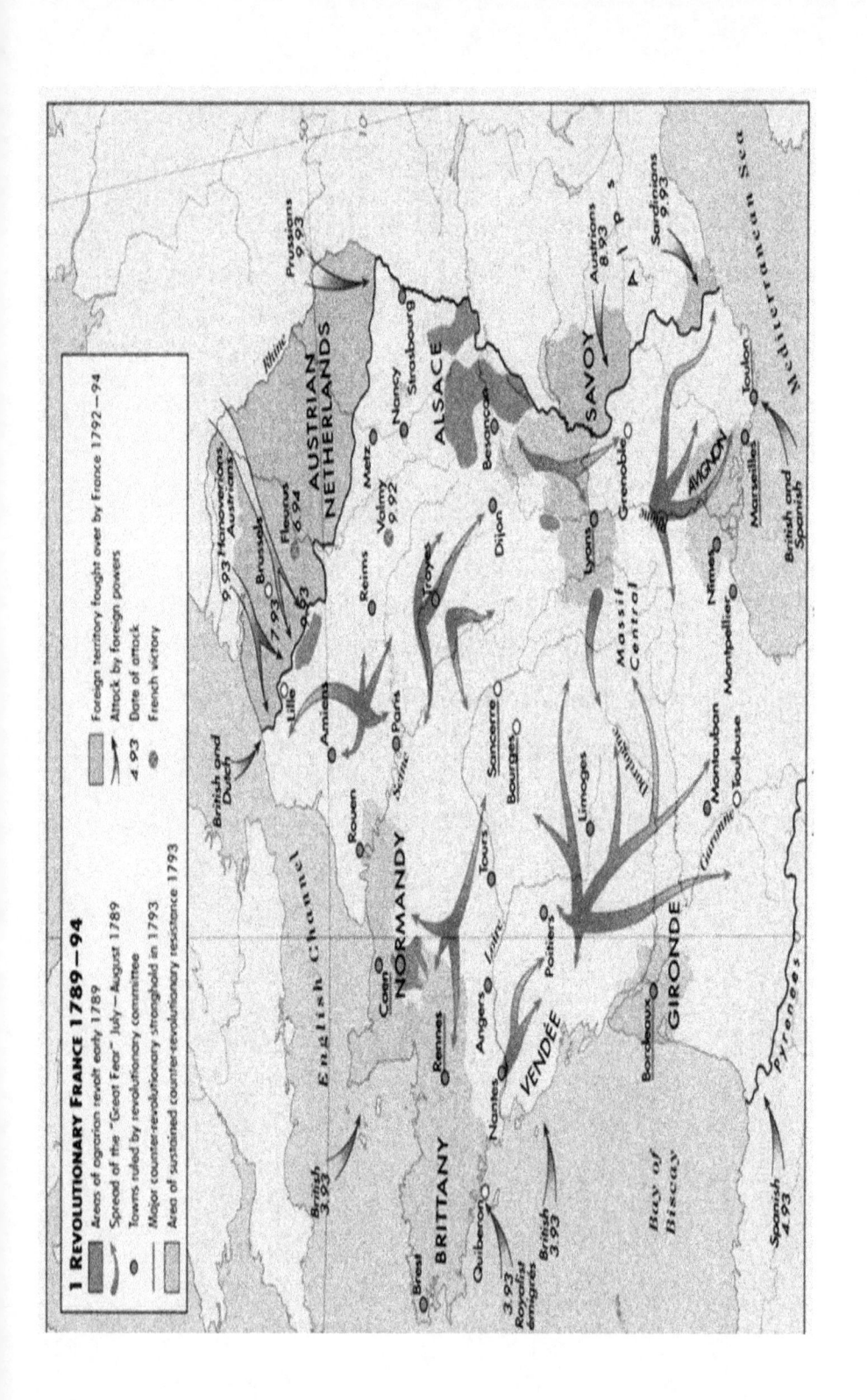

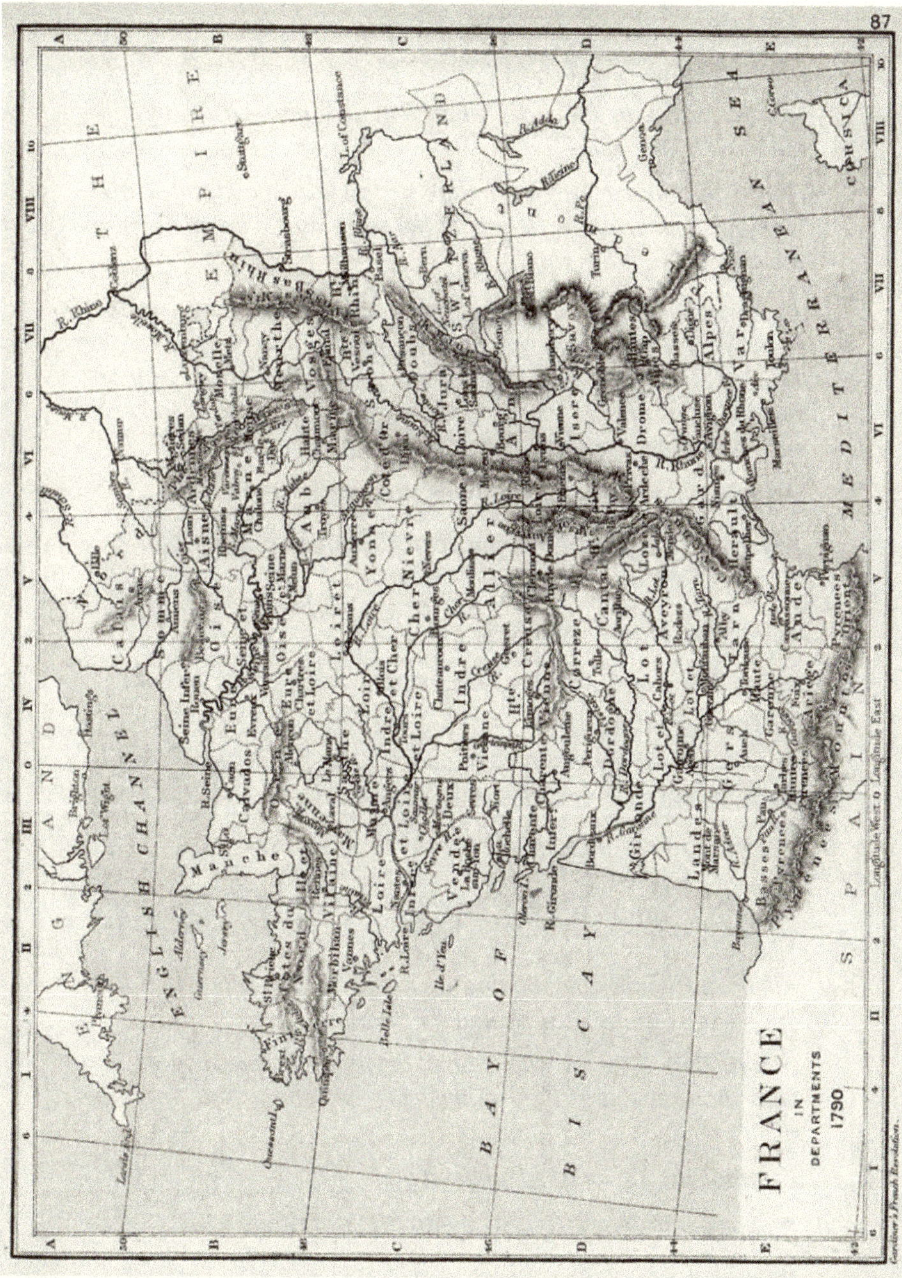
FRANCE
IN
DEPARTMENTS
1790

GLOSSARY

Aback: *refers to the sails when they are pressed aft against the mast by the wind.*

Abaft: *the hinder part of a ship, or towards the stern. It also signifies farther aft or nearer to the stern. For example behind the ship is abaft the ship.*

Abel-wackets: *a jocular punishment among seamen whereby a blow is rendered on the palm of the hand with a twisted handkerchief, instead of a palmer or ferula (a piece of iron at the end of a cane). Seamen sometimes play cards for wackets, the loser suffering a stroke for each lost game.*

Abeam: *on a line at right angles to a ship's length.*

Abreast: *off or directly opposite, for example two parallel ships with their heads equally advanced.*

Acting Rabbit: *a baked meat pie.*

Adam Tiler: *a pickpocket's accomplice who scours off with the stolen goods.*

Admiralty: *the government department in command of the Royal Navy.*

Aft: *back of the ship, the stern.*

Aground: *when the ship's bottom, or any part of it, rests in the ground.*

All in the wind: *the shaking or quivering of sails when they are parallel to the direction of the wind.*

Ark ruffian: *Rogues who robbed or murdered passengers in a boat, boarding and then plundering, stripping and throwing them overboard.*

Awning: *the top crust of a baked pie.*

Badgers: *a crew of desperate villains.*

Bark at the moon: *to agitate uselessly.*

Barky: *a barque, barc, or bark, a class of sailing vessel with three or more masts with the mainmasts rigged square.*

Barrel fever: *to kill oneself or cause ill health by excessive drinking.*

Beam: *the widest point of the ship, the midpoint of its length.*

Beam ends: *the sides of a ship. A ship "on her beam ends" means she is over on her side about to capsize, perhaps listing 45 degrees or more.*

Beam reached: *see "Reaching".*

Beat to Quarters: *drum is beaten to signal prepare for battle.*

Beating: *sailing into the wind in a zig zag course (also known as "hauling").*

Bleeding cully: *someone who parts easily with their money.*

Board and board: *ships come so as to touch each other, to lie side by side.*

Bob Cull: *an honest good natured quiet man.*

Bold shore: *a steep coast permitting the close approach of a ship.*

Bonfire Night: *an annual commemoration known as Gunpowder Treason Day or Guy Fawkes Night following the plot to assassinate King James I on 5 November 1605.*

Bowsprit: *large piece of timber, standing out from the bow of a ship, to which the forestays are fastened.*

Box the compass: *recite the 32 points on the mariner's compass, backwards or forwards and be able to answer any and all questions respecting its divisions.*

Brail up the sails: *Brails are small ropes used to haul in or haul up the leeches or bottoms for furling. The command is also "Hale up the brails". The operation of thus drawing them together is called brailing them up in order to gather the sail close to the mast, spill wind and thereby slow the ship.*

Brig: *a sailing vessel with two square-rigged masts.*

Bring-to: *to check the course of a ship by arranging the sails in such a manner so that they counteract each other and prevent her from either retreating or advancing.*

Bringing by the lee: *the ship inclines or turns suddenly to leeward, so as to lay her sails aback. To broach-to is the opposite where the ship turns to windward.*

Bristol Milk: *a Spanish wine called sherry.*

Bread basket: *stomach.*

Broach-to: *the ship inclines or turns suddenly to windward against the helm, thus her side is facing the wind (which endangers the masts). To the contrary, if she turns the other way so as to lay her sails aback on the side which is the lee side, it is "Bringing by the Lee".*

Broad: *wide in appearance. As ship "broad off the beam" is sailing with her side in view. Opposite is "fine", where either the stern or bow are only in view.*

Broadside: *a discharge of all the gun on one side of a ship, all decks.*

Broad reached: *see "Reaching".*

Bruiser: *a boxer, usually skilled.*

Bubble and Squeak: *Beef and cabbage fried together, which will bubble up and squeak whilst over the fire.*

Bulker: *a pickpocket's accomplice who jostles the person they intend to rob.*

Bulkhead: *the sides or wall of a ship below the decks.*

Bulwark: *the sides of a ship extended above the decks.*

By: *into the wind.*

By and large: *a ship that handles well (by) into the wind and (large) with the wind.*

Caffan: *cheese.*

Captain: *commander of a ship, usually with rank of master, lieutenant, or captain.*

Chief cock of the walk: *leading man, the best boxer in a village or district.*

Clagger: *the top crust of a baked pie.*

Clakker: *the top crust of a baked pie.*

Clear the anchor: *to ready it for dropping, to get the cables* *off the flukes, or stock and to disencumber it of ropes.*

Close hauled: *beating, sailing into the wind, close to the wind direction as possible.*

Close reached: *see "Reaching".*

Cock-and-bull: *a tale which is fabricated or untrue.*

Cool tankard: *wine and water with lemon, sugar and burrage.*

Coppering: *the practice of protecting the under-water hull of a ship from the corrosive effects of salt water and biofouling through the use of copper affixed to the outside of the hull.*

Crafty clinker: *a crafty fellow.*

Cramp rings: *Bolts, shackles or fetters.*

Crook my elbow and wish it never come straight: *an expression to add great weight and efficacy to an oath.*

Crop: *to be knocked down (a crop). Cropped is to be hanged.*

Crying cockles: *to be hanged, refers to the noise made whilst strangling.*

Cuddy: *nickname for the captain's cabin.*

Dancing at Beilby's ball: *to be hanged.*

Darts: *a straight-armed blow in boxing.*

Dead lights: *a shutter to cover the windows in the stern of a ship, to block out the weather.*

Dicked in the Nob: *Silly, crazed.*

Dickey box: *the front of a carriage where the driver sits, on a box or a perch, usually elevated and small. This is also the term used for a seat at the back for servants. The small platform at the rear is a footboard used by a footman. The seat behind the body is a rumble.*

Dished: *to be ruined.*

Diving busman: *a pickpocket.*

Dogvane: *a small weather vane mounted within sight of the helmsman used to indicate the wind direction. Sometimes improvised with a scrap of cloth or other light material. Also known as a "Tell-Tale" which is moreover a light piece of string, yarn, or rope attached to a stay or a shroud.*

Dogwatch: *a period of duty, or watch, upon the ship. This watch is two hours long and the first dogwatch commences at 16:00 or 4 pm, the second dogwatch commencing at 18:00 or 6 pm.*

Doodle: *a silly fellow.*

Doubling upon: *the act of cannonading from both sides of the ship or enclosing any part of a hostile fleet between two fires.*

Dub the gigger: *open the door.*

Dustman: *dead.*

Ebb: *the outgoing tidal current, flowing away from shore. Opposite is "Flood".*

Eighteens: *a cannon capable of firing an eighteen pound shot or ball.*

Empty the bag: *to be forthright and tell all.*

Fall off: *denotes the motion of the ship's head from the direction of the wind. It is used in opposition to "come to" (denotes the motion of a ship's head to the direction of the wind).*

Fall not off: *the command to steer in order to keep the ship near the wind.*

Fair: *prison.*

Fence: *to pawn or sell stolen goods.*

Figging law: *art of picking pockets.*

File: *a pick pocket. Also known as File Cloy or Bungnipper. To file is to cheat or rob. The File keeps company with an Adam Tiler and a Bulker.*

Fine: *narrow in appearance. As ship "fine off the beam" is sailing with either her bow or stern in view. Opposite is "broad", where the sides are in view.*

Fire Ship: *a woman infected with the venereal disease.*

Fish eyes: *a version of Tapioca Pudding.*

Flash Panney: *a brothel.*

Flimsies: *a certificate from a commanding officer as to conduct and performance. Usually it is provided on a thin or flimsy piece of paper.*

Flip: a small beer, brandy and sugar.

Flood: the incoming tidal current, flowing towards shore. Opposite is "ebb".

Flotsam: floating cargo or wreckage.

Fore: front of the ship, the stem or head.

Forecastle: the upper deck in the fore part of the ship, pronounced "fohk-sil".

Fork: a pickpocket.

Founder: to sink at sea by filling with water.

Frenchified: infected with the venereal disease. See also Fire Ship.

Full and before: sailing large or with the wind, ensuring the sails are kept full.

Full and by: sailing by or into the wind, although not as close hauled as might be possible, which ensures the sails are kept full.

Gage (of a ship): the ship's depth of water, or what water a ship draws.

Gage (weather): a ship to windward (or upwind) of another is said to have the weather gage, meaning she has the wind in assistance to be able to approach.

Gangway: place to enter the ship.

Give a bottle a black eye: to empty it, drink it all.

Goosewinged: sailing directly with the wind, the sails set on both sides of the vessel, the mainsail on one side and the jib on the other, thus maximising the canvas.

Gone to the diet of worms: dead and buried.

Great cabin: the captain's berth or cabin.

Gruel: a dish composed of boiled oatmeal, with a little butter.

Gunwale: top edge of the hull where it meets the deck. The bulwark extends above. Also known as gunnel.

Gullgroper: usurers who lend money to the gamesters.

Half seas over: almost drunk or inebriated.

Haul the wind: *to direct the ship's course nearer to the point from which the wind blows.*

Heave-to: *to slow the ship from going forward. Hove-to is to have stopped.*

Heave out: *to heave out the staysails is to unfurl or loosen a staysail. Distinguishable from the command to "loose the topsails".*

Helm: *the wheel and the tiller, used in steerage of the ship.*

Helm-a-lee: *the command given to turn the ship bringing it closer to the wind. This will slow the ship so it may tack.*

Hold: *a ship's compartment for carrying cargo.*

Hornswoggling: *to deceive.*

Horse Guards Parade: *a large parade ground off Whitehall in central London.*

Hoy: *a particular kind of vessel. For example a powder hoy, carries powder.*

Hull-down: *a vessel with only its upper part visible over the horizon.*

Hulled between wind and water: *cannonaded and shot under the waterline.*

In irons: *forward momentum is lost while heading into the wind, unable to steer.*

Interest: *is to have support, usually from someone of high society or a position of influence.*

Jack: *a sailor. Also refers to the union flag.*

Jack Adams: *a fool.*

Jack at a pinch: *a poor hackney parson.*

Jack in the box: *a sharper, one who lives by their wits, or a cheat.*

Japanned: *to be ordained and enter into holy orders, a clergyman who adorns the black cloth, similar to the black colour of the japan ware.*

Jingle Brains: *a wild, thoughtless, rattling fellow.*

King's College: *the King's Bench prison.*

Kiss the gunner's daughter: *to be tied to a cannon and flogged on the buttocks.*

Laid up in ordinary: *a ship out of service for repair or maintenance or a ship no longer required for active service, awaiting a recall.*

Landsman's wind: *running directly before or with the breeze, a dead (straight) run.*

Lap robe: *the blanket used in a carriage to cover a passenger's legs.*

Larboard: *left side of a ship, upon looking forward towards the head. Known as port.*

Large: *to be sailing large is to sail with or before the wind, so that wind is on the quarter or abaft the beam.*

Lee shore: *a shore upon which the wind blows towards.*

Leeward: *the side down wind or away from the wind. Opposite is windward.*

Letter of Marque: *a letter from a state or power authorising action by a privateer.*

Lieutenant: *the British Royal Navy traditionally pronounced the word as "luhtenant," whilst the British Army pronounced it as "leftenant" and the American pronunciation is "lootenant".*

Listing: *a ship's side that is inclined or heeling towards the water, usually due to the addition of weight within, such as taking on water.*

Live lumber: *what sailors call soldiers or passengers on board a ship.*

Log (to heave): *throw the log overboard, to calculate the speed of the ship's way.*

Long Tom: *a paint brush lashed to the end of a long pole, used for painting places which are difficult to access.*

Louisette: *a machine for execution, or louison, named after its inventor, French surgeon and physiologist Antoine Louis, but later it became known as la guillotine.*

Luff: *pointing the ship closer to the wind so as to lose wind* from the sails which in turn eases pressure on the canvas. To "luff up and touch her" is to bring the ship so close to the wind that the sails flap and shake. The ship will slow.

Mad Tom: *a rogue that counterfeits madness.*

Master: *an officer, primarily in charge of the navigation.*

Master's mate: *senior petty officer who assists the master.*

Masthead: *highest part of a ship's mast.*

Merry Andrews: *or Mister Merryman being the jack pudding, jester or zany of a mountebank, usually dressed in a party-coloured coat, a person who clowns publicly, a buffoon.*

Merry-begotten child: *a bastard, born out of wedlock.*

Milch cow: *someone easily tricked out of their property.*

Milling Cove: *a boxer.*

Monkey: *a small cannon. Boys who fetch powder from the magazine are called "Powder Monkeys".*

Muzzler: *a violent blow on the mouth.*

Neap tide: *when the moon is at the first or third quarter each month, the sun and moon are at right angles. The gravitational forces cancel each other out resulting in lower high tides and higher low tides.*

Nigmenog: *a very silly fellow.*

Off the hooks: *unhinged to the point of acting silly.*

Offing: *distant to seaward from the land, towards the horizon.*

Panam: *bread.*

Peeper: *a spying glass.*

Peg Trantum's: *to go there is to die.*

Penny-wise and pound-foolish: *thrifty with small amounts of money, but not with large.*

Pluck: *Courage.*

Pooping: *in a tempest before the wind, the shock of a high heavy sea upon the stern or quarter of a ship, resulting in scudding.*

Pope's Nose: *the rump of a turkey.*

Ports: *openings or windows on the outside of a ship. A square-port is square window/opening.*

Post Master General: *nickname for the Prime Minister.*

Powder Monkeys: *boys who fetch powder from the magazine.*

Press: *the act of forcing men into service on naval ships, usually against their will.*

Quarter lights: *the side windows of an enclosed carriage.*

Quartermaster: *the helmsman.*

Rake: *to cannonade a ship through the stern (aft) or through the head (fore), so that the balls scour the entire length of the decks.*

Reaching: *there are six points of sail referring to the course of a ship in relation to the direction of the wind. Reaching means the ship is sailing across the wind. "Close Reaching" is about 60° to 80° (slightly into the wind), "Beam Reaching" is 90° (perpendicular to the wind, a "soldier's wind") and "Broad Reaching" is about 120° to 160° (with the wind).*

Read in: *the customary practice of the newly appointed commander reading his commission, or orders, to the crew.*

Report: *a sudden loud noise, an explosion or gunfire.*

Rum bite: *a clever cheat.*

Rum-cully: *a rich fool.*

Sailing, by: *into the wind.*

Sailing, large: *with or before the wind.*

Scullery: *a small kitchen.*

Sea daddy: *a senior in charge of other seamen to guide as well as instruct them.*

Ship of the line: *a ship which takes part in the naval tactic known as the line of battle.*

Slack: *the entire period of a tidal current's low speed just prior to and just after its turning of direction. Not to be confused with "Stand".*

Sloop: *a sailing boat with a single mast and a fore-and-aft rig.*

Sly boots: *a cunning fellow under the mask of simplicity.*

Soldier's wind: *sailing across the wind, beam reaching (perpendicular to the wind).*

Son of Prattlement: *a lawyer.*

Souse: *not a souse, as such, not a penny.*

Sovereign's parade: *the quarterdeck.*

Spoon: *to take in the sails and drift with momentum.*

Spring her luff: *a ship is said to spring her luff when she yields to the effort of the helm, by sailing nearer to the wind than before (also see "luff"), which spills wind from the sail.*

Square-port: *a square window or opening is known in the Royal Navy as a port or square-port.*

Stands: *the direction a ship is heading. A ship "standing toward us" approaches.*

Stand: *when the vertical movement of the water ceases at both high or low tide.*

Stem to stern: *from front to back, from fore to aft.*

Stem: *the fore-part or front of the ship.*

Stepney: *decoction of raisins and lemons in conduit water sweetened with sugar and bottled.*

Stern: *the after-part or back of the ship.*

Stern light: *the glass at the back of the ship.*

Strike: *used emphatically to denote the lowering of colours in token of surrender.*

Suds: *in trouble or difficulty.*

Sugar Sops: *toasted bread soaked in ale sweetened with sugar and grated nutmeg. Usually taken with cheese.*

Tom: *a cannon.*

Top heavy: *drunk.*

Topping it: *an act of pretence.*

Touched (in the head): *insane, mad or crazy.*

Tormenter of Catgut: *a fiddler. Also known as a Gut Scraper.*

Toss pot: *a drunkard.*

Tradesmen: *thieves.*

Turnkey: *a jailor also known as a gigger dubber.*

Twaddle: *perplexing or confusing (speech). Also a "bore", a tedious, troublesome person who bores the ears of his hearers with uninteresting tales.*

Twenty-fours: *a cannon capable of firing a twenty-four pound shot or ball.*

Water bewitched: *very weak punch or beer.*

Wear: *to turn (or tack) the ship when going with the wind. The opposite is "going about" or tacking into the wind.*

Weather deck: *an upper deck with no overhead protection, above the water line.*

Weigh anchor: *to heave up the anchor from the bottom.*

White Ribbin: *gin, an alcoholic drink.*

Whitehall: *a road in Central London hosting the location of many ministries. Recognised as the centre of the Government. The word is also used as a figure of speech for the British civil service and government.*

Wild rogues: *rogues trained to steal, from birth.*

Wind's eye: *point from which the wind blows.*

Windward: *towards the direction from which the wind blows. Opposite is leeward.*

Yard or Yardarm: *the timbers upon which the sails are spread.*

Yellow Jack: *the tropical disease, a virus, known as yellow fever.*

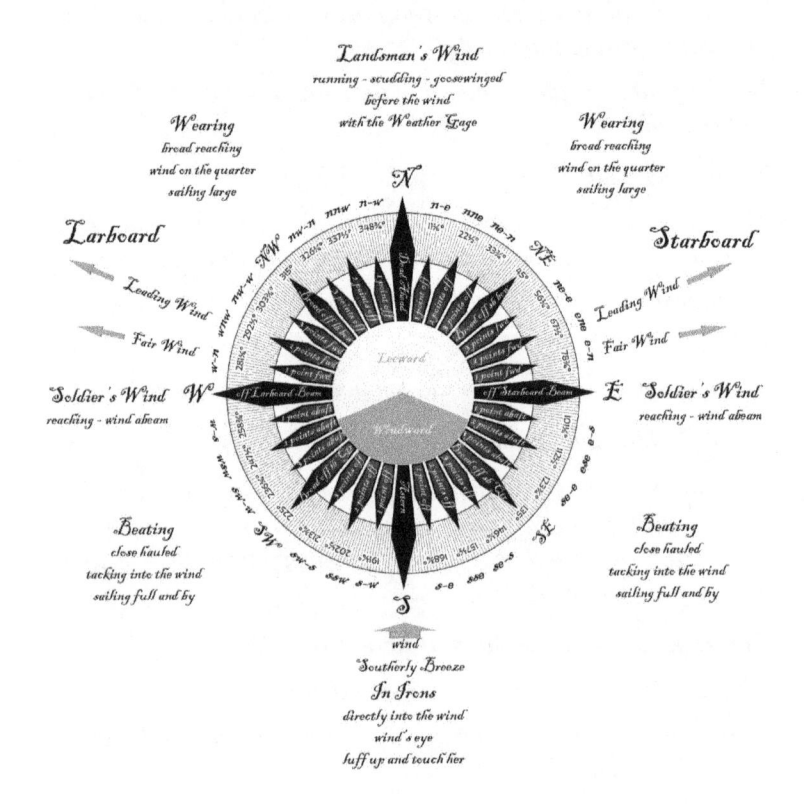

POINTS OF SAIL – COMPASS ROSE

Prologue
Of Murky Waters...

Skulking about the thickened haze, there lurked the sum of every jack's most mortal fear. Already whisperings had begun. Nigh upon the rolling banks, the ship of war leisurely made her way, carefully and quietly, the captain long before having ordered the master to fall off. It was expected. The brig was surrounded. Helplessly the crew grieved as the bow became as one with the fog. Entangled about the rigging, collecting upon the decks, ever clawing, the wispy clutches of mist haphazardly descended. Bit by bit was the ship consumed. The captain swore under his breath. Yet even for an old salt, there was naught he could muster, except but to stand tall and keep steady their way. He could not recall a thicker pitch of soup, or so he calmly recounted when pressed by the first lieutenant.

A prodigious fog it ever proved, a vile serpent no jack rightly beholding his senses would ever dare to conjure. All sight of sail, even the blackened beams barely afore had wholly disappeared. The eldest jacks had never seen the like. How they stirred within, somewhat disturbed. The vapour ever lingered, wilfully leaking below. It crept upon the planking, it dragged upon the gunwales and oh how it crawled upon the rigging, intent upon devouring whole its prey. Even the nearby reaches of yonder planking all but disappeared, the jacks afar now ghostly apparitions fading to obscurity.

An unnerving disquiet festered upon the quarterdeck and worriedly concerned glances were idly exchanged. Yet whatever the captain felt, he stood as stone, resolute, his withered eyes verily fixed fore and aft, a grim wince barely offering proof of life. To run aground and founder, or to hazard and stray unknowingly, or god forbid to have a pirate wickedly bear down and take them a prize would mean only one thing, the very end. It was a dark thought, a notion ushered with the unsettling certainty of an icy death, cruel and heartless. It was a poor fate indeed, no less a vile torturous demise, no doubt suffered long before the wicked imposition of drowning.

They were officers of the Royal Navy and little else but duty drove their hearts. Britannia ruled the seas. Indeed had she ruled for some years now. And though it was a time of peace, ever still did she proffer forth her valiant souls. Into certain peril were they flung, obligated to weather the hazards upon the backs of their own account. No doubt this was one of those times, the fog wisping against the gunwales, the decks darkened fore and aft. Yet such were the hearts of her sons that ever did each and every one clamber to be the first.

The lookout sat worriedly within the masthead, all but shivering, his eyes washed within the eerie calm. He searched hoping for the Channel's early morning respite. It would never come. The brig had slowed, hardly making way, barely a breath of wind afforded. The fog lingered cruelly, a pale shark circling, enveloping her in a world she ought never to have been. It was deathly quiet, the crew barely holding to hope, one hundred odd souls desperately struggling to retain the wits of their vocation.

'Captain? Sir, just then, I thought I heard something?' the master worriedly reported. He held fast to the helm as his head tilted,

Ships of War — Murky Waters

straining to discern the source. 'Sounded like something, maybe, like a whispering?'

'Sir!' the first officer added, now pointing into the misty haze. 'Hear that? Sounded very much like a hatch squeaking, resonating from larboard, perhaps directly abeam?'

'Good god! Ring the bell!' ordered the captain, fearing the worst.

'Ship ho!' cried the lookout above. But the captain had already seen her and openly he swore, ruing the tardiness of his man atop. His good eye remained upon the fog, the other reserved for the wrath he would later lay upon his lookout. It was an unforgivable act, perhaps even an unpardonable sin and the jack atop knew it, much to his chagrin. A tolerant first officer might argue that hardly was the man to be blamed. After all, such was the soup before them, no less than the dragon's breath, the murk utterly masking the outside world. It would be an argument sorely lost.

The entire weather deck scrambled, the eyes of each officer steadily fixed upon the looming presence. Indeed from the banks had the fog parted and a great darkened shape emerged. The captain expected the worst, a crazed bull charging from the woods and there they sat, limping, nowhere to go. He at once recognised her, a large brig moving quite briskly, but curiously it was not her bowsprit he first beheld. Rather had she turned, now safely running abreast, which is to say parallel with their heads equally advanced.

'Thank god!' the master's mate cried, an experienced hand who once before had suffered his ship to be rammed. Yet jubilation turned to horrid dread. The whites of his keen eyes widened and a paralysing consternation took hold. A row of cannon bore directly upon them, darkened sentinels protruding the gloom. Afore the ghostly ship one by one the long snouts came to bear, evil slits bulging within the vapour, emerging from the hatches as hounds curiously sniffing their prey. About each barrel the mist haplessly wafted, the heaving snorts of a great herd of wild beast, moreover a bevy of seething demons readying to spark. 'Captain, sir!' he gasped. 'She is a pirate!'

The report came in a rolling wave, one shot sent meticulously after the other. It was a moment in time hopelessly dragged, a deafening myriad of mayhem, a horror truly attesting the madness of men. Into the abyss all spoken word descended, consumed and strangled, forever muffled as man and ship despaired within the relentless fury of many an eight pound shot. The decks trembled, desperately shuddering as the iron passed easily through her timbers. Each fiery shot laid true its waste, eventually stifled within the bowels of her hull. She splintered from fore to aft, chips flying violently amidst the chaos. A terrible confusion reigned, holier than a winter's storm bearing wildly upon a festering sea. Indiscriminately did men fly, hideously plucked from their stations, some thrown directly into the sea whilst others soaked red their dye upon the decks. Amidst their scattered cries the storm all but gathered, fearing never to relent. The thunder ever growled, blazing sparks promoting the might of every thump. With every flash thereafter tallied a horrid boom, attesting to each murderous strike the fury within. Blow after blow continued, felt deep within the hull and the ship rocked forcibly, helpless to stay the undeniable might of each unwanted incursion.

 As suddenly as it had begun, the rattling spray of hail ceased and profoundly did the din of battle subside. From the smoke she limped, battered, left lying utterly helpless, a winged duck stranded upon the pond. Her planking continued to ache, grumbling and whining in the weakness of its offended state, the ship hopelessly rent. Yet the masts somehow still held, even the canvas. It was a mocking curiosity, a feeble whim to those with breath still beholden to their lungs. Storming aboard in torrents the sea indignantly washed the decks, the ship fearing to list as the icy hands of the beast swelled upon each and every jack. Oh how the meandering flood slithered through the timbers, a great serpent wrapping its prey, strangling its coil. Cruelly did it wring her, the ship filling until at last the hull surrendered under the final weight of its relentless grip.

 Still perched above within the masthead the lookout helplessly cried, the ship gently slipping into the deep, the product of his ineptitude laid verily before him. The jack's every being, his every effort, scrambled in vain to somehow avoid the inevitable. Hungrily the seas clawed the heights of the mast, eager to seize its prize. He swore one last time as the chill first gripped him. His breath stiffened and a cruel silence ensued. And so from god's earth did he and his ship hopelessly depart, almost as if they had never been.

Arrested aimlessly upon the sea the mist toiled in silence, creeping and crawling, forever searching. Into the depths of its banks did the ghostly brig slither, a hound from hell slipping idly back into the belly of her master's domain.

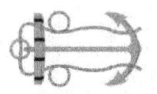

"Si vis pacem, para bellum"
If you wish for peace, prepare for war...
Royal Navy

An angered blade is a blade rarely blunted...
Kensei Hiro

Chapter I
Portsmouth – 1791

A knock on one's door can often be quite telling and this broadside was no exception. Even and yet heavy, dragging with the moderation of three distinct thumps, squarely each bang boomed, almost professionally one might think. It was verily enough to mostly awaken the dead.

'Good grief Coops! Is the rent paid?' gasped Spencer as he shot out of his armchair, anxiously righting himself as if battle had been declared.

'Quite,' Cooper calmly responded, only for a moment lifting his nose from the latest naval journal to thoughtfully eye the door. The hearth before him was warm and in turn his gaze bore deeply upon the random flickering within the embers, the casual wandering of a sharp mind. An intrusion it definitely was, not quite an unannounced French invasion of England, but an intrusion of some proportion nonetheless. Never, not in their wildest dreams, were they expectant of company and in consideration, Portsmouth's early months of 1791 had produced a most astonishing and most bitter cold. It was irrefutable. Only a mad lunatic recently escaped would be out. Nonetheless, Cooper railed through the logical choices, his mind tinkering before finally dismissing the worst. Well, what did it really matter he thought. His cottage was comfortable, albeit somewhat small and undeniably quaint, nonetheless a saving grace if truth be told. And though it was evenly shared with his particular friend, it was a grand manor in comparison to the officers' berths that more or less acquainted their lives at sea. He detested such commotions, such intrusions, but the villain soon enough would be uncovered. To be sure, probably some beggar not worth waiting on he finally considered and eventually he motioned to the door. 'Be a good fellow would you then, Spence?'

Spencer cautiously levered back the lock. Even as officers in the Royal Navy, they rarely had the honour of receiving guests, lest it be collectors of debt or arrears in rent. Times had been hard, the buzz of the last war some eight years distant now. Most ships had been paid off and summarily had His Majesty's men scattered to the four corners of England's best bars, pubs and houses, never to be seen again. It was true from time to time an old shipmate might stumble on in, scrounging for work. After all, it was Portsmouth, a shipping port of some considerable note. Unfortunately, the prospect of employment was scarce, let alone good employment. Indeed, it might prove refreshing to receive a guest, hopefully one bereft of frostbite of course. But the likelihood was hardly high, especially considering their lowly stations as lieutenants in the navy, not to mention the annoying imposition of continuing peace, an unfortunate nuisance which had set their careers nigh upon a lee shore.

Spencer barely knew what to think. It was late and it was cold. What the blazes, surely not another effrontery duel! Please no, not that again he silently grumbled and he peered out into the waning daylight hoping for the best, very much expecting the worst. Oddly before him stood a diminutive but officious looking fellow, a little plump as most often these gents are, but splendidly dressed. In one hand the fellow attempted to clean his rounded spectacles, whilst in the other he proffered a sealed letter. Spencer at once recognised the wax seal, the Admiralty of the Royal Navy, his attention now duly collected.

'And who might you be sir?' enquired the man sharply, adjusting his spectacles to take immediate examination of him.

'Oh, Lieutenant Charles Prescot Spencer, sir, of the Royal Navy,' he stoutly replied, a little miffed. 'And you sir, are?'

'Here for Lieutenant Cooper,' he asserted, quite deficient of any semblance of cheerfulness. 'I have come a long way, directly from the Admiralty,' he pompously added. 'Good god, is it supposed to be snowing out here?' he grumbled.

'Then you must come in sir,' Cooper interrupted, now standing beside Spencer. 'Take a drink perhaps, it is deathly cold. You have had a long journey? Allow me to introduce myself, I am Lieutenant Hayden Reginald Cooper, at your service.'

'Quite, very well, alright then, but first the dispatch,' he insisted, shoving it into his hand, before quickly making his way to the hearth. He looked about as Spencer offered him a glass, only to find himself comfortably seated. 'Perhaps some brandy or a port, if you please Lieutenant?' he begged, rubbing his hands.

'I regret, deeply, as officers beached on half pay with little prospect, we unfortunately have neither on offer. Perhaps, rum?'

Cooper broke the seal and read the dispatch. His eyes drew swiftly down the page, glancing the obligatory wording to which he was quite readily accustomed, *"required and directed...fail and answer the contrary at your peril..."* and of course, the complimentary close *"By Command of Their Lordships..."*. It was abundantly clear. It was summons.

'Sir, I am Fredricks. May I have your answer?'

'Aye, yes, yes, of course I will attend,' he quickly returned, still wandering over the particulars of the letter. 'Inform Their Lordships that I will attend at my earliest convenience, most definitely in the next day or two, weather permitting.'

'Oh dear,' Fredricks lamented, shaking his head. 'I dare say sir, oh dear, that will not do. No, it will just not do.'

'But the orders do not stipulate a specific time?'

'Indeed, they never do, do they.'

'And the winter of good Portsmouth has turned shockingly

bleak. Bewildering is it not? You may have noticed, but there is even snow on the ground. Snow! Can you believe it! Outrageous!'

'Nonetheless, I am to take you back directly sir, tonight.'

'Upon my soul man, what the blazes for? Am I to rush to Whitehall in the extremes of my own risks in this godforsaken weather, only to waste around for days, nay maybe weeks, withering in the Admiralty waiting rooms! It behoves me to wonder as to why this dispatch was not sent by the regular means. After all, we are not at war and what the living hell could they ever want with me? Meanwhile, there are some good positions on some very good ships which will be petitioned tomorrow. Do you hear me, tomorrow and tomorrow only sir!'

'Of course you are right. And I am sorry naturally as to your predicament, but there you have it. I have my orders. And yours, sir, now sit before you. If you are to accept the order, you must come with me tonight, if you please, sir.'

'If I am to accept the order? If I am to accept the order!' he indignantly bellowed. 'Are you sure you're from the Admiralty or even the navy? Have you not gone mad! This is the Royal Navy man, the parchment is a rhetorical courtesy, lest one wants to hang! And disobedience would surely see the end of my half pay and reserve status.'

'Not to mention the hanging,' whispered Spencer casually.

'Quite! And they would likely throw Spence in with my lot as well, just for the pleasure of proximity. Hell, they might even nab Larboard here, our scrawny little cat, just to be sure. What's one or two more 'ey, dangling from the yard! I do wonder, what the devil is going on?'

'Indeed Coops, it's got to be eighty miles!' added Spencer.

'Seventy three and one-half miles Spence, my dear fellow, from here to Central London and best guess, we won't be there until evening tomorrow, not in this muck. Now sir,' he pressed to Fredricks. 'Am I to see Their Lordships in the morrow evening? Really? Come now, madness!'

'Your answer, if you please sir?'

'Very well, very well,' he reluctantly announced, shaking his head with a polite huff. 'It seems we are outgunned and must strike. Spence, I see no other course here, time to weigh anchor.

Ships of War — Murky Waters

Let's get the cottage battened down and make our usual arrangements.' Lastly, he turned to Fredricks. 'Well then, lead the way my good man, to Whitehall. We have not a moment to lose!'

Chapter II
The Admiralty

It was a sombre stroll, the final steps upon arriving at the Admiralty a grave reminder of the peril lying in wait. More naval careers had been sunk here than in battle at sea, a subduing and most sobering thought. The building itself was imposing, no less than a hundred and twenty gun first-rate leading a squadron. It appeared simple enough, but in essence had been slyly commissioned with intimidation wholly in mind, no doubt a shrewd attempt to cool the heels of the most tenacious commissioned officers. Even though the hour was quite late, Cooper remained vigilant, mindful that prominent figures may well be about. It was prudent enough too, as one's naval career, indeed one's fortunes, might sink or swim depending upon who was lurking about.

The Admiralty stood as the stalwart almighty, prestigiously positioned between Whitehall, Horse Guards Parade and The Mall, right in the heart of London, no doubt a hive for senior naval officers and government officials. Nonetheless, it was a small joy

Ships of War — Murky Waters

for Cooper to be back in London, no doubt quite conscious of his extended absence. It was true he had not ventured these hallowed grounds for some considerable time, not that he really cared and why should he, or so he rightly considered. He was indeed a lieutenant, but so low on the seniority list it would only prove a grand waste to stalk the halls of the Admiralty. No, his time was better served scrounging for berths, the practicality of feeding himself more prevalent. Indeed, endeavouring to find suitable employment at sea was paramount and the only place for that was in a port, a good port such as Portsmouth.

As he beheld the Admiralty entrance he halted to peer upon the building and its peculiar shape. What a grand feat of architecture, but it definitely wasn't what he had recalled. There seemed to be a pale coloured extension behind the small courtyard on the left, a three storey building, constructed of yellow brick, the rear facade facing directly onto Horse Guards Parade. Ah yes, he suddenly recollected, they had announced this in the London Gazette, the official residence of the First Lord of the Admiralty. Admiralty House, or so they called it, a moderately proportioned mansion built in eighty-eight, featuring interiors of neoclassical design, whatever that truly meant. As he recalled, the main or original structure was a three storey u-shaped building surrounding a grand court yard. Indeed this was a most handsome arrangement, but not so recent. Most likely was it built in the twenties, so he guessed. And there was more, from the street one would usually discern all three sides of the inner parts of the structure, including a goodly sized courtyard. But here today before him, a great screen now blocked the way.

'Interesting,' he whispered, admiring the additional works and the effect it had on the building and its grounds. 'When in blazes did they add that?' he further mumbled.

'It was in eighty-eight,' a familiar voice attested from behind. 'To be sure, it was no less the wild concoction of one Robert Adam. Our original architectural hero, Ripley, of course passed in fifty-eight, a good year though I can personally attest, so he is none the wiser, may he forever roll in his grave.'

'Captain Nelson, sir!' Cooper exclaimed. 'How grand it is to see you again!' firstly saluting before shaking his hand profusely.

'I have not attended the Admiralty for some time, yet that fact is plainly obvious to one as astute as yourself. And sir, my belated congratulations on your extrication from that dirty business in Antigua, with Boreas. I regret not having the pleasure of attending to you since, before she was paid off in eighty-seven.'

'Indeed, thank ye Lieutenant. And 'twas dirty business indeed,' he agreed. 'But in the end patience and tenacity won through, not to mention a tiny bit of interest, not that I had any other course. The courts served them a mighty broadside they shan't soon forget, one hundred and twenty gun if I was to gauge. The battle was won, but alas, the action did not leave me unscathed. I regret, deeply, that I have not had the honour of another command since.'

'Oh, I am profoundly sorry to hear that sir.'

'Beware the damned bureaucrats of peacetime Lieutenant, for their aim is ever so true and be damned if I didn't pay for it. A lesson learned, most unfortunately.'

'Aye, but I assumed the Admiral might perhaps step in for you sir? Oh, how he loved you so. Surely he would steer a command your way?'

'Oh, Hood,' he smiled. 'Do not be too hard on the old barky. His hands were tied and I assure you peace can do that most handsomely, even to an admiral. No, it was my own fault. Bear witness Lieutenant, it's not about being right or wrong. It's about being able to win, to win through and ultimately withdraw with honour.'

'Quite, sir.'

'Alas, but I shall not keep you a moment longer, especially as it appears you have business with Their Lordships. Now straighten that button, check that hat. The devil man, don't let them see that hole now! Never mind the cold, tuck it under your armpit, aye, there's a good fellow.' And he looked him squarely in the eye and offered his hand. The gleam in Cooper's returning smile fell strangely disturbed, the sensation of a small piece of paper now tucked inside his palm. He bid farewell and as he gathered himself towards the Admiralty doors he surreptitiously helped the note into his pocket. He looked about and with all good purpose strolled up to the steward, ready to beg admission.

Ships of War — Murky Waters

The Admiralty steward eyed the lieutenant as a last meal not quite prepared to his liking, reluctantly showing him to a waiting room. There were many waiting rooms and unfortunately over the years Cooper had experienced most of them. Of course they were all somewhat memorable considering the immeasurable expanse of time spent in each. It seemed naval officers were indeed required to be men of absolute discipline, lest they turn barking mad, lost to the cavernous catacombs of the Admiralty rooms. He sat and readied for a most arduous wait.

He at once retrieved Nelson's note and was now studying it carefully and ever so curiously, as was his duty. For his old captain to go to such pains definitely suggested something was seriously afoot. Well he knew, even respected, the ploys and antics of Captain Horatio Nelson. Over and over he read it, checking for hidden meanings or some subtle code. The note simply read: *"Wish you joy... Attend all haste in the regular hour..."*. With a sigh he knew immediately he was at the right place. Nothing much changed in the Royal Navy. Whether it was a time of peace or war, being required and directed by one's superiors was definitely a common theme.

Cooper barely wasted even a moment before setting about deciphering the meaning of it all. It was without doubt a coded message. He immediately noted the existence of the two messages within the one. To the first, he had no idea why joy was being wished upon him, very odd. To the latter, he was to attend, an easy tell, a meeting of course. No mention of where or when though, but at least he was confident of the *"who"*. He of course noticed the subtle existence of the three dots after each part of the message. This was an old familiar tell. It clearly meant the writer assumed that the recipient most definitely knew all about the particulars of that part of the message. Hence, they would not regurgitate it again by spelling it plainly out on paper for all to possibly decipher.

'Well, my secret message has been somewhat solved, at least in part,' he silently rejoiced. 'Now, if only I knew the why, the when and the where, it would be most helpful and a tad less disconcerting.'

'They say this room is particularly haunted,' a voice sparked looming from the darkened corner, much to Cooper's surprise. Another officer sat waiting, no doubt in the same predicament. 'Lieutenant Shillings, sir.'

'Lieutenant Cooper, sir,' he responded, as is the custom. 'What do you mean, haunted?'

'Oh yes indeed, haunted,' he oddly accounted. 'Of course the obvious remedy firstly springs to mind. That is, perhaps some poor wretch, a forgotten lieutenant no doubt, lingered too long in here and well, there you have it, over he keeled. Alas no, nothing of the sort. In fact, it is a woman you know.'

'A woman?'

'Aye, the entire house is reputed to be haunted, by a lady called Margaret Reay. She was said to have been killed by her lover. She was purportedly the mistress of the Earl of Sandwich who, as you must know, was in residence. Apparently she embarked upon an illicit affair with a penniless army lieutenant, one James Hackman. Can you fathom that, an army lieutenant, hopelessly penniless mind you! But she would not marry him, rightly so of course. So he left the army and became a clergyman, no doubt a vocation just as equally impecunious. Defies reason, does it not? Then one night in April of seventy-nine, madly jealous outside a theatre in Covent Garden, he shot her stone dead with his pistol. Of course he later claimed he had decently intended to only shoot himself, as long as it was before her eyes. Witnessed by virtually the entire theatre audience, he could not in any circumstance escape his guilt. Later upon being found officially guilty, he was sentenced to death and subsequently executed. He is gone, but rather it seems she still roams the halls and rooms.'

'Indeed? I see,' Cooper granted, now silently appraising the sanity of the man before him, perhaps fearing the worst. 'And sir, how long have you been waiting, may I ask?'

Ships of War — Murky Waters

'Oh, all of yester week and that of today, the standard average I would submit. It won't be long now. Ah, here's the steward!'

'Lieutenant Cooper?' the steward curtly announced, his cheek rolling to a wince. 'Sir, come with me, if you please,' he gruffly insisted, much to the chagrin of poor Shillings. 'Their Lordships will see you now.'

Chapter III
The Board Room

Cooper, as youthful as he was, prided himself as a bold but shrewd tactical officer, especially when it came to warfare. And meeting with the Lords of the Admiralty indeed qualified as warfare, a skirmish he could ill afford to lose. Should a gale blow, should he be forced to strike his colours, he might easily find himself wrecked or beached indefinitely, his reserve status revoked and his pay summarily discontinued. Destitution, it fairly seemed, loomed but a door away. He must not waver or slip and oh how he must choose his words, or so he wisely considered.

Upon first receipt of the dispatch from Fredricks he was not alarmed, not in any way. However, his state of being had now unquestionably altered. After all, he had waited only the sum total of thirteen and one-half minutes before he was summoned. Never had he heard the like, especially pertaining to a lieutenant. Poor Shillings had been there a week and very much looked ready to

Ships of War — Murky Waters

forthrightly hang himself. It is a good thing, he rightly observed, that arms were not permitted past the cloak room of the Admiralty doors.

Cooper collected his thoughts, rummaging for any possible grievances to which they might bring against him. He wasn't so sure, maybe there was something, maybe not. Damnation, perhaps they mean to execute me he wildly accounted. His mind immediately evoked the nasty business with Byng in fifty-seven, a naval officer tried and shot for *"failing to do his utmost"*. And Byng was an admiral, so what hope might a lowly lieutenant hold should even one finger be pointed his way? He shuddered at the thought.

Cooper prepared himself as he was ushered into the board room, a meeting place commonly used by the First Lord. What a grand room it was, supporting a monstrous fireplace amidst a row of elongated hung windows. Magnificently did the light draw, emphasising the delicate architecture of the ceiling. In the exact middle of the room sat a great oaken table. Alongside, a well-stocked library shrewdly crafted itself into the walls. Upon a shelf, built cleverly within the library, a great spinning globe sat and upon another table a host of naval charts and maps lay idle. Most definitely, it was a room fit for a naval king.

Waiting before Cooper sat the Right Honourable John Pitt, 2nd Earl of Chatham, First Lord of the Admiralty and of course brother to the current Prime Minster, William Pitt. It immediately struck Cooper that Lord Pitt was a relatively young man, especially for such a rated position. He could not have been more than thirty-five years old, not a great deal older than himself. And holy hell he cringed, Admiral of the Fleet, John Forbes, was sitting right next to him. Cooper well knew this man and his reputation, for he was the commander of the entire Royal Navy, serving ever since Lord Hawke passed in eighty-one. Admiral Forbes must have been nigh on eighty years old by now he guessed, but how earnest and dignified the man remained. Well, he sarcastically wondered, who might pop out next, perhaps the Prime Minster or even the King himself? Indifferent, he stood awaiting instruction, clandestinely dredging the far reaches of his memory in the hope of recalling the very etiquette required of a lowly lieutenant when confronted by the First Lord and the Admiral of the Fleet.

'Aye, sit down Cooper, sit,' Lord Pitt hastily motioned. 'The Admiral hasn't so many years left that we can muck around now, can we sir?'

'Don't you worry about that,' Admiral Forbes protested. 'I have enough in me for a few more broadsides. But indeed, let us get on with it, the late hours hasten and don't forget our supper arrangements.'

'Well Lieutenant,' Lord Pitt started. 'I confess I have never actually heard of you before this month.' He peered deeply, blank muted eyes worthy of a great reptile. 'But I dare say, you have come highly recommended.'

'Indeed, sir?'

'Does that surprise you?'

Cooper always detested these kinds of questions. Open ended, always proffered to illicit some telling response. In point of fact, any response tended on the subject would be far from helpful to his cause. It was of course part of the First Lord's strategy, or so he guessed, to flush something out, to assess his character.

'I have always endeavoured to do my duty, sir,' he evenly stated. '...to the utmost,' he quickly added, thinking of poor Admiral Byng. 'But alas, I remain unmarried and have no family interest or any other influence within the gentry to support such a recommendation. Not that I know in any case. I was born of a clergyman, a decidedly large family of which I was eighth.'

'Hood? A man of no influence you say?' Lord Pitt tested, eyeing him as if he was already dining upon this evening's eye fillet. 'It is he, in fact, whom has reported to Their Lordships upon your presence. And it seems he has mightily commended you, with some glowing remarks.'

More like mightily condemned Cooper thought. Surely the First Lord wasn't reading it right. It really didn't make any sense. It was true Hood had been his commander-in-chief, but as a lieutenant he had very little direct contact with the Admiral and that included the many dinners that so went hand in hand with such fleet cruises.

'Admiral Hood, sir? Indeed, he was my squadron commander, when I was third upon Albemarle, West Indies, sir.'

'Aye, Albemarle, under Captain Nelson of course. But it says

Ships of War — Murky Waters

here you were second, not third?'

'Aye sir, I commenced as the third lieutenant and later due to, well sir, due to the normal circumstances which creates such vacancies, I was subsequently promoted acting second.'

'And you had your share of command I see, from time to time?'

'Aye sir,' he nodded. 'That is, mostly with the prizes, bringing them back to port, in course.'

'Safely back, of course?'

'Aye, sir.'

'Says here you sank a pirate within five minutes of engagement, upon one of these prizes? Is that true Lieutenant, even with such a limited prize crew, as it were?'

'Aye sir, I had command of a sloop, eighteen gun, bringing her into port and we were set upon suddenly by another sloop, eighteen gun. They had laid in wait beyond a local island. They were brimming with men ready to board, had the weather gage and without warning bore directly upon us.'

'Good god man!' interrupted Admiral Forbes, astonished.

'If I may sir, they were not good seamen and even though they were only wearing the ship, that is with the gage upon their back, they overdid it a tad and brought themselves to, almost to a founder. With a small tack, we were able to position our broadside, if we could call it that, directly upon her stern.'

'Raked her, stem to stern, 'ey?'

'Aye, sir, but we had not enough crew to fire all our cannon, so every man including myself manned a gun, firing it and then leaping to the next, until all shots were away.'

'So, you would not have been able to reload, what, more than even one gun?' surmised Lord Pitt.

'Aye, sir.'

'Mother and Mary!' swore Admiral Forbes.

'But, here you sit, Lieutenant?' queried Lord Pitt.

'A lucky shot, sir, but in actuality, a horrible one, direct to her powder. She instantly exploded. No survivors, I regret to say.'

'Oh, come now. What a fellow you are Cooper! Let us damn those devils to hell, 'ey,' Admiral Forbes smiled. 'Good seamanship and English zeal will always win the day.'

'I am sure Captain Nelson was very pleased not to lose his prize, to which you were wholly responsible. Tell me, what think ye of Captain Nelson, if you do not mind telling of course?'

Cooper cringed at Lord Pitt's question, so much, his insides turned. Another detestable poser he thought. It was indeed common etiquette in the service that one most definitely would refrain from openly vilifying their captain, even if it was deserved, lest one be forever tarnished. However, His Majesty and the Lords of the Admiralty all but expected lieutenants to report negatively about their captains. Otherwise, why would they require each and every one to maintain a separate ship's log and to hand it in at the end of each cruise. And it was somewhat obvious that with each captain vilified, the more chance a lieutenant might promote to post. The incentive was there, but to the contrary, one must not over glorify their captain, lest it smack of self-promotion and vanity, traits most unbecoming a naval officer. Cooper felt himself drifting upon a lee shore with nary a boat to be had.

'Not at all, sir, happy to oblige,' he smiled. 'It was an honour sir, to serve under Captain Nelson. He is a prolific seaman and a master tactician, as can be attested by the many prizes taken or burned during his cruise.'

'I see,' Lord Pitt confirmed, who sat there nodding and smiling. 'We think so too, not that we have been able to do much for him of late. But that is his own damned fault and he knows it, or so I would beg to suggest. Would it surprise you to learn that he too was born of a large family and his father was a clergyman?'

'I had no idea, sir.'

'Yet,' Admiral Forbes interrupted, 'He had the good common sense to be born into a family where his mother was the grand-niece of Sir Robert Walpole, First Earl of Orford, whom was once the de facto first Prime Minister of the British Parliament.'

'Quite, sir,' agreed Cooper smirking.

'Do you always smirk, Lieutenant, in the presence of your superiors?'

'No sir! Never, sir!'

'Lieutenant, it is clear you are a fighting officer, a loyal one at that. In addition, you most definitely fit the profile we require. A full explanation is due of course, but will have to wait. In short, we really need someone of fighting worth. I must make that clear, but it must be someone who is not so well known, not so compromised by their own public successes to date.'

And expendable of course Cooper immediately surmised. Someone they can disavow should the whole thing come a cropper, whatever it was. And whatever it was, it must be quite the commission. One thing was sure he carefully contemplated, his career this very day was likely over, either to be lost in some fool's action, disavowed, or drummed immediately out of the service for not taking the job in the first place.

'I can assure you sir, no one else is even mildly aware of me, or I mean to say, of course, aware of my career highlights to date.'

'Quite. And possessing no interest in the gentry, your naval career has not advanced in any haste of course, notwithstanding skills you might possess or even deeds well done. So, you do understand. That is good. As such, I must conclude you fit the profile and may be suited for our proposition. Furthermore, I must tell you, there is game afoot, big game. Now, might you be further interested?'

Another rhetorical question he loathingly considered, this one begging an obligatory response of course. Naturally he could say no and at the same time simply leave his coat and rank at the door and become a homeless rat catcher begging the next street corner. He could beg to think about it, with much the same outcome. Or, he could answer in the affirmative and at least go down honourably with his ship. This really wasn't such favourable news, but he was dished, caught between an enemy squadron and a lee shore.

'Sir, it would be an honour.'

'Splendid. Then let us perhaps share with you some intelligence which succinctly appraises where we are at. It goes without saying that anything hereby learned or spoken, must never leave this room, lest you answer the contrary to your peril.'

'Of course, sir.'

'Now, we have here a letter from Leopold II, whom has the honour of being King of Austria. It seems he has had enough of the French and their so called revolution. We honestly wagered this thing might just go away by itself, but damned if it hasn't. As you know, it has been going on now since eighty-eight. For the love of Mary, three god damned years! And of course, Leopold isn't the only one fed up.'

'Well Pitt, don't forget that our Holy Roman Emperor Leopold is, in point of fact, the brother of Louis XVI's Queen, Marie Antoinette,' Admiral Forbes added with a sly nod. 'I am guessing there is a might annoyance at the scant treatment of his beloved sister.'

'Quite. And indeed most of Europe is just sitting back now, waiting and watching, albeit most carefully. Leopold is insisting, quite clearly, that England ally together with Austria, Prussia, Spain, Russia, Sweden and a host of other smaller nations. This would form a European military coalition, if you will. He even suggests we might, together I hazard to assume, chance to invade France and reinstall the bloody monarchy. He calls this letter the Padua Circular. Now, it's not official, not a bloody soul has read it yet, except for a chosen few. He so intends to send the letter perhaps in a few months' time, maybe in July. Of course, we have the letter now, but that's just the way these regents work naturally. No good sending a letter if the answer is no, right?'

'In course, sir.'

'And here is a draft, rough mind you, of the Declaration of Pillnitz, jointly crafted by Leopold II and Frederick William II, King of Prussia. This, it seems, is meant to be released shortly after the Padua Circular. It's a tad more formal, as you may note. But we, that is, King George and England, are not quite convinced about the timing. After all, it's February now and five or six months is not long enough to properly ready for any real military action. And I assure you, action is no doubt assured. We cannot go rattling the cage and expect the bird to sit still. So, whether England is ready or not, it is our considered opinion that war is all but coming.'

'I understand, sir.'

'And not that anyone really knows it, but this bloody business has been going on right under our noses. Indeed for some time now, a great bloody time!'

'Aye, pirates! Dirty damned so called pirates!' Admiral Forbes cried, thumping the oak with his fist. 'Well, that is what the Frenchies expect us to believe, bloody pirates! As if I was born

Ships of War — Murky Waters

yesterday! Cooper, do I look like I was born yesterday?' eyeballing him in all seriousness. 'Now Pitt may have been born yesterday, but he isn't one to be fooled either.'

'Quite, thank you Admiral,' Lord Pitt commended. 'Now, I hear you have a sharp mind Lieutenant, good with numbers and such? And you speak four languages it seems, with mathematics being the fifth? Also, I am told you know France and her waters like the back of your hand?'

Cooper sat quietly.

'Well come on, no time for modesty man,' Admiral Forbes boomed. 'Is it true or not?'

'Aye, sir, it is accurate.'

'Well then, let us test you perhaps?' Lord Pitted posed. 'Would you do us the honour of having a little glance at something?'

'Of course, sir.'

'This is a list of English shipping which has been recorded as unaccounted, overdue or lost. All of them are traders and such, goodness such a god damn waste. The chart attests their positions when they were taken or at least where they likely should have been. There is a side legend setting out their cargoes, including the port of departure and destination, dates and whatnot. Have a good look now and take your time. In the meantime, the Admiral and I will partake in a sip of something, perhaps a white ribbin for me.'

'Aye, but no gin for me Pitt. A bristol milk, if you please.'

'Very well, a spot of sherry it is. Now Cooper, when you are ready, apprise us of what you might make of it, if anything?'

Cooper poured over the figures, swiftly and efficiently. This was his forte of course, the study of maths, logic and navigation. The numbers stood out, the positions upon the chart eventually obvious. A number of patterns started to evolve. He ran his fingers along the routes. He measured spots upon the coastlines, including the rough distances from the nearby ports and the last known locations of each of the English ships. His mind rattled through the known sea productivity of each vessel, each according to its class. Next he compared the sea miles required of the more capable French ships such as corvettes, frigates and even ships of the line. It was as clear to him as a summer's day, a French one of course. With some ink and parchment he would quickly prove his theories.

The Admiral and the First Lord, for the first time, were standing. They sensed he was onto something and they crowded about the chart, keenly watching as if a young master was working his craft. Sipping their drinks, they marvelled silently as Cooper edged his notes upon the chart, whilst notarising the enemy ships and their probable ports. He even started to list by name potential French ships, mostly sloops, corvettes and frigates. The smaller corvettes were marked most heavily, though there were quite a few frigates in fact and even one ship of the line. He gradually explained his theories. For the moment, politely yet correctly, he disregarded the enormity of the two flag ranks before him. It held him in great stead of course, a moment which did not go unnoticed, for senior staff had very little time for grovellers or for the larks of frightened sea rats.

'Sir, if I may, the losses of shipping are wholly unacceptable, for peacetime that is. It is far greater than the expected norm, by many more points than the allowable variance. It cannot be just the French either, for the number of ports required to support such piracy counts far wider and greater than she presently affords. The quantity of attacks, the widespread nature of the locations, the winter weather together with the type of shipping lost, is all a great tell. Most definitely it suggests that the pirates used multiple bases. They could be as widely spread from the far reaches of Spain through even all of northern France. They leave a distinct trail, very traceable in fact. With time, I believe I could pinpoint the exact number of ships, give or take a few here and there. I also believe I might be able to include each ship's probable class and most definitely their likely base of origin.'

'Come now, Lieutenant, you are not just making this up, are you man? In the last few months of discerning, even our best analysts have failed to draw any such conclusions, which you seem to have arrived at in less than sixty god damned minutes, indeed!'

'I am certain, sir. It grieves me to hear our analysts have not made headway, to be sure. But I cannot overlook the obvious, not for the sake of their honour. Allow me to put ink to parchment and thereafter perhaps put my findings to any test you deem necessary?'

'I am convinced already Pitt!' Admiral Forbes boomed. 'The

lad appears sound in his reasoning and should his maths prove out, which I am thinking I will not wager to the contrary, then we have our puzzle solved. It doesn't take much to guess who is behind all this, the bloody Girondins and that other mob, the Society of the Friends, the bloody Jacobins. But the Spaniards as well, this is indeed news! It's a god damned prelude to war! Take out our trade, weaken us in the frost of our winter months and in they all bloody well flood!'

'Either way, it seems England will have to act. We cannot have our trade preyed upon. If it is only pirates, then we will deal with them and peace will continue as is, for now. But if it is in fact French or Spanish privateers, bearing Letters of Marque, then war cannot reasonably be avoided I am afraid.'

'Aye, forsooth!' barked Admiral Forbes.

'The Spanish! I guess we should have known better? Hands down, it seems they never forgave us for that business in Nookta Sound last year in ninety, in May to be precise.'

'Precise? Sir, you do not have to be precise,' Admiral Forbes attested. 'Old Howe cruising around Ushant in peacetime with thirty-five line of battle ships for a good month or two is something I wouldn't ordinarily forget. I wager being stuck in port with the sharks circling may have somewhat unsettled our old dago friends and might perhaps have served to raise their annoyance with us? And what the hell came of it all, nary a shot fired!'

'Bloody diplomats!' Lord Pitt cursed. 'They stepped in of course. We should have gone in and finished them all, right there and then.'

'What?' Admiral Forbes mused. 'The diplomats, sir? Or the Spanish?'

'Ha! Perhaps both, now I come to bloody well think of it.' They all had a good chuckle together, even Cooper who did his best not to raise his station too obviously in such esteemed company. 'Lieutenant, allow the Admiral and myself a short recess. Please continue your analysis. We will leave you here in peace and return shortly. This, so far, has been most illuminating, indeed most enlightening.'

Bradley John

'We are going to offer you a command Cooper,' Lord Pitt started as he re-entered the board room. 'Now, it must be understood from the outset that it is indeed only an offer, not an order. The order will come later. For now we will hash out the details, in course, but I advise you carefully weigh your options.'

'Aye sir.'

'Alright, if you are willing, listen, weigh the offer and simply stay seated. If you are seated at the end of our discussion, we will take this as your indication in the positive. If it is your intent to withdraw, at any time hence forward during our discussion, simply stand. You need not say anything and your honour and your reserve status will remain intact and you may then leave.'

How civilised he considered, much more than he reasonably thought possible. The First Lord seemed quite forthrightly genuine and somewhat less than duplicitous. To accept, all he had to do was stay seated. He was of a mind of course, that even should the building catch fire and fall to rubble he would hold to his seat, even if he had to withdraw with it still attached to his backside. This was his chance, finally, a great wondrous chance, a chance one dreams of, yet very rarely comes. Now it was here, it was real. A ship, his own command, hunting in the Channel no less! It would be dangerous dirty work, he knew that. If he somehow managed to survive, there would be the prospect of promotion to post, not to mention prize money from taking a ship or two. With this command he would now be able to afford his particular friend Spencer a position and the chance of promotion. He would secure wages for himself, no less than the full rate pursuant to the acumen of master and commander. Indeed, this was a great chance, one he fully intended to secure with all his might. He was of a mind that he would do anything, even take on a line of battle ship with no more than a row boat, if they so ordered.

'Do you understand sir?' Admiral Forbes confirmed. 'No matter your choice here today, words so uttered are not to be repeated, at all, upon your own peril. And I assure you, I can dream up some pretty decent peril!'

'Aye Admiral, sir,' he responded evenly. 'I fully understand my duty. And thank you, sir.'

'Very good,' Lord Pitt interrupted. 'Now let us make this arrangement clear for the written record, which I assure you Lieutenant, not a damned soul is ever likely to see.'

'Understood, sir.'

'Do you, Lieutenant, agree that England is presently not at war?'

'Aye, sir.'

'And as such, as an officer of the Royal Navy, you must understand that we, meaning King George and England, are somewhat restrained in the legal sense you know. Meaning, we are very much limited when it comes to acts of aggression and indeed, violence upon the seas. And sufferance of such, indeed we, meaning King George, England and most definitely you, will be held accountable.'

'Aye, sir.'

'Then we propose your commission, sir,' Admiral Forbes officially announced. '…to take or burn or destroy any ships of piracy, as you see fit.'

'This will be a damned dirty business. And it must be a principally secret business. Most likely you won't be eyeing your name in the London Gazette. And should any senior officers get a sniff of what's going on, there may well be some significant resentment, very significant. Many of them are beyond destitute. They won't fathom why they are left sitting on their backside, beached on half pay, whilst a mere lieutenant, one without a whiff of interest mind you, has been given a peacetime command. They do so enjoy clinging to the seniority list you know. You will need to perform out there Cooper, or they will no doubt organise against you some form of moral reprisal in protest. Good god man, I wouldn't put it past some of them to go as far as to even arrange in some way as to call you out.'

'Have you ever been out, Cooper?' asked Admiral Forbes.

'Sir, if you mean challenged, that is, due to some effrontery of honour, then aye I have been out, on occasion.'

'I have been out myself, so I know how that feels, damned dirty business, detestable really. So, on occasion you say, more than once or twice?'

'Quite, sir.'

'Pistols, I assume?'

'Not quite sir, I strictly insist upon the blade.'

'Indeed do you? That's quite personal isn't it? Well, I expect when you are the one called upon, you are no doubt afforded the prerogative of choice, correct?'

'Aye, sir, indeed.'

'I take it you are handy with a cutlass, then?'

'I regret sir, that I cannot use a cutlass to much proficiency. I know it is the standard norm for naval officers, but with it I am horridly inept. Rather, I have a different style of blade, of which I have been privately schooled.'

'Indeed, fascinating, do tell?'

'If I may explain sir, it is steel from the Orient. Very similar to a cutlass, though it has a longer handle, so it can be wielded with two hands. It boasts a slightly curved tip harbouring a modest blood groove along the length of its back and is renowned for its proclivity to never break. The steel, if I may explain sir, has been folded more times than perhaps a lunatic with a wild fancy might ever dare to imagine. It is quite sturdy, light, well balanced and most heartily able to carve through almost any known body armour, even steel and rarely needs to be sharpened. I had the good fortune to acquire it in the West Indies upon where I had the honour of learning from a master of its art, a most interesting seaman from the Orient, whose life I chanced to save sir. I later discovered that we had found him after some wreck, his lot being lost at sea during a local battle of some note. It seems in his country he was a royal guard of some renown. Peculiar fellow, had we not come along he would most definitely have killed himself, as it is their custom when they lose in battle and become masterless.'

'We could use a bit of that in the Royal Navy,' mused Admiral Forbes, having a little chuckle.

'And you have been out with this thing, whatever it is called, how many times?' probed Lord Pitt.

Ships of War — Murky Waters

'It is called a katana by their language, sir. And aye, I have been out with it some nineteen times, each time I assure you, most regretfully. But may I add, if you please sir, not once did I request such a calling and each and every challenge did I resist... to the utmost.'

'And not one did you bloody well lose either, 'ey?' snorted Admiral Forbes.

'But nineteen, seems somewhat above the norm?' added Lord Pitt.

'If I may, sir? And I do hazard to be humble here, but I am most prolifically successful in the playing of cards, especially when it is for money. Following, I am often accused of cheating, most unfortunately.'

'And do you cheat?'

'Never sir, unless of course the proficiency of calculating mathematical chance, surmised by watchful observation, accounts as such?'

'I believe it does not.'

'If anything, I have been called out mostly because I have a hankering for mathematics, which is invariably confused with the accurate counting of cards, that is, from those cards tossed or summarily discarded from the game.'

'And a great big bag of cash summarily taken from the offended,' added Admiral Forbes snickering.

'Nonetheless, you are responsible for the loss of nineteen able bodied souls of His Majesty's empire,' Lord Pitt reminded. 'Even if it was legal!'

'Sir, I am content to say that not one man was lost. All nineteen left the field, able bodied, with their honour intact and air full in their lungs, each matter settled in noble tradition. May I offer that I do so regret the manner in which each and every one did call upon me, though of their honour and their opinions, I cannot hope to control.'

'Not one dead, Cooper? Amazing. Well, you must show me your sword and your method? I am most intrigued, as I am sure is the Admiral and you cannot hope to leave us now without our satisfaction.'

'It lies in the Admiralty cloak room this very moment.'

'Oh joy!' Lord Pitt exclaimed ringing his tiny bell to order his staff to bring the sword immediately, much to the steward's look of utmost shock and indecent displeasure. 'And understand Cooper, we don't condone this practice you know, but we cannot very well stop it. It is very much engrained in our system these days.'

'Rest assured sir, should I be called out, I will be fine.'

'I am hardly worried for you good sir. Last thing we need, with war coming, is to see good officers cut up by this... cat did you say?'

'Katana, if you please sir.'

'Aye, cut up with this cat, when we need them readying for the Frenchies. Let us pray nothing comes of it and that nineteen is the end of it.'

The sword was presented before them. Lord Pitt and Admiral Forbes immediately stood to gather about it, running their watchful eyes along its length. The sheath was truly bleak and unassuming, its sole purpose to conceal the blade within, which Cooper quickly explained was the custom of the Orient. With permission, Cooper stood, took the katana and drew out the blade slowly and surely, with an absolute precise hand. He glided about the room, his movements barely discernible to his audience, a serpent slithering side to side to mesmerise its prey. Suddenly he lunged swishing at a nearby candle, taking no more than a whisker from the top.

'Ha!' screeched Admiral Forbes joyously.

'Aye! Impressive Cooper!' Lord Pitt commended. 'Aye, yes, please sit back down. Had I blinked I fear I might have missed your exhibition. Absolutely splendid! May I?'

'Nineteen!' Admiral Forbes rejoiced as he watched the First Lord wielding the katana, testing its balance. 'Damn Pitt, I think we have our pirate hunter well and truly selected, don't you? Nineteen and not a scratch! I have never heard the like! But I believe it wholeheartedly, oh yes indeed! Now Cooper, or I should say Captain Cooper, bring me nineteen pirates and their ships intact and I'll see you make admiral one day, ha, ha!'

'Aye sir! And may I add a hurricane amidships could not displace me presently from this chair. I, if I may be so bold, am your man sir.'

'Indeed? Good, very well then Captain,' Lord Pitt commended. 'This will be no ordinary command I can assure you. Hunting pirates and Letters of Marque in peacetime will prove very precarious and not just for England mind you. You may recall the predicament Nelson found himself in, with Boreas in Antigua? Courts in peacetime, goodness, aye indeed, very bloody precarious.'

'I understand sir,' Cooper offered. 'But I have no wealth to speak of, which is to say, nothing to lose.'

'Ah yes, but what about debtors' prison? We would be hard pressed to intercede on your behalf should it come to that.'

'Aye sir, but I would wager my shipmates would never allow it. At the very worst I would be confined to quarters on board, unable to step upon land. The debtor bailiffs cannot board a ship of His Majesty and hope to leave unscathed and intact.'

'Especially if our good captain has his bloody cat with him,' jested Admiral Forbes.

'Ha! Quite!' Lord Pitt agreed, looking for the steward. 'Call for His Lordship, should he be so inclined, if you please!' he bellowed and he rang his tiny bell. 'It is time for a late sup and a much needed chat. Apart from entertaining us, Cooper here has been most forthcoming with all this business and I would like to share his preliminary findings with our esteemed dinner guests.'

A side door opened and Admiral Lord Howe and Admiral Hood casually entered the board room. Cooper stood at once, which was quite acceptable of course, no harm done as he had already accepted his commission. He saluted Admiral Lord Howe directly, a fighting admiral of some distinction. He had always admired the Admiral. Howe had also been First Lord of the Admiralty prior to Lord Pitt. No doubt he was the likely candidate to succeed as the next Admiral of the Fleet. Cooper turned to Admiral Hood who had his hand out. It was an honour of course to be recognised by such seniority. Cooper knew Hood, his old squadron commander, but also he knew him as the reigning First Sea Lord, appointed in eighty-nine after retiring from his command in Portsmouth. A First Sea Lord, not to be confused with First Lord, is of course the professional head of the Royal Navy and is a man who definitely wielded untold power. The room now accommodated the four most powerful men in England, bar one. Each and every one could make or break a career. Not to be completely disappointed, but Cooper's eyes suddenly widened. Holy Mary and Joseph he screamed inside, Lord Pitt's brother was in company, the Prime Minster himself.

'Good luck Captain,' Lord Pitt bade. 'Your written orders will be forwarded to you directly. In the meantime, there's a new blue frock coat and a white waist coat, your size, waiting for you on the way out.' And he paused to eye his hat, wincing as he detected the small hole. 'And you may want to purchase a new hat, god speed now!'

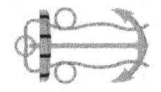

Chapter IV
Inn All Haste

Cooper resolved to make good his way from the Admiralty along Whitehall. The shadows deepened and the streets eventually darkened, but there was still a small buzz of folk milling about. As he navigated the waning light the prominence of his new blue frock kept him in good stead. To his utmost surprise, more than just a few hats were cordially tipped his way. Nonetheless, he had business to attend. Should he have encountered a wild squall in a robust sea he would still know exactly where to go, or at least he thought he did. Should his navigation prove precise, it would not be much farther. In fact, his destination should fall just ahead he calculated, directly afore a much acclaimed tavern known as The Garter.

In the near distance The Garter loomed, lit up almost with an obscene extravagance. It was a brothel of course, one which had stood since the thirteenth century. Yet interestingly enough, the place had at one time been reputedly rumoured to hold favour with

His Majesty, Charles I. It may have been a brothel, but it was also one of the best taverns in town. And it had become such perhaps nigh on a hundred years past, so it was when the son of a politician acquired it, licence and all. He did not own it long and quite rightly of course. Cooper eyed the inn as if it were a lighthouse revealing the shoals. In course he at last chanced to uncover the very front door of his intended destination, the Inn All Haste. Now this was a modest yet respectable looking inn, definitely not a brothel and never would one find rabble in this establishment. Of late, its patronage was more frequented as a tavern though, rather than an inn and to be sure, it definitely had a distinct charm.

'Welcome, sir?' greeted the innkeeper with a polite nod.

'Captain Cooper, ma'am,' he formally announced, pausing for just a moment to realise the enormity of his new title. He could not help but grin. 'A table, if you please, for two?'

'Captain? I see,' she said warmly with a knowing smirk. 'Welcome to the Inn All Haste. I am Missus Smythe,' she cordially added, introducing herself. 'I will be at your service tonight, sir. And your table is already waiting, a private room specially picked and may I add, cleaned for you both. Your esteemed colleague is already seated. He has since started with the port I dare say,' raising an eye and she paraded him through the tavern, a most prominent guest for all to see of course.

'Captain Cooper, I presume?'

'Captain Nelson, sir!' he smiled. 'Indeed!'

'I see you have deciphered my note, no small task either I must admit. Take a glass sir, not a moment to lose,' and standing he held his glass high. 'Allow me to officially give you joy of your command and your promotion,' and they downed their port and profusely shook hands. 'Now, have a seat, if you will, most comfortable this place, most comfortable.'

'I admit, it took a while this time sir, the note that is, *"Attend all haste in the regular hour..."*. But then it dawned upon me that without commas to intercede the words *"all haste"*, it may in point of fact be a noun and therefore most logically a place. We of course have attended here some years ago for a similar officers' meeting, at this very hour if I am correct?'

'Aye Coops,' he congratulated. 'It was this very hour. But if I

Ships of War — Murky Waters

recall we were a door or two up, in the other place lit up like a bloody lighthouse, you know, the house of disrepute, ha, ha!'

'For king and country, sir, in course!'

'And how long *"a while"* did it take exactly, this act of decrypting?'

'Oh sir, I am mortified to say it was a good twelve minutes and one-third, to be sure, though I was terribly put out of sorts by a lieutenant waiting in the same room, poor wretch.'

'It is good you have retained your wits, for you shall need them. Now, I have taken the liberty of booking this private room and ordering us some late supper, pork suckling if you please. And I have something for you!' Nelson drew from his pocket a sealed parchment which he offered most wholeheartedly. 'Your orders, Captain!'

Cooper managed to contain his exuberance, but only just. Without a moment to lose he broke the seal and poured over the wording. It read:

*To Lieutenant **Hayden Reginald Cooper** hereby appointed **Commander** of His Majesty's Ship **Agamemnon**.*

*By Virtue of the Power and Authority to us given We do hereby constitute and appoint you **Commander** of His Majesty's Ship **Agamemnon** willing and requiring you forthwith to go on board and take upon you the Charge and Command of **Commander** in her accordingly strictly Charging and Commanding all the Officers and Company belonging to the said ship to behave themselves jointly and severally in their respective Employments with all due Respect and Obedience unto you their said **Commander** and you likewise to observe and execute as well the General Printed Instructions and such Orders and Directions you shall from time to time receive from us, from **Captain Horatio Nelson**, or* *your superior Officers for His Majesty's Service hereof nor you nor any of you may fail as you will answer the contrary at your peril. And for so doing this shall be your Warrant.*

*Given under our hands and the Seal of Office of Admiralty, February 1791.
By Command of Their Lordships.*

It was the standard wording, as he much expected. The excitement buzzed, but upon finding the end he couldn't help but feel a little deflated. There was no mention yet of his intended cruise in the Channel. No mention of pirates, or of his mandate to take, burn or destroy. Nonetheless, he smiled and nodded. Here was proof irrefutable he had been granted his first actual command, a commission from the Admiralty. He was finally to captain a ship of war.

'Oh sir, thank you!' Cooper acknowledged. 'They mentioned Admiral Hood as my proposer, of whom I had no idea he even knew I existed. But sir, I knew immediately it was all your doing. They mentioned you too, in course. I shall not let you down!'

'My oath, Coops! I know you will not let me down, 'tis why you have been chosen.'

'How grand, sir,' he reflected, looking over his orders. 'Did your first letter affect you some, upon being given Badger, if I may be so bold as to ask?' And before he could allow Nelson to respond, it suddenly hit him, no less than the full weight of a broadside unawares. 'Good god sir! Agamemnon! My ship, sir!'

'Indeed,' he nodded, smiling as the penny finally dropped.

'She's a sixty-four! A third-rate and barely saw service out of the docks. Aye, she was built in eighty-one, just before the end of the war, Ardent class out of Buckler's Hard in Hampshire, technically a ship of the line! Captain Caldwell had her if I recall. Oh what a ship, sir, a draught of about seventeen feet, very good for shoals and chasing along the coast after smaller craft. Not to mention a broadside of five hundred and seventy-five pounds! Very handsome, sir with a deck of twenty-fours, a deck of eighteens, a

Ships of War — Murky Waters

quarterdeck full of four pounders and a couple of very nice nines on the forecastle. Those nines will come in very handy in the chase. I remember her sir, in the West Indies, she was uncommonly fast for her class.'

'I dare say you do remember her!' Nelson commended, his brow drawing in astonishment. 'You are right, of course. She was uncommonly fast, paid off late in eighty-three and as I understand it, she was subsequently laid up in ordinary. They have pulled her out of the docks for our little enterprise. But what you do not know, lest you run an organised spying ring of course, is that I have personally afforded her a new hull, copper sheathed from stem to stern. Cost a pretty penny, but if you thought she was fast before, wait til you stand upon her quarterdeck and let fly. She will outrun any seventy-four, which you may very well be in need to do and she will run down any of the latest frigates. And dare I say, not even the luckiest and fastest of sloop will ever sneak away, lest they ditch all their iron and even so, I believe it may not be enough. She's a pirate killer now Coops!' and he slapped his leg as he grinned and jigged in his seat. 'By god, I wish I was going with you!'

'Sir? You are not going with me?'

'Beached, I am afraid.'

'Beached? Alas, sir, they failed to warrant you a ship?' he protested. Of course Cooper was much relieved to firstly learn that Nelson was to be his senior in this endeavour, but this news was most unsettling. How indeed was that going to come about if his commander didn't have a ship? 'But sir,' he griped.

'Aye Coops, I am still licking my wounds it seems. Of course they all wish me this and wish me that, but hands high up are tied in this matter, for now anyway. I am too prominently high on the Captains' List they said. Can you believe it, ha, *"too high"* to be given a ship, for the love of Mary. But I must not be ungrateful Coops. No, not at all, for that would not do. Their Lordships have afforded me a position of commodore, second class, in this endeavour. But this second class commodore will be one who directs his squadron from shore, which accounts as a first in naval history I fear. So Coops, I will not be putting to sea. The silver lining, thank god, is that I will never fear discomfiture of the position, as it is to be maintained as a closely kept state secret of the highest proportion. As such, you are not permitted to address me as commodore, lest we are at sea. And I may not wear my commodore's uniform, again, lest we are at sea. We will not see our names in the Gazette, lest it be a complete pile of fabricated rubbish. Damn the secrecy!'

'Quite, sir!'

'However, in the meantime, I may afford my old shipmates, the ones of worth and loyal to a fault of course, the esteemed honour of position, of command, the chance of promotion and the great fortune of prizes! Do not fret, I will succeed, provided you succeed. Handsomely as well, my split of any prize generously set at one quarter.'

'Upon my soul, sir, that is more than most admirals are afforded!'

'Indeed, a *"silver"* lining,' he grinned, admiring his own pun. 'But no admiral wants anything to do with this endeavour. It's a career breaker, or maker, so you see. To take, burn, or destroy in peacetime is mostly frowned upon I am afraid, especially should one choose unwisely with their target. The truth is Coops, both you and I will be most expendable in this commission.'

'Nonetheless, nothing ventured sir, nothing gained,' he judiciously suggested. 'They chose you wisely sir. If anyone can do it, you can.'

'Perhaps, Coops, perhaps.'

'Sir?' Cooper prompted, standing with his glass. 'May I give you joy of your command, a commodore no less! Yet in any event, dare I say, but Their Lordships have fundamentally made you admiral, for what it's worth!'

'Thank ye Coops,' he acknowledged, smiling. 'Indeed.'

'It is up to our enterprise now sir, to see what your squadron can make of it. May I ask sir, how many other ships do we afford?'

'Oh? Other ships? Why, Coops, we have no other ships,' he announced most sombrely. 'We have but Agamemnon to complete our task.'

Cooper died inside. The fate of his old captain, now his commodore, lay solely upon his singular success at sea. A lot can happen at sea. Even a second-rate, a great ship of the line, can be lost

Ships of War — Murky Waters

by many a different circumstance. Storms, shoals, lee shores, uncharted reefs, rocks, indeed not to mention the numerous pirates he knew to be scourging the Channel, all and any, could happen upon him without a moment's notice. And Agamemnon was only a third-rate and she would be alone, most worrying. Nelson had seemingly invested heavily upon the enterprise, not just his waning fortunes but also his reputation and perhaps even his career. The weight of the world gathered and so it piled upon Cooper like a gargantuan squall falling fell upon a tiny sloop.

'I see sir.'

'Do not agonise Captain, for I have a plan,' he added, beaming as if he had just landed a flush and the pot was maxed out. 'Let us discuss it in full, perhaps on the incoming tide of the next day's morrow? That should afford you enough time to get there. Say, early morning aboard our flagship?' he grinned.

'Aboard our flag, ha!' he smiled. 'Of course sir.'

'She's down at Chatham.'

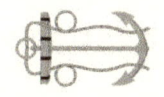

Chapter V
Agamemnon

Cooper stood expectantly upon the cobble. The coach arrived and he immediately levered the door for his commodore. The morning was brisk, the heavens were uncommonly bright and the wind near dead. A distinct eerie stillness filled the Chatham dock. It was deathly quiet. A red haze sank within the horizon, one Cooper had been admiring actually for some time, patiently anticipating the arrival of Nelson.

'Morning sir.'

'Well the early bird snatches the worm, 'ey Captain,' he complimented and they commenced a leisurely stroll down the dock. He looked about at the sky. 'Red in the morn...'

'...sailors be warned,' Cooper finished for him, with a grin.

'Indeed. And I must confess, when I first saw you last evening, I imagined your colour might be a tad more pale. After all, it is not often, or ever for that matter, that lowly lieutenants meet with the First Lord and the Admiral of the Fleet, especially at Whitehall and especially to decide our nation's woes. But you appeared quite in command of your faculties, so I must commend you. Lord Pitt can be quite the testing tyrant you know, yet it appears you have weathered his broadsides. I wonder, did Hood and Howe eventually attend, give you the once over, 'ey?'

'Aye sir, they did, as did Lord Pitt's brother.'

'What's that? The Prime Minister!'

'Aye, sir, the Post Master General himself!'

'Well Coops, now you have lived, been to hell and back one might say, but here you stand unscathed,' and he nodded, looking him up and down. 'You are going to be alright my lad, indeed. Good god, you have just met personally with England's entire war cabinet! Well, I guess it makes perfect sense,' he jested. 'Since presently, you and your ship ostensibly comprise, in whole I might add, the entirety of His Majesty's British war fleet, ha!'

'I believe sir, I could be feeling a tad more pale now.'

'Ha, quite!' he teased. 'But I must say, the new uniform suits you Coops, quite dashing. I noticed you still cling to that monstrosity of a sword. Did they insist to see it? They can be most officiously childish sometimes, I fear to admit.'

'Aye sir,' he replied, somewhat stunned. 'How did you know?'

'A calculated guess, based of course upon Lord Pitt's propensity to gouge information. Tell me,' he smiled. 'Did you do the candle thing?'

'Aye sir, ha, yes I did. How well you know sir.'

'It is good Coops. They respect a captain who knows his job, who weighs the chances quickly and goes straight on in, a fighting captain. I imagine your katana would have made quite an impression to this end, bloody scary thing if I may.'

There were not so many ships docked at Chatham and Cooper spotted Agamemnon directly. She was riding high on the water and her three masts towered higher than he reasonably thought possible. Her lines appeared quite appealing. How manoeuvrable her hull must be he ventured. This was a well-built ship he decided almost immediately. She even looked as if she had just come off the yard. It took his breath. It was basically a goliath of a frigate, or rather a small ship of the line. Of course, it was commonly thought most sixty-fours couldn't actually stand in the line, the consideration being that they just couldn't match the weight of a returning seventy-four. No, the sixty-four was built to move in battle, manoeuvre its victories with agility and skill, rather than slug it out.

'Beautiful, sir!'

'Aye, I cannot lie, I am most jealous Coops. It is a ship to my liking I find. But you will have your work cut out, if we are to get her ready for sea in time. Spring is almost upon us and you must be under way by then. As you can see, there are no cannon aboard, no spars, no cloth, not even a tender. She is nothing more than a skeletal frame. There are more than a great many items that need to be acquired in order to get her in shape, not to mention a crack crew.'

'Aye sir, five hundred I believe is her intended complement.'

'Indeed?' he said somewhat surprised. 'That many? Finding those directly will be our biggest struggle I fear. Let us repair aboard. We should have adequate privacy in the great cabin,' he urged and he paused for just a moment to survey the surroundings. 'I should not expect much activity here at Chatham. Apart from the Leviathan, a seventy-four last October and the Rattlesnake, a sixteen last month, there has not been a whiff of action. And I am told from Their Lordships, moving forward she likely won't be launching a damn thing. Goodness, a perfectly good dockyard just sitting wasting itself, fairly well doing much of nothing.'

'It's perfect sir!'

'Indeed, isn't it so Coops!' he grinned. 'Perfect!'

The great cabin was spacious, that is, for a ship of war. It had been entirely stripped. Only a small table sat modestly before them with just two spindly half broken chairs limping about it.

'We shall have to rectify this too of course. Nonetheless, let us sit and I'll outline our situation.' Nelson pulled out the very charts Cooper had notarised at the Admiralty. 'They are very impressed

Ships of War — Murky Waters

with your summations Coops, as am I. The experts were too, much to their chagrin of course and very much wish to meet you. I dare say some are genuinely impressed and wish you joy, whilst the rest in point of fact just wish to see you forthrightly lynched. Now, last night I mentioned I had a plan and it was no idle boast. But I fear to say that our endeavour much depends upon the first encounter. So, for what it is worth, this is what I propose.' Nelson stood as if he were commanding a legion of captains in a great fleet, entirely focused upon the charts and the delivery of the plan. He was rather diminutive in stature, but right now he appeared some seven feet tall. 'We will put to sea and we will immediately chase down our first target. Our course will naturally be wholly based upon your summation of the active attacks. I submit that our first target must be one of utter insignificance, the smallest if you will, perhaps a schooner, sloop or even a yacht.'

'A yacht sir?' he responded, quite dumbfounded.

'Indeed,' Nelson smiled. 'For, it is my intention that we do not burn, we do not destroy, but sir, we definitely are going to take! We are going to take and take, until it hurts. Naturally, we will need funds, more than you can imagine and don't think Pitt is going to steer even a halfpenny our way, not a souse. Prizes will have to provide the necessary gold. We were lucky to get Agamemnon, to be sure but already have they penciled in the cost and it is up to us to balance the ledger. I am told she came off the docks at twenty-four thousand pound and all told they have already spent another twenty-six thousand pound on her, minor repairs apparently.'

'So we are in for fifty thousand, sir?'

'Almost, but best you add another thirteen to the pot.'

'Sir? For the coppering?'

'Aye, a product of my being penny-wise and pound-foolish I fear.'

'Sir, you have put in thirteen yourself?'

'Yes and then, no. Let us say a great portion, is on loan.'

'I see sir,' Cooper responded, immediately weighing the gravity of the situation. Not succeeding would mean certain bankruptcy and disgrace for Nelson, perhaps even debtors' prison. It was a detestable predicament, one Cooper could only avoid by engineering complete and utter success upon the sea. Naturally he was immediately resigned to ensure the debt would be repaid, at all costs, the fate of all held now within his grasp. 'Then we most definitely must succeed, sir and swiftly.'

'I am sure I would be most grateful in course,' he thanked. 'To that end, our immediate goal will be to capture certain classes of ships, should they present themselves. This is especially important at the outset of our cruise...'

'Sir?'

'Indeed, for how else are we to build our squadron?'

'Our squadron, sir?' he excitedly replied.

'Aye Captain!' he cheekily confirmed. 'If Their Lordships are not willing to provide us with a fleet, nor a penny to get one, then by god, we will provide our own. Once we have a fleet, I deem our enterprise will have much less chance of failure, a hedged bet if you will.'

'Agreed sir, brilliant!' Cooper applauded, very much respecting such cautious stratagems and the men who contemplated them. 'We will have the power to overwhelm and to be sure, we will not be so easily scuttled by any one pirate.'

'Very well. Let us agree to commence our takings with a nice sloop, something which can scout, go back and forth in haste with dispatches and such. She must be very fast. Next, let us see about adding a frigate? A forty at least would be most grand or even two twenty-eights would suffice. But we must beware. We do not want so many ships that our fleet is suddenly noticed. And the speed and efficiency of our entire endeavour is paramount. We just cannot be weighed down. Our fleet must be a wholly mobile one, with the utmost speed. In course, let us wish for a fleet which comprises a sixty-four with two modern frigates and a nice fast yacht.'

'Indeed, that's a tidy number, most manageable and if I may sir? I would suggest one other,' he offered with a sly grin. 'We should at the very outset arrange to acquire one of these packet style ships.'

'What? A merchantman, really? Well, I am intrigued, but what the hell should we do with that? Do you want to run it into Brest as a fire ship? Good god man, the First Lord would skin us alive! If we are lucky, such a vessel might boast perhaps one, maybe two cannon, nothing of real use. And the purpose is to take, not burn, in case you really were thinking of a fire ship.'

'Aye sir, agreed, but to catch a rat, we will need cheese.'

'Ah, I see,' Nelson replied, pausing in deep thought. 'I think I like where you are going Captain, indeed!' he grinned. 'Let us make it so. But I think we will have a small legal issue. We are not at war. In our effort to capture such a ship, we cannot hope to account any such prize as a viscous pirate who set upon us and thereafter so keep her. French merchantmen only tend to be stocked with an obligatory four pounder here and there, nothing worthy of staring down our fleet or robbing our cradles. Nay, Coops, let us go one better. I will purchase us a merchantman, a good solid British looking piece of cheese. Five hundred pounds should do it.'

'Indeed sir, but it will have to be fast, to keep up with Agamemnon. And that may fetch more than a pretty penny. And it shall have to look like she has expensive tastes, to entice our rats?'

'Very well, make it so.'

'I shall look into this, directly.'

'I shall wait with bated breath,' he teased. 'Now, for the crux of it all, our ultimate aim, so to speak. Once we have established our fleet, we will cruise after the real targets which might return us some real funding!' and he stopped short as he eyed the charts before him. 'Goodness Coops, it says here on your footnotes there's a bloody ship of the line prowling about. You are sure?'

'It is most likely Pompée, a French seventy-four sir, Téméraire class ship. And she's new too sir.'

'New? How new?'

'Well sir, she was only recently laid down, out of Toulon, in fact about this time last year. And I would have rightly guessed that she couldn't possibly be launched until at least this May sir. But I am thinking something is going on and somehow she has been commissioned a tad early.'

'Indeed?' he warily responded. 'But you are sure?'

'I am only guessing about this, but aye, the mathematics bears it out and there are no other ships capable. The vectors and the distances and the area of sea, all point to a larger ship. I know this area and I know she is being built there sir, according of course to the French naval journals which I have come to acquire.'

'Indeed? I find that most enterprising, Captain, most enterprising!'

'She's a beast sir, thirty-six pounders!'

'The devil she is! We will leave her alone then, til we are ready. Whilst I might be inclined to wager upon the Royal Navy at the outset, we cannot risk such an engagement one to one. It would not be a fair match, by any means and should we chance to lose, they would hang us.'

'Sir, the French surely wouldn't...'

'The Admiralty, Coops...'

'Ah, of course, sir.'

'Now let us work on the particulars. This isn't normal of course Captain. As you know, in course we would just employ you to a ship, issue you some general orders and you would work the rest out yourself, or suffer the peril. But this will be complex. We will have to gather the right men, furtively. We simply cannot go around sticking posters up everywhere about a grand pirate hunt! There are bound to be French spies about. No, it will require a delicate hand. We will need to gather some cannon and a goodly amount of dry powder. We will need to furnish the ship with the right amount of stores. We are operating close to home, so it is well we can possibly lighten the ship somewhat. In all of this, the need for secrecy is paramount. We cannot be loading her up in plain sight, as if we are going off to blockade Brest. Your official orders will indicate that you are to be a packet, for the general correspondence and such. This will afford you the privilege of ignoring the orders of detention by ships of seniority. Simply fly the packet flag if challenged. We cannot have you boarded, ever, understood.'

'I understand sir.'

'Now, let us discuss frankly what has been going on. I suspect you probably already have a handle on things, considering your proclivity for spying,' he grinned. 'As you may know, the French are building dissent against their crown. Soon enough they will revolt. It is true that to date their revolution has not taken up arms, not officially, but we can see all too well what is happening. These things always follow the same course. And the so called pirates it seems are wildly prevalent. Our trade and shipping has been quite harassed and very much reduced. With only a small percentage of our military fleet operable, we cannot hope to protect much of anything. Were we to suddenly bring ships out of dock and into service, it would be very much noticed. Our escalation would give the French the necessary reason to act in kind, to build their fleets and in turn, to send them to sea.'

'But our spies thankfully have put two and two together now,' Cooper added. 'Or so the Admiral told me.'

'Aye, they are good at that,' Nelson casually jeered. 'Finally, we are now the wiser. But we cannot in good conscience start a war, not just yet, for we are not ready. But by god, when it comes, we can damned well finish one. In the interim, we must endeavour to diminish our enemy, if only to prolong their inability to strike us. The more French ships we take, the more British ships we safeguard and likewise, so will it all account in the grand scheme. So Captain, it is Their Lordships' wish that we are to silently prepare for war. And it must be silent, you understand. We cannot go throwing the likes of a Captain Nelson out into the Channel on some guard duty or some packet runs, not without heads turning. They just won't swallow it. But if we send some unknowns, all good up and comers, then it will look like peacetime business as usual.'

'Brilliant, sir.'

'So, is that you Coops? An unknown?'

'More than you can ever not know, sir.'

'Up and comer?'

'Up is the only direction I can physically go, indeed, sir,' he smiled.

'No doubt, the French spies will be looking, especially when a few of their ships don't come home. Aye, they will looking, but they won't see what is going on, not if we are careful. As you know Captain, you have no interest and not a penny to support you. And I have seen where you rate in seniority on the lieutenant's list. Good gracious man, bent my neck swooping that far down the page! So you see, the French will not see. We have been provided with a ship, a decent one and Their Lordships will make your commission public too. It will be portrayed as something necessary, something of the mildest importance, like the packet run.

But in point of fact, you will be hunting our so called pirates!'
'Indeed, sir!'
'So there you have it. I will afford you the honour of course of selecting your officers. I will not intervene. You are the captain of Agamemnon and it is wholly your prerogative. If you get stuck, of course I will be willing to provide some names. Let us fill our ship with the finest England has to offer. There is little time with much to do. Good luck Captain!' and he wholeheartedly shook his hand and smiled.

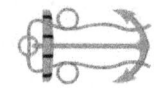

Chapter VI
Crispin Inn

Captain Cooper, in the fashion of any seasoned naval officer, waited quietly and patiently, assessing the situation. His eyes drew down upon his target, a split second to weigh the most likely, indeed the most advantageous method of its destruction. The possibilities brewed within his mind's eye, infusing a furious broth of wild notions as he carefully played out the encounter. He raised his hand, the blade within professionally poised, glistening. His grip held firm, his aim true, the sharpened edge hovering for one last moment before down it came. This was likely the best acting rabbit he had seen for some time he thought. He was salivating to be sure. With the tip of his knife, he carefully flipped off the awning, or what some might call the clagger or the clakker, those being the curious names with which a seaman commonly accounted for the pastry top of a baked meat pie. The flakes melted in his mouth, forcing his eyes shut as he swilled the juices. It weighed as a rare moment, one a poor naval officer might eternally savour.

Cooper usually tended to judge eating and drinking as tantamount to some unnecessary distraction, even an annoyance. But not this time, for within all his planning had he foremost selected this particular inn for this very reason. And now he could afford it. Apart from a handsome meat pie, a delicious ale and a comfy berth, it was here he might furtively base his operations. The first order of business was to properly acquaint the situation with his particular friend. To that end had a vague note to Spencer been dispatched, encrypted in his own personal way, but nonetheless official. Forthwith was the Lieutenant required and directed to attend the Crispin & Crispianus, an inn on London Road, exactly at eight bells in the afternoon watch. For a seaman in the Royal Navy that would amount to the start of the first dogwatch which, for a landsman, would be exactly four o'clock in the afternoon.

The note simply read: *"Watch first the dog's start... at St Crispin's Day..."*. A rather cryptic naval summons to be sure and perhaps one more befitting a gang of spies spoofing in a war time dispatch. Of course England was not at war, but to any naval officer the preponderance of risk and secrecy was always necessary, at any time. Cooper wholly trusted the message would be aptly understood. To his mind, it was a forgone certainty French spies were lurking about. They could be most anywhere, as they usually were. Peacetime England had already known a ship or two to mysteriously catch fire, even sink right in front of her dock. And further weighing his mind was an Admiralty adamantly insisting war was a matter of *"when"* and not *"if"*.

It may have been prudence or it may have been paranoia, but whatever it was, Cooper welcomed it as one would a fat enemy sloop brimming with gold, languishing downwind to leeward. Of course, to lose Agamemnon in port would not be his peril to legally bear, having not yet been read in, which is to say he was yet to officially take command. Nonetheless, he would ensure every precaution. He had even found himself subtly glancing twice at each and every person in the vicinity. If there was a spy, he would sniff them out. To bear the damning consequences of the loss of his ship

Ships of War — Murky Waters

before he even sailed would be to enter the fiery pits of hell and never return. If it were not for the busy refitting, he was of a mind he would already be suitably berthed within the great cabin, virtually a frothing rabid dog guarding his coop.

Cooper pondered the situation as he bore down on his pie, in true naval form his attack straight at it, allowing no quarter. He washed the flavour with his ale and as etiquette demanded, he sat back after each bite admiring the fine character of his surroundings. He was most definitely a man who engaged perpetually in thought, examining and calculating odds. It was a dogged curious quirk and oh how he presently brooded upon Agamemnon, not that it might show. He was determined to see his ship to sea as soon as practicable, prudence and logic all but demanded it. All he had to worry about then would be pirate cannon balls, unknown reefs and shoals, wild unannounced storms and of course the inept blundering of poor sailing in a crew just barely joined.

Cooper knew he risked much whilst Agamemnon sat in port. All told, the Admiralty could just up and change their mind, pull the ship for other duty, change the commander, or just flat out cancel the cruise with no explanation or warning. Crews often tended to view port as the proverbial Red Sea they had to part, running off or even just forgetting themselves in fits of drunkenness, never to be seen again. Without good jacks to run the ship, his command would be forfeit before it even started. And neither had he forgotten that the ship's stores would have to be preciously guarded, another weak point. And he would need guards for the guards. Thieving, mysterious loss and accidents were all common place in any naval vessel at port and each new day would see a new instance. Any one of these problems meant one terrible outcome, more time in port. It all weighed rather heavily.

Ponder indeed did Captain Cooper, for the paths to his perilous destruction were roads busier travelled than the one lonely route open to his salvation. Overall, it was a most precarious time and he knew it. Europe was in turmoil, England was all but waiting for war and French spies no doubt already had designs upon his ship. A peacetime port was far from an ideal place. Aye, sabotage would be a much easier proposition for an enemy, rather than take on a sixty-four gun ship in all her glory at sea. His thoughts were clear and his determination grim. It was his will against theirs and he would prevail, which is why he was presently sitting within the Crispin Inn. Handsomely situated in the midst of Rochester, the inn lay just three miles to the dockyard, which is to say just three miles from his new ship, Agamemnon.

The inn may have been in close proximity, but it also had some other necessary advantages. In particular, it was an inn well known for its generous hospitality to naval officers, especially certain naval officers. Moreover, he and the publican, Rufus Day, were already acquainted, albeit from some years before. Cooper's need for a trusted innkeeper was as necessary as employing a good bosun. He had even chuckled at the idea of making Rufus an honorary warrant officer, for the inn would feature heavily within the schemes of all his planning. It was here he was hopeful he might catch his spies, given the right amount of honey. Rufus would get wind of planned desertions, learn the local scuttlebutt and for a reasonable bargain, exchange the information for some coin. Rufus would ensure Cooper could meet in exacting privacy with his officers and, all in all, allow a tight grip to be maintained upon Agamemnon's operations. Indeed Cooper considered a trusted innkeeper in his back pocket was akin to a sharp eye in the masthead, a most necessary ingredient to any successful battle. To be forced to lower his colours before he even launched would be the greatest tragedy he could possibly imagine. Not only he, but his commodore would be completely destroyed. There would be no loose lips if he had anything to do with it.

'Thank you, Rufus,' Cooper kindly acknowledged, as the publican ushered Lieutenant Spencer into their private room. Rufus smiled back, with just a telling nod. He was definitely a pillar of secrecy for his acquaintances of old, especially those who kept him swimming in coin. By now Cooper had completely routed the acting rabbit, laid it on its beam ends and summarily sent it to the bottom of his belly. Only some crumbs persisted, the flotsam remains of the wreckage as it were. Presently he had the honour of the house ale in hand, no doubt a portion from Rufus's special stash. It was a local brew of some distinct quality and oh, he thought, how delicious it proved, another small luxury. He sipped it as if it were the last known drop in England, the froth creamy

Ships of War — Murky Waters

and the body full. Barely could he drag his eyes from under his lids, the acknowledgement of his particular friend's arrival still pending.

'Ah, Coops!' greeted Spencer with a smile, not sensing how terribly he had just interrupted him. Cooper nodded, reluctantly breaking off from the engagement. Finally he eyed Spencer with a look of inspection, before drawing a qualified smile.

'Welcome Spence, do take a seat. We have much to discuss.'

'What are you doing man?' Spencer interrupted, looking Cooper sternly up and down. 'Are you top heavy? Have you not gone mad? They will hang you if they catch you in that uniform!'

'Ha, no Spence, I am neither drunk nor maddened,' he smiled. 'Our fortunes have changed. I have been made, well, commander at least.'

'Strike me blind!' he swore. 'Please now, you're not hornswoggling me, are you?'

'Commander I am made, may I crook my elbow and wish it never come straight.'

'Well,' he blankly replied, somewhat paralysed in disbelief, prompting himself to snatch up the nearest mug. 'Then, if we are not to be dancing at Beilby's ball, hanged as such for impersonation, may I wish you joy, Captain Cooper, indeed, joy of your new command!'

'Thank ye Spence. Don't worry, I have my orders and my commission right here,' he assured and he put them upon the oaken table. 'But first, before I can discuss any of this business with you, I must put to you directly a proposition. In which, you are to choose, immediately,' Cooper insisted, eyeing him now as a superior officer, forthright and straight to the point and neither did he wait to receive Spencer's acknowledgement. 'As such, I formerly request you answer in the affirmative or the negative, if you please. Lieutenant Charles Prescot Spencer, will you accept a commission, boarding a ship of His Majesty with all rank and privilege bestowed upon such, as deserving the rank of lieutenant of the Royal Navy, including full pay and thereof, serve at His Majesty's pleasure? I do not know where you will sit in the seniority upon the ship, so I cannot answer as to your exact position, except that you have one, if you so desire.'

'You're topping it aren't you? A ship! Full pay! Is this a bloody trick question? Of course I will be answering in the affirmative!' he excitedly rejoiced, although Cooper continued to silently scowl, unmoved until the subtle message of a superior, as it were, was finally received. '...er, sir!' he quickly remedied. 'Aye, sir!'

'Very well. You will in course receive your orders and commission from the Admiralty, no doubt in a timely manner. But I must stress the need for the utmost confidentiality. You understand? There is to be no loose talk, which is to say, there is to be no talk at all. We won't be offering out what ship we have, or what our mission entails, or with whom we sail. I can say right now that it will be most uncommonly dangerous, physically and dare I say, even politically. I intend to gather what officers we can muster and then meet on board our ship in three weeks' time. She is docked at Chatham, only three miles down the river. In the meantime, you will be acting first lieutenant and indeed have much work ahead of you. Now, let us discuss the particulars.'

'I see. What ship did they give you?' he exuberantly quizzed. '...sir?'

'Agamemnon.'

'A sixty-four! A third-rate!' he cried in a whisper, almost jumping out of his chair. 'Well, that almost explains the enigmatic extent of your note, that is to say, your summons. I must admit it took me a few sweet minutes to sort that one out.'

'Indeed?' he mused. 'More than fortunate you are now here, for without, mayhap your backside might have been left on the beach.'

'Goodness, well, it is all plain as day, now I come to think about it. The first part, *"Watch first the dog's start"*, very easy of course, our meeting set for the first dog watch and all. The latter and importantly the only other part, *"at St Crispin's Day"*, was true brilliance may I say. Of course it had to be *"the where"*. There has to be *"a where"* and the note was quite short. And it could not be *"the when"*, as Saint Crispin's day is in October and I am sure you did not mean to meet some months from now. And lastly, due to the extreme cryptic nature of the note, I could only but assume there was not a moment to lose. Thus, our meeting naturally would take place on the next available dog watch. That only left where and I have never forgotten the old Crispin Inn or our friend Rufus,' he finished, now grinning in admiration. 'But the hidden irony did not escape me either. I congratulate you upon the subtle reference to Saint Crispin, that being Shakespeare's *Henry V*, calling his band of brothers to arms, at Agincourt, if I rightly recall.'

'You do rightly recall Spence,' he confirmed with an admiring grin. 'And now here we are at Crispin's Inn, a glorious band we shall ever be!'

'By George, Agamemnon, a sixty-four! How the devil did you rate such a ship, for the love of Mary, in peacetime!'

'I cannot disclose that presently. But suffice to say, we have a heavy job ahead of us. She has been laid up in ordinary for some time and is barren of basically every item necessarily prerequisite to our sailing. For now, I have prepared a list for you to fulfil. And I expect some in-roads upon these before next we meet. I know of no other in the entire navy who can scrounge like you, so I will accept no excuses. Keep a low profile if you please, but you will be happy to know, most of the items will be able to be gotten quite legally this time.'

'Quite,' he rejoiced. 'How refreshing, sir.'

'And I want you to find us a good master, as it is my full intent to employ a master, rather than perform the duty myself. We have a ship of the line and irrespective of my rank, we shall operate in course with the seniority of our ship.'

'I agree, sir.'

'Our master's main duty will of course be navigation. But we require an experienced hand here Lieutenant. Our cruise will likely take us up and down the Channel and into the Mediterranean, not that you will disclose this fact. But we will undoubtedly sail in close proximity to the coastline, perhaps one might say, even perilously close. And may I say Lieutenant, not our coastline either, if you grasp my meaning?'

'I understand, sir,' he acknowledged knowingly.

'In addition, I expect our master to take the ship's position daily and set our sails as appropriate for each required course. So there you have it. In course, he will educate our young midshipmen, as well as the master's mates, so far as in taking observations of the sun and the maintenance of the ship's compass. I expect him to ensure the ongoing goodwill and maintenance of the rigging and the sails. The normal duties will also apply, such as the stowing of the hold, inspecting our provisions, taking in stores and placing said stores to the greatest effect for optimum trim. We cannot afford to be improperly weighted so as to sail ineffectively, lest you enjoy the gruel so served at French prisons. He will be wholly responsible for reporting defects as he sees fit, directly to myself as captain, or to another so acting as captain. As such, he will personally supervise the entry of the official log, to record weather, our position and our expenditure. I do not think we will have too much issue with the preponderance of the English sailor to take to heavy drink, considering our cruises will likely be short in duration. But nonetheless, our master will ensure the security and fair ration upon the issue of rum on board, to the good health of the ship first and the crew second. Understood?'

'Aye sir and I know just the man we need!' Spencer immediately offered, his head down, furiously scribbling to note the fullness of his captain's orders. 'Aye, providing he ain't swimming with the fishes, I'll get him for us. Damned if he doesn't know every rock, reef, shoal and inlet, without a look mind you and speaks a number of the dialects of local lingo.'

'Very well, sounds a most prodigious master,' he complimented. 'Now it is paramount, Lieutenant, paramount that the ship's ability to make way is maximised. We will need men of knowledge in their craft, for each and every station. To that end will you locate our senior most rated man of the deck department, our bosun, who will of course act as the foreman of the unlicensed deck crew. He will be most responsible for the components of our hull, which as you may appreciate directly affects the speed we might make. He must be more intelligent than to which we are commonly accustomed as I will expect him to wholly supervise planning, scheduling and the assignment of work as well as provide the ingenuity to craft every ounce of haste.'

'I understand, sir.'

'Outside the supervisory role, I will insist he inspect the ship regularly. He may perform, with full permission, a variety of routine duties in order to maintain all areas of the ship, that is,

Ships of War — Murky Waters

those areas not so managed elsewhere, such as cleaning and painting. He must maintain our hull at all times, as well as our deck equipment. He will be responsible for the ship's colours, anchors, cordage, deck crew and the ship's boats and whilst in dock, the rigging. He will operate the ship's windlasses when letting go and heave up the anchors, god forbid to his great peril should he ever lose one. I fully expect a solid working relationship between the bosun and whomever you choose as carpenter. We cannot have strife on board due to some personal grievance. You will afford the bosun the first choice. Before engaging our carpenter, see to it the bosun is in agreement. I know it's not usual practice, but we cannot afford to blunder. Too much is at stake.'

'Of course, sir,' he agreed, without actually understanding the entire gravity of what might be at stake. Obeying his captain's orders for now was quite enough.

'I already have a gunner in mind, I think you know who.'

'Indeed sir, is it perchance Shaw?'

'I have already sent for him. By god, if he can get our crews' cannon work down to two minutes, we will be unstoppable. And I expect he will have our lubberly landsmen shooting dead eye within a month, lest he feed them to the sharks, ha, ha.'

'Landsmen, sir?'

'Aye, live lumber,' he confirmed. 'There's nothing else for it. We have some five hundred souls to berth on board. They won't all be seamen, not in the time allotted to put to sea. We will have to suffer a few landsmen of course. But let's get them into shape, see what they might do, before we swing them from the yard,' he smiled. Spencer listened intently, at the same time tasking to browse over the list provided. He had made the necessary notes and had aptly discerned the necessary flavour of the orders. He was a good officer. And apart from being astute of mind, this was his particular skill of course. Of scrounging and of providing, he had the honour of a most colourful history and had proven to be especially enterprising in most of his endeavours. 'All in all we will need fighters Spence, strong men good with a cutlass and men who can handle cannon with commendable speed. Agamemnon had twenty-fours as well as eighteens, so you and our gunner have hard work ahead.'

'Goodness, sir,' he replied in astonishment. 'Are we... at war?'

'No, is the official answer, for now. But nonetheless Spence, fighters, if you please,' he insisted. 'Now, let us toast,' he suggested, struggling to think for just a moment. 'Let me see...'

'It is Friday sir,' assisted Spencer politely, with a practised whisper.

'Good god, no, is it? What the bloody hell is the date?'

'Sir, rest easy, it is most definitely not the thirteenth.'

'Of course, thank you Spence, it's been a long week,' he accepted with a grateful smile. 'Let us toast, *"to a willing foe and sea room!"*.'

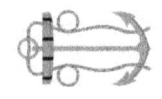

Chapter VII
Chatham Dockyard

Three weeks in the Royal Navy would see mountains moved, especially when the disposition of a captain fell inordinately upon his command. A captain without reasonable quarter and naturally not a moment to lose was a fearsome beast. Of course a seaman would be hard pressed to ever find a situation where they actually were afforded a moment to lose, such was naval life. And by and by a captain standing tall upon the quarterdeck conjured one almighty presence, holier than thou most seamen might say. He is the law, a terrible tyrant, his word absolute, his wrath irrepressible. He is the maker and the breaker. To report failure, to exude tardiness, is but to most definitely invite terrible peril.

Obedience and deference to command no less serves to measure a good naval officer, absolute trust an unequivocal necessary prerequisite. So, all in all, it seemed Captain Cooper had chosen wisely in his selection of first officer, for his particular friend Lieutenant Charles Prescot Spencer indeed brandished all of these traits, to a point of honour.

Spencer was not unlike Cooper in many regards. They had served together of course and both were typically bereft of interest, which is to say they carried no favour with the gentry. Certainly, they nary held any semblance of a worthy ally within Whitehall. They were both single men, unencumbered upon land with the looming threat of matrimony floating far from range to windward. Spencer was the junior officer of course, but he definitely possessed some singular skills, much to Cooper's silent admiration and esteem. Scrounging and arranging for almost anything seemed to be second nature. Ordered to find a golden egg in the nearest barn, more to the point, Spencer would emerge with the hen that laid it. When it came to his ship, he would arrange almost anything and presently, that foremost included employing able seamen, in the hundreds.

In a time of peace it was always a grand notion to think a ship could be handsomely manned. And it wasn't that you had to convince a jack to ship to sea. No, not at all, the entirely steeper challenge was to firstly find them, the good ones in any case. They hid away like cats in the rain, with hardly a twitch or a squeak to ever give them up. And if you were fool enough to come upon them without proper warning, hide nor hair would you ever see again. Ever skittish they proved, beyond measure in fact, a creature which very much required subtle coaxing. Spencer was akin to this practice, but hardly could he post the regular advertisements professing the usual promises of action, adventure and prizes. Secrecy had definitely served to becalm his best efforts. Jacks were mostly pirates at heart and hardly could they bathe in the taking of a prize without the standard legality a solid war offers. Thank the heavens that he knew every bar, house and shack throughout London and well into the south of England. Sailors were a particular breed with particular habits and these days it seemed only a good sailor could find another good sailor. His strategy was sound enough, wrangle a few of the very best, a sweet deal proffered and for him would they simply haul in the rest, especially the old salts. Jacks were a proud breed. They relished the thought of good pay and they detested any sailor who got in the way, especially ones who didn't pull their weight. With good officers and able seamen, the work to refit would progress in haste. Spencer knew time was short, as it always was and to this end had he been most industrious, scrounging like the dog of the sea he naturally was.

Cooper arrived on the dock eager to assess the progress, a light buzz of excitement filling each step. He had been careful not to interfere in his first lieutenant's domain, or even the other officers, not that he had even met them yet for that matter. He looked up at the rigging, as if to inspect the works, but he was really sneaking a grand peek of his new ship. Agamemnon towered over the dock, the River Medway within which she sat made to look now somewhat diminutive in respect. Oh how he yearned to get under way, to get his sea legs once more. He strolled onto the planking only to be halted and immediately challenged. The grim face of a jolly stood before him, unwavering and mute, all intentions clear. Cooper gazed upon the undeniable shiny red coat and the white fencings, noting the insignia of the regiment. The Royal Marines had finally arrived and no less than a crack regiment, all courtesy of Commodore Nelson. Thank god for the jollies, he silently rejoiced. He approached the gangplank and the guards came to immediate attention, as did a stout looking officer slightly afore them.

'Sir!' greeted the officer in course.

'Ah, McFee, I presume?'

'Aye, sir, captain of the marines, assigned to Agamemnon. My commission and my orders, sir,' he added and he offered the parchments, already at hand. Cooper smiled as he beheld the unmistakable scrawl of Nelson. In his very short walk from the cobble had he already made up his mind about these marines. Without a second look, without even a how do you do, he immediately wagered the ship would be in expert hands. It was not lost upon him either that Captain McFee was already waiting at the gangplank, in full dress uniform, with his flimsies, fully expectant of his arrival. Curious indeed, as Cooper had made a point of not sending any warning, a small whim to perhaps test their worth. Either McFee had stood there all day, which he highly doubted, or the man had been alerted somehow. If it was the latter, then this was a shrewd operator, one who would fit nicely into the fray of Agamemnon.

'Very well, Major,' Cooper commended, addressing him with the courtesy title afforded a marine captain once assigned on board. After all, upon any ship of war, there can be only one captain. 'You have come well recommended Mister McFee, a pleasure,' he cordially replied as he paused to subtly inspect the man, a man who might at some point likely hold the entire fate of Agamemnon in the roughness of his crusty palm. McFee was a strong looking fellow, somewhat grim, but rather older than usual for his rank. He supported a most guttural accent. 'May I ask, from which part of Scotland you hail?'

'Why, sir, only the most violent parts,' he grinned knowingly, as Scots often do when pressed about their heritage. Oh how they so enjoyed adorning the carnage of their country as a badge of honour. And it was a forgone certainty, left to their own devices, they would have you educated quick smart as to from whom they had descended. Curiously, nine out of every ten were all direct descendants of the great William Wallace, as if the man had stopped at every hut, house and barn on his way to each battle. Pride aside, Cooper well knew them as a renowned people, much celebrated for their warring skills. McFee didn't know it yet, but Cooper very much admired the Scots. 'Aye, hailing from the clan Campbell, sir.'

When it came to warfare and fighting, the Scots were hardly modest about their prowess, but in reality they were in fact everything they purported to be, indeed most terribly formidable. They so enjoyed a good scrap, almost too much. Presented with having absolutely no one to fight, no doubt they would commonly just fight each other. Cooper actually knew quite a bit about the clans of Scotland and he well knew the Campbells, a clan far from the pages of obscurity. They boasted a notoriously colourful past, the usual warring and such. Their infamy perhaps rose when they were at odds with clan Gregor, over land of course, a matter thankfully well and truly settled centuries before. In very recent times they were nothing less than the talk of the entire nation, their third earl passing without an heir. That was in eighty-two Cooper recalled and at the time it was a cause for great concern, clan war all but assured. But curiously, no madness came of it and as Cooper understood, it was a young nineteen year old John Campbell who assumed the title of Lord Breadalbane, without even a breath of opposition. Cooper well knew, indeed so was it common knowledge, the clan Campbell were all presently holding up under Lord Breadalbane, some talk of forming a regiment of fencibles. It begged the question as to why McFee was not with them. Cooper was suddenly at pains to try and make sense of McFee. Scots were parochial to a fault, blood for blood and brothers in arms. Indeed it begged a good question, but one that perhaps could wait.

'The Earl of Breadalbane's clan, if I am not mistaken?'

'Aye, sir,' he confirmed, somewhat surprised.

'Indeed, then I compliment you on a capital heritage Major,' he offered. 'One to be lauded, but if I may, am I to understand you are McFee, not Campbell?'

'A minor defect of my parentage, sir,' he added with a smile.

'I see,' Cooper grinned, knowing full well what he meant, immediately asserting he must have been born a bastard, by definition a child born out of wedlock. In such cases he well knew it was not uncommon for there to be an alternative family name. Cooper was somewhat intrigued. 'You will no doubt find yourself in fine company here Mister McFee,' he added with a devilish smile.

'Thank you, sir.'

'Now sir, I wish to compliment your command, if it pleases. The dock seems most adequately guarded, as is the larboard side of our ship and may I say, guarded without throwing out unwanted attention. However, might I enquire as to your protection to starboard, to the river? Do you have jollies stationed aboard thus, looking over the river and her movements?'

'Aye sir, and more,' he grinned and he began to stroll abaft Agamemnon. 'If it pleases, sir,' he added, beckoning his captain to follow. 'I have a man in the rigging,' he whispered and Cooper peered skyward. More like two men he thought, there being an additional man stationed to watch over the territory to larboard, on and past the dock. Cooper grinned as he suddenly realised how McFee had been alerted to his arrival. That lookout must have the eyes of a hawk he thought. 'And I have a man every fifteen paces starboard and please sir, feast ya eyes aft,' he lastly whispered, without a point or even a glance. It was with enormous surprise that Cooper in fact eyed a boat. There were no marine uniforms within, only poorly clad swabbers and painters. But at close inspection he could discern they were anything but that. In fact, they were well-armed marines who seemed very poor at swabbing and painting. 'In guise I have issued each boat with a long tom, although please sir, do not expect much actual painting to be done, none that is any bloody good.' True to his word, Cooper spotted the long toms, long poles with the paint brushes fixed on the end like long bayonets. At closer inspection he could see muskets strapped to the poles.

'Very clever, Mister McFee, outstanding,' he immediately complimented. 'And should any raiding party arrive, let us hope your men are not so far round the bend they might confuse the long toms with their bayonets.'

'Ha, ha! Aye, we live in hope, sir,' he mused.

'I must admit,' Cooper candidly offered. 'I could not even see them til I got here now, capital indeed. Sir, I leave you to your duties, for which I can see you need no schooling. Good day.'

Cooper silently eyed the surrounds and the progress upon Agamemnon as he made his way aboard. To his satisfaction, she was almost looking like a ship of war. The spars had been lifted and even rolled sail cloth adorned them. She was riding low in the water. He rightly surmised the cannon must have been delivered. The deck supported a number of boats now and what was that smell he wondered, powder? By god he thought, they must have snuck the powder hoy in during the night. He was about to compliment his first officer when he was abruptly halted by a long beastly groan, a farm animal baying it seemed. And then a pungent smell overcame him, his head turning sharply.

'Ah, a few beasts sir,' confirmed Spencer gingerly.

'God awful smell, Lieutenant,' he replied, thinking it might be a tad early in the process to be loading such stores.

Ships of War — Murky Waters

'Precisely the idea, sir,' Spencer whispered, so as to inform his captain discretely, so the penny might drop. How cunning Spencer had been Cooper thought. 'But they have only just arrived sir, so you may still be able to smell the powder, apologies.'

Of course, Spencer was the only officer who vaguely knew about the intended plans for Agamemnon. And for now the lieutenant remained intent on keeping it that way, even from the other officers. It was by command of course, Cooper for now choosing to withhold such information. That is to say, he had Spencer lie to them. As far as they were all aware, they were refitting the ship for another crew. Eventually she would sail to the West Indies. Perhaps she would even continue to Captain Cook's new colony on the far side of the world, likely never to be seen again for some untold count of passing years. So it was understood, the ship, together with her complement of marines, would be taken out into the Channel and summarily handed off to an incoming crew at Portsmouth. As far as any spy might be concerned, this was good news, another British ship ferried far from the real war, conflict all but bursting to erupt. Whatever it was, it was a good yarn, quite believable. And it had seemingly taken hold, the tale blabbed back to Cooper at the Crispin Inn and even the other local taverns, The Bull and The Coach and Horses. Naturally, his crew would all eventually hear the truth of the real orders, but only when they were safely at sea, the scuttlebutt of the town left far behind.

It may have been Cooper's first command, but already was he proving a shrewd tactician. In nothing would he put his trust, except perhaps god and very little else would he ever rely upon. Perhaps the unimpeachable discretion of his first officer was of course one exception, whilst the continued expectant devilry of the French spies was perhaps the other. Indeed he was counting on these spies to be dubious and doubtful, as is their kindred nature of course. And any spy worth their salt immediately might scoff at the blether of a West Indies cruise. Such a cruise was hardly farfetched, indeed most credible and that in itself made it all the more outrageous to swallow. A good French spy would always be dubious, dismissing the first thing they hear directly out of hand. It was the natural reaction upon which Cooper was hoping. Next, these spies would likely be sniffing around for solid confirmation, which wouldn't be forthcoming and so the seeds of suspicion would be sown. Soon they would be frantic to discover the truth, perhaps assessing some great secret behind it all. And Cooper would give it to them, but not without some effort on their account. In some parts had he already let it slip that Agamemnon's cruise was in fact just as suspected, a complete and utter pile of invention, a story of cock-and-bull. Instead, they would hear Agamemnon was earmarked a packet, albeit another barefaced lie, yet upon all accounts, the real cover story.

Cooper had always found the second lie to be more believable. Sailing large, they would cruise the Channel ports without interference or sufferance of the regular delays. Agamemnon would pick up secret packets, deliver messages, dispatches and perhaps even haul some choice goods. Naturally, this was a dish too juicy for any spy. With their initial doubts vindicated, their suspicions proven right, they would be mice onto his cheese. This was how he played at cards too. Lure them in, no less than the master of a devilish hand, adding levels of trickery and deceit to each new bluff, the truth buried right before their eyes.

His officers lined the deck and to his great pleasure and utmost surprise, he was even piped aboard. Naturally, naval etiquette demanded that any captain received to larboard should, in honour of their rank, be piped aboard. Some crew milled about, their hats off with a knuckle upon their forehead, all curious to get the measure of their captain. To them this man was either a godsend or the architect of their doom. Their success depended wholly upon the captain and his skills. A captain's shyness was a hated thing with any jack, that is to say, a captain who might do his very best to avoid a fight. But a fighting captain was a man they would love, a man for which they would necessarily bleed.

Spencer summarily dismissed the gathering, quickly returning them to their duties, perhaps some silent recognition that he was utterly aware there was not a moment to lose. Cooper entered the great cabin ahead of Spencer, a private update from his first lieutenant most definitely overdue. In the midst of the cabin sat a wondrous oaken table and some handsome chairs. Even the sideboards were stocked with some sherry and port, a tidy stack of glasses supporting the decanters. The entire cabin had been spotlessly cleaned and tidied, the furnishings worthy of an admiral.

'Lieutenant, a seat if you please,' Cooper ordered, hiding a discrete smile. 'Before we discuss our present position, I would commend you on a number of matters, one being the wondrous condition of this cabin. Next, you will be pleased to know that I have heard our *"mission"* bantered about in the taverns, as has Rufus, so well done. The less important we are perceived, the less chance we have to be blown to kingdom come sitting here helplessly in port.'

'Aye sir, to be sure, would be most regrettable.'

'Quite. And I commend you on the beasts. They have now aptly hidden every damned smell at all, including our new powder.'

'Aye sir, I apologise for the inconvenience. Once we are preparing to get under way, I'll have the master stow them properly. Sea air will sort it out.'

'The master, Thornton, isn't it?'

'Aye sir, found him napping not far from here.'

'Well, good fortune early. As promised, he comes recommended as an impressive master, so they say, provided he stays sober. I thought it was he you were chasing upon. Well done. But as you know, the master will ensure the security and fair ration upon the issue of rum on board, my orders specifically to the good health of the ship first and the crew second. Perhaps, I will amend those orders. Perhaps another officer may be in charge of the rum stores? And let us ensure the stores are preferably guarded.'

'Aye, sir, I have already made the arrangements with Mister McFee and I have slyly left a token bottle half hidden about for Mister Thornton's secret pleasure, watered ten times to one. That should keep him from looking too far afield.'

'Very well, but if we cannot keep him sober, he will have to go, as much as it would pain us to lose him. Let us assign another to watch over him perhaps?'

'Aye sir, but the master is rated a senior wardroom officer, so it will take some convincing. Perhaps one of the master's mates, or a quartermaster might do? Perhaps it will take once I explain the biting pain of wallowing leisurely in a frozen sea, all brought about because the master had one too many a tot and missed the shoals. I will immediately see to it.'

'I must say, the ship, appears as if it has progressed beyond what I ever imagined possible and, I can imagine quite a bit. Please do inform me about the cannon?'

'Oh sir,' he happily started. 'They are most handsome, pick of the litter. All of 'em darts, straighter than a virgin handing out choir courses. If I may, I had gone to some pains to find our twenty-fours and our nines. I shan't make a fuss just now, but I will be most interested in how you judge the performance of our nines.'

'What, the chasers?'

'Aye sir,' he grinned, almost stupidly.

'I see,' he nodded somewhat intrigued. 'Virgins you say?'

'Freshly plucked sir, so much, even the madam of the house might gasp. Shaw, our gunner, has been liaising with Thornton and our bosun sir.'

'Our bosun, Waters I believe?'

'Aye, sir, a good man, fought in the war. All three of them have been at it, as to the positioning of each cannon, all with the haste of the hull in mind. It seems that not each cannon weighs the same, curious is it not?'

'What is curious is how the bloody hell did they know that to begin with? It seems we have a crack crew!'

'Aye, sir,' he chuckled. 'A right set of badgers!'

'Badgers? Indeed, then let us hope they focus their villainous ways upon just the French. Do any of them have any idea about our cruise?'

'Not a one sir, except maybe Shaw? But then, he is on old salt, a lifetime gunner. He ain't one to be giving much away either. Peering into his mind is much likened to being thrown into a darkened swell with a night storm bearing down and sharks swarming. Nonetheless, I get the feeling he knows something is afoot, but he hasn't uttered a word of course.'

'He is an old hand, most experienced, sailed with Nelson as you well know. He ain't quite a bob cull, but I believe he is honest enough. I better have a word with him. What of our crew?'

Ships of War — Murky Waters

'We are short on good hands sir, dare I say, the West Indies story has 'em a little off, you know with the yellow jack and all.'

'Ah, of course, the thought of one's kidney slowing melting into irretrievable mush amidst the irrepressible onslaught of agonising pain and endless vomiting, with the only joy forthcoming that of eventual death? Indeed, it is time for us to float our next story, about us being a packet and let them know it will be here in the Channel, far from yellow shores.'

'Aye, grand, sir and I believe it will do the trick.'

'Very well, make it so. Now, you will be pleased to hear I have an important errand for us to run,' he announced with some subtle excitement. 'The question is, when might we be able to take her out, for a short spell, if you will?'

'Sir, it is my honour and pleasure to inform you, for a short spell, she is in fact presently ready.'

'Presently ready?' Cooper grinned. 'But it has only been three weeks? Confound me body and soul man, presently ready!' he rejoiced and he slapped his leg.

'We can sail on the next tide, should it please?' he happily informed, beholding a cheeky smirk.

'Should it please? It most definitely pleases! Lieutenant, muster the men, what you have that is. We shall take her out on the morrow, on the morning tide.'

'Aye, aye, sir, morning tide it is, four bells in the forenoon watch.'

'And be sure to let our landsmen know the correct time.'

'Aye sir, ten o'clock in the morning it is, of course, sir.'

'How civilised. Our cargo will arrive most likely just after sun up. And our package should arrive upon the start of the forenoon watch. Here is a list of our cargo. Make the necessary arrangements. And Spence, best you be on your toes. I cannot say any more than that, but duly have you been warned,' he added cryptically with a knowing grin.

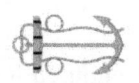

Chapter VIII
Four Bells

His Britannic Majesty's Ship Agamemnon sat serenely within the privy of the Chatham Dockyard, the rising flood of the Medway endlessly lapping upon the lines of her bow. The rising sun had barely brushed the horizon, the first rays stealing within the dockyard, venturing to rush the great cabin. Cooper was already seated, head knee-deep within his papers. Finally a slither of light slipped through the stern glass, sneaking upon his desk, an unofficial call to the breaking day. This winter's morning was brisk, more so than normal and the captain of Agamemnon could not be more pleased as he took a moment to survey the world outside. It was a feast to any seaman's eye, a fair sky, the run of a calm brisk tide and the hint of a light steady breeze. It had given him pause. Upon reflection, especially considering it was still quite early, a stiffer breeze in the offing might wholly be forthcoming. Winter by all rights should have almost passed, but the morning's frost was still biting hard and a latent mist wafted translucently across the Medway. It was a scene which might burn for long in his memory, perhaps even for as long as he might live, providing of course his life endured long enough to warrant such reminiscence. He beheld the scene with reverence, a good omen. It was utterly picturesque, verily befitting the inauguration of his very first command.

Cooper secured the square-port, tight, preferring to leave the dead lights ajar so he might still admire the view to the rear of the ship. He was particularly glad to have his wool he thought, a precious item for which he had saved his coin for some months. Of course he was quite accustomed to the cold, especially at sea. Oh how he verily enjoyed the time just before and just after dawn, especially in winter. Within it the world seemed a quieter and somewhat more reserved place, fresh and perhaps born anew. All in all, it was a moment in which he could contently sit, contemplation of the highest order endlessly afforded. It was almost as if the sins of yesterday were washed away, forgiven as they perhaps were each Sabbath. For a moment he pondered his sins yet to come. After all, was he not sitting within the great cabin of a sixty-four gun, commander of a most formidable ship of war, all but readying to kill French pirates?

Contemplate the early hours he had, but with the sun upon the horizon, duty topside would soon call. For long, perhaps even before the morning's twilight emerged, had he been immersed deep within the bowels of the ship's paperwork, navigating the bookkeeping of his new command. It was a detestable affair for most captains of course, the proper handling of funds no less treacherous than the encounter of shoals, reefs and hidden rocks. It was going to require a delicate balancing act, if only to make the very most of the paltry funds he currently afforded. It was some comfort the lieutenant's half pay upon which he and Spencer had barely survived would now thankfully be a thing of the past. As a serving commander he would be paid twice as much as a lieutenant. And he would need it all. After all, he was captain of a third-rate and with that came a financial responsibility to keep his cabin well stocked and in order. A man of his station was looked upon to provide a fare of high quality, not to mention good wine, sherry, port and perhaps some cigars. Hosting dinners for his officers, receiving visiting captains and even pandering to the odd dignitary would be a regular occurrence of course. He would have to limit the frequency no doubt, lest funds were somehow to arrive from another source, such as a prize he instantly thought and to this he quickly knocked the nearest wood.

It was less than five minutes into his budgetary calculations where in utter dismay he ultimately found himself. His annual pay may have been a handsome sum of around £200 per annum, but in actuality, he was receiving far less. In course he would lose a portion to the obligatory deductions imposed by the Admiralty, such as the Officer Widow Fund, the Greenwich Royal Hospital Fund and the Greenwich Chest Benefit. Notably, a rather sizeable portion was also being retained until decommissioning, a practice the Admiralty thoroughly enjoyed for the obvious reasons, but mostly insisted upon because they could not trust the behaviour of their seamen or expect the safe return of their very expensive ships. All told, with what he deemed the bare minimum of his expected expenses as captain, he was of the unhappy opinion he would be lucky to have left even one shilling. Should any unforeseen instance arise, he would actually be put in the compromising position of requiring a loan. It was precarious, a situation he would have to well think upon.

Four bells rang in the morning watch, two chimes together with a small pause in between. To the people of Chatham it was now six o'clock and for Cooper, it was past time to venture topside. With coffee in hand, he headed for the quarterdeck, the sacred retreat for officers. A busy morning was brewing, a true test with barely only four hours left til the tide turned. He knew stowing the cargo would prove no simple task, especially considering its bulk. Yet, all going well, this would be the day and oh how he buzzed as his steps echoed healthily upon the planking.

As he arrived on deck it was oddly peaceful. Before him a sullen deathly still presented itself. Suddenly the shrill pitch of the bosun's call unexpectedly broke. The call, which was really an elaborate whistle, was the ancient means with which commands could be passed, or piped, to the crew. As you might imagine, this was indeed a totally necessary practice, one which wholly ensured the clarity of each and every order. Passing any order proved no simple matter on a ship with a crew of hundreds, especially when the sea was pounding or an ocean breeze was howling. There were many different calls of course, but this morning's was strong and distinguishable, the long high pitch to *"still"*, that is, to bring the crew to silent attention. If it had not been for the piping and the sight of a few hundred men blinking blankly back at him, Cooper would have sworn every man, jack and jolly had deserted. Apart from the odd cry of a gull, the distant echo of a rickety cart, or the hungry wash of the Medway lapping upon the hull, not a single sound was stirring.

The first officer had been quite busy, the crew already formed into divisions. It seemed the entire ship's company had been waiting for their captain, including McFee and his jollies. It immediately struck Cooper as to how grand they appeared, some four hundred men standing in absolute serenity, obediently awaiting the next order.

'Bloody hell, is it Sunday?' Cooper whispered to Spencer, somewhat dumbfounded, perhaps now thinking it was time for their weekly religious service, article one quickly coming to mind, *"the commander shall cause the public worship of almighty god, according to the liturgy of the Church of England, to be solemnly, orderly and reverently performed... and that the lord's day be observed according to law...".* 'Damnation, the lord's day be observed!' he frantically thought. 'We won't be able to take the ship out if it's Sunday, the jacks would never forgive me!'

'Sir,' Spencer reported. 'All hands present and accounted, ready for the reading in of her new captain, should it please. And may I suggest sir, perhaps directly following, may we also read in the articles, thus dispensing the need this coming Sunday?'

'Very well,' he evenly responded, concealing his absolute pleasure and his utmost relief. He was now thinking how fortunate he was to have such a capital first officer. Spencer had the makings of a good captain already, his rationale and strategy always a few steps ahead. Cooper was regularly at pains to ever find anything to correct. Yet in this case, it seemed Spencer had overlooked one item, indeed an item ever so crucial to the reading in of a captain. For such an important ceremony, perhaps it may well have been more prudent for the captain to be warned in advance. 'Lieutenant...' he softly whispered, leaning in so as no one could hear, his tone somewhat beckoning and wholly surreptitious. But before he could continue Spencer subtly handed him a copy of his commission.

'Sir, for the reading,' Spencer whispered back. 'Or at least a good enough copy, that is to say,' he added confidently before turning to face the ship's company.

'Ah,' Cooper acknowledged, realising he had been dished once again. With a deep breath and the look of a tiger about to eat its young, he eyed the crew and began. 'Very well, to Hayden Reginald Cooper...' he started in a loud distinct voice, not that it mattered as it was early morning and the entire crew were quieter than a pack of rats thieving the last biscuits in the pantry. '...by virtue of the power and authority to us given, we do hereby constitute and appoint you commander of His Majesty's ship Agamemnon... nor you nor any of you may fail as you will answer the contrary at your peril...' and he peered up at that bit, devilishly exaggerating the depth of peril before finally finishing with the Admiralty's authority, '...by command of Their Lordships.'

With those last words it was official, Cooper was now the commander of Agamemnon, a third-rate, sixty-four gun, line of battle ship with over four hundred souls, its sole purpose to serve his every will. And in turn would he serve at the pleasure of His Majesty, King George III. But now, not even an admiral could order him how to sail her. The helm was his alone and so would he live and breathe with the well-being of his ship. Should she capture a handsome prize, he would enjoy in a healthy one quarter of the spoils. But should the hull unexpectedly explode, or should sea water suddenly breach, should she be lost in any way, he would now be completely answerable, a court martial proceedings mandatory. Some captains had even been known to suffer death upon the loss of their ship and no captain would ever forget poor Admiral Byng, who indeed suffered death, shot after a court martial having not even lost his ship.

Spencer proceeded to read the Articles of War, a firm reminder to the crew of their obligations, its contravention resulting mostly in the pressing sufferance of death.

'*...Five: All spies and all persons whatsoever, who shall come, or be found, in the nature of spies, to bring or deliver any seducing letters or messages from any enemy or rebel, or endeavour to* *corrupt any captain, officer, mariner, or other in the fleet, to betray his trust, being convicted of any such offense by the sentence of the court martial, shall be punished with death, or such other punishment, as the nature and degree of the offence shall deserve and the court martial shall impose...'*

Spies thought Cooper, a beast more treacherous than finding himself suddenly caught to leeward under the gun of a vastly superior ship. And the skunks had to be out there, hiding like a dirty blue water high tide rock just waiting for the ebb. He was of a mind to have Spencer read that one over again, if he could.

'...Twenty-five: Care shall be taken in the conducting and steering of any of His Majesty's ships, that through wilfulness, negligence, or other defaults, no ship be stranded, or run upon any rocks or sands, or split or hazarded, upon pain, that such as shall be found guilty therein, be punished by death, or such other punishment, as the offence by a court martial shall be judged to deserve...'

To that particular article he immediately pondered, for it really need not be read. Death was a most likely result of any wreck and should the crew somehow manage to not freeze or drown, the captain would always be the one to suffer court martial. It was true a tribunal might include the master as well, but the captain was ultimately responsible and wholly culpable, even in the instance where he was absent from his ship. It had been known to happen. The seas, the channels, the oceans, even the rivers had constantly proved to be an unpredictable entity, a mysterious precarious beast for which upon every moment demanded the utmost respect and diligence. If Cooper could somehow cure the illness long known as slumber, nothing would prevent him from standing watch every day and every night. To avoid destruction and the customary peril that followed, much would depend upon his choice of officers and their handling of his crew.

'...Thirty-five: All other crimes not capital committed by any person or persons in the fleet, which are not mentioned in this act, or for which no punishment is hereby directed to be inflicted, shall be punished by the laws and customs in such cases used at sea...'

In conclusion, the bosun's pipe sang, high for just a second only to sharply finish low, the distinct call to *"carry on"*, the crew summarily dismissed.

Whilst in port, Cooper tended to favour the starboard side of the quarterdeck, presently because he enjoyed the serenity afforded by the view of the Medway. The quarterdeck was as a holy shrine for any captain. It served as a place to observe, to think, to immediately strategise and most importantly, to be clearly seen, which in Cooper's mind, was to be clearly feared. He was also finding that there was some practicality in herding his officers to larboard, affording the optimum view of the dock and the work so carried out. He found it interesting as to how his officers had drawn some imaginary line upon the planking, splitting the space between them and their captain. It was as if the vengeful hand of god might suddenly strike them dead, should they as much as even dare think of crossing. He was once one of those officers of course and now it made him grin. High upon the quarterdeck, sneaking a look over the bulwark, Cooper could discern the tide sucking in even harder now. To his satisfaction the wind still favoured the ship. It would be a capital start and he would pray it should hold, for he had no immediate need to test his crew just yet, especially with a difficult exodus. No, there would be plenty of time for that in the offing, out to sea within the safety of the Channel and most importantly, far enough from discerning eyes. A landsman's wind, being one which comes directly astern the ship, is what he would most welcome.

'Sir?' a squeaky voice interrupted. Cooper peered down with a smile. It was Midshipman Jarvis Thomas Holt, a young gentleman from a most prodigious Westminster family, posted to the ship from one of Nelson's circle. It was quite common of course, all part of the process of becoming an officer. Young gentlemen, those who were the sons of naval officers, were actually permitted to enter the service at the age of eleven, rather than the standard age of thirteen. Holt appeared about fourteen, fresh and uncommonly bright. To make lieutenant was any midshipman's goal and Cooper was wagering it was also Holt's goal, especially considering the pressure brought to bear by his family. He wondered if the lad even wanted to be here, such is the case amongst many a midshipman. Time would tell, as firstly the lad would need to prove six years in the service, two as such in the rating of midshipman or mate. Cooper could only admire the tidy dress of young Mister Holt, an aspect which said much about him. In actuality, the lad was in fact moreover the honourable Lord Holt. And of everyone presently aboard, he was the one most likely to ever make admiral, or failing that, maybe prime minister. Until then, his rank would rightly progress faster than the bilge rats clearing unguarded cheese in the wardroom. It was also probable Cooper would one day be saluting this young boy, that is, depending upon who made post-captain first. 'It's Mister Spencer sir, begging your pardon. He ordered me to inform you that the lookout has something to report. The lookout felt it prudent sir to pass the word silently, sent one of the monkeys down. Mister Spencer, sir, said it was most pressingly important.'

'Pressingly important he says?' Cooper remarked, now somewhat intrigued. After all, they were in port, inland some matter of miles in fact and unless the French had declared war at four bells and snuck their fleet up the Medway unannounced, he was at a complete loss as to what could be so damned important. 'Which lookout, was it the one they call Mister Eagle?'

'Aye sir, that's him, one of the jollies.'

'I see,' he nodded, now thinking worry may be in order. If Eagle was up there and had seen something, he would tend to believe it. What an eye this jolly had, Cooper now thinking that if the second coming of our lord suddenly proved true, the man would undoubtedly see it first. 'And pray then, where is Mister Spencer?'

'Oh sir, he is up the main top, in the masthead, stopped there on his way to the nest.'

'Nest? I see,' he nodded. 'Hang on, what bloody nest?'

'Aye sir, that's what they are calling it, Eagle's Nest. Seems he has made some kind of housing up there sir, way above the top.

Quite clever really, keeps him tucked in nice and safe, appears quite comfortable too for which I gather he could stay up there as long as he wants.'

'Above the top? Good god!' he replied and he strained to look up the main mast, searching for the so called nest. Finally he saw him, right at the very tip of the mast. Cooper had never seen the likes of it before. 'Is that some kind of barrel? How the hell did he do that?'

'Sir, Mister Spencer begs your forgiveness, but says it's mighty important. Says he can come down to report, if it pleases?' Holt added, looking eagerly for his orders. Cooper knew Spencer well enough to know the last comment was a subtle insistent hint for his captain to consider attending directly. 'Sir? Should I...'

'That will be all for now Mister Holt,' he interrupted. 'I commend you. You have well performed your duty,' he added with a smile. 'Now young sir, would you please tell me, if you would be so kind, do young gentlemen climb?'

Cooper arrived at the masthead, a flat square platform fixed just above the lower yard, evenly split between the deck and the nest above. Spencer braced his captain, ensuring he could not slip. In fact, he had him nicely hemmed in. Never could Cooper fall, not in a gale force storm or even in a wild fit of lunacy for that matter. For Spencer to lose his captain right now would undoubtedly see the end of his current commission and likely the end of his naval career. He would be scrubbing bilge from the tarnished copper of slipped ships for the rest of his miserable life. Holt's cheesy grin appeared upon the masthead, the young midshipman beside himself in joy as he made the climb up the rigging, no less right beside his captain.

'In no uncommon way sir, would I have ever thought I'd be racing my captain up the rigging on our first day!' he cheekily announced. Cooper grabbed young Holt by the scruff of the collar, not unlike a kitten being hauled by the mother. Of course, in turn, to lose Holt would mean the very end of every officer on board. His father, the honourable Lord Thomas Holt, friend of the King, would likely not be amenable to the death of his son, let alone a senseless death. Never though was the lad's safety in doubt, for unbeknownst to Holt, Cooper had one of the older jacks, a sea daddy in fact, carefully follow the youngster up.

'Sir, my peeper,' beckoned Spencer and he quickly handed over his spyglass. It was a very good piece too in fact, one with a greater range than most, handed down from his father after the War of Independence with America, no doubt worth a pretty penny. 'Four points sir, broad off the larboard quarter,' he directed, which brought his gaze directly abaft the ship, thereafter adding exactly forty-five degrees further to the right. The directions brought his glass overlooking the streets. 'You may note our cargo arriving, sir.'

'I surely trust this is not what you hauled me up here for Lieutenant?'

'No sir. But if it pleases, cast the glass to the rear of our cargo, about a quarter of a cable's length. May I say, sir, it appears that our cargo be great bloody cannon, sixty-four pounders, if I might guess?' Cooper lay silent for the moment, wondering how his first lieutenant might know about the cannon. After hovering the glass over the carts, his question was summarily answered. Damnation was his first thought. And who the hell organised this great bloody street procession was his next unhappy thought. Their cargo, which was meant to be secret of course, was not only late, but it formed a line of carts that might bring every boy and man curiously out thinking there was a parade. He moved the glass fifty yards abaft the carts, searching. 'As I mentioned, there is a curiosity to the rear of the carts, a gentlemen, ruffled shirt, neckcloth, fancy hat, dark blue coat, looks very much like one of the gentry, sir.'

'I see him now. And what is so curious, if you please?'

'Look to his pace, he walks no faster than the carts, obviously a young strong fellow and there! See that old woman passing him.'

'The rascal is following our carts!'

'Aye sir, most curious, is it not?'

'A tradesman?' suggested Cooper thoughtfully.

'A thief? Not sure sir. Could well be a thief, but his attire doesn't fit.'

'One moment, let me see, he stops here and there, looks around, dark features, perhaps Spanish, a gentleman's attire,' he continued. 'Ah, there, we have him!' he exclaimed, handing the glass on to the young midshipman. 'Tell me Mister Holt, if you please, you are a gentlemen in the making, one who has had the fortune to mix in the circles of your father. What do you notice about this fellow?'

'Well sir,' he started, pausing to peruse the man. 'Fancy hat it is and if I may sir, he is most definitely a gentleman but then, not a regular gentleman. It is curious. The way he holds his strut, the way he stops to smoke his cigar and the biggest tell sir, the boots. Those are not the most handsome boots, very practical though, one more likely to be worn by one of my uncles when they ride, sir. But, I must say, he is otherwise dressed as a gentleman. It is a mixed bag, if I may say, most curious.'

'Most definitely a gentleman, but not a gentleman...' repeated Cooper, now eyeing Spencer.

'A sly boots?' suggested Spencer.

'Indeed. That man is likely a spy,' he confirmed, smiling at Holt.

'Mister Holt,' Spencer ordered immediately. 'At once, scamper down and instruct Mister McFee to take a detachment, three men should suffice and quietly now, detain that man.'

'Belay that Mister Holt. I have a better idea. Spence, we have the advantage here for once, for well do we know our opponent's hand. Perhaps we could use this to our advantage. Aye, it is true we can call his hand now and the pot is ours. Or, we could stoke the pot and take a much bigger win, if you get my meaning.'

'I believe I do sir,' he grinned most devilishly. 'Indeed.'

'Do you play cards Mister Holt?'

'Not so much, sir.'

'Then, I shall teach you, for when you are Admiral of the Fleet with a singular wit for strategy and a wily nose for battle, may you think well of your poor old captain and perhaps afford him a berth somewhere in your great armada.'

Ships of War — Murky Waters

Cooper and Spencer huddled on the dock together with McFee, ready to formerly accept the cargo. McFee had a small detachment of three marines, his best in fact, all sharpshooters and devilishly handy with a bayonet. Not that he needed them though, as McFee was no less than a wild Scot, much accustomed to violence and if Scottish truth be told for once, a straighter and truer marksman there never was.

'This shipment was meant to be delivered at four bells, on or before sunrise,' Cooper angrily lamented. 'There's plenty of twilight this time of year and I do not appreciate our endeavours being laundered for all to see. When I find the corked-brained dunderhead who sent our cargo in broad daylight, I'll have him flogged, hanged and skinned! And not in that order either!'

'Aye sir, it was quite a procession to be sure,' McFee added. 'And even a raving madman could not fail to discern the existence of cannon under the sheeting. But sir, I fail to gather the importance of this. It is peacetime. We are a ship of war and cannon are quite commonplace.'

'Look here, Major,' Cooper directed and he pulled back the sheeting to partly reveal one of the cannon. It was a monster, a sixty-four pounder. McFee's eyes immediately widened, suddenly realising these were far too large to be housed upon a ship. This then begged the question, what the hell were they for? 'Have you ever seen such a cannon mounted on a third-rate sixty-four gun Major?'

'Nay, surely would send it asunder, sir.'

'But your man, Eagle, it was he who spotted our unwanted guest following the carts. And he has made some kind of cuddy up there, remarkable. Eagle is proving a most capital fellow it seems. The idiots in ordinance may as well have planted a bonfire upon the carts and shot some fireworks off every bell, for all the good they have done. I cannot go into it now Major, but our commission is not as you might think.'

'Aye sir, I never thought this barky was going to the West Indies.'

'Which it ain't,' confirmed Cooper immediately.

'Aye, I already know, sir, we are to be a packet of some sort, not your regular packet now, some kind of secret packet. After all, when has a sixty-four ever been a regular packet?'

'I assure you Major, that is also not the case. We are not commissioned as such to be packet. Explanations will come later. Secrecy is tantamount for now. Presently, we must deal with this situation. There is likely a French spy out there. Now he knows about the cannon. Even if they cannot put two and two together, they will hound us til they know more. If we are not careful, the whole French Foreign Service will descend upon us and once we are at sea, we will be dogged day and night. No, no, no, this will not do. But I say, in lieu, we have been dealt a winning hand here. We know about our friend out there, unbeknownst to him. We can use that and we must sweeten the pot before we call our hand. Now listen Major, this is exactly what I want you to do...'

McFee marched his jollies outside the dock, together with Midshipman Holt. They found their quarry right in front of one of the local merchants, lazily leaning against a building. He seemed to be in the act of casually browsing the latest Gazette, a genuine enough endeavour, though who could really tell. McFee's jollies marched right up to him, suddenly snapping to attention with the synchronised stomping of boot and musket. McFee meandered through the line to stand before the man, a thoughtful look of arrogance preceding what seemed to be an obvious challenge.

'Sir?' announced McFee trying to get a rise. The fellow gradually tore his gaze from the Gazette, perhaps more in polite curiosity rather than startled concern. Holt was somewhat impressed and was almost thinking perhaps they had now made some grand mistake. This was one cool clinker. Surely a spy would react. Bereft of even the faintest sliver of apprehension he reeked of innocence, somewhat worthy of a new born kitten, not even an ounce of worry. McFee held his poise for the moment, half expecting the awkward silence to send the crud running.

'Yes, may I be of assistance Major?' he responded evenly.

'Ah, very good, would you be the owner of this house? I am looking for some cigars, capital ones of course, for my captain.'

'I am not unfortunately, but I too have come to this district in search of a good cigar. I am so terribly low presently.'

Ships of War — Murky Waters

'I see, then, if you are not from around here, I am sorry to have bothered you.'

'It makes me wonder Major, why you would need to stock cigars at all. Are you not bound for the West Indies?'

'Oh no, we ain't going there. I had heard that one too, funny how these things get wind. More like up and down the Channel for us, easy service and if we're lucky, maybe as far as the Mediterranean. So you see, we must find the very best, for otherwise our captain will have us flogged, ha, ha.'

'I would not try this house sir, but I have heard the one a few doors along may quite suffice.'

'Oh, grand, how many doors along exactly, these houses all look the bloody same?'

'Just two doors, in fact.'

'Please pardon an old Scot?' McFee feigned, pretending not to understand. 'Too much highland living I am afraid, perhaps for far too long. Still am I getting acquainted with accents down here you see. Did you say two?'

'Yes Major, two,' he happily confirmed, holding up his hand to signify. 'And should they stock any from the Caribbean, I would be most grateful if you would do me the honour of not taking the last one.'

'I think we can arrange that. Good day sir.'

'Before you go Major, I would like to offer your captain the last of my personal stock, should you be unsuccessful. I could not help but notice your carts arriving before, with your cannon, what a grand procession. From this, I gather you might be attempting to ship out soon, especially with the tide nigh upon us. I should be very grateful to sell you, at a fair price, whatever cigars I have left, should you fail to procure any from the merchants along here.'

'Well, that is mighty generous, sir. But it's very doubtful we will be able to load our cannon in time and we have such a terribly long trip ahead. I am guessing we will miss the tide. I am almost glad of it, gives me one more chance for a solid meal at the local club.'

'Would that be the Lion?'

'Indeed sir, you know of it?'

'Oh, I frequent the establishment from time to time, when I am in need of course.'

'Aye, I do believe that is the very place our captain mentioned.'

'May I recommend the ribs Major, surely the best in England if I may be so bold. But do stay away from the tables. There are sharks larger than the deep blue swarming there. And it is serious money I dare say, hardly are they playing for abel-wackets, if you please. You will find all of them, their pockets well breeched and of course gullgropers nearby ready to lend gold, always at an outrageous stipend. There are no swindlers of course, but indeed beware, for low tide can come quite rapidly at the Lion, Major.'

'Indeed?'

'Should you prefer something other than the ribs, may I recommend the bubble and squeak or the pope's nose, both capital dishes. Personally I am partial to the turkey, splendidly succulent.'

'Aye, I am with you there, for a good pope's nose is hard to resist. But beef fried with cabbage is a Scot's delight too. Well, thank ye and good day then.'

Cooper waited patiently as McFee and Holt returned. They looked mighty pleased he thought, perhaps with some happy news forthcoming.

'Oh sir, it was brilliant,' Holt piped, before anyone could say a word, the lad quite excited. 'Mister McFee played him like a Scottish fiddle.'

'Ha, ha, thank ye lad, but it is the only way I know how to play, a good tormenter of catgut, especially a Scottish one. The trick, Mister Holt, is to let them think you are a little simple, not exactly dumb, but ripe for some picking. But I do believe the Captain might be requiring the senior officer to firstly report, as is customary,' he softly corrected.

'Quite,' Cooper confirmed. 'No harm done. So, I take it our

cheese is set?'

'Indeed. I'd heavily wager he is a spy sir,' McFee reported. 'The man is definitely not a local, hinted his affairs were in a state of the utmost good fortune, but those boots I just could not fathom. He's a cool one to be sure, calmer than a priest on Sunday and he addressed me as *"Major"*, which even no gentile landsman would know to do. He well knew the turn of the tide too. I have to say sir, I really don't know where he's from? He sounds more English than the King, but he ain't. Held up his thumb and first finger he did, to signify two, just as you planned sir.'

'Thumb and first finger was it? That clinches it, European, most likely France or Spain.'

'I have to say, it was absolutely magnificent, sir,' McFee congratulated. 'How the hell they count from the thumb first is beyond me. I can only get to three, ha, ha, before my hand cramps.'

'Then I would not recommend counting as such in the Orient, which is curiously in reverse of the French.'

'And he knows about the cannon and it's a good guess he knows they ain't ship cannon. He asked about us shipping out to the West Indies, so I let it slip sir that we will likely miss our tide and that we are a packet headed up and down the Channel, just as you ordered, sir.'

'I believe sir, he is most definitely French,' Holt surprisingly added, much to the astonishment of all present. 'The inflection on his h's was very good, albeit somewhat practised, excepting on one or two accounts.'

'Well, I didn't bloody well notice that,' protested McFee.

'You speak French Mister Holt?' Cooper asked, himself now conversing in French. 'You are so very young of course, so it begs the question as to how much French you might know and how much you might really understand?'

'Yes, sir, I am fluent,' he answered in perfect French, much to the shock of McFee and Spencer, who had not a bloody clue what anyone was now saying. 'In fact, I learned it before English, from my nanny. She used to sing to me too and we would write poetry and sketch. When we drew, she insisted it was in French as well. She was from...'

'Brittany?'

'Yes sir, how did you know, sir?'

'Your Breton accent Mister Holt, but of course, a beautiful distraction from the usual French we commonly hear. Now, listen to what I say and see what you think?' Cooper went on for a short time, the young lad ever so focused.

'Oh sir, magnificent! You speak it with so many regional accents, as well as Parisian, the language of the nobles, all in perfect fluency. And sir, was that old French and even Breton. How is that possible?'

'I will teach you, if you like,' he said smiling, finally returning to English. 'Now let us speak the King's English, so as not to bore Mister Spencer and Mister McFee. Gentlemen, I am convinced, at this stage, to accept Mister Holt's notion that our man is a Frenchman. It seems our midshipman here is not just a capital climber, but has the ear of angel,' he added with a grin. 'And now Mister McFee has provided the necessary honey for our bee. I am most curious though Mister McFee, did he really warn us off the tables there at the Lion?'

'Indeed he did sir. What should we make of that, I wonder?'

'All part of his gentlemanly façade I believe. What better way to get your captain to the tables, if anything but to emphatically tell him he must not try. And the Lion should be jammed with naval officers tonight, as well as the usual circle of gentry and of course the incessant climbers of society.'

'I'd wager a month's rum ration our friend will be in attendance sir.'

'As will we, Mister McFee. So, let us all adorn our best dress and endeavour to prevail upon the Lion tonight, that is of course, provided we have in fact missed the tide,' Cooper prompted, who in point of legal process could not now do anything except sail on the tide, his orders so logged with the port authorities. 'We would need a substantially good reason to not sail of course,' he helpfully added and all eyes fell upon the first officer, who did not disappoint.

'Oh sir, those cannon are just topping it the harry with the blocks, all ramshackled. We are most definitely in the suds. I most humbly apologise that it appears we won't be able to sail on today's tide. Of course, I will properly advise the appropriate shore authorities and amend our log.'

'Very well and after, Mister Spencer, see to the purser and withdraw twenty pounds if you please.'

'Sir?' he worriedly returned. 'Twenty pounds?'

'Yes, you are quite right, make it a neat fifty.'

'Fifty pounds sir!'

'Oh do not be concerned, just some playing funds. It will all be returned of course.'

'Of course, sir,' he sternly lamented. 'That is, I mean to say, if it is not returned, indeed all of us will be dancing at Beilby's ball.'

'Oh don't be ridiculous Mister Spencer. Goodness, what a fellow you are sometimes. All of us, hang? How absurd,' he scoffed. 'Now I am quite certain they will surely not bother to hang young Mister Holt here,' he added with a wry chuckle.

Four bells rang in the forenoon watch and the ebb at last overpowered the slack water. This was the appointed time for Agamemnon to make her way out to sea and an official decision had to be made. The cannon may have been on board, but they were still attached to a pyramid of blocks, dangling precariously above the weather deck. Cooper smiled. In no way could he risk moving the ship whilst the cannon lay unsecured. It would not look so good on the log though and should the Admiralty bring him up on the matter, there could be a reprimand. It was always the small things such as this of course which ever niggled a lieutenant's chance of making post. He knew it was a career risk, but to his mind dealing with this spy took absolute precedence. In no way could he fathom leaving the crud to his own devices. Who knows what amount of mischief might pile up with a loose Frenchman about. The last bell rang and he offered Spencer a knowing look, the order for the ship to stand down. However, the entirety of the exercise was duly interrupted by the sudden arrival of a courier.

'Sir, it must be the package we have been expecting.'

McFee brought a parchment up and delivered it to his captain. Cooper paced back and forth reading the note, its scrawl immediately identifiable, a wry smile finally coming upon him. The note was from his commodore and simply read: *"Captain Cooper, with apologies, the package has been delayed. Expect its arrival on the morrow at six bells in the forenoon watch. I have notified the shore authorities in course."*.

'Mister Spencer, stand the ship down. Our package has been delayed. Note it so in the log, immediately and add this parchment as evidence. We will depart on the morrow's tide, which by my reckoning will be six bells in the forenoon watch.'

'Aye, aye sir,' he confirmed. 'Standing down for six bells in tomorrow's forenoon watch, that being eleven in the morning for our landsmen, sir.'

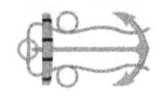

Chapter IX
The Lion

From midday to midnight it was fair to say Rochester was commonly a community abuzz with fashion, flare and fragrance. Indeed, it hoarded many a fine establishment. As it turned out, the very best of these were in short proximity to Agamemnon, all seemingly no less than a cannon shot of an elevated twenty-four. The Coach and Horses, the Royal Oak, the Cooper's Arms and the Bull Hotel were but some of the most highly regarded houses, not just by the locals, but moreover by the many travellers who found themselves transiting from Central London. However the most prestigious, by reputation and renown, the place to be as it were, was unequivocally the Lion.

Of all the inns and houses the Lion was actually a traditional gentlemen's club, which is to say it was much frequented by the officials of the district and consequently, very much preferred by the local gentry who meant to grease them. Of late, due mostly to the annoying imposition of unending peace, the place had been tormented with a deluge of beached naval officers, all looking to procure interest and ultimately a position. With eight in ten naval officers on half pay or less, it was quite an understatement to suggest that entry to the Lion had become a dogged snarling contest. Mind you, not just anyone could enter. The Lion was, in every sense of the word, a club and one had to be a member, or be invited. To inadvertently invite some troublemaking beached officer would be a rueful decision, the standing member unceremoniously removed right behind his guest. The prevailing opinion of most members, indeed their very inclination and practice, was to not invite unemployed officers, of any kind, even if they were well-known friends. Oh, it always started out innocently enough, but they all seemed to morph into wild devil hounds, sniffing mindlessly about for employment until madness finally took hold.

Naturally, a certain amount of business was conducted behind the closed doors of the Lion, but fine dining was the foremost attraction. Of course there was a strong tendency to dabble with other pleasures, such as the Lion's fine selection of cigars and her extensive cellar, not to mention the den of gaming tables. To dine, to drink, to banter and, most importantly, to horse trade had for long been the standing practice amongst England's elite. It was a custom that happily resulted in no less than the most productive mingling of interests. Should a beached lieutenant dare be admitted, it was true their career could most definitely be made, but it was much more likely to be forever broken.

Cooper needed no invitation, his captain's uniform served to swing open the oaken doors not unlike a saint venturing the pearly gates. He waltzed through the entrance with the poise of an officer who had just stormed Brest and taken down the entire French navy single-handed. In reality, he of course was desperately in need of procuring some real interest, not that it presently mattered. Yet by and by, he had only one target in mind and his eyes subtly rolled around the room, searching for the Frenchman.

Cooper had been most loath that morning to delay Agamemnon's departure, a substantial risk to his career in fact. In the end, it was a great relief to find the excuse of Nelson's note promptly presented, albeit with not a moment to spare. Nonetheless, stalking this French spy was always going to take precedence. It seemed the trail had led his hunting party to the Lion and curiously, all at the subtle behest of their spy. It was a grand place to venture of course, with nary a complaint from any officer, but hardly had he undertaken such a course just simply to enjoy a festive night out. He would beg to enjoy the club, should the opportunity present and should any high powered official somewhat sympathetic to their cause offer their services, he wouldn't exactly be turning it away. At least as a serving captain he could happily secure conversations without the slightest risk of some disastrous snub. In fact, he could prevail upon almost any member of the club, should the fancy take him. He was still a hundred souls shy in the ship's complement, of which included a handful of lieutenants and at least ten more midshipmen. Should the word get out, there would be a handy stack of well-to-do gentlemen clambering his way, all anxious to see their boy safely to sea whilst the peace still held. The more he thought, the more it seemed likely the members of the Lion might fast be approaching him. He wouldn't have to lift a finger either. Even flag officers were likely to press him, full knowing it was his every prerogative to refuse them, a most interesting turnabout in his state of affairs.

'Captain?' Holt interrupted. 'I do believe winter is pressing longer this year,' he cryptically remarked, which in point of fact was the prearranged verse to signify that the spy had been located. 'Sir, may I say, it seems to be warmest two points off the starboard beam,' he further directed only to add a landsman's touch with a whisper. 'Far right sir, third gaming table.'

Cooper had heard of spies attending the clubs across London, a damning network or so he had been told. It was with absolute impunity too that these clusters had most cheekily progressed and all right under the nose of the Admiralty. It was of course a capital place to collect the prerequisite tidbits of intelligence, mostly talk loosened from too much wine or the innate need to impress. He had heard that these spies often lost substantial sums at the tables, thus ingratiating themselves to their prey. Or sometimes they would fleece them like the sheep they were, thus currying certain favours for debt forgiveness. Their ploys were most clever and Cooper knew he would have to be most diligent, high stakes indeed laid before him.

'Ah Captain Cooper,' beckoned one Captain Horatio Nelson from across the room, delicately poised beside a most distinguished gentleman.

'Ah very good,' he whispered.

Yet Cooper's eyes widened when he beheld Nelson's guest. Mother and Mary he thought. He smiled back, making his way briskly, but respectably. The Frenchman would have to wait til later he immediately reasoned. The crud wasn't going anywhere of course and after all, if he was indeed a spy, nothing less than his utmost attention towards each and every one of Agamemnon's officers might reasonably be expected. Nelson greeted Cooper like a long lost brother.

'How very good to see you Captain,' Nelson played, loud enough for all to hear. 'It has been quite some time. And my congratulations upon your commission and your new ship, Agamemnon! Allow me to introduce my esteemed friend, His Royal Highness, The Duke of Clarence and Saint Andrews, Rear Admiral, retired, The Prince William...'

'Thank you, sir,' Cooper prompted with the correct nod. 'But The Prince William needs no such introduction,' he added courteously.

'Ah, indeed, but he very much delights in the regurgitation of his many titles aloud,' added Nelson cheekily, much to the mirth of Prince William.

'Your Royal Highness, a pleasure indeed sir, Captain Hayden Reginald Cooper, Agamemnon, at your service.'

'New command now is it Captain, Agamemnon? Oh yes, I know her, great lines, can turn on a dime and a fast beauty too. Such a pure ship, not a great blustering seventy-four with barely a rat's chance of engaging even so much as a barn and happily, if I may say, not a frigate which might be sunk by the first lucky barrage to nick the hull. I do believe I am almost jealous! I heartily congratulate you, sir!'

'That is most kind. Honoured and thank you. Sir, may I present my first officer, Lieutenant Spencer, my captain of the marines, Major McFee and this young gentleman is Midshipman Lord Holt.'

'Lord Holt? Ah, I thought that was you Jarvis! How grand you look in your midshipman's uniform. I had only just dined with the King and your father last week. He is most proud indeed that you are putting to sea, could not stop squawking and he kept sprouting on about how you will be made captain soon.'

'Captain? Captain! Bloody typical,' thought Cooper inwardly, who of course was already much resigned, condemned even as it were, to endure the rest of his dreary days as a lowly lieutenant.

Oh naturally he was a captain for now, but unless he made post, it would all slip away. And that wasn't going to happen without some great feat, a feat mostly unachievable in peacetime. And before him stood Holt, fourteen years old, a lad who had barely laid foot upon Agamemnon's weather deck, the naval experience of a seagull and already were they planning his promotion to post and with it one day an admiral's flag assured. But as much as it disturbed and forever annoyed him, he was one who could never bring himself to hold it against the lad. There was something pure about Holt, something realistic, something almost angelically unwavering, unlike the other young gentry to which he was very much accustomed.

'Your Royal Highness,' Holt returned. 'It is a pleasure and thank you sir. I will do my very best, but I assure you that father is being presumptuous and boorish of course. I still have quite a few years before I am even permitted to sit for my next promotion and I should very much like to know well my job first. Should I be so fortunate, I will be most pleased to firstly serve as a fighting lieutenant. I have not been with my captain for more than one day, but already I believe he is a superior officer who will teach me well my duties.'

'Is that so?' Prince William remarked, his good eye squinting at Cooper somewhat. 'Now Jarvis,' he whispered in Parisian. 'Should he ever beat you, you will have to let me know.'

'Sir,' he returned in French. 'You do not yet know my captain, but if I may, I beg that he will never do such a thing, for he is professionally restrained and very much a man of honour. In addition, ever will I endeavour to ensure my good conduct. Moreover will I represent myself honestly and as such never will I put my captain in such an unfortunate position,' he astutely replied, now turning to Cooper, still speaking in French. 'I hope I do not overstep my standing here Captain?'

'You are quite right Mister Holt and if I may, well said,' Cooper confirmed also in French, much to the surprise of Prince William. 'But His Royal Highness is also quite right and you must always listen to him. Should I or any other officer ever dare beat you, it would be considered an offence and as such, you have every right to inform him, or any other authority you so choose.'

'Captain! You speak French and what beautiful French it is!' Prince William delightedly exclaimed. 'Oh, sublime. Now sir, are you sure you are one of us?' he jested. 'And what a grand manner you have,' he added, now returning to English. 'But I do get the feeling we have crossed paths before, West Indies was it not?'

'Aye sir, you have a capital memory. It was in eighty-six and I was lieutenant under Captain Nelson when you were captain of Pegasus,' he smiled outwardly, yet inwardly he was cursing. He had never actually met him before. Neither did he harbour any ill will, but there was not a naval soul in all of England who did not know about Rear Admiral The Prince William. Promoted to lieutenant in eighty-five, post-captain in eighty-six, rear admiral in eighty-nine and thereafter summarily retired from active service in ninety. It wasn't that anyone would begrudge saluting a potential future King of England, but following, it meant that even a great tactical commander such as Nelson would now absurdly be forced to defer to the Prince's lesser naval knowledge. It was a blessing he had retired thought Cooper, but being the third son of the reigning king definitely had some benefits. All part of the course though, that is, for those with interest.

'All of you must dine with us!' Prince William insisted, looking to Nelson. 'Is this permitted Horatio?'

'We are at your service sir,' Nelson happily confirmed. 'I am sure Captain Cooper and his officers would be honoured, as I always am of course.'

It was with interest and shock that Cooper learned of the most recent pirate attack, this time claiming not only a fat merchant, but also a ten gun brig which was assigned to protect her.

'Right in the mouth of the Thames you say?' Cooper lamented. 'And both hopelessly sunk?'

'In the midst of the soup, such a report of fog they have never before seen apparently. All hands lost I am afraid, except one,' added Nelson.

'Indeed, outrageous is it not?' offered Prince William.

'And we have only been apprised of the event, merely because one survivor somehow miraculously found his way back to shore,' Nelson lamented. 'Damned fortunate one might say. Every other soul either drowned like rats or froze to death.'

'That's right and he is some odd fellow too I believe, a lieutenant?'

'Shillings, sir, I believe, a lieutenant.'

'Shillings?' quizzed Cooper in disbelief.

'Aye, you know the man?'

'Oh, no sir,' he quickly corrected. 'I had just met him briefly in the waiting rooms of the Admiralty.'

'Aye, apparently he spent more time in the waiting rooms than that upon his ship before she was blown out from under him, poor devil.'

'Was it a frigate sir?'

'No, apparently they were set upon by a large brig, some eighteen gun. She came suddenly out of the mist, quiet as a mouse yet damned with the speed of the devil, so he says. Even the lookout didn't see her til the cannon were thumping away. Not a scratch of rigging either did they hit, just hulled her and she went down like a bloody stone. Our man Shillings was sent flying off the ship in the first report, found himself upon some driftwood and somehow managed to stay out of the water. Damned lucky fellow, if I may.'

'Well thankfully nobody saw it of course, but from all accounts the scuttlebutt has already started. I mean, this Shillings has returned holier than thou as evidence to the contrary that the ships were hardly lost at sea in a storm. The whole fleet will soon learn they were preyed upon. They will want their pound of flesh, mark my words.'

'Tricky business then, sir.'

'Well, we have already assigned our Lieutenant Shillings to another ship. Best we get him to sea quickly, away from the prying which is sure to come.'

'Be damned if the fellow isn't some lucky charm, the lone survivor, quite incredible.'

'Aye, perhaps, yet not so lucky for his shipmates though?'

The fine dining with Prince William had not in the least dragged upon Cooper's patience, but he was finally glad to put that part of the evening behind him. After all, he had a spy to wrangle. The delay played right into Cooper's hands of course and it did seem the Prince was quite taken with the new captain of Agamemnon. Cooper's career could use all the help he could get and he was sure Nelson had thus cleverly arranged it. His commodore was a commander whose heart would bleed right next to his men, do anything for them and grind to see them afforded every opportunity. The Prince spent some time with Cooper, fawning over his linguistic skills, discussing the likely points of sail in Agamemnon, even ruminating their shared cruise of the West Indies to the point of comparing the antics of their past commander who seemed mildly amused to be sitting right next to them.

It very much now appeared that Cooper had made a new friend, one who could be most influential, should the inclination take him. It may have been Cooper's honest charm, but it moreover stemmed somewhat from the close friendship Prince William and Nelson had for so ever enjoyed. The Prince however was not so active in the politics of England. As the third son of the King, there was very little chance he would ever ascend to the throne. He would not only have to outlive his older brothers, but both brothers would also have to be barren of legitimate children and he knew very well his father was pressing his older brother George ever so much to marry. Oh no, it would never happen. It seemed therefore reasonable that the Prince should do everything he could in life, everything except perhaps partake in his official royal duties that is. And part of his adventure most definitely included dining as much as possible with his particular friend, Nelson. Nonetheless, Cooper was one to never look a gift horse in the mouth and he welcomed the Prince and any favour that accompanied it with open arms. You can be sure as well, his status with McFee and Holt just rose in currency somewhat. It appeared their captain was no ordinary sailor.

'Captain,' Nelson started, quite knowing what he was doing.

'If you might excuse His Royal Highness and myself, we have some small business to attend. But I believe we will repair to the tables later perhaps,' he added, cueing Cooper to attend to his real duty this night. All night Nelson had played it brilliantly too. For now it was certain the spy was well aware of Cooper and his apparent importance to England, not just as the new captain of a sixty-four, but also to his apparent social standing. In doing so, he had made a mark of Captain Cooper, a juicy tidbit no spy might resist. It had its risks of course, for if the spy failed to nibble, he might slither away, free to cause harry and mayhem.

Holt for some time had been slyly examining the gaming tables, appearing boyishly interested but altogether portraying a mild state of confusion. And he quite cheekily tended to prevail upon the closest post-captain or admiral with innocent questions about the game. They didn't mind either, for they not only knew his father and the power so wielded with the King, but they had just witnessed the lad chewing on a prime rib with the Prince.

'Sir, I am no card player,' he admitted, 'But, if I may be so bold, I feel I have the mathematics of the game in hand.'

'Your maths is sound then, Mister Holt?'

'I beg forgiveness to say sir, but it is perhaps a little better. I have been watching our friend here for some time and Mister McFee has been kind enough to fill me in on the rules.'

'As have a few admirals I see,' he remarked with a wry grin.

'Winning, so it appears, seems plainly dependent upon firstly positioning what cards you have sir, mustering a mob so to speak. It is possible to win outright as such, but I have found thereafter that most importantly one must draw picture cards, or a corresponding card of ten? Am I correct, sir?' he probed and they both watched the current game unfold, the Frenchman seemingly making his move. 'The way I see it sir, he will call for one more card and he will now win.'

'What do you mean, he will now win? Surely he may draw any card and the outcome a factor of chance?'

'Well, sir, it is my summation that he is in need of the cards which count ten.'

'Yes, of course and...?'

'Well sir, the deck, as you might attest, is quite low. But I assure you there's lots of them,' he explained only to be drowned out by the buzz of onlookers celebrating as a queen fell. The Frenchman threw his hand down in victory, cheerfully adding another win upon his side notes.

'How the bloody hell did you know that Mister Holt?'

'Well sir, I was counting...'

'Shhh, sir!' Cooper quickly hushed. 'Mister Holt, I know you are new to the game, but did Mister McFee not explain? Not that anyone can possibly count such a stack of decks in any case, but it is strictly forbidden, at least in England. In fact, it is actually considered tantamount to cheating.'

'Oh? No sir, he didn't, but then I didn't ask either.'

'Of course,' he smiled, the lad as loyal as a three-legged hound. 'Can you really tell how many face cards are left?'

'Thereabouts, sir and I am sorry sir, I assumed it was permitted. After all, the Frenchie is doing it.'

'What? What! The Frenchie is doing it! Is that so? How can you tell?'

'Oh, he has a small system, hardly discernible. See how he is stacking his hand in a certain formation each time a picture card falls.'

'Indeed, and you have never played cards before Mister Holt?'

'No sir, but I think I might like to.'

'I think I might like you to as well,' he grinned. 'Let us test your skills on the next game. Look, they are shuffling the decks,' he announced and they continued to observe in the guise of interested spectators. True to his form Holt was accurately picking the remains of the deck. Cooper quickly brought him up to speed on the strategy, no different really to organising a hasty plan of battle upon a busy quarterdeck. The lad was attentive and willing and Cooper was now thinking Lord Holt's faith in his son to make post in the next few years might hardly be misplaced. 'We will sit in upon the next game and I will stake you of course. You will play your hand as you see fit, without fear of reprimand, understand? Now, our plan is not so much for you to win, unless I have folded my hand. Don't worry at all should you lose, for when I win, we will get back your losses in the same pot. You will soon see, it will

Ships of War — Murky Waters

be to our advantage to strategically lose. You will ultimately transfer the pot to me and my power in the game will be amplified. Your main task of course will be to signal the remains of the decks, being high, low or indifferent.'

'Aye, aye, sir,' he confirmed with the maturity of an ageing admiral.

The Frenchman had the table drawn and quartered in quick time, the seats before him thereafter readily vacated, sent packing as it were. Cooper sat down with a smile, fifty pounds laid upon the table.

'Ah, Captain, how handsome and I bid you welcome. Lord Pendleton sir, at your service and allow me to introduce my associate, Mister Rose, who will be my second. But, you do not have a second? I can arrange a handsome player for you, if it pleases?'

'Oh, of course, how forgetful of me, but no matter,' he nonchalantly remarked, turning about the room. 'Ah, Mister Holt, please join us, if you will.'

'Captain? Are you sure sir, this is a game for large stakes and one not so much for the young at heart. I fear the youngster may put you at a disadvantage, which is not how I intend to take your pot.'

'That is very civil of you sir.'

'I must be frank and suitably warn you sir, for I am considered a formidable hand here at the Lion.'

'*C'est la vie*, as they say across the Channel. But as you say, it is just a game of course. The lad must learn sometime and I am prepared for either outcome. After all, it is but a game of luck.'

'Luck?' he replied, somewhat aghast. 'Perhaps, Captain, but with a sprinkling of skill attached. Very well,' he agreed. 'But first, I have a gift for you, if you will permit,' he politely announced and he laid some fine cigars upon the table. 'For your upcoming journey, I hope you do not mind. I had the honour of meeting your marine major today, as your cannons were loaded and he apprised me of your predicament.'

'Oh, capital! You are very kind. I will save them of course.'

'Of course, such fine cigars and may I say, such fine cannons Captain. They will make a handsome addition to your armament. But it surprises me as to where they would be stationed?'

Cooper smiled as he could do little but admire the genius behind Pendleton's question, most clever indeed. It was no less than a two-edged blade and might easily have succeeded on a captain of unassuming nature, its final destination revealed. To the contrary, it perhaps would oblige an astute captain to reprimand the enquiry as too intrusive, whereupon Pendleton would merely feign ignorance and insist he only meant where they might be stationed upon the ship. This was one crafty clinker Cooper heartily determined.

'The cannon are sixty-four pounders, too large for any ship sir. You would never house one upon a wooden brace, lest the force destroy its housing and the mere deadweight would no doubt send the iron through the hull. The ship would sink sir, directly, after barely one shot.'

It was interesting as to how subtly Pendleton slipped in his questions about the cruise, the ship, the cannon and anything trivial at all it seemed. If he was not a spy, he definitely was a nosy social climber with a heavy broadside of scuttlebutt, ready to rake Cooper at a moment's notice. It took time, but Cooper was now detecting his accent, ever so slight and barely discernible. He also noticed the incorrect use to describe the local plural of cannon, which of course is never *"cannons"*. But more than anything it was his mannerisms and if he was an English lord, then Holt was a runaway street snipe. Holt had been surprisingly precise in his initial appraisal it seemed, but a man who is actually French pretending to be an English lord did not by itself a spy make. At the very least Pendleton was a con, taking money from the gentry. But in Cooper's mind it all started to add up to much more, especially with Pendleton's associate now exposed. Upon scrutiny, Cooper was certain the man would prove to be an accomplice.

Holt played his part brilliantly, without fail losing almost every hand, much to the mirth of many onlookers. But unbeknown to all, he was flawless in his efforts to clandestinely signal the status of face cards left in the deck. He was most imperceptible, so natural that Cooper could have easily pinned Holt as some kind of spy himself. Nonetheless, the game was somewhat at a stalemate, for it seemed Pendleton was indeed counting the deck with the same precise exactness. This was what Cooper was planning all

Ships of War — Murky Waters

along of course, for now he would play the man on skill, to which he perceived Pendleton's lay only in his ability to count. Onlookers gave a hearty cheer as Cooper knocked Rose out of the game, of course joining Holt who had been served up by Pendleton a few hands before. The vanquished sat helplessly admiring their partners, patiently waiting for their man to win through. It was not unlike a matched ship action with a seventy-four and a frigate on each side, with both frigates languishing after being forced to strike. A larger crowd had now formed, a coliseum of onlookers, the obvious skill of the two seventy-fours something not to be missed. In the spirit of old Rome, Naval officers were belting for Cooper and the local gentry for Pendleton. Side bets were rife in the taking, a flourishing trade. The table stakes now stood at their highest thus far and undoubtedly it appeared to be the last hand, the pot being mostly all laid down. Pendleton laid down his cards, a handsome hand, one almost beyond assailment. With it had he raked Cooper from stem to stern and was now boarding, the very end seemingly inevitable. But Cooper hardly moved to strike his colours, laying down his hand with a steady eye upon his opponent. The crowd fell into a rowdy panic, some groaning as if they had all but fainted. Cooper's hand was no less than the last barrage of grapeshot cruelly fired upon the boarders. He had cut Pendleton down, a final blow. Pendleton sat back aghast, eyeing the hand, calculations shooting through his mind. He had most definitely meant to win and he could not fathom how Cooper had come to his hand.

'You have cheated sir!' Rose angrily accused and the onlookers hushed in disgust. Whatever had happened, it hardly mattered now. This was an ugly unwarranted scene, one which could only lead to something far worst.

'Sir,' Cooper snapped. 'The customary response when one loses is to say *"well played"*.'

'I agree. You did play us well, indeed, like a milch cow, a sixty-four pound pot! I see now the integrity of the Royal Navy, or should I say, lack thereof!'

'I will assume, sir, for the sake of your own well-being, your bluster is perhaps only offered because you are half seas over with your wine tonight.'

'Damn you sir! Hardly am I near drunk, a pastime I am hardly partial in any way and I ain't no bleeding cully who is going to let you just waltz out of here with my stake!'

'Please Mister Rose,' Pendleton interjected. 'We must not cry over spilled milk. The Captain is the victor. If you had thought there was something untoward, you should have brought it up well before the game had ended.'

'Most outrageous!' Prince William exclaimed, intervening. 'Never have I seen the like! Cheating you say? By a naval officer? And the very one before me whom I know to be of good character and conscience! Sir, your words offend. Damned if they have not offended everyone here present! You have offended Captain Cooper and you have offended me sir! Unequivocally have you offended every naval officer in England! Have you not gone mad? I demand at once you retract your remarks and beg forgiveness.'

'Is that your wish Captain?' Rose vehemently challenged. 'You wish to hide under the skirt of the King's son?'

'Mister Rose!' Pendleton protested. 'You go too far sir!'

'No sir, The Prince William has no right over his subjects, no right whatsoever, not in matters of honour. This man has cheated and I will have satisfaction. He will apologise before everyone present and he will hand over the pot to you, sir.'

'I will not,' stated Cooper calmly.

'Then sir, I suggest you put your affairs in order. I will have my man call on your man.'

'As you wish, but my man is already here,' he coolly offered and he looked to his first officer who was now quite drained whatsoever of any colour. Spencer reluctantly stood forth as second, a position to which he had been accustomed some nineteen times before. 'May I present Lieutenant Spencer, my man. Please make what arrangements you deem necessary.'

'Not tonight,' Prince William interjected angrily. 'Lieutenant, for this matter I beg you stand aside. I will be the Captain's man.'

It was no less than the ugliest most horrible scene one could ever feign to conjure, but not so uncommon to gaming tables and hardly uncommon to such a gifted strategist as Cooper. Right or wrong, Rose's actions had crossed a line for which the Lion had

Ships of War — Murky Waters

no tolerance. The caretaker summarily appeared before Rose and so was his immediate departure requested. Begrudgingly he left, but not before he and his man had arranged the duel, in principle any way.

'Captain, I regret terribly my associate's behaviour,' Pendleton pleaded. 'I will beg him to steer away from this course of action, or I promise you sir, thereafter he will not have my favour. In no way have I thought our game was anything except an even handed ever brilliant challenge. You sir, are indeed a worthy opponent and I assure you that I am hardly out of pocket from the loss. Much to your credit, you have bested me with no less than poor Lord Holt bumbling at your side. I would esteem it a pleasure sir to play you again, for any stake you deem fair.'

'Very well Lord Pendleton. However, should you dissuade Mister Rose from our day out, please understand that he has in fact slighted me not only in front of the entire club, but also in front of The Prince William and my former commander Captain Nelson. He has but two options now, either apologise in front of these men, or proceed with his lunacy.'

'But surely sir, is it not forbidden for a ship's captain to engage in such duels of effrontery?'

'It is. But even post-captains, to which I am not sir, are duelling day in and day out all over England, like mice feeding in an alley. No sir, should Mister Rose insist, I will afford him his honour.'

'But I must warn you Captain, he is as good a shot as he is hot headed. I sincerely fear for you sir.'

'I too am a worthy shot and very much accustomed to the end of a musket pointing my way. Sir, do not worry, I will practice. We put to sea tomorrow, but we will return in some weeks of course. We just have to deliver these damned cannon.'

'Indeed, a delivery?' he openly noted, his eyes surprisingly wide open. 'It seems beneath your station sir, if you do not mind my saying, a line of battle ship carting goods. Could they not bother some lesser officer?' he sympathetically added and Cooper inwardly laughed, for if only Pendleton knew, he was indeed already the lesser officer.

'Oh, I very much do not mind sir. We are going where it is

most cold though, which is something unfortunate of course. I heartily thank you for the cigars. I will put them to good use. And I must say, I very much enjoyed our contest tonight and I will afford you a rematch, upon my return.'

'Provided, Captain, that you are indeed the better shot,' he worriedly added and for just a moment, Cooper was almost in full belief as to his sincerity.

'Duelling, like cards, is also a game of chance. I will take my chances and either way, my honour will remain. I bid you good night sir.'

'The devil, sir!' McFee burst as they strolled out of the Lion and along the Rochester cobble. 'Never have I seen such a thing. Good god! The temper of that man! And all in front of The Prince William and Captain Nelson, not to mention a Lord of the Admiralty and a handful of admirals,' he spouted. 'Good god sir, good god! That went exactly to plan!'

'Indeed,' smiled Cooper.

'But sir,' Holt pointed out. 'Now you will have to fight Mister Rose. If he truly is French, which seems likely, he will undoubtedly attempt to kill you.'

'Undoubtedly Mister Holt, but even captains on the quarterdeck must stand tall and fight,' he openly reassured, looking thoughtfully at the young lad. 'How are you with a sword Mister Holt?'

'Uncommonly average, I regret to say.'

'Then I must teach you.'

'Sir?' Holt thoughtfully quizzed, appearing somewhat confused. 'How did you know Rose was going to call you out for cheating?'

'Well,' he smiled, his brow twinging. 'Because young sir, in point of actual fact, I did most undeniably and most unequivocally cheat.'

And for the next ten minutes McFee could not hold back the gurgling laughter of a mad highlander, now thinking his captain was more a wild Scot than even he ever was, forever swearing upon his life to follow the man into the depths of hell and back.

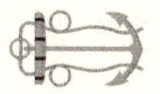

Chapter X
On The Tide

Six bells in the forenoon watch and it seemed the morning had been somewhat kind to the Medway and by extension, Agamemnon. The ebb had arrived and soon would the great ship make sail and navigate her way up the Medway into the Thames and out into the Channel. The first officer of Agamemnon knocked firmly on the door of the great cabin, to which he was immediately granted entry. Captain Cooper sat pensively behind his table, shuffling the last of his horrid paperwork, of course fully expecting the arrival of his first officer to save him. Spencer hesitated and perhaps even gulped a little before he began, a worried look pressed upon his brow.

'Well man, come on, out with it? If it is news unwanted, best you spit it out now. I know that look.'

'Quite sir,' he sheepishly replied. 'It seems your package has arrived, or should I say packages.'

'Indeed,' he questioned. 'But this is good news, especially when you see what the package is. Oh my word indeed, ground breaking to say the least.'

'Sir, I have already had the opportunity of seeing one, but not the other and may I say the former is hardly ground breaking, although I felt like breaking the ground when I laid eye.'

'Seen one and not the other, did you just say?' he pressed, somewhat confused. 'There's only one package expected Lieutenant. Now, what the devil is going on?'

'Perhaps it is best I bring in the packages, sir?'

'Very well, at once,' he barked, somewhat out of patience. Spencer returned immediately with a man holding a sizeable canvas satchel, hugging it closely, as one drowning would a buoy. Cooper immediately recognised the face. The alarm building almost all at once dissipated. It was only poor tubby Fredricks, the courier who had so boorishly dragged him from Portsmouth to Whitehall just some months ago.

'Captain Cooper, we meet again, Fredricks,' he loosely announced. 'I have a package of the utmost import from Admiral Lord Howe, marked most secret. I understand you are waiting upon it. As I said to Lieutenant Spencer, this package must be delivered direct to your hand, or not at all. If you would be so kind as to inspect the contents and thereafter, I will require you to of course sign for its receipt. And oh, best close the door Lieutenant, quickly now,' he directed, much to the displeasure of Spencer's mounting frown. Cooper nodded and Spencer locked the door, but before Cooper could reach for the satchel, let alone sign for it, Fredricks had cut it open. A swag of flags spilled out of the canvas, sprawling themselves over the decking. They were mostly numbers, but there were some others, typically with patterns of different sorts. 'Here are your instructions, all there, quite detailed it seems,' he openly commented, proceeding to now brazenly read the contents.

'Look well Spence,' Cooper urged, ignoring Fredricks for now. 'This is a ship to ship signal system, a concoction of Lord Howe no less and the first of its kind. It is a code of numbers, designed to be quickly sent up and down the main. Imagine the benefits. No more needlessly halting upon every ship we come upon just because they are bored or curious. But mainly, think of a squadron with instant command and communication, the privilege of its consorts peeking over the horizon and immediately reporting back. We have been chosen to test it as part of our cruise.'

'Intriguing, sir.'

'I know what you're thinking, in that we have only one ship. Don't worry, we will be able to test it and not only, but we will go one step further and develop our own rendition of the signal's code. Now, Lieutenant, you mentioned a second package?'

'Ah, here it comes,' warned Spencer and he motioned to Fredricks.

'And here are my papers,' Fredricks interrupted. 'Orders I believe you call them.'

'Is this some kind of a joke Mister Fredricks?' Cooper sternly queried, his face still buried within the wording of the parchment. 'It says here you are assigned to Agamemnon, but I don't recall interviewing you. I definitely have no record of your prior request to serve aboard this vessel. And it says here you are to be considered for the position of captain's clerk or steward!'

'Indeed, it does,' he glumly agreed.

'Sir!' Cooper sharply barked. 'It is *"sir"*. You will address me as sir, whether you are a member of this crew or not!'

'Yes sir, very sorry.'

'Aye, aye! You will say *"aye, aye"* when given an order, one aye to indicate your response in the affirmative and the next aye to signify your intent to then carry out such order. Or you may say one aye and verbalise the order back, thus confirming your understanding. Do you understand?'

'Aye, aye, sir.'

'No, no, no, Mister Fredricks,' Cooper corrected again, shaking his head. 'When indicating your understanding as to the affirmative, upon where there is no other action required, one aye will suffice. Good god man, are you sure you are in the Royal Navy? Even aboard a ship as big as this, it is a hard life, even for the privileged, to which you ain't. Food is dished sparingly and there are some five hundred souls packed aboard a handful of decks, the largest barely one hundred and sixty feet by forty-five. It's tight living and sailors can be quite cruel to the uninformed landsman. It's their domain and they'll tear apart any man who, for it, lacks the appropriate respect. Do you even know which side of the ship is larboard and which is starboard?'

'Starboard is the left, no right, no left...'

Ships of War — Murky Waters

'Damn you sir, starboard is to the right, whereupon standing at the helm and looking forward. Come now Mister Fredricks, sailors have perished for want of not knowing or understanding something as simple as to which side of the ship might be on fire and which side ain't. No, no, no, this simply will not do. We must send you back I am afraid. Please fear not any reprimand. I will make it clear to Their Lordships that these positions are already full.'

'They said you might say that, sir. So they instructed me to tell you that should you have no use and should I be sent back, that they would have no other course but to hang me, even showed me the rope.'

'Hang you? Goodness, what the devil for?'

'Aye, sir, for I had snuck a peek at your package. I did not know that no one was allowed to see it.'

'Bell, book and bloody candle man!' Cooper swore, shaking his head. 'But it is clearly marked *"most secret"*! If you did not have the prerequisite authority in this matter, why the holy hell did you open it up in front of us?'

'And read the instructions?' added Spencer.

'Indeed! Are you not mad, insane? No one could be so dull as to be that bereft of the consequences! Perhaps hanging is too good I am now thinking, much too good!'

'Sir, perhaps keel hauling?' suggested Spencer evenly.

'Perhaps, but it is over so quickly.'

'Then sir, what about flogging around the fleet?'

'Oh, capital, now that would do the trick. But we don't presently have a fleet?'

'But I only peeked in to see if it was something perishable.'

'Sir!' Cooper corrected. 'I say once again Mister Fredricks, it is sir! Failure to address me properly on my own ship is tantamount in failure to recognise my authority, an authority given to me by King George! Should you dare do so one more bloody time I will have Major McFee most definitely haul you around the keel! Thereafter will you spend the next ten minutes drawn above the deck by your neck! And should somehow you still miraculously draw breath, I will have you confined to a small basket and dangle you from the bowsprit until you properly starve to death. Unless of course you take the sharp knife afforded and either slice your wrists or the ropes or both, whichever takes your fancy!'

'That's the pointy stick that protrudes afore the ship,' explained Spencer calmly.

'Sir, aye, sir! Sorry, sir,' Fredricks profusely apologised, his head down. 'I am not a sailor sir, never wanted to be one, too chubby, sir. It was my father's vocation, his dream not mine, sir. The ocean and I don't see eye to eye, sir, know what I mean, so to appease him I sought employment at the Admiralty. I didn't mean to offend and I didn't mean to open the package just to be curious, only to preserve its safe cartage to you, had only good intentions sir. But it seems they say I am some security risk now. If you cannot take me, I honestly believe they will hang me. They said I could do England no harm if I went with the package of course and stayed aboard. I am very sorry sir, very, very sorry.'

'Captain's clerk sir,' Cooper roughly announced. 'I cannot imagine you be fit for want of anything else on the entire ship, judging this book by its cover. Nonetheless, I warrant your endeavours with the quill might be just the thing? I must admit, you were able enough to venture the biting cold of Portsmouth and summarily complete your assigned task with my return to Whitehall, all most very promptly. You had planned the route, arranged the carriages so required, including the stopovers and other logistics. You may not be as useless as you think. Now tell me man, quickly, as captain's clerk, would you be of service to this ship and her endeavours?'

'Sir, I cannot be sure, to be honest I feel...'

'Uht!' interrupted Spence, sternly eyeing Fredricks to illicit the required response, his right hand slowly mimicking a noose pulling his neck, his tongue poking out a little with each tug.

'Oh, sir,' Fredricks announced with some renewed confidence. 'I believe sir, I would be a most capital choice,' he assuredly restated, looking back to Spencer whose expression was now stone cold, mute as a parliamentarian being asked for coin. Spencer's eyebrows rose, his eyes widening, a silent indication of the necessity for something more. Finally Fredricks understood. 'Oh and sir, I shall not let you down, sir.'

Ships of War — Murky Waters

'Very well, but if you do Mister Fredricks, I assure you it will be to your very peril. I will appoint you as captain's clerk. Should you fail this vocation, you will be scrubbing pots for the cook and doubling up as bait for the sharks. There will be much you need to learn about a ship of war, especially a third-rate. I will assign a sea daddy to instruct you. Whenever off duty, you will not lounge about. Rather you will afford to learn everything you can about this ship and your new life in the Royal Navy. You will start by reading the Articles of War, noting the penalties imposed for failure.'

'Aye, aye, sir.'

'Well,' he happily added, noting the correct usage of the affirmation. 'It seems you have made some progress Mister Fredricks. Now, do your duty and don't put your captain in the precarious position of having to flog or hang you. You will report directly to Midshipman Holt. Lieutenant Spencer here will draw up your orders and Mister Holt will help get your bearings. Bear in mind that Mister Holt, albeit a young gentlemen, is an officer candidate and is in every sense your superior. You will address him accordingly, otherwise to your immediate peril.'

'Aye, address him accordingly, sir.'

'And one last thing, you must not mention what you saw in this satchel to anyone on board, even including myself. Should it come out in your sleep, should the man next to you suddenly talk of it, should you tell of it even to the ship's rat, I will have you flogged, drawn, quartered, keel hauled and feed to the sharks. Do not test me on this, now get out of here. Dismissed!'

'Sir?' Spencer remarked, his face in the pensive stage of still deciding whether to be in mirth or in shock of Fredricks. 'Do you really think they showed him the rope?'

'Of this, Spence, I have no doubt. He is lucky they didn't hoist him up in the middle of the Admiralty waiting rooms and use him as a piñata, a warning to the many fools who frequent.'

The one advantage of peacetime and there were very few, was the abundance of able seamen and availability of competent officers, provided you could firstly find them. They definitely had the skills to hide away too, scattering like leaves to the four winds if they were of a mind. Cooper was thinking he had the pick of the litter, thankfully with some modest help from Nelson. But mostly the credit lay with the ingenuity of his particular friend and first officer, who amongst all scavengers ranked no less than Admiral of the Fleet. Without Spencer it was likely Agamemnon would still be in the throes of fitting out. Good men made all the difference and the water now flowing under the hull as Agamemnon made her way all but served up a cautionary reminder. It seemed clear, now more than ever, good men were going to be in need.

It was often thought that navigating the estuaries of England was a far more dangerous prospect than being at sea. Oh, if Agamemnon ran aground on some inlet or bank, no one would drown of course. The ship wouldn't even likely be damaged enough to break or sink, but it was a sure thing it would not go unnoticed. Everyone would see it and of it everyone would gossip. The log would reflect such an instance as well. Indeed no one would drown, but later a court martial might see quite a few hanged, Cooper now pondering the old adage for a captain choosing to go down with his ship.

With the random possibility of destruction or imminent death all but a blink in time away, Cooper made it his business to stand tall upon the quarterdeck, inwardly checking the steerage and the actions of every officer. The jacks hustled about the weather deck and scrambled up the rigging like fleas gnawing a dog's tail. Agamemnon surprisingly made her way, quite easily, all under very little canvas. It made sense of course. She was barnacle free with a new copper bottom, all courtesy of Nelson and his benefactors. Cooper however was not expecting any tremendous speed. He recalled Nelson somewhat bragging about it of course, but for him, no amount of money could change the laws of physics. In port he had applied what scruples he possessed to trim whatever he could out of her, studying her lines whilst also applying the weight of his cannon and cargo to suit the best draught. He had even personally chosen the best sailcloth on offer, light yet sturdy and recently dressed down. Only the best wax would bring them back to life and he had personally chosen that as well. It was more a case of soon enough we shall most definitely see. He could hardly fathom what Nelson's sum of exactly £13,844 was actually going to procure, a sum mind you which would take a commander some seventy years to ever physically earn. Eleven knots at best, maybe twelve, was her previous best and he had heard that this was achieved under some very kind conditions. Most ships would be lucky to make ten of course. Yet with a new bottom, touch wood and cross fingers, maybe, just maybe he would wring thirteen or fourteen out of her. Wouldn't that be grand, especially considering what he reckoned the French could barely muster. If he could steal away even one extra knot, he was of a mind it would be worth double Nelson's pot, with interest. Where he was going and for what they had him doing, every knot would count most heavily and in the scheme of any action it might very well mean the difference between a knighthood or French prison.

He laid his good eye over the crew. They were already beginning to come together, cohesive, productive and happy, much more than he had expected. It had come none too soon either he considered, as sailing a river upon the outgoing tide was no cup of tea. The water was threatening its lowest mark and even though the ebb was gently carrying them, never was there a more hazardous time to be cruising the Medway. So far so good he thought, admiring the light wind running the lines of the ship, the smoothest run he had ever seen. Apart from the risk of running aground, he was feeling contented. He had Eagle up in his nest checking the runs of the river ahead. If there were deviations not depicted upon the charts, perhaps shifts in the banks and shoals, Eagle would see it. The constant toot on Eagle's whistle was some comfort indeed, chirping every cable's length, his affirmation that all was well. It was like clockwork. Cooper was thinking he would need to meet this marine sometime, a most satisfying and functional member of his crew. But for now, until some danger haphazardly presented itself, there was very little for a captain to do, except silently pass judgement as his first officer barked orders and the ship gradually made her way.

Agamemnon had some six hours allotted to make her way to

the Channel before of course the tide turned and the weight of the incoming flood chanced to trap them. They still could escape to sea, but much depended upon the wind. To sail with the tide would all but assure success. Sheppey, an island sharing the mouth of the Medway and the Thames, was finally looming to starboard. He could almost spy the entrance to the Swale, a channel which separated Sheppey from the mainland. Cooper immediately knew he had made it, with time to spare. Nothing left but a short haul from the Medway, a sprint into the Thames and out into the safety of the Channel. Most satisfied, he tucked away his glass and prepared to repair to his cabin. But the sound of his steps upon the plank suddenly ceased, replaced by a shrill call from the nest. It stopped him cold, a surging alarm striking every inch of his being. He looked up immediately to find Eagle tooting heavily on his whistle. It was a call he dared not want to hear, at least not just yet.

'On deck, ship action!' called Eagle.

'Where away?' shouted Spencer, running forward to attend the report in full. You can be sure he wasn't the only one who had heard it either and a bevy of bearded jacks looked up with a telling grin, gold weighing the wickedness sparking their good eye.

'Sir,' Spencer reported, rushing back to the quarterdeck. 'Lookout reports a ship action.'

'What? Did you just say *"ship action"*?' he questioned in astonishment. 'We aren't even out of the Medway. What the devil?'

'Aye sir, that is the report. Two points, broad of the starboard bow.'

'Soon to be almost dead ahead, if I am not mistaken, for are we not meant to gradually bear to starboard in the next few cable's lengths?'

'Aye sir, once we clear Sheppey,' Spencer agreed, laying a chart down and running his finger along the course. 'So that puts them thereabouts in the vicinity of the mouth of the Thames, directly north-east of Sheppey.'

'The mouth!' thought Cooper aloud, immediately recalling the recent loss of two ships to pirates.

'We cannot see them yet on deck, but of course the hills of Sheppey are presently blocking our view. Also sir, it was Eagle who spotted them, so they might even be over the horizon.'

'Indeed, our present speed?'

'We are running at four knots sir, but we barely have a scratch of canvas up, being that we are still in the Medway.'

'Order to make sail, immediately, full and bear away. In good time, put us directly before the wind, Mister Spencer. And I will be wanting to know the tidal drift of the Thames, if you please. Have Mister Thornton advise the exact time we might expect the slack and the returning flood. It cannot be far away. And sundown Mister Spencer, an exact time if you please? Mister Thornton is a competent master and should have no quibble. Lastly, ask Mister Holt to accompany me, directly.'

'Aye, aye, sir.'

'And let's get some clarity here Mister Spencer, best you ask Eagle what ships? And get his opinion of the exact distance, if you please?'

The ship was abuzz. The jacks were literally licking their chops. Had to be pirates of course, what else could it be, lest it was something which didn't involve prize money. They weren't at quarters just yet, but the more experienced jacks had everyone primed, all but waiting upon the order.

'Both two mast, brigs, sir,' he finally reported. 'They are on the horizon, both hulls in view. One is running from the other sir, attempting to make the Thames.'

'That one must be ours, standing for safe harbour.'

'Aye sir, but it is very hard going, they being close reached, almost beating directly into the wind. And sir, the masthead still reports no ships in sight. They can barely see over Sheppey, so I am thinking the brigs must be right on the horizon.'

'Ah,' he remarked, thinking upon the calculations roughly in his head. 'Indeed, Sheppey can rise as much as two hundred odd feet, especially near Minster I believe. Mister Spencer, how high up is Eagle's nest, if you were to hazard a guess?'

'Have to be two hundred feet sir, that is, being from sea level.'

'God bless that Eagle. He must be some seventy feet above the masthead! And if our masthead cannot see them yet, then it is a good bet they cannot see us either, unless they have their own

Eagle! I am guessing we must be around thirty thousand yards out, some fifteen sea miles.'

'Sir?' begged Holt politely. 'If I may be so bold sir, Eagle is exactly one hundred and ninety feet above the sea, as I had him measure it this morning.'

'You had him measure it?'

'Aye sir and seeing how the hulls of each ship are partially visible, then our maximum distance should be thirty-two and a half thousand yards, which is sixteen sea miles, or eighteen odd land miles as it were. Ardent class ships can maybe at best make twelve knots, and we have a fair wind directly abaft. Very soon, we should be able to make a direct run to the brigs, as the crow flies. Mister Thornton informs me the wind will pick up slightly as we make the mouth, so we might make up some time there. Provided they don't change tack and head to sea, we will be board and board in approximately eighty minutes, a tad less with a favourable wind.'

Cooper and Spencer both took pause to look upon Holt with some kind of stupefied amazement, their visage wrapped in indecision and wonder. Holt was either a prodigy or an escaped madman. Never had they witnessed any officer boldly make calculations as such, not without thinking for some considerable time and even then, it would just be some hopeful approximation. Cooper's calculations were catching up in his head, as were Spencer's.

'Mister Holt, I believe you have omitted to factor in the tidal drift!'

'Likely running at three knots,' assisted Spencer quickly.

'Very well, adding three knots in assistance,' Holt confirmed, continuing his thoughts with a slight mumble. 'Let's see, aye, deduct approximately sixteen minutes. Sir, sixty-four minutes to boarding range!'

'Mister Holt, sir, by the devil's horns, you are certain?' Spencer pressed. 'You didn't even...'

'He is right Spence. Be damned if he isn't right!' Cooper excitedly declared. 'Mister Holt, you will prove your calculations with Lieutenant Smythe, on paper sir, and report back directly. For now, do you swear on its quality?'

'Aye, sir.'

Ships of War — Murky Waters

'Very well. Mister Spencer, be so good as to ensure the ship continues to run within the cover of Sheppey, for as long as we can. We will hug her coastline and use every effort to mask the ship with the shore,' pointing to the chart. 'We have a draught of just on eighteen feet, but let's not get too fancy. If we run aground, we are of no use to anyone, so have a man checking abaft for foul water. The first sign of mud, he had better holler. Have a dogvane erected, she will show us the true wind. Let's continue and navigate our point where we can put her directly before the wind, a dead run to the brigs if you will. Line us up neatly now. I wish to hide the length of our sails and the number of masts from their view, so they cannot perceive us to be a ship of war, or a ship of greater weight and definitely not a ship with four hundred maddened poverty stricken jacks wildly bearing down on them.'

'Aye, sir,' confirmed Spencer, now grinning.

'You say they are broad on our starboard bow, close reached, trying to make the Thames? Being broad and close reached means they will not, any time soon, be getting closer. Very smartly will we approach, fine off their beam. We won't even have to wear the ship. They will be exactly dead ahead and not know what is coming. Should they see us and try to run, make ready to haul the main to larboard and the jib to starboard.'

'Goosewinged! Aye, goosewinged and both sheets aft it will be sir,' he happily acknowledged, thinking how grand the ship might look with her sails spread wide. 'And sir, beating to quarters?'

'Not just yet. Let go and complete hauling the sails first, trim them like they've never been trimmed before. Let us rest what men we can for now, but heave the log, immediately. I need to know how much way we are making, at every step.'

Agamemnon snuck around the shoreline like an African cat slinking about a waterhole, waiting hungrily on its prey. They were in the shadow of Sheppey now, the sun rapidly descending almost directly behind them. The ship started to make way considerably, the bow nodding heavily in descent and ascent, determined to scythe deep the murk of the Channel. The jacks were not ignorant either of their captain's cunning. He had been as slippery as an old hand nicking the rum. It would take a lookout of some quality to now spot Agamemnon running fine in the afternoon shadow with the sun squarely disappearing. It was a point of honour to serve with a captain who was no fool and how they buzzed as they weathered the speed of the ship making way. The far horizon deepened, finally falling dim. Underneath the flash of battle flickered haphazardly, Thor's hammer sparking within a darkened cloud. They could hear the cannon fire now, much the same as a faint thunder breaking the distance on a stormy night. The jacks popped up their good ears, waiting and listening, some older hands counting the intervals to attest the cannon crews' skill, others immediately insisting they were six pounders on one brig and eight pounders on the other.

Cooper took the time to settle his thoughts, play through the relevant and most likely scenarios. A British ship was under fire, running for their very lives. He was required to render immediate assistance, there was no other course, lest he enjoyed hanging. But he had not a full complement and there was an uncertainty in the crew, something to which he couldn't shake. They were new and were yet to fight together as such. Some had not been aboard a ship for years. This wasn't the prudence for which he and Nelson had painstakingly planned. Should he come up on the action and suddenly find a seventy-four, or a squadron of pirates, all could be lost. It was a good guess no pirate would wait around to take charge of a third-rate with some four hundred men. No, indeed, they would be of a mind to just sink her and be done with it. And with that, Cooper would also be sunk, his career and livelihood abruptly at an end, that is should he somehow manage to even survive.

'Sir, I have the reports you requested, if you please and here's your coffee?'

'Damn good coffee!' Cooper remarked, sipping it like he had just personally witnessed the second coming. 'Damned fine indeed, who the devil made this?'

'Oh and here it comes. You won't like it sir,' warned Spencer.

'No, please, not that tubby lard Fredricks! Please tell me you didn't let that man near my food? Not after the scrubbing I gave him.'

'Had Holt test it first sir and aye, it's Fredricks.'

'Good god, not Holt! No, no, no, perhaps use another mid next time, or the ship's mutt!' he worriedly exclaimed. 'Did Fredricks really make this?'

'Seems his belly is somewhat proportionate to his skill of fine cuisine, but the cook very nearly took to him with his gutting blade, says there's no place for that kind of posh grub in the scullery.'

'Indeed,' Cooper grinned, unable to hide his mirth, the picture of the cook chasing poor tubby Fredricks around with a great shiny blade happily embedded in his mind. 'Very well, now, what of your report?'

'Confirming three knots of tidal drift sir, directly abaft the ship, as is our breeze. The breeze, may I happily add, is stiffening somewhat. We have barely another hour before the slack and then thirty minutes before the flood hits us. But we will lose the light just before that anyway sir. No moon. And most happy to report, the ship is presently making eighteen knots.'

'Eighteen knots!' he wildly cried, the coffee spitting from his lips as if a burly cove had just cracked him hard on the back. 'What the devil! Eighteen knots! By what god, no, eighteen, it cannot be? They must have got it wrong, the lubber heads.'

'Had them check the log twice sir and the third time I did it myself with Holt, to show him the ropes,' he grinned, admiring his pun. 'It is correct. And if I may say sir, the jacks can feel it. I have heard them talking. There's a real buzz out there.'

'Very well,' he finally accepted. 'By all that is holy, never have I been on a ship at even fifteen knots, let alone eighteen, outrageous! How the hell are we getting eighteen? It feels swift enough, but it's oh so smooth.'

'I pondered this myself sir. It will be something for us to study.'

'In course, we will now need to recalculate our arrival.'

'Aye sir, in expectation, I have already reworked it. I have us at fifty-three minutes from time of sighting. That puts us only twenty-five minutes out. I took my time too sir, on paper, to be sure. And may I say, of the original estimate, Holt was bloody well spot on, he was.'

'Mister Holt, over here if you please sir,' Cooper sharply beckoned. 'We have an adjustment to our calculations. The ship it seems has been running at eighteen knots.'

'Oh sir, of course,' he paused, standing upright, his eyes sliding sideways in thought. 'Best take off another eleven minutes, which makes fifty-three and a half minutes, sir, that is, from the time of sighting.'

'Very good Mister Holt, return to your station,' he ordered, looking knowingly to his first officer. 'Well, well, well, Spence, it seems you were out by half a minute, shameful.'

'Mother and Mary!'

'Beat to quarters!' cried Spencer, a wild flicker in his good eye.

'Three thousand yards,' reported Smythe.

'Closing fast Captain,' Spencer added. 'And it appears we are in luck. They have not the canvas set in order to run. I think they have hardly bothered to see us.'

'They stand directly to leeward sir,' Smythe happily piped. 'We have the weather gage!'

'Indeed, but that is only all well and good if they are of a mind to fight,' Cooper corrected. 'But these old Frenchies, they have never really fought much with the gage you know and I think this captain might be one of them.'

'But sir, surely...' offered Spencer.

'Dissect it Spence, they instigated their attack from leeward, which means they had to chase whilst beating directly into the wind and current. Why attack as such? It's a slog. It's because they use the gage to allow themselves to turn and run, should the fight sour. They can turn downwind anytime and then it's one ship's speed against the other. But they are soon in for an eighteen knot surprise!'

The brig was most assuredly a pirate, fighting without national colours flying, which in itself was a crime punishable by death.

Ships of War — Murky Waters

The experienced eyes were already of a mind that any ensign offered was likely going to be French, not that it mattered thinking in any case never would they strike, only a noose awaiting them if they did. It was a large brig, some eighteen gun. The front was styled in the French way, not that this by itself meant they were French, ships continually being captured or traded over the years. Cooper could spy the captain through his glass, a well-dressed man in what he considered to be the French style. They were busy alright, so busy they had not seen Agamemnon. Cooper was thinking they were in for something of a surprise. He peered to the rear of the ship, the words La Hasard barely distinguishable.

The English brig, His Majesty's Ship Resignation, was much smaller, only ten gun, mostly six pounders and as such, so was she hopelessly outmatched. Nonetheless, they had been aware of Agamemnon bearing down on the action for some time, her captain cleverly manoeuvring to keep the eyes of the pirate away from shore.

Cooper could not fathom how Hasard had failed to spot a third-rate barely a cable's length away. He was laughably considering he might have to bunt them with the bowsprit to wake them up enough to strike. It wasn't until the shadow of Agamemnon loomed over her before some notice took hold. It was a feat of absolute seamanship to be sure and every man and jack aboard felt the pride.

'Fire over her bow, one nine on the forward chaser, if you please,' he ordered, calculating Hasard might actually just strike right there and then. It seemed the only plausible course of action, a sixty-four bearing down, both decks of cannon running out, all in readiness to fire. What else could the brig hope to do. Surely there was no choice. The gun boomed and the jacks cheered, swinging their fists. Cooper waited for the fall of her colours, or more to the point, the fall of the bland curious flag attached to her rear.

'Surely she must strike?' vexed Spencer.

Hasard fell to panic as Agamemnon bore down directly. Cooper had all but to steer hard to starboard, luff her sheets just enough to spill the wind and she could lazily drift with thirty of her larboard cannon pointing right down the brig's throat, a broadside weight of some six hundred and seventy-eight pounds.

Cooper would not damage his prize of course, for it was much too valuable. At this range, he figured he would only need one or two eighteen pounders, such a ball likely to penetrate around three feet through the planking.

'Luff up and spoon, Mister Spencer,' Cooper ordered. He was indeed slowing the ship so he could drift and fire. Agamemnon steadily began to pivot, Hasard would soon be directly off her beam. This was surely the start of the very end, one way or the other. Cooper made his calculations and they proved true, down to the second. Oh how he yearned for the next moment, a prize and he hadn't even barely left the Medway. 'First volley, high, if you please! And the first rat who hits the hull will know not the taste of rum til the next coming! Eighteens only, Mister Spencer.'

The captain of Hasard bellowed frantically, no less her men ordered to run. They were not going to strike, not just yet. It was a bold risk, for one ball from an eighteen could very well sink her. A ship her size would go down faster than a polished stone too. Agamemnon was almost in line and Hasard knew it, the seaman aboard scurrying about like mice scampering from the cat.

'Sir, she is not striking.'

'Quite, have Mister McFee's sharp shooters open fire, clear those men from the deck and their duties. They mean to run, cheeky fools!'

A volley rang true, the result appallingly apparent. McFee's jollies knew their work. Lastly a lone shot cracked, a distinct bang from Eagle's nest and an officer upon Hasard's quarterdeck fell directly thereafter. Not only Cooper and his officers, but the entire weather deck took note, more than half the crew straining their neck to catch a glimpse of Eagle. It did not seem possible of course and they shook their head in wonder, some hoping Hasard didn't by chance have their own Eagle sharpshooter. Another volley rang, more Frenchmen cut down from their stations, one even horribly caught by his foot in the rigging, the poor sod left to dangle lifelessly in the breeze.

The cheers from Resignation could now be heard, for they had taken quite a beating and were looking for some recompense of their own now. Agamemnon's first cannon loomed, finally bearing and Cooper graciously gave the order.

Ships of War — Murky Waters

'Fire as you bear! Aim for her masts!' he urged. Now, it would be all over. All over indeed, except however for the want of a few seconds, which is often the privy of war. Hasard should have been finished right there and then, the first balls poised to take out every scratch of rigging and most likely the masts. This was her cue to strike and escape utter destruction. But a few seconds were all that stood between that and a second chance. She had quite cleverly heeled and was now surging forth into Resignation, almost uncontrollably. It was a surety the brigs would now likely collide. Resignation was now savagely trading musket fire. This was not the handsome scene Cooper or Spencer had imagined. 'What the devil! Belay firing! At once!' Cooper ordered, much to his absolute disgust, but he knew he had no other choice, for he well knew Resignation would be sent to the bottom at the first wayward ball. 'Belay firing! Damnation! This lunatic will see his crew killed! Mister Spencer, board and board! Put us in close, jam us right in there. Prepare to board!'

Resignation, not sensing the situation and rather, the fear of being rammed very much taking hold, did veer wildly to make room. Immediately both Cooper and Spencer swore, for this was the last thing she should've done. Hasard, until now, had been hemmed in and had they stayed the course, the French brig could not avoid being boarded, by both vessels in fact. Unless they had some five hundred men stashed below, they would be forced to strike or see British steel tended to their bellies. McFee readied fifty marines, his entire complement. The ships would bunt, grappling hooks would be slung and they would storm the brig like wild animals stampeding to feed. But it would never happen. Hasard had her chance now, a perfect line back out into the Channel, poor Resignation blocking Agamemnon's cannon. Agamemnon would now be forced to fill her sails and wear ship around the brig, which Cooper quickly judged as no small feat either, time permitting. And this would all have to happen well before she could bear upon her or hope to even give chase.

'They are moving away, sir!' reported Spencer.

'Damn, damn, damn, the stupidity! What in hell was he thinking! She will have a handsome head start on us! Fine luck that was, damned fine. Spence, get us going, prepare to wear the ship, just enough to slip around the brig. Good god! Is that a boat in the water?'

'Aye sir, I see him, already making the necessary correction!'

The boat was floating haplessly, directly between the brig and Agamemnon's intended line. Spencer took the helm, swinging it hard over, savagely veering the ship as Cooper called the mark of each turn. Barely, only barely did they miss, a testament to the skill of their seamanship. They looked up thereafter, fully expecting to see the sails of Hasard making her way to the horizon. She most definitely should have been on her way, well back out to sea, but to their surprise she had changed tack. Her gun ports bore her teeth, her cannon poking out directly abeam Agamemnon, but no less still on the far side of Resignation.

'What the devil!' lamented Cooper.

'She means to fire on us sir!' Spencer warned. It was a perfect shot of course and they could not miss. Agamemnon could not return fire, Resignation broad off the beam still blocking the way. They were at the mercy of an eight pounder broadside, virtually at musket range. It was going to hurt and Cooper weighed his option to fire. Perhaps better to end it now he thought, even if Resignation takes some collateral damage. The disdain Cooper harboured for the French captain almost inclined him to chance it too. In the end, the hundred odd British lives directly in the way succinctly brought him to his senses. Hasard was quite brisk and was proving no stranger to warfare, turning efficiently and safely, exactly when necessary. Why they weren't heading out to sea was beyond both Cooper and Spencer, but they were soon to find out. 'Prepare to take cover,' Spencer ordered, but Cooper had already flushed out what Hasard was up to. Now all he could do was watch helplessly as she changed course once more.

'Belay that!' Cooper ordered. 'No, no, no!' he yelled in frustration, his pulse right upon the situation. Hasard was hardly going to run and she wasn't about to waste a perfectly good broadside on a sixty-four she could barely scratch.

'She ain't running sir and surely she is to fire on us?' Spencer surmised, until finally he understood all too well the mind of the French captain. 'Oh sir, by god, she is steering directly abaft Resignation. I don't think Resignation have picked up on it.'

Ships of War — Murky Waters

'They mean to rake her, fore and aft,' Cooper reluctantly confirmed, evenly and coldly.

'Strike!' Spencer frantically whispered, albeit to himself. 'Why don't she at least strike her colours, for the love of god!' It was worse than a bad dream. Hasard slipped around the stern of the helpless brig, most handsomely luffing her sail to slow her way. Resignation's colours finally fell, but it didn't matter. The cannon let go one by one and Hasard elegantly passed in a haze of smoke. Even if Fredricks was pulling the lanyards, they could not miss. Each ball hit home, methodically and accurately, ripping right through the length of the ship. Wood chips flew high into the sky, balls exiting the ship even as far up as the bow, the damage absolute, the result catastrophic. 'The devil sir!' Spencer lamented. As the last few shots held true, Resignation all at once ripped apart, a savage explosion, sudden, deafening and somewhat surreal. Agamemnon jacks quickly turned away, the shock rippling the length of their ship. The eruption of a blinding spark struck, beholding to such carnage perhaps only attesting such magnitude as to the end of days. Upon turning back, not a scrap was afloat. The entire ship was gone, her last bits wafting in pieces as a molten shower from a devil's sky. Of the crew, only naked bodies floated here and there, the burned garments ripped from their very backs. 'Good god!' Spencer cried. 'Poor devils!'

'Such evil,' Cooper vexed. 'There are six things the good Lord hates and seven that are an abomination to him, most of all evil hands shedding innocent blood.'

'Fret not,' Holt sombrely added. 'For they shall soon be cut down like the grass and wither.'

'You can count on that Mister Holt. Blast that whoreson to hell!'

'Must have hit the powder sir,' Spencer correctly surmised. 'All done for, every last poor sod.'

'Not all, they had men in a boat, somewhere?'

'Oh sir, there's no boat, not no more.'

'Very well,' he quickly pondered, eyeing Hasard's run, the brig now making her escape ever so quickly out to sea, a dead run neatly down wind. She already had over a thousand yards on Agamemnon and the sky had mushed into a gloomy mess melting against the deepening sea. She would soon be out of sight. 'Lieutenant, stand the men down, we will make our search for survivors.'

'Sir?' he questioned, full knowing that it was in fact the only real choice. The pirate was as good as a French needle in a field of Prussian haystacks. Never would they find her as the darkness gathered. 'Sir, the brig?' he begged.

'No Spence. We would be rabbit hunting with a dead ferret. He has played his hand all too well, the devil. He knows we have him by the jib if it's a race and he full well knows anyone in the water is as good as dead in barely ten minutes, it being so cold. He knows it's turned dark as Davy Jones Locker, there being no moon til later and he can slip away whenever he chooses. He's a clever one. Upon turning to rake Resignation, he all but ensured we would heave-to, as we cannot risk lowering a boat in this darkness. We might even catch our rat, but upon returning, we'd never find our boat of course. In my mind, there's no doubt, we'd likely lose our rat in the first bell. No Spence, let's search, do what we can, whatever poor souls might be out there do not have much time. I have had a good look at our French friend, don't worry, there'll be another time.'

'But the crew sir?'

'They will understand.'

Of course, that would be mighty wishful thinking. Captain Cooper made his way along the weather deck, a deck with hundreds of souls upon her and if there was even one mouse scurrying, you'd hear it sniff and scratch before it squeaked. They had their hats off but their eyes fell upon their captain in distrust and contempt. Not only had an English ship been savaged and sunk, but it all happened whilst they were in musket range. Making eighteen knots, they all knew who would catch who. They would see the pirate captain hanged before the next day broke, or there would be hell to pay. But now the brig was gone, long gone, slipped away without so much as even one shot being fired.

Two survivors were hauled aboard, both of whom had been away in the boat. The first was a young lad, not quite Holt's age, barely a scrap of clothing to hide him. He had almost succumbed, his body shivering uncontrollably. Cooper took one good long

Ships of War — Murky Waters

look at him and then another, his curiosity very much taken.

'Take this boy to the great cabin,' he immediately ordered, much to the shock of some nearby crew. Normally, a captain might afford to send him to the cockpit, being the surgeon's cabin, perhaps with a loblolly boy and eventually be tended by the surgeon's mate. 'Have Mister Holt go with him, bring him some clothing and let's see if we can't get him warmed up then.'

A short while later a lieutenant, or so it appeared, was hauled aboard although it was most difficult to ascertain his rank, his uniform most terribly savaged in the explosion. He had been most fortunate as well. Eagle had only just located him moments before it went completely dark, far from where he should have been in fact. The force of the blast had sent him far from his boat, a boat which was now all but reduced to kindling. He was conscious, but weak and they dragged him up onto the weather deck scuffed like a drowned kitten.

'Shillings?' Cooper declared. 'God damn man, is that you?'

'Aye sir,' he feebly responded, looking up to see his saviour. 'Ah Lieutenant Cooper! Beg your pardon, Captain Cooper. I thank you sir.'

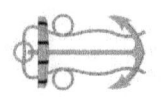

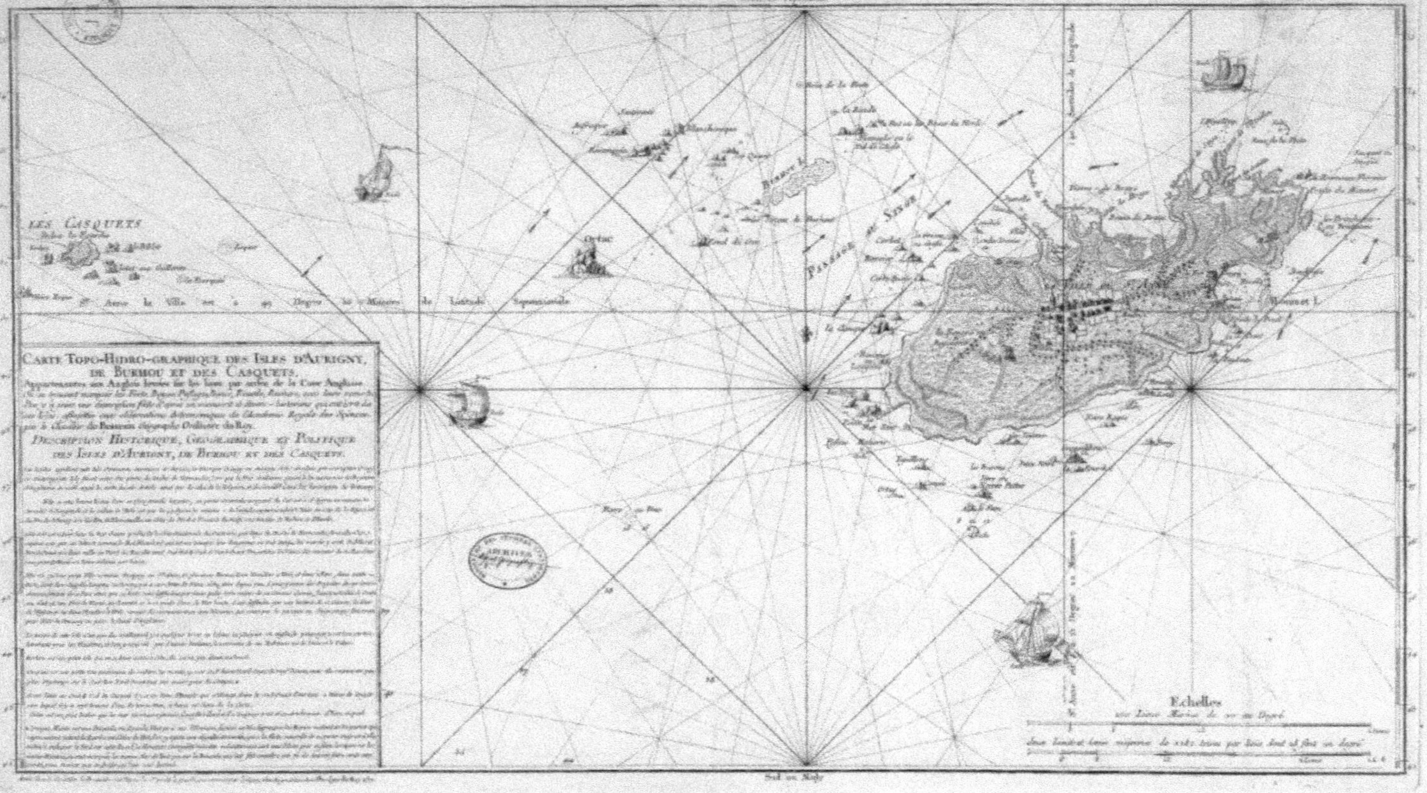
Nord ou Septentrion
Les Casquets
Carte Topo-Hidro-graphique des Isles d'Aurigny,
de Burhou et des Casquets.
Appartenantes aux Anglois levées sur les lieux par ordre de la Cour Angloise
par le Chevalier de Beaurain Géographe Ordinaire du Roy.
Description Historique, Géographique et Politique
des Isles d'Aurigny, de Burhou et des Casquets.
Ortac
Burhou I.
Passage du Singe
Sud ou Midy
Echelles

Chapter XI
Ortac

Cooper was cognisant of the feelings amongst the crew. He had some idea what they might be thinking and perhaps even saying. His decision to break off the attack and search for survivors had cost them the French prize. Of course that is to say, it had cost prize money, easy money which hardly was going to present itself so handsomely again. They weren't privy to the Admiralty's plans. They had no idea they were to be pirate hunters and they definitely knew very little about the politics of Europe and that war could break at any moment. They only knew one thing, it was peacetime and they had come upon a pirate. The prize was right there before them, barely a cable's length away, Agamemnon faster and more powerful. All they had to do was fire a broadside and the prize was theirs. But no, their captain had just let it scoot off, scot free. And for what, to rescue a boy and one lone lieutenant, an officer they were starting to think hardly seemed worth it. It was a hard pill to swallow, especially after witnessing the horrid destruction of Resignation, a cruel act even by wartime standards. Vengeance ruled a sailor's heart and Cooper knew there had to be a reckoning, or they would never forgive him. It was the inherent nature of a jack of course and Cooper well understood it. They would despise him, for now, but in time he was sure he could win them back, with any luck hopefully before they ran the ship onto the next reef in protest, or took a cutlass to his throat.

Since the action, Cooper had mostly confined himself to the great cabin. Out of sight, out of mind, so he was thinking. Let them cool off a bit. He had laid in the course and was now just waiting upon his first officer to announce their arrival. Of course he had not told them where they were going, or what they were doing, only that it would be apparent when they arrived.

'Sir?' Spencer offered, about to knock on his door, only to be met face to face before even a single knock was half managed. 'Lookout has reported sir, a great bloody rock on our course, permission to veer?'

'Ah, very good. Now two things Lieutenant, firstly, you have navigated most precisely, admirable indeed. Secondly, we are here. The great bloody rock, as you put it, is in fact our destination. Clear the anchor, hide the ship as close as you dare and bear in mind that it is my wish to take our fine cannon atop the rock, perhaps tomorrow. Once we have dropped anchor, you may stand down the crew. No one is to go ashore yet, but they may rotate on light duty so they may fish, swim and sup of course.'

'The sixty-fours sir! Atop the rock?' he fretted, only to be met by a stern unmoving expression, his captain assuredly far from prepared to discuss it. 'Aye, aye, sir!'

'In addition, it is my wish to invite the officers to dine in my state room, if you would be so good as to make the invitations for me. This will be our first dinner together and it is time to unveil our plans. Oh and please ensure His Lordship is also invited.'

'Aye, aye, sir. And does that include our new guest too?' Spencer probed, fearing the worst. He eyed carefully his captain's silent reply. 'It's just that it will not be popular sir. The man has, how should I put it, aye sir, he has a knack of imposing the most candid annoyance.'

'Well, the man was just blown out of his boat and suffered the loss of his shipmates, in entirety. And I beg you to remember that he was the lone survivor of last month's obscene calamity, a disaster of which we have only recently been apprised.'

'Sir, of course, regaled at the Lion. I have not forgotten.'

'He has damn well survived two wrecks now, in as many months. What a lucky soul he must have. I am sure he deserves a good meal and some company. If we have to, I think we could indulge Mister Shillings for now, don't you?'

'Aye sir. But you should know, the jacks have taken a disliking.'

'Indeed, how so?'

'Aye sir, they blame him for the prize getting away, seeing how we had to break off and save him.'

'Ah, the lost prize money no doubt?'

'Aye sir and that's not all. There is this business of his surviving the wreck of Retribution, upon no other soul excepting the boy, who doesn't count being he is not a sailor. It is not sitting well and may I say sir, it's damned improbable. And they are saying he's the cause of some mishaps. There's been a few on our journey since, just small things, some injuries and equipment failures, you know the regular stuff. But, to be sure, the jacks have got it in for him and it's catching. Even had to flog one of the landsmen just today sir, insubordination, failed to raise his knuckle.'

'For the love of god, please don't say they think him a Jonah? Please tell me they aren't saying that?'

'Wish I could sir, but that's what they're saying and more. They are blaming him for Retribution, seeing how it was his boat which prevented us making way. And sir, somehow they know about his previous ship and her fate, again he being the only survivor. More to their point, only a Jonah could have brought that much bad luck upon a crew and the proof is that he himself survived.'

'Bugger their souls to hell! Good god, next he will be a witch because he didn't drown!'

'Aye sir and the weather just turned mighty cold too and where we are presently, it should be a tad warmer.'

'Blaming him for that as well?'

'Aye, sir.'

'Blast! Damn the jacks and their superstitious twaddle! Just what we bloody need thank you very much. I will need to think on this. Well, one thing, at least they ain't blaming their captain so much.'

'As to that sir, it is mixed,' he hesitated. 'The more experienced hands have nothing much to say, good or bad, which is about right of course. There are some, more so the ones who have been to war, who have stepped forward with some praise sir.'

'Indeed, such as?'

'First, never have they seen a third-rate sneak up on a brig like that, so cool you could reach out and tap the French captain on the shoulder, which is how they said it. And never have they seen a captain get eighteen knots out of a sixty-four, not even a frigate, so slick your locks mopped up before you could blink. They also said something about how you had put your own money into the barky. Not sure how they came to think that, you being poorer than a jack at a pinch on Sunday. And a right proper seaman they say you are sir, veering a ship of the line around Mister Shillings's boat, without even a how you do as if you was out for a Sunday row. But the pacifier to be sure and I'm glad there's one, is that they are saying you know exactly where the Frenchie is and it's only a matter of time before we go and get her.'

'Indeed?' he remarked raising his eyebrows at the last comment. 'Anything else?'

'Pretty much the usual, you know, laying blame on the devil and the deep blue sea sir, for letting our prize slip away. Said only the devil could've arranged such luck, or a Jonah, which is where they started on Mister Shillings. The jacks, the ones who have been to war, they all knew we had the game done until Resignation most unfortunately veered off. A brig captain ain't a real captain they are saying, not like a sixty-four's captain, which is a right and proper one.'

'I see, but?'

'But there's a small muster sir, mostly misfit landsmen, maybe a few others too, who are saying you are to blame. They are saying you are the captain and you should've headed after the prize and then come back for Mister Shillings and that you didn't because you didn't want to fight.'

'Didn't want to fight? What, I didn't want to fight an eighteen gun brig, with my sixty-four? Are they touched in the head?'

'Sorry sir, but they also brought up some scuttlebutt about you being called out by Lord Pendleton's man for cheating at cards. Don't know how they know, but they are saying you refused to fight him too.'

'Refused to fight him? But to fight him was our whole bloody plan!'

'Sorry sir, they are going about saying you is shy, that you are somewhat wanting in pluck, beg my pardon.'

'Damn their insolent hides!'

'And sir there's one more thing. I am somewhat loath to bring it up, but I think you need to know. It's about the lad sir, the one we pulled from the water. Well, there's some talk, same muster sir. They are saying not only are you shy, but you're a might soft sir, is how they are saying it.'

'Soft?'

'Well, seeing how you sent the lad direct to your cabin instead of the cockpit and they haven't seen him since, they are saying you are soft on him, using the lad as your cushion, if you get my meaning, sir.'

'What!' he bellowed in absolute outrage. 'Do you mean to tell me these misfits, these landsmen, are telling everyone their captain is buggering that lad! Is that what they bloody mean?'

'Aye sir, told you I was loath, most loath.'

'Give me a name Spence!'

'Aye, sir. The ringleader from all accounts is Cross, a landsman, one Jebediah Cross. He is a known trouble maker I am afraid.'

'I will splay them alive!' he menacingly swore. 'I will personally skin them and then splay them and I'll make every man and jack bloody well watch! Spence, you will accompany me at once. There's something you need to see before dinner! Bloody well go get Mister Holt too!'

Cooper, Spencer and Holt entered the great cabin to find the young lad cheekily sitting behind the captain's desk, casually reading. The lad glanced up with almost a shy grin, perhaps a modicum of some latent acknowledgement, not that Spencer took much interest. All the first officer angrily saw was a cabin boy remaining firmly in his place when he should be on his feet showing a knuckle. Spencer's sudden jolt of annoyance surely showed and immediately he thought to correct the lad, properly explain each shortcoming and then have him before the mast to be suitably flogged.

'On your bloody feet lad, or I'll have you kissing the gunner's daughter!' Spencer angrily bellowed. 'It is your duty and custom sir to show respect whenever the Captain is present!' he further attested, his eyes wildly fixed awaiting the required response. However, it was hardly forthcoming. The lad blankly blinked somewhat unknowingly, wholly reminiscent of a night owl wincing amidst the dead of night and just as enlightened as a landsman fumbling the rigging knots. The lad passed his blank look towards Cooper before laying the book upon the desk and sheepishly standing. Spencer was just past boiling and about to start when his captain conveniently intervened.

'Lieutenant Spencer, sir, I present to you His Royal Highness, Louis Joseph Xavier François, a Fils de France or *"Son of France"*, Dauphin of France, heir apparent to the throne, the twenty-sixth crown prince of the Valois and Bourbon monarchies and oh,' he added with a wry grin. 'Our most special guest it seems.'

'Sir?'

'This is the elder son of King Louis XVI of France, his mother being Marie Antoinette. He is the future King of France, the Dauphin.'

'God bloody well fetch me sir!'

Ships of War — Murky Waters

'Indeed! Quite a nice young fellow actually, but he speaks absolutely no English,' he sympathetically added, turning to the Dauphin to introduce the first officer in his native tongue, to which he made a most elegant bow in return. 'So you can see why I have had him locked away down here, with only Mister Holt in attendance.'

'But sir, I heard the Dauphin had died, consumption, in eighty-nine?'

'Aye Spence, curious is it not that the revolution then commenced only one month later? They knew it was coming. His apparent death was all a cunning ruse it seems, to hide away the Dauphin from the hands of the many lunatics and madmen no doubt preparing their run.'

'Why, sir, he cannot be any older than...'

'Ten, Spence,' he finished for him. 'The royal family has been trying to escape France since the revolution began. In fact, the Dauphin has informed me that his family will soon attempt to escape from Paris to Montmédy, to an ancient but very strong citadel in north-eastern France. It's quite close to Austria, his mother's homeland of course. It seems his father, the King, wishes to initiate a counter revolution, no less at the head of loyal troops under royalist officers, which it seems are all somewhat concentrated at Montmédy. The Dauphin has been on the run from his oppressors since he was eight, but it was only recently they found out he was still alive. It's why Hasard was not giving up that fight you see and it's also why Shillings was in the boat. The captain saw Agamemnon and had rightly sent the boat away knowing it was only a matter of time before Hasard overwhelmed them, fully expecting the cruds to board and retrieve the Dauphin. He ordered Shillings to get the Dauphin to Agamemnon, by any means. It was working quite brilliantly really, as they never once realised he was in the boat. Of course, neither did we. Now, they will naturally think he really is dead, which is going to work in our favour somewhat.'

'Good god sir!'

'So, as you can see, I am not *"soft"* on the lad.'

'Oh sir, I will have those mutineers flogged to an inch of their lives.'

'It can wait for now Spence. It may not even be so necessary soon too, so I am thinking. In time, the crew will hear what they need to hear and shame will be those mutts' bedfellows. For us, the jacks will do the work upon them, in abundance.'

'I am astonished sir, the future King of France, by all that is holy!'

'Now, come to think of it, I think you are right. I will leave Shillings to dine with the Dauphin tonight.'

'Gentlemen, a toast,' Cooper solemnly suggested, sitting at the head of the table with his glass held high. 'Being that it is Thursday, let us drink to, *"a bloody war or a sickly season!"*.' Happily he received the customary *"ayes"* in response. Having been given the seat of honour next to his captain, it was of course Holt who immediately sought to find out why they would wish upon such a horrid thing. Of course, the young midshipman so admired his captain he would drink to the dismembering of his favourite puppy should he so order it. 'Now who here would like to explain Thursday's tradition to our young midshipman? We must of course excuse Mister Holt. As a young and budding king's officer, he is not yet practiced in the ways of proper naval drinking, a disorder we shall soon rectify, may he one day successfully pass for his lieutenant's exam!' he candidly added to the rumble of hooting laughter.

'Mister Holt,' Spencer started. 'Young sir, we drink to such maladies because it is our most vehement and deepest wish to one day be promoted. For without such maladies striking down our superiors, our chances of promotion are of course no better than a cat in hell without claws, which is to say no chance at all.'

'Oh,' he blankly replied, not knowing what to think.

'Begging your pardon Mister Spencer,' McFee challenged. 'But is not that analogy reserved for one who enters a dispute or a quarrel and the opponent is greatly above his match?'

Spencer stared blankly at McFee, as if he had been caught out, the table quietly awaiting his opinion. Holt felt anxious, perhaps thinking it was the start of some disagreement, but in fact Spencer was merely biding his time, for dramatic effect.

'But of course Major,' he finally agreed. 'And when has the matter of promotion by Their Lordships ever been anything but a dispute or a quarrel, they always being greatly above our match?' he smartly responded, much to the mirth of the entire table, including McFee who then sought to insist they all drink to larger claws.

'Hear, hear,' McFee praised. 'Oh though, to be born with some interest, rather than some skill and thus not require such claws,' he light heartedly added, before he suddenly realised the comment may have insulted young Holt, implying as such the lad would promote in spite of a want of skill. 'Oh, please Mister Holt,' he very quickly corrected. 'I did not mean that towards you of course.'

'Indeed,' Cooper added. 'For our young midshipman is not dining with officers tonight because of his much lauded station. He is here because he has, from the first day aboard, performed his duty in the most admirable fashion, well above what is due his rank and age. Even though His Lordship may enjoy the biggest claws here, I do believe he needs them not to succeed. Mister Holt, we will all be watching your progress, with some *"interest",*' he lastly added with a wry chuckle, barely holding back a wild grin, to which everyone gurgled at the play on words. 'Mirth aside, rest assured, you will not be promoted by me without first knowing your job, without first showing courage, without first showing skill and without first, to be sure, a lot of other withouts!'

'Hear, hear!'

'Aye, Mister Holt, please accept my sincerest apology for any slight this old Scot may have inadvertently made.'

'It is quite alright Mister McFee,' he graciously and most evenly responded, modestly unveiling his future potential and station as a lord. 'I was never in any way slighted, but I am decidedly going to have you flogged anyway, as soon as I make captain,' he very cheekily teased, smirking at the old Scot altogether with a truly wicked smile that no soul might reasonably resist.

'Oh no, Major!' Spencer quickly added, mortified. 'By my reckoning, that's barely only a handful of months away,' he jested, the room now in an uproar of merriment. 'Best you get your affairs in order and prepare for the *"cat"!'* he most cleverly added, the last play turning the room inside out.

The dinner was proving a great success for Captain Cooper and it had to be, his stores hardly at a level which might promote any more than one invitation a week. He may have chortled along with his officers, but he was watching most intently each and every one and barely did he partake more than a sip of his wine. They were a unique bunch he had decided, a crew he could shape and perhaps eventually even trust. With the servants finally sent from the room, it was time for port and cigars and the unveiling of his plans, or at least the first stages.

'Gentlemen, when we toasted earlier this night, to *"a bloody war"*, it was unlikely any of you had any inkling as to how nigh upon us that might be. I am happy to inform you that war with France is most definitely coming,' he boldly announced, much to the immediate attention of all. 'We, upon Agamemnon's back, are the very first chosen few to spearhead England's defence. I will have you know that before we sailed, I was summoned to Whitehall, whereupon I had the distinct honour and privilege to meet not only with Right Honourable John Pitt, 2nd Earl of Chatham, First Lord of the Admiralty, but also Admiral of the Fleet, John Forbes, Prime Minister William Pitt, Admiral Lord Howe and Admiral Hood.'

'Holy mother of god!' exclaimed McFee.

'Not quite, but close Major,' he teased. 'As a consequence, we have graciously been placed under the command of one Commodore Horatio Nelson, who is presently without ship, our de facto admiral if you please. It is with absolute furtiveness however that we must now operate. We cannot be uncovered, or be found acting contrary to any international law. If we are, we will be disavowed and hung as pirates. I warn you, to speak of this even to one soul outside this room would only invite such peril...'

'This is for the main, of course, as to why we did not bother to chase down Hasard. Gentlemen, you will soon find out in great detail, but for now, know this, I have been given the absolute prerogative to cruise and roam wherever we so please. Our mission insists upon this premise. I suspect you may now be guessing we are not a packet, boorishly destined to sail mindlessly from port to port. No, no, no and as such, I promise you that our French friend Hasard will be in our sights. I think I do not need to tell you that she would have duped us in any case, for the night was far too deep and she a ship far too small and fast...'

'Our commission, from King George himself, is to rid the Channel of these pirate attacks, which we believe are in fact French Letters of Marque in disguise. Oh they will argue patriotism, right up to the time the noose is placed around their grubby necks, but to us, gentlemen, they are just dirty damned pirates! And I believe we have just seen our first, Hasard. La Hasard by the way means *"hazard"*. And I can tell you that immediately upon laying eye I had recognised the vessel, it being a French brig, eighteen gun, Hasard Class...'

'The foremost in her class then?'

'Aye, the lead in her class, because when hunting English shipping in peacetime, you are not going to do it with anything lesser. You may be interested to know she displaces one hundred and eighty tons, is thirty yards long with a draught of less than four yards, a complement of approximately a hundred souls and bears eighteen gun comprising fourteen six pounders, the rest being four pounders.'

'Sir, if I may, but for the main, weren't they eight pounders? And if I am not mistaken, the rest being thirty-six pound carronades?'

'Very good Mister Spencer, for indeed they were. But that class of brig is meant to have sixes. Somehow they have mounted heavier gun without a discernible loss of speed. Did you notice her as she departed, quite swift and brisk and with short eights, quite the scourge one would think...'

'May I say, continuing, the state of Europe is as such that the Admiralty strongly believes war is imminent. I am permitted to tell you that even as we speak certain countries are readying to confront the lunacy sweeping over Paris. The French King is all but powerless now, the Girondins and the Society of the Friends, being the Jacobins of course, are in fact the ones actually ruling. When war breaks, we will not be fighting a royalist France. No, no, no, more likely we will be fighting the mob. And who is to say how the mob might fight? Possibly might they throw down and discard all etiquette and all honourable rules of war, like the dogs they are? The reality is plain. They are secretly murdering their own countrymen, day in and day out, for far less...'

'The recent action with Hasard and Resignation was regrettable, most regrettable. As you may appreciate, Agamemnon did her duty, to her utmost. If it were not for the judgement in error of Retribution's captain, we would have easily boarded and taken her a prize. None of you are to blame and so has it been reflected in the log. But I promise we will still yet catch her, mark my words. The fact of the matter is, I have been privy to the record of all pirate raids which has prevailed for the last eighteen months. To this, had I already prepared a list of potential ports from which our pirates operate. I am most certain as to where Hasard holds up. And may I add, it is not far from this very position, in Alderney. Gentlemen, Agamemnon will have her pound of flesh, provided we remain patient...'

'I have our ship's log here, attesting to the destruction of Resignation. You will note it to be a fabricated story of sorts. The simple matter is, England has been caught napping. We in no way are ready to go to war just yet. Naturally, should the truth of Resignation's fate come out, perhaps published in the Gazette, there would be such an outrage that King George would have to declare. We would take a bad licking upfront I am afraid to say, seeing how we are undermanned and somewhat unorganised. But rest assured, the Admiralty is quietly mobilising, quietly recalling and quietly strengthening our forces on land and sea. I will now read aloud our public report:

"Regret to inform, His Majesty's Ship Retribution, a brig of ten gun, appears to have been driven ashore and sank at Great Yarmouth, Norfolk. She was on a voyage from Rotterdam, Dutch Republic to Great Yarmouth. There were no apparent survivors.".'

Ships of War — Murky Waters

He paused, sternly eyeing each of them.

'And now my private letter to Their Lordships, which is the official record of the action, the entire truth of the matter:

"10 April 1791. Sighted French brig La Hasard, eighteen gun, just on nightfall, on horizon, sixteen sea miles north-east of Sheppey, without colours flying, chasing His Majesty's Ship Retribution, ten gun. Upon Agamemnon closing to a cable's length, regret to inform Your Lordships the complete and utter destruction of Retribution by explosion, a cruel raking at the unforgivable mercy of La Hasard, all hands lost, save one Lieutenant Shillings and the Crown Prince of France, the Dauphin, His Royal Highness, Louis Joseph Xavier François, intent upon escaping to England. La Hasard immediately proceeded into the moonless night and was thereafter rendered most unfindable, much to our utter dismay. Your servant, Captain Cooper, Agamemnon".'

The entirety of the room was stunned, somewhat quieter than the average church mouse and they looked at each other attesting whether their captain was perhaps still in a state of jest. It certainly explained quite a lot and in silence they remained, attentive as nuns to a virtuous choir.

'Their Lordships will know of the action, in full, as you all can now attest. The public report will of course be temporary. They will likely release the factual report once war is declared. Until then, your silence is very much demanded. Please do not despair, for as I have already attested, I know Hasard's likely port and even her habits. Once we are set comfortably here at Ortac, our squadron is going to make a nice meal of her, but first of course we need to get the Dauphin back to the safety of England.'

'Captain, sir, did you just say the crown Prince of France?'

'And sir? Did you just say squadron?'

'Indeed, on both accounts,' he grinned. 'It seems we have plucked the next King of France from the claws of the revolutionists. He is a grave threat to their cause of course, should he remain with the living. And to the latter, it is my utmost intent that any ship we take a prize be installed into our service. We can hardly take on France with just one ship, as grand as Agamemnon is. It is my every intention that we will operate as a small squadron and such said operation will commence forthwith on Ortac, with a small fort. We will use our fort to spy on shipping in and out of the Channel Islands and also those out of Alderney. I have already arranged for cargo ships to dock regularly in order to furnish supplies, thus allowing Agamemnon to hunt indefinitely and our fort to be sustained. Commodore Nelson and myself have come to the great conclusion that we should start small and work our way up. Whatever ships we take will be bought into service, but most handsomely will they be retained for our squadron. So I suggest no one is to get overzealous on the direction of our cannon when the prize is before us. And I must warn you, there are spies in England, so we must avoid bringing any prizes back home to refit. Gentlemen, there you have it, we are to be pirate hunters...'

The room was murmuring like a pack of private school brats who had just discovered they were all immediately elevated to prefect, their first duty to hunt down any scallywag they might find loitering, a hefty prize for each head in recompense. It was a grand surprise, one which could only lead to fame, fortune and absolute promotion, unless they failed of course and their naval careers would all be over, their future draped in destitution and disdain.

'Eyes gentlemen,' Cooper sternly announced, attempting to belay the happy murmur, laying down a chart. 'I give you Ortac Island, a small uninhabited islet exactly three miles west of the coast of Alderney, most near the islet of Burhou. It is a small island which I believe will serve us well, it being two hundred and thirty feet by one hundred and sixty-four, the latter of which curiously is perhaps almost the exact length of Agamemnon's gun deck. But most importantly, Ortac rises seventy-nine feet above the sea. She is solid rock and any French cannon could bang away all day and night before they might reduce barely a loose pebble. Our cannon, in contrast, will hide away within the rock, sixty-fours no less. The only way to take the island will be to storm her by way of one small entry point by force in small boats, an overwhelming force of men. I assure you, with grapeshot loaded and only one way in, it is quite the impossible feat...'

'Three odd miles did you say captain?' enquired Spencer. 'How curious?'

Ships of War — Murky Waters

'Aye, three miles is the prevailing international law for a nation's right to the surrounding water. So, we can legally be here, should the French discover us.'

'Three miles, sir?'

'Aye, Mister Holt, because that is the expected range of the largest cannon that might be mounted and even then to reach she would have to be some three hundred feet above the sea. At three miles they cannot hit us and we cannot hit them. And you may all appreciate this next tidbit. It has been said the French have at some time in their history known Ortac as *"the Eagle's Nest"*, a good omen gentlemen, no less. It has also been suggested that Ortac originated from the Norman language, meaning a large rock at the edge. Well, how true, as we are but one cannon shot from the island of Alderney, a French land of course. I expect that shipping will not come so close either considering that between Ortac, Verte Tête and Burhou Island, there are scattered many dangerous rocks as well as ledges among which the streams run with great velocity.'

'Capital sir, this position will allow us to spy in the shadows of the French empire...'

'With much impunity,' Cooper added. 'Work will commence tomorrow. Major McFee and myself will scout the island at the outset. Mister Spencer will arrange for our cannon to be sent over, together with our stores and shelters. Our builders and carpenters will arrange a natural fort from the rockery and utilise the natural cave said to be there, to which I am told is presently sizeable enough for all our stores. A complement of marines of course will be left to man her, together with one naval officer. And one last item, a matter of the utmost secrecy in fact,' he warned, pulling out Fredricks's satchel. He jiggled the flags out onto the table, the officers crowding to get a good look. 'I present the future, gentlemen, our new signal system to which we are the very first to utilise. We can thank Admiral Howe for this concoction, a simply brilliant innovation. As you can see, they are mostly numbers. It is my intent to assign the officer with the most mathematical mind to undertake the design of a private code, one for which we will use to communicate with Ortac, even from well over the horizon!'

The officers parted and each one turned to nod at young Mister Holt, who was immediately all but painfully quite aware of his youth, right there and then.

'Ah but sir,' Holt protested, perhaps mildly attempting to weasel out of the enormous responsibility. 'I am not an officer, perhaps...'

'Ah, soon to be rectified!' Cooper grinned, belaying the lad's well thought out objection. 'Congratulations Mister Holt, you are now acting fourth lieutenant of Agamemnon.' And the officers immediately cheered huzza thrice and drank to the lad's promotion, slapping his back whilst McFee grabbed his hand checking it for claws. He was not yet of age, but he had the aspiring mind of a young Galileo. 'I believe Mister Spencer has a uniform which may be appropriate, it having already been shipped by your father, Lord Holt. And oh, just to be sure, there's a captain's uniform in there too, bless your father. Be a good chap and put the right one on would you.'

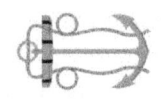

Chapter XII
Ortac Games

It would be hard work at Ortac and Cooper knew it, especially with the crew somewhat disgruntled. An unwilling jack was a useless jack, especially in peacetime. Oh they would still do their duty, at least their version of it. Something had to be done, short of just telling the entire crew that the ship was actually readying to hunt pirates.

'Mister Spencer, it is my most immediate wish that the ship be ready, on the morrow sir, to engage in some gunnery exercises. We will split the decks and arrange our cannon into groups of three, each group with their own gun captain or officer. From this exercise will we decide the proper ratings and the better men will enjoy some time off with some extra rum to fulfil it.'

'With real powder and shots, sir?' he hesitantly questioned, knowing full well how expensive it was.

'Indeed, for it is the only way the balls may fly, lest young

Holt has invented some alternative. I will recompense Commodore Nelson out of my own pocket, should we ever be fortunate enough to in fact one day perhaps capture anything larger than a river barge.'

'Oh, how splendid sir!' he complimented. 'This should set a fire under the jacks. They like nothing better than to let go, especially with their favourite Tom.'

'Furthermore, to the endeavour of our games, we will promote some other activities which will also figure in the ratings. For this, let them contest in divisions, a healthy rivalry if you please. We will have the standard stuff, you know, chasing to the top and whatnot.'

'Aye sir, we can have a rigging race to the top, boat racing around Ortac, boxing and even some pistol and musket competency?'

'Boxing?' he questioned, a squint in his eye. 'Jacks only of course?'

'Aye sir, of course, my boxing days are well and truly over.'

'Very well, for we must get them motivated. They are still whining over Hasard and we cannot allow that on a ship of war about to go to battle.'

'Perhaps, sir, we could just tell them?'

'I have considered, to be sure, but we must return to Chatham once more and I am mindful of the secrecy required. No, no, no, the men must know their work, irrespective. The cannon crews can start practising today, dry runs though, no powder. Let's see if we can get their reload time down to something resembling a crack crew.'

'Aye, three minutes it is sir.'

'Closer to two and a half Spence, would hit the mark.'

'Goodness, three shots in five minutes!' he gasped. 'Aye, sir.'

'Also, I will see that man Eagle, with Major McFee present of course and yourself.'

Ships of War — Murky Waters

Eagle presented himself most handsomely. He was a smaller man than most, but a grim solid fellow. Upon being required to attend the captain's cabin most men usually fell to wild panic, naturally fearing some reprimand. But Eagle stood stern and politely disciplined, bereft of any nervous inclination whatsoever. Cooper was starting to think the man was perhaps made of stone. He peered inquisitively upon him. The man's eyes listed, a virtual sea of solitude, his slits washing blankly within a dull muted expression. It was a look well more suited to a rogue of high stakes gambling, or perhaps a murderer of the serial persuasion, nonetheless all highly commendable traits for either a jack or a jolly.

'Corporal Eagle,' Cooper started quite sternly. 'Am I to understand that it was you who blatantly fired upon and felled one of the French officers standing the quarterdeck of Hasard, killing him stone dead I believe?'

'Aye sir, that I did.'

'And who gave you permission to target an officer? And whilst we are at that, who gave you permission to haul that barrel of yours one hundred and ninety feet up my main mast and make a bloody nest?'

'Sorry, sir,' he pleaded. 'Begging your pardon sir, I have permission from nobody, on both accounts. I alone am to blame and as such will I accept all the consequences, sir.'

'Indeed? Well, so be it Sergeant! Of each and every consequence will you alone bear the burden, mark my words, every bloody one of them!'

'Sir, if I may,' he very politely interceded. 'But I am only rated corporal, that is, lest I am to now be disrated in reprimand.'

'Presuming to correct your captain?' snapped McFee.

'No sir, never in life, sir!'

'If I say you are sergeant, then you are sergeant,' Cooper confirmed with a grin. 'Now, Sergeant Eagle, upon leaving this cabin, you will form a squad of the best men on board, be they jacks or jollies. They will act as Agamemnon's new lookout brigade, under your command. You will approve every man and you will train every man, personally do you hear, in scouting and in marksmanship,' he added vehemently, his eyes detecting a small crack of approval within the squalid blankness Eagle so ever naturally har-

171

boured, just enough to convince him that his orders had been most happily received.

'Aye, sir,' accepted Eagle, lightly nodding with a most mischievous wry grin, more like a rapscallion banker about to foreclose.

'Your new brigade will be the eyes and ears of the ship and as such, will have much responsibility in keeping her safe. They will also be required to go off ship, on certain scouting missions, an advance squad if you will. So your men will need to have their wits about them.'

'Aye, aye, sir,' he evenly replied, still lightly nodding, his grin much expanded now, perhaps of a mind to wage war the moment he left the cabin.

'I heartily commend you Sergeant, upon your craft as a sharp shooter and also in your zeal to protect the ship with your nest, which you have done many times already. You are a credit to your regiment and to Major McFee. I also commend your ingenuity as to even think to create the nest, a feat which I have never seen nor heard of in all my years in the Royal Navy, most extraordinary. In addition to what I have already laid down, you will next report to Lieutenant Holt directly. He will instruct you upon our new signal system. He is a young officer, but he has the mathematical prowess of a bevy of hardened professors. We will be testing the new signal system on the morrow, between Ortac and Agamemnon. And to note, it is a matter of utmost secrecy.'

'Aye, thank ye sir!' he acknowledged, coming to attention before departing. 'I will not let the ship down.'

'One last thing, Major McFee has very graciously thought to distinguish your men's uniforms with the addition of a single feather, of which may be added wherever each man pleases. That is all.'

Ships of War — Murky Waters

Agamemnon cruised about Ortac like a great white circling the murky depths. In the distance a school of barrels bobbed about, a more than moderate day upon the Channel sending them end upon end. The order, prepare to fire, belted forth as the ship bore down upon the targets, the barrels now sitting some three hundred yards directly off the ship's beam. The gun crews were licking their chops. Their ratings, which is to say their wages, were very much on the line and of course more importantly, some recreation time and the promise of unending rum. The more experienced jacks hovered about their cannon, more cautious than an old street peddler slipping the local lord's watch. Carefully they set their barrels, checking and rechecking the elevation required to compensate the day's wind and the distance adjudged. There would be ample enough time for the first shot, but the following shots would have to be managed by approximation and some luck. It was a battle drill with battle conditions and as such, each gun captain had been given very little information, except that they were to utterly destroy the barrels before them.

'Listen up,' Shaw barked, the ship's gunner. 'On the first run, attack only the barrel flying your flag. You have one barrel and you have three cannon afforded per team. You will get two reloads. You must take down your barrel. Upon your second and third shots, provided your barrel is down, you may proceed to attack any other target. Destroying another's barrel will knock that crew out of the game.'

The eyes of each crew were sliding sideways. They glanced at each other more like black coves, readying to slip a dagger steadily in from behind all whilst whispering sweet dreams within the softness of their victim's lobes. They all knew they had to get the first barrel down, or they might be out, which is to say, any chance of rum would be out. The eighteen pounders were going first with both sides of the ship firing at the same time. What a grand show it promised beholding to those spectating upon Ortac. Agamemnon boasted twenty-six long eighteens, there being thirteen larboard and starboard respectively. Cooper realised that with three cannon making up a team, there would be four teams each side, with one cannon per side left over. He casually approached the last cannon, much to the amazement of the gun crew.

'Lads, even though you have drawn the short straw, I cannot allow you to miss out on the chance of rum. If you are willing, today I offer myself as your gun captain?'

'Honoured, sir, but we only have one gun to every other's three?'

'Indeed, then is not everything right in the world? We must most definitely be serving our king in the Royal Navy. For the life of me, I cannot ever remember a battle where my ship had more gun than the other. In fact, the only time we ever really got to truly fight was when we were hopelessly outgunned, the enemy otherwise usually running like frightened hares. One cannon is enough lads. And if we were to only ever be left with one cannon on the entire ship, know I would fire til it was taken from us.'

'Welcome sir!' Holt excitedly greeted, his crew languishing directly behind him, the older hands looking like a crusty pack of homeless rat catchers about to crack a safe. 'Oh sir, what a cracking day for it, is it not?'

'Indeed Mister Holt, but is this not your first time, firing a cannon?'

'Sort of, sir. My father used to let me watch them bang away on our estate. Once, he let me fire the lanyard, cannot wait, sir!'

'I suspect these are a tad different to your father's. They are Blomefield cannon,' he happily announced. 'God bless Thomas Blomefield, a man with a vision.'

'Thomas Blomefield sir?'

'Aye, he was our Inspector of Artillery in eighty you know, virtually reproofed half the cannon we had and when he couldn't get a cannon made to his liking, he bloody well went and made his own. By eighty-seven he had made some significant alterations to the old Armstrong design. See the breech there, more rounded now. And secondly, the first reinforce was made virtually cylindrical, the second reinforce strongly tapered and the chase somewhat strengthened. See the ring there, which he cleverly added to the cascabel. It allows free movement of the breech ropes and now the gun might be trained at an angle to the side of the ship without the recoil breaking her free. One thing which sets them aside though, a real difference in accuracy, is the firing of it with a flintlock. No time waiting on the thing to let go, not like it is with the old touch holes. Those were cannon you could never love unfortunately. Ah, but these beauties, they are the future.'

Cooper glanced thoughtfully at Holt's team. He looked over each of the breech ropes, his eyes following down the ring bolts from their fixture to the ship's framework back along the rope to the cascabel, especially eyeing the knob on the rear of the cannon, ensuring it was all braced properly. He could ill afford to lose the lad, especially in training. An old hand knowingly winked back at him. Cooper immediately recognised the old salt from Boreas and instantly he knew Holt was in capable hands.

The order came, bellowed down the deck, the order to fire as she bears! There were five bobbing barrels and Cooper's was the last. He was happy with this arrangement. His keen eye would seek to rate the flight of the other shots and estimate the behaviour of the swell. As he laid first eye upon his barrel, he quickly sought to approximate the angle and the surging sea against the amount of charge and elevation required. He noted the swell and the time it took for the cannon to sway up to the horizon and back down again. He was calm, his breathing even, his focus that of a wild cat stalking.

'Quickly lads, down one on the wedge,' he ordered. The crew sought to adjust the elevation cognisant that the first cannon at the front of the ship had just let go. 'With haste lads!' he encouraged and the hammer was pulled back to half cock.

Strangely enough, one of Holt's cannon let go early, the ball harmlessly sent well wide of each and every barrel. Cooper smiled. It was a natural mistake of course, young Holt of course succumbing to the roll of the swell, his lanyard stretched too tight. It had happened to most officers and it was hopefully a mistake from which the lad might likely learn. Holt's target loomed and Cooper could hear him firing his remaining cannon one at a time.

'Ready lads,' he steadied. 'Hammer full cock!' Cooper was now counting in his head, the swell finally lofting the point of his cannon up above the target. 'Fire!' and he pulled upon the lanyard. The hammer clicked creating a spark and the priming powder fired, igniting the main charge. The shot propelled out of the barrel and the gun hurled violently in recoil, only to be safely halted by the breech rope. Without the rope, the cannon would likely have kept going some forty-five feet, which incidentally was the entire width of Agamemnon.

'God fetch us sir, you took off the flag!' one of his crew excitedly complimented. They had almost taken the barrel on the first attempt with only one cannon and oh what a capital shot his crew thought. Motivation was now assured and they busied furiously to reload. A good crew would do it in three minutes or less, which would afford three shots in five or six minutes. 'Don't worry sir, we'll have it up in less than three minutes, god willing!'

'Serve your vents!' Cooper bellowed, the lust of battle high in the wince of his blood sodden eyes. The gun was swabbed out, a sheepskin wad soaked in sea water dunking every bit of flame before any new powder might be inserted. 'Swab it neatly man, lest you are on your way to kingdom come! Handsomely now, the ship has almost come about!' They loaded the powder, a small cloth cartridge and a cloth wad followed directly to hold it. Another slammed it home with his wooden rammer. Cooper felt down the touch hole in the breech of the gun, searching for the flannel cartridge with his pricker, a small length of wire. 'Home!' he shouted as he made contact and pierced it. 'Shot your gun!' he added and a round shot was loaded into the barrel, followed by another wad, a necessity serving to prevent the ball from rolling. They rammed it home. 'Run her out you dogs, pull!' he affectionately screamed, lustfully maddened by the excitement. The crew hauled it up to the gun port, aching their arms upon the gun tackles. In short time the front of the gun carriage was hard up against the ship's framework, the barrel protruding out of the port.

'Congratulations sir,' Holt complimented with a hearty nod. 'Right on three minutes, so I believe.'

Cooper sighted the wooden barrels bobbing in the distance, his target an easy find, it being without any flag. It was then he noticed there were only four barrels left. It was wishful thinking of course to think that any crew who hadn't been to war for years could hit a target half the size of a man, first shot mind you at three hundred odd yards. In fact, to see one barrel destroyed was something of a joy to behold, a thought that brought some mild hope to Cooper's heart. He counted each flag before suddenly realising it was Holt who had taken down the barrel. He couldn't believe it. The lad had never fired any cannon before, let alone one at sea with rolling swell and all under the utmost pressure to perform in very little time. It suddenly dawned upon him that Holt was now free, under the rules of the game's engagement, to now take out his opposing crews' barrels.

'Mister Holt, I commend you on your first shot young sir. Be it known that the barrel without a flag is your captain's,' he subtly suggested with a knowing look of mercy, hoping the lad might take some pity on his barrel and leave it be.

'Captain, sir?' protested one of his crew.

'It is quite alright lads,' Cooper whispered. 'This is war remember and those of us dogs who have only one cannon must seek to stay alive by any means possible and I mean to do it.'

His crew sniggered. He would make scoundrels of them yet and so he sought to play with his rope tackles, training his cannon left and then right. But in the midst, he could not but help to notice Holt with something strange in his hand. It was a stick of some description and he had his good eye lined up upon it, much like a painter with his thumb out, staring down the canvas. How odd, but there was no time to dilly dally and he quickly had his crew adjust the elevation once more, noticing that Thornton, the ship's master, had sneakily veered the ship in a tad closer this time. His crew worked furiously with their crow irons. They raised the breech and moved the quoin, the wooden wedge. Over the touch hole Cooper laid his priming horn, already brimming with powder. He grinned as he admired his own personal concoction of the fine powder mixed with a spirit of his own store of wine. 'Hammer at half cock!' he warned and the bobbing barrels loomed in sight. 'Hammer full cock! Ready! Fire!'

The shot hit home and his crew cheered as bits of the barrel splintered into the yonder sky.

'No time for that! Let's reload, we are still in this!'

'Sorry sir, but the barrels are all down. At least we got ours!'

'All down? All down!' he silently rejoiced, for that to be true meant only capital gunnery. He was thinking his crew was not as rusty as he originally expected, that is, until the word came down. No one had hit anything, except for Holt's crew, who had taken down three barrels with his second broadside.

'Well, Mister Holt, I believe you have made up for a shaky start.'

'How's that sir?'

'The first ball, of course, it went off early.'

'Oh no sir, I was just wasting one so I could gauge the performance. I've never fired one at sea you know, but I had an idea though, just needed to test my thinking.'

'You just wasted one?' Cooper intoned, silently stunned. 'I see, well, thank you at least for leaving a poor captain one barrel to spit at.'

'Honestly sir, you shouldn't. I did like the look of your barrel, but seeing how you only had one cannon and the others had three, I reasoned they were the immediate threat, even though you were the experienced gun amongst us. I knew you were trying to trick me sir, a neat test!'

'Indeed! I see, saving me to gloriously finish me off last, ha, ha! So you are a fine tactician as well as a capital shot. Well done sir, well done! But if I may Mister Holt, what the hell was that stick you were holding? It's not bloody religious is it?'

'Oh, you noticed that sir? Aye, it is something I came up with yesterday, to approximate the range of a target at sea. Since I have been out in the Channel, I have had a hard time distinguishing distances. It's quite an art to be sure sir. I really cannot fathom how you accomplish it so competently. So I made this stick for close range. You see sir, you hold the top on the horizon and the lines below signify the distance to target. Upon knowing the relative distance, I then calculate the shot required with the appropriate feet per second, the inclination of the gun, all weighed together with the sideways speed of the ship in feet per second. Of course, it is just an approximation, sir.'

'Just an approximation!' Cooper declared in astonishment. 'Well, sir, you sure did approximate the hell out of those barrels, indeed, there's not a bloody splinter left!'

Ships of War — Murky Waters

The cannon exercise had brought back some much needed life not only to the crew, but to its captain. Hardly any of them had managed to hit a bloody thing, but the reports were mostly solid. Crews may have missed, but it wasn't by much and when laid alongside a target somewhat bigger than a barrel, they would be capital shots. Cooper was more interested in the reload time of course with just on three minutes the best and the worst at nearly five minutes. It was something which he wholly intended to fix.

Holt had proved a good choice for acting lieutenant and nobody could deny it, especially now that he had triumphed in the eighteen pounder cannon exercise. The final had been a real contest as well, with Holt facing down his captain and two of Nelson's old hands from the war. To say every man and jack were astonished to see the young inexperienced lad best them would be a gross understatement. But they all had the camaraderie of a pack of river pirates, patting the lad on the back and insisting he immediately tote some rum. Holt was a good sport and indeed curried some substantial favour when he generously divided his rum out to the crews he had fought against in the finals.

It was a page out of the Roman Empire Cooper thought, the emperor wielding the mob's favour with the gift of the games, a little less bloodletting though of course, but the exhilaration was there. The twenty-four pounders were banging away now and the crew were all but on the edge of their seats as it were. In point of fact, of course, most of them were up on the edge of the rigging or the bulwark, vying for the best vantage point.

'Sir!' yelled one of the hands quite frantically, running up to his captain with a hasty knuckle. 'Mister Spencer requests you come most directly to the lower gun deck. There's been an accident, one of the officers, at Mister Shillings's gun, sir.'

'Tarnation!' he grumpily swore and then almost immediately he thought of Holt who had been assisting poor Shillings with his gunnery. 'No, no, no, not Holt!' he thought and his stomach churned as he quickened his pace. 'Sharply now, locate the Doctor, get him down there and I'll come directly.'

'But it is the Doctor sir! He's been killed. One of the breech ropes let go, bad tackle and he was crushed by the twenty-four, sir!'

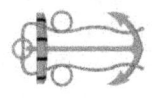

Chapter XIII
Twenty!

Agamemnon slipped quietly into her old berth at Chatham. The incandescent shine upon her hull receded, lurking dull within the shadows of the morning sun. In contrast, the sheets above wildly beheld the fiery depths of a deepening red sky and soon her masts would once again fill Chatham's vista, as if she had never left. It was almost dawn and she had timed her entry to port most handsomely, riding the flood right up until the stand of the slack ventured to settle softly about them.

The first voyage of Agamemnon under command of Captain Hayden Reginald Cooper had been a mixed bag to be sure. He thought about it in great detail as he imagined presenting his pending report to Commodore Nelson. Barely had he ventured out of the Medway when suddenly battle presented itself. Outrageously had he amassed eighteen knots, sneakily navigating sixteen sea miles in complete stealth only to cheekily arrive no more than a cable's length away, still without his enemy aware. He subsequently had twenty-six cannon with a six hundred and seventy-eight pound broadside trained point blank upon the Frenchman. His commission was very clear, to cruise the Channel, to seek out pirates and Letters of Marque and by any means possible, destroy, burn or take them a prize. Yet, in all his endeavour and zeal, he had managed to fire not a single shot upon his enemy and by all accounts, stood idly by whilst His Majesty's

Ship Resignation exploded into thousands of tiny bits, Agamemnon so close that bodies littered her deck and fire bristled her sails. Instead of doing his utmost to destroy an obvious pirate, a ship he well knew would continue to take British lives, he had allowed the prize not only to sail away very much unscathed, but he had not even bothered to give chase. Of course he rushed valiantly to rescue two survivors, one of which ludicrously turned out to be in fact the Dauphin, the Crown Prince of his enemy. Nonetheless, thereafter pushing on, had he proceeded to take possession of Ortac Island, whereupon he could only manage to build half a fort before embarrassingly running short of materials. In good time he exercised the crew and upon doing so had used valuable powder before finding that hardly a jack could manage to hit anything smaller than a barn. Still remaining short a hundred souls of a full complement, he then proceeded to thin his ranks. Firstly, a good gunner's mate lost, horribly mauled and eaten by a shark. Secondly, a landsman albeit not of much use, hopelessly drowned in the necks of the rocks, then mauled and eaten by the same shark. And lastly, the ship's doctor being one of the most essential men on board, utterly crushed by a loose cannon. To add indignation to what was already a debacle, the good doctor's body was ceremonially laid to rest at sea, as is the custom, only moments later to have been eaten by the shark. To balance the account in his defence, he had acquired a new officer from Resignation, one Lieutenant Shillings. However, the crew think him a Jonah and directly must he be put off the ship for fear his mere presence will serve to sink Agamemnon, undoubtedly without warning, the expectation of said event all to transpire in what the crew might consider the very next available moment.

 His commission was likely over. There would probably be a court martial, a tribunal of peacetime captains presiding mind you, all eager with some bungling relative ready to take command of Agamemnon. He would be most lucky if they did not hang him, or even shoot him on the weather deck like poor Admiral Byng. Perhaps in the whims of Admiralty justice they might in fairness simply just adjudge that he should be summarily fed to said shark. He might as well summon Holt and hand the lad his commander's jacket and coat, for the lad would definitely be the only soul

Ships of War — Murky Waters

aboard likely acquitted of all charges.

'Messenger, sir!' called the officer of the watch.

'But we haven't even docked yet?' Spencer protested, snatching the parchment, immediately ferrying it to his captain. 'And the sun is yet to even come upon us!'

'Of course,' Cooper confirmed, now noting the seal. It definitely had a particular flare about it, most flamboyant. 'Oh, it is about our old friend, Mister Rose, from his second Lord Pendleton. His Royal Highness, The Prince William, has most politely forwarded the summons. Oh charming, look here, Rose desires to meet forthwith, upon the ship docking, at the sun rising, along the dock, in front of the ship.'

'The cad sir, he means to diminish you before the entire crew!'

'Aye, he knows his business.'

'By god's blood sir!' he exclaimed. 'The lookout's pipe is a tweeting. Look, it's The Prince William already! I best muster the watch!'

'Belay that, His Royal Highness is also an admiral, albeit retired and he knows better than to come aboard. It's not the piping, but we'd have to fire off god knows how many cannon in salute. No, he won't impose that upon us. I expect he will wait on the dock. Be a good man Spence, go fetch my duelling kit. With all the bloody sharks, drowning and cannon crushing, not to mention a few other mishaps we have suffered, I am thinking I am presently in a right mind for this man, damn his French insolent hide!'

'Of course sir,' he reluctantly huffed, Spencer no stranger to his captain's penchant to attract duels. 'But you're not really going to fight him here?' he urged. 'Not in front of the men, sir?'

'I would have it no other way. It's time to show these layabout landsmen who's bloody shy and who's bloody soft! You make sure that cove Cross gets a front row seat. They will see I mean business. Now, it is also my wish that you fetch Mister Holt and have him escort the Dauphin down to the dock. Make sure the Dauphin is dressed appropriate to his station. Oh and Spence, just to be sure, be so good as to get that bloody Shillings off my ship.'

Cooper marched down the gangplank, together with his first officer. They found Prince William standing most regally upon the dock, fully dressed in his royal attire, a most dazzling sword by his side. Commodore Nelson was naturally in company and for the first time, adorning the splendour of his commodore's uniform. Nelson was a slighter smaller man, but oh how monstrous and powerful he now appeared. McFee was already there, for he knew his business, a small detachment of marines already mustered to secure the dock, hovering about as wasps swarming the nest. It seemed a grand affair indeed. Now all they required was Pendleton and Rose to arrive and rest assured they were going to be received most handsomely.

'Captain, it appears you have made quite an impression upon Lord Pendleton and his man Rose,' Nelson immediately warned. 'The man has been boorishly going about town informing everyone that he is going to most definitely kill you, stone dead, the moment you step off the ship. It is of no doubt now that even the Lords of the Admiralty would perhaps know of it.'

'And you should know Captain, he is no longer welcome at the Lion, nor that Pendleton, so I am told,' Prince William added. 'I even heard the man has been outrageously telling everyone you snubbed him, refused to fight, hiding away on your ship behind your rank, the impertinence!'

'Sir, your most obedient servant,' Cooper welcomed, turning to address Prince William. 'I am right heartily glad to see you. But you cannot risk yourself here, not on my account. Perhaps Lieutenant Spencer can step in for you as second? It, in itself, is a dangerous station. After all, seconds have been known to disagree and as such they then must fight it out too.'

'Oh, I am counting on it Captain, indeed, which is why I have brought my finest blade and pistol set!'

'Sir, I would not wish to burden England, should something ever happen to you.'

'Nonsense, I will be fine Captain. But notwithstanding, I have already drafted a note, should I be cut down, absolving you of course. It sits here in my pocket should you need it. And my particular friend, Horatio here, has most generously agreed to immediately kill Pendleton, dead as a dog mind you, should he get the better of me, ha, ha!'

'But sir, the King, your father?'

'Oh, if my older brother can get away with it all, then so shall I.'

'His Royal Highness Prince Frederick, Duke of York, sir?'

'Aye, with that Colonel Lennox, they had it out. And my brother is the Crown Prince god forbid. I will never take the throne of course, so no one is going to mind about me.'

'Sir? Your brother, he really duelled?'

'Indeed he did, but they had kept it quiet of course. Can't go letting every cad and swine know they can just step out with the next King of England whenever they take the fancy. Goodness, when would we ever have time to breakfast! Lennox was lucky my father didn't have him drawn and quartered, just for insisting. But there, there you have it. I am of a mind to tell every soul of it now though, the excitement being so exhilarating. Oh, how I wish for war and a fast ship!'

'Sir, really, your brother?'

'Oh, back in eighty-nine Captain, this Lennox called out my brother after he had accused him of making, how did he put it, yes, making *"certain expressions unworthy of a gentleman..."*. All was denied of course and after demands for a retraction were refused, he demanded satisfaction. They met with pistols on Wimbledon Common, about this time of year in fact. Lennox then proceeded to shoot off my brother's royal curl! Oh, ha, ha, ha, can you imagine, can you imagine! Oh, to bloody well be there! But my brother, a stubborn soul, god bless him, refused to fire back. He informed Lennox that he had been called out to give satisfaction and it having been given, the matter was closed. Lucky bastard of course, my brother would not have missed and the man would have found himself no longer of service, except to the deep blue sea and the devil below, ha, ha, ha!'

'That kindness is not going to happen here, sir.'

'No, quite. I must say, I am of the absolute belief this Rose will most definitely try to kill you. I have heard he is an expert shot and he has been practising for weeks,' he forebodingly added.

'Indeed?' chuckled Nelson who immediately glanced at Cooper.

'Oh?' Prince William quizzed. 'Something humorous, Horatio?'

'Aye sir, but I will not dare to spoil the surprise.'

'Commodore Nelson, sir,' Cooper pressed. 'Whilst we wait and whilst I am still able, would you be disposed to hear the report of my cruise?'

'Oh, I really think it can wait til after, don't you? Anyhow, how much could really have gone on, such a short cruise.'

'Quite, sir,' he politely remarked. 'Ah, here is Lieutenant Holt, what timing. Thank you Mister Holt, you may return to the ship, muster the men in divisions upon deck, if you please, all of them. And you may leave our new friend here with us.'

'New friend?' Prince William sounded. 'And who might this young gentleman be?'

'Indeed, sir. Allow me to present His Royal Highness, Louis Joseph Xavier François, Dauphin of France, elder son of King Louis XVI of France and Marie Antoinette.'

'What the hell did you just say!' Prince William spluttered. 'Good god, the future King of France!'

'The very same, sir.'

'Captain,' Nelson worriedly intoned, firstly eyeing the Dauphin before his curiosity turned to gaze upon Cooper. 'Maybe just a quick rundown in report is in order 'ey, whilst we have time?'

The scuttlebutt on board moved like wild fire and grapeshot through a splayed rigging. Every man, jack and jolly crowded the deck, some even clambering the rigging, all the way to the top. They had heard some outrageous talk, which is commonplace upon any ship of war, but the main of it was their captain had been challenged to a duel. Even Eagle had come down from the nest to find a prime spot. For Eagle, it seemed no bustling was required either, the crew arranging a most handsome viewing point for their favourite sergeant. He leaned happily against the rail, right next to Holt in fact, almost as if a guest of honour.

Ships of War — Murky Waters

'Seems like a bloody parade!' hooted one of the jacks and the crew buzzed in jocularity, pointing and sniggering.

'That, lads, if I may, is His Royal Highness, The Prince William,' Eagle rightly pointed out, much to the utter shock of everyone nearby. In a hush, the scuttlebutt quickly passed and soon enough the entire crew was gawking like a colony of stunned monkeys hanging in the spindly branches of a splayed tree. 'And which, of course, is why our jollies are out there, shinier than a brass cup on Sunday.'

'The Captain is going to duel The Prince William?'

'No,' Holt answered. 'The Prince William is the Captain's second.' It was beyond belief of course, firstly that their captain was going to duel, strictly against regulations and secondly, that not only did he know the potential future King of England, but was his second. A sullen new respect for their captain washed over the crew, a knowing nod or two exchanged. 'See the young boy, the one we rescued, that's the Dauphin of France.'

'The who of what?'

'The dolphin,' one jack answered annoyingly.

'He don't look like no dolphin?' another questioned unwittingly.

'There ain't no dolphins in France,' added another.

'Well, not in the rivers anyways...'

'The Crown Prince of France, you simpletons!' Eagle added. 'That's right lads, His Royal Highness, Louis Joseph Xavier François.'

'Elder son of King Louis XVI and Marie Antoinette,' added Holt with a mischievous smile.

'That's right lads, the Captain had to rescue His Royal Highness's arse, which is why we didn't chase the prize. If he had left him in the water, you would all be crying cockles swinging the yard right now!'

'What the devil, is that Mister Shillings down there?'

'No, he'll Jonah our captain!'

'For the love of Mary, someone get him out of there!'

'Steady lads,' Eagle reassured. 'A Jonah is only a Jonah on the sea. Captain knows that, which is why quick and nimble he has had him put ashore, mark my words!'

'Look, someone is coming!'
'Aye, now it's a bloody parade!'

Lord Pendleton arrived with Rose, both strutting upon the dock as if they outranked the King of England. Rose's eye was most definitely fixed upon Cooper, the glare of a wild ravenous predator. Pendleton approached Prince William, the reception worthy of a Roman colosseum.

'Your Royal Highness,' Pendleton cordially greeted. 'Sir, may I humbly commence, pleading for Captain Cooper to apologise?'

'He will not, sir!' Prince William returned immediately. 'And allow me to humbly continue, as such and plead for Mister Rose to retract his allegation and apologise?'

'He will not, sir,' he regretfully returned, most sincerely in fact, a sullen remorse filling his visage. He chanced to glance at Cooper. It was then that Pendleton laid eyes upon the Dauphin, casting a longer look than what might be considered usual. It was what Cooper had been waiting upon and the revelation in Pendleton's gaze immediately gave him away. It was a serious gamble of course. Pendleton and Rose, suddenly realising the Dauphin was alive and only some few yards before them, might very well trade their lives right there on the dock, especially if they knew their game as French spies was over. Nonetheless, it was some mild proof that Pendleton at the very least was a Frenchman. 'What a charming young gentleman? Should he be in observation of such proceedings though?'

'My cousin, sir and his royal blood is well acquainted with such barbarity. Now, before we commence, let us choose weapons and then retire, naturally, for the mandatory period?'

Prince William opened the kit and to his surprise and very much to his absolute mirth, there was not a pistol to be had. He cast a knowing glance at Nelson who was grinning like a wildcat perched high upon its rock. The kit offered only a variety of swords, most magnificent, each and every one. Indeed it was a collection fit for a king he thought.

'But sir, these are blades, not pistols?' protested Pendleton.

'Sir, you have a particular sharpness of eye to which I must commend,' he dryly mocked. 'However, in course and pursuant to the prevailing rules of duelling, your man has been afforded the honour of choosing when and where. And I compliment the choice of course. As such, my man is afforded the choice of weapon. It is clear, plain and quite unequivocally simple, the choice is before you. You may choose any, or for that matter, as many, as you see fit.'

'I protest sir, for men of worth fight with pistols!'

'Then, am I to understand your man wishes to forfeit? This is his right of course, but he cannot withdraw without first apologising to my man and begging forgiveness, which naturally I make assurance to be granted.'

Cooper had only one choice, his katana. For an Englishman, it was a most strange and obsolete looking sword, definitely heavier and by definition, likely slower. Never could they have appreciated it was quite capable of hewing a man in two or that it would sever the steel of another blade with oh so little effort. Barely an Englishman alive had ever seen one in action and, most importantly, not a soul had the slightest comprehension that the English captain before them was moreover an accomplished hand. Never would Rose and Pendleton have guessed Cooper practised religiously, day in and day out and for that matter, for the sum of many, many years. Never in their wildest dreams would they have conjured to think him a master of its every virtue. Yet, it was all true. Long had he laboured, unveiling the blade's secrets, all under the watchful eye of none other than the Emperor of Japan's esteemed Head of Royal Guard.

Rose, if it was even possible, appeared even more infuriated than before. Yet, upon Cooper selecting the katana he subsided with a knowing grin. Aggressively he shuffled through the choices afore him, carefully testing each before discarding those deemed unworthy. His final selection was split, ultimately hovering between the choice of a rapier and a smallsword. The rapier was quite a bit longer than the smallsword, perhaps almost four feet to the smallsword's three. His thoughts weighed heavily before eventually settling upon the smallsword. He grabbed it up, swishing it sideways, twisting it, weighing its balance, until lastly he bent back the blade to test its ultimate worth.

'A splendid choice sir,' Cooper commended knowingly. '*Épée de Cour*, a smallsword of French making, much favoured by the aristocracy and the Court of France I believe?'

Rose ignored the comment and promptly returned to his second, as did Cooper now brandishing the katana by his side. It would not be long now, only the nuisance of an obligatory period of waiting lastly required. The time would soon enough pass, quite solemnly in fact as is the practice, this being the last chance to call off the contest before facing each other. Cooper took his mind to a place he well knew, lightened the tips of his fingers, the irrepressible restlessness building within now tempered by the measured steadiness of a disciplined breath.

'Blades, 'ey?' Prince William whispered, much enjoying the ruse. 'Indeed, I commend your ingenuity, for Rose did not see that one coming. A beautiful collection too Captain. Are they for ship actions only or am I to assume you have been out before?'

'I deeply regret to inform you sir, this will be my twentieth occasion.'

'Good grief man! Twenty!'

'Our captain is a popular one, sir,' Nelson added, turning to Cooper with a cunning grin. He was about to wish him the customary good luck and fortune, when the sight of the Dauphin hugging terribly upon Cooper's leg served to bring him abruptly by the lee. The lad appeared quite upset.

'Captain, this man, I know him,' whispered the Dauphin, a tear clouding his eye, straying in order to hide his face.

'Indeed, which one? Please, he cannot harm you now.'

'The second,' he confirmed, quite frightened. 'You must not fight this man Captain,' he pleaded. 'This one I have seen many times at court and in our games has he never lost. For long, he was Champion of France and now he is one who chases my father. Please Captain, you must not.'

'I see,' he softly thanked, immediately thinking it was now

Ships of War — Murky Waters

really Prince William who was no doubt in the greatest peril. 'But I am not to fight him. I will fight the other.'

'Now, thank you, Lord Pendleton,' Prince William announced. 'Please ensure, as second, pursuant to the prevailing rules, that you are armed as well. You or I will be afforded the right to intervene, but only in the case of cheating. No man may start before time and no man may attack once fallen, such an act signified by the contact of one's knee to ground. Gentlemen, I implore you one last time to meet face to face and consider deeply your position with an apology. I urge you to leave your swords sheathed, lest the second be forced, precipitously mind you, to cut you down.'

Rose marched forth, the devil in his eye. Cooper by contrast was quite calm, his mind churning the possibilities of what had already transpired. He had not all the facts before him, but enough to ensure he was of a mind to be wary, now more than ever. This was no simple duel and should Rose prove even half as proficient as Pendleton's reputation, it might very well be his last.

'Apologise? I will not, sir!' Rose confirmed vehemently, not once taking his eye from Cooper's. 'This day Captain is your last. Breathe your last breath sir and not only your entire ship, but all of England will see you as the rat you are!'

'The only rat here is you,' Cooper cleverly goaded in return, now whispering in Parisian. 'Your game is afoot, I know who you are. You and Pendleton are finished here in England. Oh, did he not tell you who the boy is? He is the Dauphin and whilst he knows not you, he indeed knows the famous Champion of France!'

Rose looked upon the Dauphin with distaste, the only path before him now ever so clear and oh how he immediately erupted. Angrily he drew his blade spinning quickly about, the tip whizzing sideways, slashing perilously towards Cooper's neck. It was immediately clear Rose was no amateur, although those watching were somewhat dumbfounded. This was not the expected form, the smallsword reserved predominantly for stabbing. Nonetheless the slash was adept, stealthy and somewhat expert. His style was of course one-handed and as he spun, the tip could only but gather distance and speed. His arm outstretched, the razored edge found itself driving upon the small of Cooper's soft gullet.

Rose had been found out and he knew it. There was little left but to do his best to at least kill Cooper before the jollies could make their arrest. Given time, he would cut down the Dauphin as well. Everyone was aghast of course. He had started before time, an obvious cheat. But no longer was the match in any way a duel. The façade was over. He had nothing to lose. For him the entire saga was now a moot point, for whatever happened, afterwards he would no doubt hang. He was resigned to his fate. Upon dispatching Cooper, he would rush the Dauphin, perhaps even Prince William and long live the new France.

Cooper all along had intended to goad Rose, fuelling the man's anger. In all warfare he had ever known, an angry opponent was often a foolish one. He could see the white flesh rising upon Rose's knuckles, the grip tightening. It was immediately clear he had been successful. Blood filled the man's eyes, the first attack coming ever so wildly. Under normal circumstances Cooper might recoil, draw, parry and wait for an opening which was sure to come. But Rose fell upon him as a raging bull. Never was there time enough. The man was likely already arrogantly celebrating Cooper's expected downfall. The Dauphin would soon follow and perhaps, just maybe, he could attempt to disappear into the Medway amidst a likely barrage of failed musket shot.

Cooper would have been a dead man too, had his insight not served so keenly. He had expected duplicity. After all, the goading had been the catalyst, a fiery attack wholly expected. Yet hardly was he ever caught off guard, perhaps as many onlookers may have thought. Now would he seek to do his very best to disappoint poor Rose. To know of a pending attack was surely an advantage, but alas was he forced to linger, to wait upon its arrival. He could not be first to draw. To draw before the official commencement would not only see the match lost, but so lost would be his honour and position. He might as well be cut down.

Rose's eyes had widened as the smallsword first railed from its sheath. In that moment had it begun. Cooper remained dogged. He had permitted this one generosity planning thereafter to take his chances. The eyes were an easy tell and instinctively Cooper twisted his sheath, his hand having been upon it the entire time. Swiftly and forcibly his thumb levered hard upon the guard, forcing the blade to edge from its home. To his delight the blade obeyed, for often the sharpness of frost can freeze even an exceptional sword and never would it budge. Sharply his hip nudged back, an action he had practised thousands of times and the hilt sharply filled with the palm of his good hand. He lifted the hilt to eye level, the blade swiftly railing out, but perhaps only a handful of inches. There it stayed, stopping short.

To draw completely would be to test one man's speed against the other. Rose was agile, enraged and possessed a lighter sword. He also enjoyed a healthy head start. To challenge would likely see Cooper's immediate end. He was quite certain, by the time the tip of the katana cleared his sheath, the smallsword would be protruding well out his back. Nonetheless, he was otherwise prepared, his strategy already executed over and over within his mind's eye.

With one hand on the sheath and the other on the hilt, Cooper had suddenly lifted them high before his face, still only a small portion of the blade showing. Rose's smallsword hammered onto the bared steel, scarcely inches away from Cooper's neck. It was an impressive attack but moreover was it an impressive parry, immediately proving Cooper too was no amateur, no less, a man of steely eyed grit and courage. Within the confines and guard of his blade he comfortably rallied, heartily assured of his absolute safety. His defensive prowess had always been undeniable, no less the impenetrable stone of a great castle fending off all manner of cannon, ballista and catapult. It would take a prodigious combination to break the walls of his cover, short of some inopportune erring. He was most at ease in close proximity to his opponent and presently it showed.

Rose grimaced as he felt the steel between his blade and his intended target. It was to his mind improbable and somewhat unexpected. Yet not only had the attack been thwarted, most cleverly checking the smallsword's weight, but thereafter had Cooper now mustered to half trap Rose's momentum, if only for just the barest of moments. It was all he needed. His swordplay mimicked a masterful game of chess, the opponent drawn to follow but one limited action. Continuing to draw, the katana railed fully from the sheath. The sheath may have been simple and bland, but the blade proved magnificent, the ancient depth of its folds mesmerising. Cooper hovered it high above his head, the trapped point of the smallsword now accompanying its journey. It was a play to which Cooper had used oh so many times, forcibly propelling his opponent's sword skyward.

To his utter shock, Rose immediately realised he soon would no longer have control, or for that matter, a sword to protect him. His hold ever loosened, levered from his grip and the farther it lifted into the air the more he came to realise his peril. He quickly struggled to retract it, desperate to regain his balance. The fight had barely begun and now it seemed his very existence hinged upon this one act. Yet respite would not be so quickly forthcoming, not against such a seasoned swordsman. He had erred and he knew it, wholly underestimating the bout. It was inconceivable, the man before him proficiently masterful and inwardly he shook as he accounted his chances. To his credit he continued to struggle, desperate to stave off the inevitable.

Cooper had control of both blades and by his charity, charge of the fight. Before Rose could chance to even think, the counter came. Cooper spun quickly almost on the spot, the katana railing down upon the outstretched wrist, the entire exchange executed within the blink of an eye. His first strike, a well-timed downward swing, sang perfectly in splendid execution. Rose shrieked as the extreme tip of the katana scythed upon his sword arm.

'Good god! His arm is off!' came a cry from Agamemnon. For the most part had the jacks and jollies been absolutely quiet, the bout barely begun and now with hardly a breath spared, it was over. They stood stunned of course trying to fathom what had actually transpired. Some had missed it too, begging the next man to explain. 'The devil take our souls, did you bloody well see that!' a lone cry further exclaimed.

'Aye lads, take note! That be your captain there!' Eagle proudly remarked, looking happily at Holt who from the very first moment had been cringing like a schoolboy trying to save his drowning puppy. Eagle comforted Holt with a knowing nod and a mischievous grin, patting the lad reassuringly on the back. Naturally the Sergeant was also much relieved, having come to very much admire and respect his new commander. Agamemnon finally erupted. Their captain had bested his opponent in the first exchange and, much to the crew's utter delight, all in a most brutal fashion very much befitting their every desire. They tormented Rose as he clung to his lopped wrist, Pendleton now tying it with a belt.

'Sir!' Prince William rightly accused. 'Your man has sought to cheat. He has started before time, the cad!'

'It is quite alright Your Royal Highness,' Cooper insisted. 'He has paid for it, most dearly. But nonetheless, I will hear what he has to say for himself? Is our fight at an end? I await sir, at the ready, should you be any good with your left?'

'Damn you!' Rose screamed fumbling the smallsword with his left hand. Forebodingly he motioned it towards Cooper, Pendleton all but trying to rip it from his grip and dissuade the lunacy. 'Chevalier, we are undone,' he whispered in French, his eye never once straying from his opponent. 'He knows. The Dauphin knows you. He has told the English captain,' he grieved, the words falling as a great axe descending the condemned. Pendleton immediately sank in disbelief, his grip no longer upon his man. His concerns elsewhere, he retired, stumbling, gazing mindlessly about, but there was nowhere to go, a wall of jollies in every direction. Cooper stood defiantly before Rose, the tip of his katana barely off the planking, almost as if he was resting. It was a well laid ruse of course, the sword feigned in respite, an irresistible enticement. Rose was quite ready to heartily believe his good fortune, Cooper's entire body now seemingly open to an easy attack. 'I will finish this!' he cried, maddened beyond all reasonableness.

Rose gained his feet and lunged, a wild move with more gusto than perhaps good thought. Yet now the cat would play with the mouse, the expected lunge easily parried. Swiftly Rose retreated, moving in and out now to test his opponent's response. Cooper floated left and right, both hands gripped upon his hilt, the katana still laid low, now catching a sparkle of morning light. It was a most magnificent piece of steel, one which Rose, to his misfortune, had never quite appreciated. It seemed the fight would continue and as Cooper was about to discover, the man was just as worthy with his left as he was with his right. Rose attacked directly, his feet shuffling smoothly and swiftly, the traditional manner. The point of his smallsword found the line to Cooper's heart, the apparent end. The katana lifted, yet barely in time, the strength of its back deflecting the French steel, Rose again swift in his effort to most craftily retire. Cooper felt upon his arm. His clothing lay torn and a wisp of blood dribbled, a very near miss.

Empowered, Rose stalked again, in and out, preparing to charge and make the final lunge. Even so injured, the attack was swift and furious, much determined, a wild hound with its back to the cliff. Cooper again held low his blade, its back facing Rose. Suddenly it came, a most deliberate attack, the man wildly all in as it were, lunging forth in a vicious stabbing motion. For what it was worth, it was only then that Rose came to learn an English lesson in the art of fighting. With the task seemingly at hand, the man suddenly found his sight offended. The breadth of Cooper's blade had caught the morning sun, a subtle twist of his steel reflecting the brilliance into Rose's wild gaze. Wincing horribly, his eyes fell very much blinded if but for just the barest of moments and his lunge fell unbalanced. Again, it was more than Cooper needed. He deflected the heavy thrust skyward, the smallsword cannoning helplessly above their heads. Down came the katana, steel upon steel. The swing was smooth, elegant, a wisp of a whistle announcing the approach of the edge. The smallsword fell asunder, its pieces clanging as the metal splintered in tatters upon the planking.

Unlike the backward and forward motion of fencing a smallsword, Cooper throughout had rhythmically stalked his opponent, floating side to side not unlike a serpent transgressing hot sand. Not only had he arced endlessly about Rose, but indeed so had the tip of his katana. Seemingly it had a soul of its own, a breath of life undeniable, perhaps even a mind of its own. It had fallen upon the smallsword, a hot razor upon butter and thereafter did it continue, never ceasing, always motioning, hovering, circling. And so did it continue to circle, venturing upon its prey until finally the sharpened edge found its way back upon the open neck of Rose. It was a soundless harmonious strike and at first nary was there even a drop of blood. If the man had not stiffened, not a soul watching would have wagered he had even been struck at all. Then it came. Rose's body dropped lifelessly, his head suddenly rolling off, an astonished jolly unceremoniously halting it with his boot.

Ships of War — Murky Waters

Cooper continued to circle his sword, almost mesmerising, a harmonious flick of the wrist following. Whatever blood lingered, tarnishing the blade, now found its remnants splattered upon the plank. Slowly he sheathed the katana, all the time maintaining his good eye upon Pendleton, some wonderment now gracing his thoughts.

Pendleton was undone, uncovered. He was a wild animal, his tail swishing, stiffened and hunched with the hair upon his back raised, a cornered beast. What would the man hope to do now Cooper silently pondered? Pendleton peered upon the decapitated body of Rose and eventually back to Cooper, a muted unmoving expression. Their eyes met. Cooper knew at once, a gaze he had seen many times before, Pendleton was planning to kill him.

'You were right to kill him Captain, for he was surely bent on killing you,' he surprisingly offered, taking a few steps towards him. 'But you have won, fairly, your honour intact, sir.'

'Stand your ground sir!' ordered Prince William.

'But, sir, is it not over? I am but only the second here?'

Cooper's sword rang from its sheath, his determination to cover the ground before him, a handful of yards in fact, no less than the greatest feat of exertion ever performed in his entire life. The inescapable flash in Pendleton's eyes had announced the intent, all but allowing Cooper a half chance. Pendleton was indeed worthy of his reputation and his title as the *Champion de France*. His rapier railed out lunging wildly at Prince William and not a soul nearby was hardly aware. His thrust was but inches from Prince William's heart when Cooper's katana fell upon his forearm. Pendleton cowered upon the planking, gripping his stump, the tip of Cooper's katana now forebodingly resting upon his gullet.

'Good god!' Prince William cried, only just realising what had happened. 'The man is as winged as a devil serpent!'

'Indeed sir, fast and twice as deceitful!'

'Perhaps even faster,' Prince William lamented. 'I hardly was afforded the chance to even grip my cutlass, let alone pull the thing out and good god, I would have been killed and not even known it!'

'I sincerely do hope sir, that I have not offended you, by interceding on your behalf and striking him down in your stead.'

'Captain,' he sincerely responded, now gazing at Cooper in some genuine amazement. 'I heartily thank you sir!'

'In any case sir, I must insist that it was never a fair fight. This man has all along hidden his true identity. Honour dictates, even in France, that one of such esteem should announce themselves. Sir, allow me to introduce Chevalier Yves Maurice Rocques du Motier de Lafayette, a famous *Champion de France*. As I said sir, hardly a fair fight, for the Chevalier here is a seasoned professional and has never once been bettered.'

'Well, he is pretty much bettered now!'

'I believe you will find that he is a spy, sir, as was Rose.'

'But hardly are we able to find anything left of Rose, if truth be told!'

'Ah, well done Captain,' the Chevalier congratulated, still clasping his stump. 'It is good you finally know who I am. I had forever wanted to tell you of course and now that I have seen you fight, more than ever. Is it not a strange life within which we find ourselves? For us, our births merely divided by little less than a stretch of water. And for England and France, our nations divided merely by the doctrine of religion. Yet beneath it all, we are much the same, you and I. You fight for your country, as do I, sir. Of course, you will continue to fight, whereas mine is plainly over.'

'But sir, I do not understand for we are not at war?'

'Oh, but war is coming Captain,' he politely warned. 'The mob of France will ensure it happens.'

'But you and I are not the mob, an honourless throng? And yet you do their dirty bidding, at the cost of your honour and now your soul?'

'Of course, you are right. Nonetheless, I do most sincerely hope for your well-being. You are a man of honour, a good man and a man of some magnificent talent. Had you been French, we could have been brothers. I laud your magnificent sword and all of your magnificent skills, for never have I witnessed such prowess. If only we had fought in France, at the games, oh how grand! But Captain, the new France will not fight as the old, something I am somewhat ashamed to admit. I never cared so much for that buffoon Rose, for he is the new France, whereas I assure you I am the old. Please apologise to The Prince William for me, he deserved better than what was given. It would have grieved me to have succeeded in killing him. Farewell Captain, sincerely. You have won and I have lost, my life now forfeit. But I am glad it is you, sir. I am ready.'

The Chevalier shut fast his eyes, perhaps to make the task much easier. Cooper knew the man would be hung or shot, if he didn't at first succumb to his wound. The honourable thing was to finish him. But for a captain in the Royal Navy, with his entire ship watching, together with his commanding officer and the King's son, legally he could not. The required action was to withdraw.

'I have thought very hard about it sir, but I believe the Chevalier may be of some use to us, under lock and key of course.'

'If he bloody well survives, but I take a dim view of someone trying to kill me as such, especially without honour.'

'This may sound strange sir, but I would not hold it against him. I believe his goal was the Dauphin here, behind you. It was nothing personal and the Chevalier indeed regrets it very much.'

'Oh does he? Well, bloody good to hear, isn't it! It is fortunate I am alive so as to forgive the bugger. Well then Captain, this all makes sense now, doesn't it?' Prince William nodded knowingly. 'Is this why you cheated at cards then, 'ey?'

'Ah, sir,' he sheepishly replied. 'You noticed that? What a capital eye you have. I sincerely regret that you are most correct. I did in fact cheat, to bring our culprits to the surface.'

'Ha! For king and country then, 'ey, Cooper.'

'Sir?' McFee interrupted. 'There's a curious little lad, a foreigner sir, says he needs to speak with you?'

'A foreigner you say?'

'Aye sir, one of those beggars from the East Indies I think.'

'East Indies you say?'

'Aye, says his name is Hero?'

'Ah, his name is Hiro and he is Japanese, Major.'

'A japanned? What, a bloody priest sir? He don't look like no priest!'

'No, no, no, Japanese, not japanned, Major. He is from an island in the Orient.'

'Oh, then you know him sir? I was of a mind to shoo him away, but sir, I thought twice about it, seeing how he's got a great bloody sword just like yours.'

'Indeed Major, that was most wise. Best you do not offend him. Please to bring him directly.'

Hiro was without doubt the smallest man gracing the dock, not much more in stature than even the Dauphin. He approached Cooper halting a good three yards short, bowed slowly and deeply, his eyes lowered. Upon his eyes meeting Cooper's he grinned and spoke in the language of his land.

'I see you have gotten a little slow, Captain.'

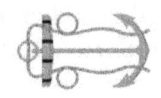

Chapter XIV
Joys of Port

Cooper and Hiro faced each other, their faces grim, stalking left and right, each sword pointed at the other, the tips barely crossing. Hiro had the darkened eye of muted shark, blank and soulless. He was one who would never hesitate, an experienced warrior without remorse. He lunged, suddenly, the strike aptly deflected. Cooper countered, an arcing swing hazarding the lower body. Hiro grinned, the tip checked with only inches to spare, its momentum now trapped. With a sly drop, spinning, he found the neck unguarded. The tip lay foul upon its destination, barely an inch from taking Cooper's life.

'Oh not again!' lamented Cooper angrily, returning his steel to his sheath whilst offering a respectful bow.

Hiro owed Cooper his very life, not only within his heart, but very much according to the legal custom of his lands. It was a debt that would never be repaid. In gratitude, ever since had he sought to make Cooper a competent swordsman and likely was there none better, in Europe at least. The katana was a proven weapon, on land and at sea. Many a battle had Hiro waged, for his Emperor, for his clan. But that was in another life, for now his Emperor lay dead, his clan disbanded, disgraced. He was now called *Rōnin* in the tongue of his emperor, a wanderer, a drifter, a masterless warrior.

Cooper never really fully understood Hiro's customs. Hiro had lived his life in service according to what he called *Bushido Shoshinshu*, the warrior code of his emperor. In fact, if Cooper had not rescued him from a watery grave, he would have no doubt committed *seppuku*, taking his own life in ritual suicide, rather than face the shame accompanied with failure. Instead, Cooper's act had served to compel Hiro to live, whether he wished it or not.

They were exchanging opinions on each other's stances, disputing the advantages and the disadvantages when a knock on the door took their attention. It was the first officer and as usual, he harboured a look indicative of a slumbering sloth knocked from his branch, most definitely irritated and quite somewhat disturbed about something.

'Ah, Spence? Might you ever venture my cabin without something of an annoyance powering you?'

'Apologies sir,' he returned, now noticing the swordplay. 'And further apologies, I did not realise you and Hiro were practising.'

'Aye, it is good to have my old teacher back. Already have I felt the surge of something new within. A session twice a day should see my timing and speed mostly return.'

'Mostly return, sir?' he wondered, his brow raised.

'Aye, I used to be somewhat fast, even by Hiro's obscene standards.'

'Sir, if I may, there were men with their eyes wide open who failed to see what happened on the dock, such was your proclivity for haste. As a professional ring fighter myself, albeit retired, may I offer it looks absolutely trump already. Sir, should we ask Mister Rose what he thinks, or perhaps Lord Pendleton?' he cheekily added.

'Quite,' he begrudgingly agreed. 'But you must try to appreciate that there's always the smallest of margins, especially when faced against the best. One can never be fast enough.'

'Good gracious though sir, there's hardly room enough in here to swing a cat!'

'Men must fight most anywhere of course and often we cannot choose our ground,' Cooper happily clarified, only to see Hiro mimicking the sound of an alley cat and motioning to swing it around. Cooper most profusely shook his head.

'No, no, no, Hiro!'

'What is he saying, sir?'

'He is in absolute disagreement with you it seems. He maintains that a cat could be swung in here, most easily. I have just explained to him that you were referring to a cat o' nine tails, being a whip with claws, not the feline variety.'

'I see sir,' he grinned. 'So am I to understand Hiro can understand English? But, I have never heard him speak it?'

'Aye, he can do both, but prefers to express himself in his own tongue, part of their culture and tradition of course. Best you keep that to yourself now. It may well be of use to us in time. Now do tell Spence, what has got you going?'

'Begging your pardon sir, but I have come to report upon our predicament to fill our quota of men, to bring us to full complement. As you know, we are a hundred shy.'

'I see, but it is peacetime of course. Perhaps we will have to just make do? For what you have already procured, I am most amazed and heartily grateful, of course. Fine men Spence, many fine men.'

'Oh no Captain, it's not that we don't have enough. The fact is, we have too many. Ever since you lopped off Rose's head, most handsomely if I may say, not to mention the dismemberment of both his and Pendleton's right arms, the bloody dock has been ripe with all sorts of men, all wanting to sail with us.'

'Indeed?'

'Aye, sir, it seems the word has got out right smart. I even heard one tale at the Crispin Inn which had you cutting both the cads in exact even halves, all with just the one swish!' he added, now amusingly mimicking the act with a poor rendition of his own imaginary katana.

'Too many, you say?'

'Oh indeed sir, they all want to sail with Captain Lefty.'

'Captain what?'

'Which is what the men have affectionately been calling you

sir. You know, seeing how your method is to chop off the right arm, sympathetically leaving them only with their left.'

'Preposterous! Really?'

'Aye, sir.'

'And the talk of shyness?'

'Oh, gone sir, without doubt. That muster, the landsmen, haven't had a fair day of it since the duel, experienced jacks been giving them a right fistful. That man Cross took quite the beating, if I may say.'

'You most definitely may say Spence.'

'The whole crew heard we had rescued the Dauphin and when the King's son arrived and acted second to your contest, there was very little left in the ship but unabashed pride. Of course, it was a most capital strategy on your part choosing to not die in the process and now, we are mostly on our way to a happy ship.'

'I see, mostly?'

'Ah, aye sir, the matter of a nice fat prize should do it.'

'Naturally.'

'Sir, of the applicants and I can tell you there's boatloads. I have to say there are some really good sailors out there, ones I'd really like to take, but we have already taken others.'

'Of course and we cannot go and throw our fish back, would not be right, not now since they have made their mark,' he passed thoughtfully. 'How many extra jollies did we get?'

'Well sir, including Mister McFee, we started with fifty-nine marines, which of course is the correct complement for a fourth rate, not a third like Agamemnon. So, it was my intent to beef that up sir, to the requisite ninety. So we should expect to receive nigh on thirty more. As it turns out, Mister McFee insists they will be here today.'

'Splendid, then it is settled. We will take no more than another five hundred men and officers.'

'Five hundred sir! Did I hear you right, for we cannot even fit that many on board let alone house them and find them employment.'

'Ah but, tell me now, are there even some five hundred to be had out there, good ones?'

Ships of War — Murky Waters

'Aye, but sir, how's this going to work?'

'Ortac, for starters,' he contended with a wily manipulating smirk. 'With some thirty more marines expected, Agamemnon only needs another sixty sailors. And for the main we are well heeled for good jacks, but we do have some dirty specimens aboard too, a few landsmen of which we might like to see their backs. Now, whilst we cannot legally put them ashore, or send them packing, we can however transfer them. It is my wish that we find good use for them, perhaps on Ortac, as part of the fort's complement?'

'Oh, brilliant, sir!'

'We must properly fill our fort with strong willing men who can shoot cannon and fire a musket. After all, we are barely three miles from the shores of France, the front line so to speak. So, should there be a nice flurry of handy souls out there, rest assured we can use them.'

'Aye sir, but five hundred?'

'I know what you're thinking, Ortac won't take more than a hundred. Don't worry, I have designs in store for the surplus. You will soon see. As long as they can fight a ship, we will have a nice spot for them.'

'Aye, aye, sir.'

'Sir?' a voice interrupted. It was Lieutenant Holt, looking energetic and chipper. 'Captain, I have been asked to tell you that an officer has just repaired aboard, wanting to see you, a lieutenant sir.'

'Very well, please, if you will,' he responded, motioning to bring him up onto the quarterdeck.

'Also sir, there is a messenger just now arrived. I believe I know the one. If I am right, it's from the King, seen him visit my father on occasion.'

'What, the King? Then it's either something quite astoundingly worthy, or it is the complete death of us all, barring perhaps one young lord. Best we deal with him directly, same Mister Holt, on the quarterdeck, if you please.'

'Aye, aye, sovereign's parade it is, sir. And sir, Mister Shillings is requesting to see you as well.'

'What, not on the bloody ship?'

'Aye, sir?'

'Inform Mister Shillings I am doing my rounds upon the dock later and he may prevail upon me then. By god's blood, don't let that man back upon the ship, the jacks will bloody well mutiny and we just got them back to being right and proper seamen.'

'Aye, aye, sir. And sir, not to hold you up, but there is also a messenger from the Admiralty and another messenger from Commodore Nelson, both waiting.'

'The Admiralty, by the horns!' he vexed, looking somewhat glum. He paused, allowing a solemn sigh to slip. 'I see. Unfortunately, this cannot be good news. Well, let us hope Mister Holt that your new captain will afford to retain your acting rank.'

'Oh please sir, they wouldn't, would they?'

'The Royal Navy is a harsh place my young friend, she is one for tough love, to be sure. But in point of fact, I let an enemy vessel escape, unscathed. By rights, they can verily order a court martial, the decision and my fate left with my fellow officers. Very well, I will see the messengers first, King's, Lordship's and then the Commodore's. Thereafter will I see the Lieutenant, unless of course either I am to be court martialled or the King himself turns up! Upon the sovereign's parade, as you so eloquently put it, Mister Holt.'

The quarterdeck of a man o' war, purposefully raised behind the main mast of the ship, was not only where the colours were kept, but it moreover lent a common place for ceremonies and receptions on board. Yet, specifically, it beheld the absolute sanctity and privy of the officer corps, especially the captain. And presently the captain of Agamemnon was very much enjoying a private space to think, one which afforded a handsome unrestricted view to properly attend the ship. Holt led the King's messenger up the ladder, an eminent looking gentleman in tow. It was with some delight and surprise, but Cooper immediately recognised the man.

'Sir, may I present Doctor Gilbert Blane.'

'Yes, yes, of course,' he happily welcomed, taking the man's hand. 'The Doctor's reputation is well known to me, Physician to the Fleet til eighty-three, accompanied Rodney in eighty, to pursue the Spanish squadron besieging Gibraltar, resulting in the Battle of Cape Saint Vincent. Honoured, sir and how may I be of service?'

'Well Captain,' he evenly responded, subtly looking Cooper over. 'More to the point, actually, how may I be of service to you? The King was speaking of you just this week and it seems he was of the faithful opinion that you were in need of a ship's doctor, yours succumbing to sharks I believe?'

'Ah, well, not to contradict His Majesty, but the poor Doctor was unlucky enough to be standing behind one of our twenty-fours when the tackle let go.'

'What? And he was thrown into the sea thereafter and succumbed to sharks?'

'Oh no sir, lower deck, crushed. Horrible to be sure, not much of the man left regrettably. But we have had our share of sharks to be sure.'

'I see. So there, there it is Captain. If you will have me, I very much esteem to be Agamemnon's Doctor?'

'You, sir?' he questioned, most surprised and even somewhat taken aback. 'Goodness, I thought you were here about providing one. Your reputation precedes you sir, no common ship's surgeon, but an honoured physician. It would verily be our honour and privilege to invite you aboard, indeed. I know you have very much improved the well-being and good health of all British sailors with your ideas upon diet and proper sanitary precautions, of which I have endeavoured to personally follow. I would count myself most fortunate sir, to have someone of your esteem. I welcome you and any choice of assistants and loblolly boys to which you deem necessary.'

'Honoured Captain and thank you,' he politely acknowledged.

'The King, you say?'

'Well, the King had heard about the ruckus down here you know, those two cads calling you out, what impertinence! He was most happy, most happy, to receive the news that you had cut them both in half with one mighty swish!' he gloriously added, now gazing upon Cooper's katana. 'Good gracious, is that the weapon sir?'

'Indeed,' he grinned now taking sword and sheath and politely offering it to the Doctor. Blane took hold gingerly. 'Be careful now sir, grip the sheath, but place your thumb upon the guard, so as to ensure it doesn't slip from its place. Many a man has been known to dismember himself upon inadvertently holding one without proper knowledge. The blade is true as none other, I assure you.'

'Indeed?' he cautiously replied, ensuring to follow Cooper's instructions to the letter. 'What a magnificent weapon sir! It is much lighter than I had ever imagined.'

'It is the balance that you discern sir, rather than the actual weight. This blade is well over a hundred years old. More recently it was last presented from Emperor Go-Momozono himself to his most loyal head of guard. Upon rescuing the same guard from certain drowning in the Indies, he presented me with this sword and later instructed me on its most proper use.'

'Intriguing sir, most intriguing!' he complimented. 'Well, His Majesty was of the opinion that your act on the dock will now likely chance to stamp out the rampage of ruffian fools from being so commonly bold. So many duels going on these days, even said his son had been called out back in eighty-nine. Good grief, who would call out the future King of England, madness! He is most mightily happy sir, indeed. Oh, I have a letter from His Majesty, for you.'

"Captain Cooper, Agamemnon. It has come to my most serene attention that you did wilfully and did most industriously prevent the most unfortunate murder of my son, His Royal Highness, The Duke of Clarence and St Andrews, Rear Admiral, The Prince William from what I apprehend to be the ignominious act of two lowly French spies. I am, as is all of England, most grateful. It was my immediate mind to create you a baronetcy, in recognition of your obvious bravery, unmitigated courage and service to your King. I, however, cannot in any good stead presently arrange this, as such, to my utter annoyance, for it would unfortunately come to pass in common knowledge what has in fact transpired and I am most rightly told that in this matter, secrecy is of our utmost prosecu-

Ships of War — Murky Waters

tion. Nonetheless, I will look upon your endeavours and act favourably to your behalf should any future deed or act so warrant my attention. For now, may I offer you a very fine replacement for the loss of your ship's doctor, whom I am to understand was recently eaten by shark. King George III..."

The Admiralty messenger handed over the letter with some distinct pleasure, casually eyeing the katana at the captain's side. Cooper was wondering if there was not a man in England who had not heard about his duel, or perhaps the messenger knew exactly what was in the note, that Cooper be immediately directed to his quarterdeck and allow himself forthwith to be shot for failing to do his utmost. He opened the note, from Admiral Hood, his squadron commander in the eighties and a twenty pound note slipped out.

"*...Captain Cooper, Agamemnon. Sir, it is with absolute pleasure that I rightly enclose these two twenty pounders, some mild acknowledgement, in part if you please, for the admiration to which I esteem upon your recent twentieth duel. Upon the chances of this occurrence, I, together in concert with Admiral Lord Howe, have in course wagered and subsequently bested Right Honourable Lord Pitt, First Lord of the Admiralty and his respected brother, Prime Minister Pitt, much to both their chagrin and absolute devastation. In course with the taking of all prizes, the captain is afforded a one-quarter share, to which we have enclosed two notes, one for each lopped arm. In course, to update our thoughts, Their Lordships have read your recent reports with much eagerness and rightly agree that we continue to maintain the utmost faith, lest you to the otherwise suffer the usual peril. Admiral Hood...*"

'Good grief!' Cooper vexed. 'Very well, who is next then?'

'Sir, may I present the messenger from Commodore Nelson. He carries with him a written note of some description.'

"...Captain Lefty, Agamemnon. Sir, it is with the utmost esteem I invite you and your senior officers to dine. Tonight, if you please, regular hour as Rufus will attest. Commodore Horatio Nelson..."

'Ah, Mister Holt, please inform our senior officers that we are to dine tonight, with our commanding officer, seven this evening at the Crispin Inn. Please to arrange some coaches, in course. Next?'

'Aye, aye, sir and next it's the lieutenant to see you.'

A tall wiry man stood before him, quite immaculately clothed no less in his best dress uniform. Cooper remained on the rail, eyeing the man up and down, waiting upon his approach.

'Lieutenant Lord Melvin James Middleton, sir,' he evenly started, removing his hat before offering some parchment and some other papers. 'My commission, my orders and these are my flimsies, sir, reporting for duty.'

'Ah, I see,' Cooper welcomed, somewhat surprised as he perused the orders. They were direct from the Admiralty. It was then it suddenly hit him, the man's examination date for passing lieutenant. Middleton had seniority. Cooper would be compelled to make this man, a man he had never met nor fought with, his first officer. This was also a man whose input to date, to ready the ship for sea, was absolutely nil. It turned his skin, for Nelson had promised autonomy with his officers and the ship was finally in a state of near happiness. It also made very little sense, but such is life in the Royal Navy and there was very little he could do. 'Very well, Mister Middleton, be so good as to settle your dunnage below, first officer's quarters and I'll expect you to attend my cabin on the next bell. Dismissed.'

It had happened before and it would happen again. It was the nature of the beast, officers proffered and pushed upon captains

Ships of War — Murky Waters

who almost in every case did not require them. A ship of war was much likened to a tight knit family and she would rejoice or suffer in the sins of her father and the ineptitude of her sons. Spencer had been a most exemplary first officer to date, almost irreplaceable, or so Cooper was thinking and further, the man should really have a command of his own. Of course the only practical way to secure a command was to be the first officer in a successful ship to ship action. To promote the first officer was very much the custom, a common almost expected practice, although not always assured. Cooper loathed the situation and he very much loathed the practice of some lord or admiral applying their interest to insert their favourite onto his ship, especially without the least discussion or enquiry with her captain. It was vexing and now this turn of events would only serve to crush his first officer, the man also being his particular friend. A solid knock upon the door sought to shatter Cooper's train of thought.

'Sir?' Fredricks interrupted, softly imposing his head around the edge of the door. 'Very sorry sir, but there is a very well-dressed and most distinguished gentlemen here to see you, an officer sir, a captain.'

'Fredricks! Damnation, man, he is a bloody lieutenant! Now I'll be expecting you to smarten up. Cannot have officers and dignitaries presented and announced in such ignorant fashion. Now send in Mister Middleton!'

Cooper remained behind his desk, eyeing the man up and down and if one could physically perceive anger as some abhorrent steam venting from one's ears, you would see it now. The man's dress was nobler than the King of England. He possessed an annoying air of superiority to match, his stance, his expression, his lack of deference. Cooper was about to begin when Middleton surprisingly started for him.

'Captain, sir, before we may progress, know that I would never dare correct you in front of the men, but I must inform you that I am Lieutenant Lord Middleton and as such it is perhaps appropriate to refer to my presence as My Lord.'

'No.'

'No?'

'Aye, the answer is no.'

'Sorry sir, but I am not sure I understand?'

'Quite, then let me make it clear. Not a bloody soul on this ship will afford to call you My Lord. They will call you Lieutenant or sir.'

'Well, I must protest.'

'No! No, you must not, sir!'

'But, it is my right.'

'You are an officer aboard the King's ship first and a lord second. Your captain decides your rights, pursuant to his rights, which you already know are many and far-reaching. When it comes to one's titles, have you not noticed that rank always precedes birthright? Even His Royal Highness, The Prince William, had insisted his men address him as Admiral whilst in uniform and on duty. No, no, no, sir, all that is required of you is for you to follow orders and do your duty. Now, it makes we wonder how you have arrived to be assigned to Agamemnon, perhaps you might enlighten me?'

'In the usual manner sir, of course, I really do not know to what you are alluding? I was ordered to repair aboard and take my post, as first.'

'As first?'

'Aye, sir.'

'Curious, and how did you know you would have seniority in fact to be first, 'ey?'

'Whatever do you mean, sir?'

'Ah, would you not be some relation of Rear Admiral Sir Charles Middleton, Comptroller of the Navy, a post he held since seventy-eight, the elected Tory Member of Parliament for Rochester, indeed this very Province if I am not mistaken, a seat he had held since eighty-four, no?'

'Sir Charles is my uncle, sir.'

'Of course he is. But it is my understanding he had since retired last year in March, not only from the Admiralty, but also from active service and all naval affairs? Well, it seems the Admiral is still very much in favour, if he was to arrange your posting here.'

'Sir, my uncle may have put in a good word for me, nothing

untoward in that, but if you will do me the honour of reading my flimsies, perhaps it will become apparent that I have arrived here due to other reasons.'

'Very well, I shall and perhaps the benefit of doubt will flow in your favour, but in case you bloody well haven't noticed, I am far from bloody well happy about this Lieutenant! Of course your presence here means you will be rated first officer. But we already have a first officer. We have been commissioned for some many months now, had to build the ship from the dockyard ourselves, scrape together what men we could find, been to sea and we have even been in battle.'

'Aye, sir, one I believe, which left you wanting.'

'You will choose your words sir, before the next leaves your mouth, most carefully!'

'Apologies, sir.'

'Should you know anything about our recent skirmish and I sincerely hope you do not, it being noted to the Admiralty as secret, you must very much keep the knowledge to yourself, lest you wish to swing from the yard for bloody treason. And do not for one moment think I will not do it!'

'Sir, I do not know all the particulars, just heard some portions. All in all, Agamemnon did not destroy, burn, or take the prize. I assumed you came upon some pirate on your last packet run.'

'Very well,' he paused, somewhat satisfied that the man had not been privy to the secret of Resignation's destruction. 'And no, Lieutenant, this ship has been commissioned at the highest level sir, the highest level! We are not a bloody packet, we are a ship of war readying for war, to which you will find out shortly. The officers and crew have been personally chosen from the outset and the ship has been afforded every luxury to prosecute speed and performance, with one goal in mind, battle. The crew have been plucked from England's finest and have since been moulded with utmost professionalism from the first officer. A first officer who has worked liked a dog, a dog, sir, to get to where we are! And where the bloody hell have you been? All the hard work has been achieved, under what I consider to be a very competent first officer, an officer who now stands to be relieved of his position!

Now did I mention I am far from bloody happy about this Lieutenant!'

'Aye, sir, but I must protest, for I am yet to even take up my duty and already am I disparaged and most poorly judged. Should it continue, I warn you I would be compelled to ask for satisfaction.'

'That sir, will be the last time you protest, or I will break you! You know full well you are not entitled to request satisfaction from your captain, so please do not pretend to do so. Also, sir, you must be the only soul in England who is not privy to the last duel fought here upon these very docks. Now, I submit you should immediately explain where the bloody hell you have been, these orders being well past dated?'

'I had been waiting upon my orders and it being so awfully cold this season, I felt it necessary to wait it out before travelling to Chatham. Upon arrival, sir, Agamemnon had already since departed.'

'I see,' Cooper paused, weighing the man's statement. 'Well, you make it easy for me then.'

'Beg your pardon, sir?'

'Lieutenant, you do realise I can have you brought up on charges right here and now, for failing to do your utmost to attend your post, desertion sir, if you will!'

'If I may sir,' Middleton offered softly, now realising his fate was legally in the hands of a man he had just threatened to call out. 'Please accept my apology. I fear I have gotten off on the wrong foot. I am certain I will exceed all expectations in my duty as first and no doubt close the gaps in Mister Spencer's shortcomings and have the ship in good order, quite smartly.'

'Mister Spencer's shortcomings?'

'Aye sir, I have already noted quite a few.'

'I see,' Cooper snuffed, thinking his rage alone would see the man eviscerated before his eyes. But Cooper smartly realised the battle here could not be won upon the first broadsides. There were two concerns. Middleton was either a good officer, so it would not matter, except to Spencer, or he would not perform and as such the door would open to be rid of the man. Cooper weighed the way forward, looking evenly at the man, a man who presently was rather cut down to size, or so it now appeared, the threat of an irrefutable court martial looming over him. 'Mister Middleton, sir, let us put this behind us, no need to be off on the wrong foot, as you say. But I expect you to show the proper respect to Mister Spencer, who in point of fact has quite handsomely done your job for you. I will with interest and eagerness look forward to weighing the performance of your duty, from this point on. I will defer my decision to press charges, for now. Now, please ask Mister Spencer to attend, so I may inform him of the situation.'

'Aye, aye, sir, but I have already informed Mister Spencer. Did you still wish to see him?'

'You did what?'

'I have informed Mister Spencer of my presence and also my seniority upon the ship.'

'You go too far sir! That is the privy of a captain. I will insist you do not overstep, not whilst your serve at my pleasure! Dismissed!'

Cooper pretended to stroll upon the dock, arms behind his back, akin to pacing up and down the quarterdeck. It was not long, as he most expected, before Shillings all but popped out from behind the nearest structure.

'Captain, good afternoon sir and might I have a word, if it pleases? I would most heartily be glad if you could consider me for any post upon Agamemnon?'

'Well, as it turns out Mister Shillings, I have nothing available upon Agamemnon, but I do have something for you.'

'Indeed, sir?'

'Indeed, whilst young, I esteem our Mister Holt greatly and he has informed me that you are something of a capital shot with cannon?'

'To be honest sir, I couldn't hit a fleet of first-rates from deck, but upon land I assure you, I can take the hat off an admiral's head at a thousand yards.'

'That is primarily what Mister Holt said, much to my utter surprise of course. So, you may remember the fort we are building on Ortac?'

'Aye, sir?'

'Very good,' he smiled. 'How are you with a sixty-four?'

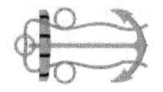

Chapter XV
Pass the Cheese

Hats were tipped and courteous nods were exchanged as Cooper waited upon the cobble outside the Crispin Inn, many a glance chanced towards his hip and his magnificent blade. It seemed he was now a well-known figure about Rochester and all it took was a few swings with his great katana, lop off a few limbs and one head.

'Ah Captain!' Nelson greeted, in the usual zest. 'I am most sincerely sorry about your first, couldn't talk sense into them. Insisted they send young Middleton, they of course being the Pitts, thick as thieves. Get him to post, all that talk naturally.'

'Quite alright sir, all part of the course,' Cooper reassured. 'I have read his flimsies, seems quite an officer, perhaps he will do nicely.'

'Oh, yes, well, the flimsies, wouldn't get your hopes up on

those. Don't be too swayed upon what you read. Did you notice how many there were? He has been shipped from one command to the next and...'

'...and how better to be rid of someone, lest each ship's captain provide the actual truth behind the man,' Cooper grieved, immediately understanding. 'I see sir.'

'In course, I am sure it will work out. I am thinking the next pirate you meet will shoot him right in the bloody head, ha, ha!'

The publican of the Crispin Inn, Rufus Day, had more or less taken it upon himself to silently join the crew of Agamemnon, or at least that was what Cooper was very much thinking. The man was as adept as any first and oh how he ensured every detail was laid down to outright perfection. The absolute necessity for privacy or the utmost confidentiality Cooper required never once had to be gouged nor even mentioned for that matter, taken by Rufus as the standard gospel whenever the officers of Agamemnon were piped aboard his inn. Not only that, but Rufus was most accommodating about his vocation as an informant. Diligently had he apprised his employer of all the activities and goings on, proving to be a spy most attentive and precise in his cunning. Cooper of course kept him swimming in coin, not to mention providing his business with a steady flow of Agamemnon patronage.

'Gentlemen, I have a small endeavour for you all to collaborate upon,' Cooper mysteriously posed, Nelson's knowing eye jauntily squinting in expectation. Cooper's gaze moved about the table. 'Aye, have you not seen her? Have you not feasted your eyes upon the beauty docked beside Agamemnon?'

The officers all moved in their seats somewhat, crowding their gaze upon each other, no one venturing to speak first. They all of course had seen the so called beauty, as Cooper had put it, a ship. The ship in question was by popular opinion a poor excuse for a most terribly beat up antiquated merchantman, perhaps more befitted to a pack of drunkard landsmen set upon their first voyage. And each and every officer well knew within seconds of its mooring that it had rudely slipped in beside Agamemnon, just this very day. It was quite an outrage of course, a ship such as that daring to berth in such proximity to one as grand as Agamemnon. McFee was most incensed, not having anyone to reasonably fight for at least the last month, insisting the cannon upon the poop be immediately trained upon her.

'Sir,' Middleton started. 'They dare to dock that old tub beside us! I will sort this out directly the moment we repair back to Agamemnon. I'll have a pound of flesh from the owner, by god and a tad more from the captain, lest I burn that tub to the waterline!'

'Well, if you must, but I confess that I know the owner, quite well in fact,' declared Cooper.

'Oh?'

'She has been delivered here in the great hope that we might make her worthy to take along with Agamemnon. So, as it were, in short, that is to say, the barge is actually my tub.'

'That, sir, is your tub, er, ship?' quizzed Spencer.

'Indeed,' Cooper grinned, looking as if he had just snatched a pot of milk from the King's own stables. 'Now, it is the Commodore's and my wish that some very important cargo be stowed for her first voyage. As you know, Agamemnon was never going to the West Indies and she is not to be a packet either, but let us keep that to ourselves, alright. We have certain skins to catch. Our first officer has only just arrived, so he will need to be brought up to speed. I trust you will all afford him some leeway, til he gets his bearings.'

'Sir, if I may, if we are not a packet, what is our commission?'

And the entire table grinned and smirked with the cheekiness of knowing a certain bet. Even Nelson was beaming somewhat. Spencer was afforded the honour, firstly outlining how they had sought to establish themselves at Ortac Island and that they were to pursue, without restriction, the pirates frequenting British trade. Middleton was quite astounded, eventually questioning if it was in fact legal, there being no war presently.

'So we will need to get the tub not only sea worthy, but she will have to be fast, moderately fast anyway.'

'Aye sir,' Middleton replied. 'But how fast could she really go, even with every luxury afforded?'

'We will have to see what we have first,' Spencer weighed. 'So, sir, with your permission may we take her out?'

'Very well, but you will find that Commodore Nelson has already made some significant contributions to her. We just need to trim her and place our cannon and our cargo efficiently.'

'The cargo, sir?'

'Indeed, you all already know what the cargo is and so have you laid eye upon it too. You just haven't realised.'

'Oh, of course, sir,' Spencer trumpeted. 'Our surplus men!'

'Aye, armed to the teeth, we shall cram a good hundred odd aboard her. Without actual cargo, she will be light and fast, well, fast enough. She is the first addition to the fleet I intend to build, His Majesty's Ship Cheese.'

'What a god awful name, if I may, sir,' remarked Spencer.

'More than you know, for this is how we will catch our rats. And her captain must be a fighting man. For it is my plan to send our Cheese to sea, verily right amidst this damned nest of piracy. She will afford our first catch, which is why we have established our fort on Ortac. Ortac will serve as a safe harbour for our Cheese to bear off, should she need to hide under some great bloody cannon, for which we have so painstakingly arranged, all sixty-fours. Of course the captain of the marines and his very finest will be neatly tucked away beneath Cheese's deck,' he added much to the utmost inclination and delight of the entire table, all nodding in unmitigated approval. 'We must ensure the trap is sound. We must lure the enemy aboard her, make them think they have found the leprechaun's pot of gold, so we may in turn board the enemy and take her a prize. All depends upon this, or they will simply break off and so very easily sink her.'

'But sir, we will have Agamemnon to support her, will we not?'

'We will not, so to speak. Well, not in such proximity that might afford some kind of real protection. I intend to hide Agamemnon upon the horizon or perhaps closer around some islet, triangulated between Ortac and Cheese, thus cutting off all chances of escape. It is not likely we will sneak up so easily again, not as we did to Hasard.'

'Indeed?' Middleton queried. 'Hasard?'

'Aye,' Holt answered exuberantly. 'The Captain had us cross some sixteen sea miles with the Frenchie none the wiser, full and before, running fine at eighteen knots, masked within the shadow of Sheppey, the sinking sun abaft.'

'Eighteen knots, please, do not be absurd young sir.'

'Was tight sailing with a draught of only eighteen feet, but most handsomely did the Captain contrive to see us there as such, quicker than you can blink. The Frenchie did not even see us til the bowsprit touched their sheets!'

'And then the Frenchie slipped away, so I am to understand?'

'Oh sir, it wasn't like that,' protested Holt.

'Indeed Mister Middleton,' Nelson interrupted. 'Perhaps a visit to the log might attest to convince your enquiry, a prudent course of action sir if I may, before you might improperly impeach the good honour of the ship you have given oath to serve.'

'Apologies sir, of course, you are right.'

'Quite, but let us not digress gentlemen,' Cooper rightly interjected. 'Of Cheese, it will spell the end of her should our game of cat and mouse be uncovered, as I am sure our pirate friends will happily sink her well before Agamemnon could reasonably present. Nonetheless, Agamemnon will be nearby, if only to ensure our rat is the right class of rat.'

'Indeed sir, what are we hoping for, a twenty-eight?' probed Spencer.

'A forty sir, indeed it's a forty isn't it?' corrected Middleton.

'Well, if you must know, our first quarry, should all go to plan, will be a yacht.'

'A yacht?' objected Middleton.

'What? A tiny weeny yacht?' frowned Spencer.

'A yacht indeed,' Cooper grinned, the whole table falling fell, somewhat disarmed upon hearing the intended catch. 'A well-armed one of course, but by all means a yacht. Once we have taken it into service, it will serve as our lookout, peeking over the horizon, as well as our packet for supplies, stores, crew and even dignitaries. And she will need a captain, naturally,' he added casually.

'Naturally,' grinned Nelson wickedly, the blood now flowing, his heart seemingly more piratical than the Frenchies they were to chase down and he eyed the officers one by one. In turn the officers hungrily moved in their seats, nodding at the thought of promotion, greed fuelling their every whim.

'Oh, it should not need to be explained, but I have weighed the resources required for us to catch the big fish. Trust me, when I say we will need a little friend. It is Commodore Nelson's opinion too in course. It will definitely make the difference between sinking and swimming. Quite happy to take on a frigate thereafter, but gentlemen, I implore you now to wholeheartedly embrace our plan. We will most desperately need a yacht.'

'And a new captain for her too,' added Holt excitedly.

'Capital sir, just capital!' applauded Spencer.

'Very well,' Cooper happily nodded, feeling his officers were in good spirits now. 'What pray tell are we drinking to?'

'It's Tuesday!'

'How fitting, let us toast *"to our men!"*.'

'Now, it comes to the point,' Nelson happily announced. 'Who will enjoy the honour of first commanding Cheese? Captain Cooper and I will afford seniority to take precedence of course, a show of arms gentlemen, if you please?'

Arms shot into the air, even Holt's, as cheeky as it seemed. The others launched their arms in an immediate race, as if they were small children before their father thinking the swiftest might be first chosen. How grand Cooper thought, the entire table volunteering with such bravado, until his gaze fell unfortunately upon one particular man. He corrected himself, the entire table had volunteered, bar one. Middleton remained silent and resolute, his arms weighed down with wine and cheese as it were, an irritating nonchalant look of disinterest set upon his sails. It was a dangerous command of course, for any pirates so encountered would tend to fight to the death, knowing full well surrendering would simply land them the noose. And furthermore, they would not hesitate to sink poor Cheese, even just out of spite.

Ships of War — Murky Waters

'Very well, as Mister Middleton has remained, Mister Spencer will be captain. He may choose his first officer, I will choose the remainder. For now gentlemen, your challenge will be to arrange our Cheese to look so ever inviting and merchantman like. Time is short, but on the morrow's tide will I and Commodore Nelson be taking Agamemnon to Ortac, to furnish the necessary supplies and finish the fort. Oh and I have just the commander for her. In the meantime, you will afford Cheese every effort and make her worthy of the rat. It seems next time we meet, we will be at sea gentlemen and by courtesy of Admiral Howe and his signal concoction, we will be able to communicate over the horizon. It is imperative that Cheese appear, from the very first, to be on her own. I assure you there are spies about, reporting our every move. To this end I have informed our publican Rufus here that Cheese will be making a run to Gibraltar, through the Channel Islands, carrying some most handsome cargo. He will let it slip. So the trap is fairly set, patience and fortitude are now required.'

'Spence, I most heartily am sorry for Middleton. Damned unfortunate luck, even Nelson couldn't do a thing.'

'It is quite alright sir, quite alright. I had never expected to be first and my time will come, when it comes. I am right happy just to be part of it all. Such a grand endeavour, if I may.'

'Quite, spoken like a true officer. Now, where the hell did Holt get to tonight? He didn't attend drinks after dinner and I am quite certain it was not his watch?'

'Oh, didn't you hear sir? Mister Middleton demoted him back to mid, seeing how we have an extra officer now.'

'He bloody well did bloody what!'

'Aye, sir, thought it was strange?'

'And the cad did this after just dining with him?'

'Aye, sir, I felt it was somewhat heartless myself.'

'Heartless? That is something of an understatement!'

'But no one would question it, thinking it came direct from you.'

'It bloody well did not! Blast that man, what has he done! Not only is it a stupid thing he has perpetrated, but indeed a wholly foolish thing considering the manner in which he has done it. Holt is much beloved by the jacks. The crew will crucify me! For the love of god, damn that man to hell! Oh my god, how is poor Holt taking it?'

'Actually, sir, he is fine. He is right good one that lad. I think I shall endeavour to be kind to him for as long as he is with us, so when he is admiral, which I esteem will likely be barely in a few years' time, I might have a job, ha, ha!'

'This vile man has come upon us at such an unfortunate time. I must act or he will sink us all, so precariously we presently sit. Spence, more than ever am I wretched to see you off the ship, even for a moment. But I am glad you are in command of Cheese. It's only a tub, but a captain is a captain.'

'Acting Captain.'

'Well, ain't we all, ha, ha!' he jested. 'But, you do realise, of course, you now outrank Middleton.'

'Sir,' he grinned. 'Never had it crossed my mind.'

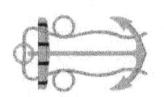

'Ha!'

Chapter XVI
Cheese and a Dirty Rat

'I stand most vigorously amazed at you sir, amazed. Before you, right verily before you, was the golden chance to become acting captain, you barely being with us for even one day. And to my utter dismay, sir, utter dismay, you turned it down, turned it down flat! I will have the reason Mister Middleton, indeed I'll have it or I'll have your hide. Now out with it!'

'Is it not obvious, sir? Cheese is a tub, not worthy of my standing or my rank, or for that matter, my time.'

'I see, I see. But now Captain Spencer is taking the fight to our enemy, with a barrel full of marines at his command, a boarding party of some distinct worth. It is a brave endeavour and most worthy, a very good opportunity to distinguish oneself. As such, now he stands but just one ship action away from a permanent promotion to master and commander. And you, you will languish here as first. If he were to capture a tidy little frigate, it will now go to him, not you.'

'Nonetheless, Cheese is very much beneath me, sir,' he reiterated, most annoyed to be discussing the subject at all. 'And with respect, I very much doubt Cheese will ever chance to catch anything, except perhaps the bottom.'

'Well, well, well, we shall see. We shall see and just so we are clear, Mister Middleton, Captain Spencer now outranks you.'

'Perhaps, in course, I imagine so.'

'Sir, last time I checked, a captain outranks a lieutenant! Damned you will be, mark my words, damned, should you not afford Captain Spencer your every deference to his new rank, a rank you allowed him to procure before you.'

'Aye, of course, sir.'

'Now Mister Middleton, with Captain Spencer and his first off ship, you will promote Mister Holt to acting lieutenant. I have asked Mister Holt to wait for you on the weather deck. You will leave this cabin and you will do so directly, in front of all the men present, willingly and loudly, do you understand?'

'Aye, aye, sir, but I must protest,' he griped, the unwavering look upon his captain now serving to attest that he should immediately find recourse within his wording. 'Ah, sir, let me rephrase, it is just that I disagree.'

'You disagree, for what reason?'

'Holt is very young, sir, very young. His examination for officer is some years away and frankly upon a sixty-four, he is somewhat out of his class, his knowledge being so limited.'

'You have not had the privilege of being aboard very long, so I will perhaps forgive your ignorance upon this matter, as utter as it is. To enlighten you, Mister Holt very much distinguished himself on our last cruise, especially in our engagement with Hasard. You will find that he has a singular skill for mathematics, most definitely well beyond that of your own and if you had not heard, he captained his gun crews to absolute victory in our ship's cannon exercise, most handsomely annihilating every other crew, many of whom were old hands from the war. He is most industrious I must say, even invented a bloody stick to determine quite accurately a ship's distance, something we are presently expanding upon. He was also of great service to me personally when we had the Dauphin aboard, seeing how Mister Holt speaks perfect Parisian.'

'The Dauphin, sir, of France?'

'Aye, there is much you have to catch up on it appears. Perhaps, you should be engaged in perusing our ship's log, before you start your next watch? As I have alluded, we are not and have never been just a simple packet. You will find that young Lord Holt is much beloved by the jacks and that by disrating him, especially in the manner so chosen, they will much despise you for it, no doubt.'

'Yes, yes of course, despise me. Did you say *"lord"*, sir?'

'Aye, did you not know he is Jarvis Thomas Holt, son of the honourable Lord Thomas Holt, close friend to George, that's George the Third, our king? Young Holt and The Prince William are good friends too I believe,' he casually added.

'Aye, of course, immediately sir,' Middleton smartly confirmed. 'Our young Lord Holt promoted and directly it is, sir, on the weather deck!'

'And Mister Middleton, I expect Mister Holt to remain acting lieutenant, until further notice, irrespective of the number of officers aboard. Should the King himself take up duty, he will stay an officer. Furthermore, I expect you to discuss and likewise seek approval with me before any man on the ship is promoted, or disrated, understood?'

'Aye, sir, understood.'

'Well, at least now you will have two supporters aboard.'

'Sorry, sir?'

'Why, Lieutenant Holt and Captain Spencer of course,' he explained, a sliver of vengeful triumph hidden within. 'Mister Middleton, did you not realise that both officers will now enjoy a larger portion of the prize pie, considering both their promotions? Mister Holt may not need the extra coin, but he is most insistently independent and will very much appreciate being elevated. And of course, as commander, Captain Spencer will now receive a lion's share of the coin, a lion's share! And considering you allowed him to take a command already earmarked as yours, he will no doubt be most appreciative of you. You did know all this of course, didn't you?'

'Oh? Aye, in course, sir.'

'Ah good, I was starting to worry. Oh what a fellow you would be, 'ey Mister Middleton to not know how our prizes are divvied? What a fellow you would be indeed, ha, ha!'

Agamemnon cruised about the Channel Islands, Eagle keenly surveying the far horizon hoping to catch Cheese. She was due to meet close to sundown and Cooper was bent upon taking no chances, beating up and down his station as if war had been declared at the last bell. Eagle had every man and jack of his lookout brigade perched upon every possible vantage, whistles at the ready, eyes peeled. Agamemnon would naturally spy Cheese first, her masts affording a longer reach upon the skyline and, her being so much swifter, she would thereafter close the gap considerably. Cooper was very much interested in this aspect actually, already postulating Agamemnon's rate of closure to the horizon, the intended arrival of Cheese offering a worthy trial. Of course they would have to sight her first and time was short. All in all, he had very much planned to rendezvous as the sky deepened and the pitch collected, the obscurity of a moonless night serving to douse and swamp every scrap of sheet. He definitely could not be persuaded to meet even a moment before, although he was well aware that if he waited one too many moments thereafter, they might never meet. It was a risk he had to take, for barely could he afford the two vessels to be seen together, the rats about tending to be less curious once the trap has been eyed.

'Beautiful, ain't it sir,' commented Holt, taking a moment to appreciate the oncoming eventide and its magnificent grandeur.

'The sun setting at sea is something to behold for sure Mister Holt, a small pleasure of our vocation.'

'Is it always different, sir, out here at sea?'

'Indeed, as is god's vision upon us all. It is a shame Commodore Nelson could not make the voyage. I think he would have appreciated the beauty of being back to sea. It has been some time I am afraid.'

'If I may ask sir, was it his ailment?'

'Oh, you know about it?'

'Ah, the malaria, sir?'

'Quite, poor soul has had it since seventy-six, reoccurs in sudden bouts from time to time, such a damned nuisance.'

'Oh, aye sir, The Prince William had confided. But only as an example of what maladies might await my career, should I push on of course.'

'And you are pushing on I take it?'

'Never in life sir would I do anything less. God willing, I will push on and may I say, much of my mind I credit to you sir. I cannot imagine being educated by any other in a manner so fine. I am for it now.'

'That is very kind and I must commend you Mister Holt, for not taking your recent disrating to heart, as brief as it was. It was never my intent.'

'Oh sir, I know it wasn't ordered by you. I have been around my father long enough to sniff out the cow and the dung. And any doubt was soon alleviated by the sight of our grand Lord Middleton promoting me on the weather deck in full privy of the entire watch. Sir, sorry to say this out loud, but being disrated was almost worth seeing that. Nonetheless, I was truly happy enough just to be a mid, sir and wait my time like everyone else.'

'But you are not like everyone else, which is why you are in fact acting lieutenant, for one part. There are two types of officer, Mister Holt, those who can and those who cannot. You sir, will be the one who can, being my wager. It is good to recognise the difference, because rank often is a poor indicator, as we unfortunately bear direct witness presently thereof. Know your fellow officer, for at some stage, your life will verily be in his hands.'

'Like you, sir and Captain Spencer?'

'Quite.'

'I very much miss Captain Spencer as our first. He has taught me so much in so little time. He even showed me how to scrounge, should the need arise, ha, ha. And I never fear for the ship whilst he is first.'

'What?'

'Sorry sir, that perhaps came out indifferently to my intent. I have said too much, beyond my station.'

'Very well, naturally, I cannot expect you to snitch on your superior, but if Mister Middleton has put the ship at risk, it's your duty to tell her captain.'

'Perhaps sir, the view from above is more telling,' he hinted, now peering up at the nest.

'What the devil? Where is the bloody nest? It's gone?'

'Aye sir, very telling,' he hinted again.

'Thank you Mister Holt,' he replied, still aching to ascertain where the present lookouts were stationed. Finally he spied Eagle in the top, in the masthead. The nest was nowhere to be found. He was now thinking aloud the necessary calculations as to how many sea miles past the horizon the lookouts had now lost.

'Around four sea miles sir,' Holt casually confirmed, guessing what his captain was doing.

'Good god lad, how do you do that? I believe I almost had it! Well, no, I lie, I was still some way off.'

'Sorry sir, I know you are most handsomely accomplished at mathematics, didn't mean to diminish you in any way. Your calculations upon the pirate chart, well, they were brilliant sir, to be sure.'

'Oh, for heaven's sake, don't go making a habit of apologising every time you know more, or are in fact a quicker study than that of your lowly superiors. You're a wonder, you are, just keep doing your duty and feel free to accommodate your captain, anytime, especially with your particular skills. That's an order.'

'Aye, sir and thank you, sir.'

'Bloody hell, four sea miles!' he exasperated, a few extra naval expletives immediately entering his mind, the mystery of the missing Cheese now all too apparent. 'No wonder we haven't seen Cheese yet!' he vexed knowingly. His faith in Spencer was such of course that he all but expected the masts of Cheese to miraculously peak the horizon, no less than exactly upon the allocated hour, at the precise minute and at the exact second. But now the product of his mathematics, calculations which would not suffer even the slightest deviation, were out by four sea miles. It immediately came to mind that night would likely now fall prior to Agamemnon catching sight of Cheese and both ships will be flailing around in a barn searching for the proverbial needle in the haystack. 'God damn that man!' he blasted, continuing to think through the problem. 'Why the bloody hell would he take down the nest? Gracious, what else has he bloody well done?' he lastly thought, now wishing some immediate act of god to suddenly rear up and save the ship from a first officer barely rated able. 'Thank you Mister Holt, indeed and I should be rightly sorry, in any case, for Mister Middleton's poor judgement in disrating you. I have had it struck from the log, so you know. The bare fact is, Agamemnon needs you as an officer. You have earned your post, fear not. Anyway, you need not fear him again. In deference, I actually think he now might fear you.'

'Sir?'

'If he asks about The Prince William, you just make out you are the greatest of friends and often go hunting together.'

'Captain, you didn't, sir?' he grinned.

'Oh I bloody well did. A good officer must use every available force at his disposal and it's perhaps rather no more than a small extension of the truth, that's all,' he blatantly justified. 'Remember, you are in the Royal Navy now and such actions and engagements are verily common place, ha, ha!'

'On deck!' came the call from Eagle, his whistle tweeting. 'On deck, ship on the horizon!'

'How the devil?'

'Look, sir, with the sun descending, Eagle has crawled to the very top, the very top sir, clinging on like a maddened cat!'

'Outrageous! Bloody outrageous! God bless that man, a man who knows more about what's going on than any officer on the ship!' he applauded. 'I suspect though Eagle might have had an accomplice in this matter?'

'Whatever do you mean, sir?' returned Holt blankly, as innocent as might a young puppy beguiling its master blinking its big brown eyes.

'An accomplice of singular skill in mathematics, is what I am thinking?'

'Well, who can tell, sir?' returned Holt naïvely, shrugging his shoulders, his gaze focused anywhere but upon the eyes of his captain.

'On deck, Cheese in sight!' confirmed Eagle.

'Finally,' Cooper rejoiced. 'Mister Holt, I will not soon forget this. Now it seems we have a squadron! Be so good as to send to Cheese, *"Welcome. Captain and First repair aboard. Dinner.".*'

Captain Cooper sat at the head of the table, upright and stalwart, Captain Spencer and Lieutenant Middleton taking the esteemed station of seniority each by his side. All the senior officers, including McFee and Blane, had been summoned. Eagerly they awaited the appearance of the feast, their best dress uniforms adorned, an air of excitement buzzing. Yet most of all, they yearned to hear more about their captain's plans and how they were going to profit from Cheese and the pirates who verily awaited them.

It was a scene perhaps reminiscent of the eve of any great battle. The dinner table gently listed as the ship rolled to and fro. The bread eerily slipped from one end to the other, nary an experienced soul giving it a second thought. The wine was flowing with cheer in the air and the mains yet to come. All the relevant charts were now presented before the gathering, the officers giddier than a swag of schoolboys readying for some drunken mischief. Haplessly the charts floated about, the butt of many a wine glass serving to corral them as a horde of attentive minds sat studiously in awe.

'Bread, Major?' offered Blane casually, the basket finally chancing to rest before him. His eyes continued to flow over the wave of documents besieging the feast, only mildly distracted by the butter now hazarding to slip past his reach.

'I do believe the butter has lost the gage?' remarked McFee.

'Now is our chance Major, whilst the thing is hopelessly aback, verily drifting before us!'

'Aye, Doctor, thank ye. Oh, what a capital texture! I must say this spread is unusually sweet too. Where ever did the Captain find this man Fredricks, something of a culinary prodigy, if truth be told? But Doctor, I cannot tell ye enough sir,' he heartily insisted, almost to the point of being somewhat excitable. 'How comforting it be, indeed how comforting to welcome a fellow Scotsman on board. You are from Edinburgh originally, sir?'

'Oh, I had studied there in my youth, at the University, though originally from Blanefield, in Ayrshire.'

'Aye, Edinburgh was always a wee bit cramped. Even with the advent of the new town has it only barely dared to alleviate the issue.'

'It is a serious issue, this overcrowding. And it has the unfortunate effect, of course Major, that disease is more commonplace. It is very much like stuffing some five hundred men into a ship of war, such confined spaces procreating all sorts of nasty vermin.'

'Of that, had I personally noted sir, if I may,' Cooper added, now avidly joining the discussion. 'Indeed had I noted the most horrendously tall buildings there, most uncommonly frightful, most prolific, stretching farther into the sky than ever reasonably thought rightly possible,' he told forebodingly, suddenly swivelling about as if he had just discovered a first-rate bearing down from a nearby fog bank. 'Fredricks? I say Fredricks there, let us have those sugar sops!'

'Indeed Captain, some are known to be over eleven storeys into the heavens, well over the masts of Agamemnon if you can imagine, a modern marvel to be sure. But with the defensive walls of the outskirts very much limiting the town's expansion, I fear it was a product of necessity, rather than invention.'

'No less, sir, yet Edinburgh remains the heart of Scottish enlightenment, does she not?'

'I believe some call her the *"Athens of the North"*, something of a major intellectual centre indeed. And if I may, the minds presently being turned out of her are proving astounding, simply astounding!'

'And gentlemen, if I may, are we not honoured to have one such mind aboard, not just an eminent physician, but one who has distinguished himself in battle?'

'Oh please Captain, much too kind for one just doing his duty. I risked much less of course than the average jack crewing a gun.'

'You have been in battle many times Doctor?' queried Middleton.

'Oh Captain, these sugar sops are magnificent! Who could have thought toasted bread soaked in ale sweetened simply with sugar and grated nutmeg could be so divine!'

'But sir, please, you must have them with cheese,' insisted Holt.

'Fredricks, I say Fredricks there,' Cooper immediately bellowed. 'Flick us some more panam and some caffan! And let us have the special spread!'

'Aye sir,' Fredricks silently groaned. 'Bread and cheese it is and I shall use the best knife to flick it. But, as for the special butter, sir, it is already upon the table, the other stores having since been long ago depleted.'

'Oh, I do apologise Mister Middleton,' Blane finally returned. 'Please forgive the impertinence of my tastebuds, somewhat foundering after that most delicious experience. But six, sir. Yes, there it is, six major engagements I believe is the count.'

'Prodigious indeed Doctor, most prodigious!' complimented Middleton, very much impressed. 'I regret that I am yet to have the honour of battle.'

'Prodigious indeed is to say the least,' Cooper quickly added. 'At the time, our Doctor here was of course Physician to the Fleet under Admiral Rodney, whom I am to understand, remains your particular friend?'

'Aye, but he is very much retired now, resting away in the countryside per my instructions. He, beyond all doubt, has done his duty.'

'And there, Mister Holt, is a man who first went to sea at the age of fourteen much like yourself, he being made lieutenant some few days after his twenty-first birthday and captain only three years later in forty-two, which at the time afforded him the honour of being one of the youngest ever post-captains in the Royal Navy.'

'Perhaps our young lieutenant will better that mark?' Blane suggested with a knowing smirk. 'Never have I seen a lieutenant so young.'

'I have just turned fifteen, sir, but I will endeavour to do my utmost.'

'Ha, ha, indeed, well said, well said,' complimented the Doctor.

'And I have read your book Doctor, *"Observations on the Diseases of Seamen"*. I was most intrigued as to the results you obtained in the matter of scurvy. And you say it was all due to the introduction of some simple lemon or lime juice?'

'Ah, if I may,' Cooper interrupted, turning to the Doctor for permission. 'Doctor, you would not know this, but I was actually part of the West India Fleet and I can tell everyone here with the utmost assurance that the services so rendered by yourself and your many reforms were of the most singular importance. The efficiency of the fleet not only improved, but it inaugurated a new era, a new standard as it were in the sanitary condition of the entire Royal Navy. Scurvy is such the devil you know, often itself alone the cause of many a failure in naval operations. It is much less commonplace now and all because of a simple sip of juice, the wickedness no longer prevailing to the lamentable extent it had so ever enjoyed. Fevers and such arising from the unhealthy state of ships also caused great mortality, one man in seven per year I believe was the figure. But again, by supplying wine, fresh fruit and such, together with the enforcement of a strict discipline over sanitary conditions, that number reduced to one man in twenty! Even Admiral Rodney himself attributed, in part, his great successes to the Doctor's knowledge and attention. Not one man upon the flag, Formidable of course, found themselves buried in six months, not one out of nine hundred souls, remarkable!'

'What is it Doctor, some kind of water bewitched?'

'Oh, it is more than just weak beer or punch, Mister Middleton. Over the years, I have chosen many forms within which to attract its ingestion. My drams are more like a flip, or perhaps a cool tankard, or even a stepney.'

'A stepney?'

'Oh yes, a decoction of raisins and lemons in conduit water sweetened with sugar and, of course, bottled up for the duration. Yet, the winning favourite amongst all sailors was no doubt small beer mixed with brandy and sugar, thereafter laced with lemon. Oh, how they snapped it up!'

'Ah, a flip!' Cooper added rightly, now reminiscing. 'I most heartily agree and you stand most absolutely correct. The jacks ever so loved their beer and lemon, though not always were they able to partake its portion with brandy, it being so hard to come by in such great quantities. I must admit Doctor, I do so enjoy a good flip, much more than a stepney or a cool tankard. I even keep a stash of brandy handy for my flips, when the urge comes.'

'Ah, well, partaking in any of them leads to the inescapable consumption of the prescribed lemon juice and as such the elimination of scurvy.'

'Fascinating, absolutely astounding, Doctor,' remarked Middleton.

'But I must point out that I am not in fact the discoverer of this remedy, merely the promoter. It was James Lind who has that honour, a Scottish physician who argued for citrus fruits, better ventilation and the enforcement of not only the cleanliness of sailors' bodies, but also their clothing and their bedding.'

'Aye, to prevent Typhus gentlemen, would be to promote a definite advantage in superiority over our enemy, especially the French,' added Cooper rightly.

'Indeed, Captain!' the Doctor nodded, somewhat impressed that the man before him was no buffoon. 'Further, Lind advocated fumigation below deck with sulphur and arsenic. It was also he who proposed to obtain fresh water at sea merely by distilling sea water, albeit somewhat problematic and impractical. Even wrote a publication in fifty-three, which from all accounts fell on deaf ears.'

'Indeed gentlemen, it is the simple things which make the difference. Take the men's beer for example. It is weak beer of course, but as it has been boiled in the brewing process, it is mostly free from bacteria and will last for months, unlike water kept in a cask for the same period.'

Ships of War — Murky Waters

'Oh, very good Captain, splendid!' Blane complimented, raising his glass. 'But of course, officers are afforded wine and brandy!' he added, to a rising cheer from the table before turning back to McFee. 'Major, I did so very much enjoy Edinburgh, but after receiving my degree, I had ventured to London of course, affording many more open doors.'

'Indeed so I have heard Doctor. Are we to understand that you are the personal physician to the Prince of Wales?'

'Oh, aye and to his brother The Prince William, who was so very adamant that I should embark with you all. Oh Captain, he had such things to say about you, such wonderful things! You really had made such an impression, to be sure. He was of the most virulent and adamant opinion that you should forthwith be knighted.'

The last comment drew a distinct rise from perhaps one eyebrow in particular. The first officer eyed the Doctor with some degree of silent dissatisfaction. Middleton had been at odds with his captain since the moment he boarded. He further insisted to himself that the man was not fit for command having failed to destroy or take Hasard. To now hear that the Prince of England harboured a knighthood for him suddenly struck within an outrage most unseemly and distasteful, nonetheless altogether obscene and to every inch of his being wholly offensive. In fact, he was now pugnaciously thinking it was something of an offence to any man who stood rightly before the almighty.

It was well that the dinner proceeded without incident, much to the happiness and preponderance of her captain. The food proved especially succulent, a product of Fredricks's promotion as the newly appointed captain's cook, a position now attested as an unbridled success. It seemed the man was most horribly and pathetically resigned to a life of ineptitude and absolute failure, except for perhaps this one vocation. His coffee had not only been fit for a king, but a French king and the appearance of freshly baked croissants had Blane comically insisting Cooper was undeniably collaborating with the French. It had been a hard pill for Cooper to swallow, but he was now of the undeniable opinion that his tubby bumbling cook was somewhat indispensable. A captain could never underestimate the persuasive power of a state like dinner when entertaining dignitaries and other eminent guests. With that endeavour in mind, he would insistently point Fredricks not unlike cannon ready to rake.

'Gentlemen, to the meat of it, it seems our friend Mister Shillings has been most productive and dare I say, even most useful. His report from Ortac just this day was most informative and altogether enlightening. Not only has he accounted seeing Hasard, but he managed to plot a fairly decent idea of her comings and goings. It seems she very much frequents Alderney and the Channel Islands.'

'Sir, perhaps Mister Shillings should repair aboard for a stint and share his report directly over dinner with the senior officers? We could send Cheese directly to fetch him?'

'Fetch him?' Cooper returned blankly, somewhat straining to conceal his mortified apprehension. The entire table, bar Middleton and Blane, appeared as if they had just broached-to and sunk, all aboard presently holding their breath awaiting the very end. 'Oh no, Mister Shillings has a fort to command,' he quickly added, much to the sudden relief of the room. 'In point of fact, we must exercise some care it seems. Mister Shillings has also accounted the passing, only just this day, of a French seventy-four.'

'By god, sir!' Spencer exclaimed. 'In these waters?'

'If I may, Captain Spencer,' Holt politely suggested. 'I believe it is quite alright, being that the Captain already knew it was out here. Isn't that right, sir? Your charts assumed it to be Pompee?'

'Indeed they did Mister Holt, although *"supposed"* might be a tad more accurate, rather than *"knew"*. Nonetheless, Mister Shillings said she came within a cable of the fort and it was in fact, Pompee. Not only that, but she proceeded to hunt and chase down a British merchantman, all in complete eyeshot.'

'The dogs!'

'Aye, verily. Now, Mister Holt, might you regale us of Pompee sir?'

'Oh Pompee, aye sir,' he commenced. 'La Pompée, Téméraire class ship of the French Navy, Toulon shipyard, six hundred and forty men with twenty-eight cannon on the lower deck being all long thirty-six pounders. There are thirty cannon on the upper deck being all long eighteen pounders. And on the forecastle and quarterdeck, she boasts sixteen more eight pounders and four more thirty-six obusiers, her expected launch date May or early June of this year.'

'Impressive Mister Holt, how is it you know all this?' queried Middleton.

'Captain has been schooling me sir, on all the French shipping, says a good captain must know his enemy. He has all the French gazettes.'

'Indeed, the Captain? And an obusier?'

'*Obusier de vaisseau*, very similar to a carronade, but made of brass, sir. They mostly fire explosive shells at a low velocity.'

'Good god, a vastly superior ship then?' noted Blane.

'Aye, Doctor, nine hundred and ten pound broadside to our six hundred and seventy-eight, but might I add, a vastly slower ship. Is that not correct Mister Holt?'

'Some nine knots only, expected maximum sir. Don't worry Doctor, we will scoot away quicker than a highlander screeching a bagpipe.'

'Of course, that is, should we so determine the need to run?' Middleton pompously insisted, much to the sullen amazement of all. The idea of taking on a seventy-four with only a sixty-four was not the most welcoming thought, a French prison or the bottom of the deep blue sea more prevalent in one's mind. 'We must do our utmost, naturally.'

'In course, but gentlemen, note the arranged launch date, June? Is that not somewhat interesting? She is not even supposed to be launched, but here before our eyes is Pompee, cruising the Channel Islands. Most curious, is it not? It seems she has been launched and fitted ahead of time, perhaps even well ahead of time, for I calculate a seventy-four has been snatching our merchantmen around here for at least the last six months. Now, our Mister Shillings also reports an additional number of brigs and small craft cruising most swiftly about, the number being much more it seems than usual.'

'Cheese, sir? They are looking for Cheese?'

'It seems the word is out, aye. On the morrow will we lay our trap and set our Cheese and so shall we wait upon our rat. Here it is gentlemen. Agamemnon will lay behind one of the islets here in the Channel Islands,' he boldly announced, his finger moving upon the chart. 'Here, this one is perfect. Our masts and therefore, the entirety of our lookout brigade, will just barely be peeking over the islet. The Frenchie will not see us, but we will see them. We will keep Cheese in sight at all times. I propose that Cheese make her course through the Channel Islands at a most lubberly merchantman pace, an inviting target. She will lay in between Ortac and Agamemnon. Should the existing winds prevail, which is very much my absolute wish, Agamemnon will lie leeward of Cheese and the prize. Should our prize *get wind*,' he cheekily tested raising an eyebrow to a room already very much receptive to any wit they might enjoy in polite mirth. 'Aye, should she get wind of the plot against her, she will likely prevail upon said wind and the weather gage to make good her escape, the French way of course.'

'The weather gage?' Blane blankly queried. 'That is, is it not, when you have the wind advantage, it being at your back? I was of the understanding it was better for us to have the gage, when entering battle?'

'Indeed, of course you are mostly right Doctor, for the gage allows the attacker to choose the moment of attack. Because the wind is in assistance, the ship need only wear, a safer and faster manoeuvre in turning her, as opposed to beating which requires some effort with the sheets, as you may appreciate. The determining advantage, I must point out, is that the attack will be carried so much the swifter and that the cannon can verily be aimed without much ado. The enemy, to the contrary, will be struggling into the wind and cannot as easily manoeuvre to match. Apart from a distinct lack of speed, they will not be afforded the luxury of so easily aiming her cannon, her being close hauled or close reached and consequently, very much unable to adjust her turn. In addition, the side of her hull will be somewhat out of the water, due to the heeling of the ship under the enormous press of sail. Oh, I do not have to tell you it is such a terrible weak spot, the planking normally below the waterline now vulnerable to cannon. Upon taking even one solid shot and consequently righting her way, the ship would naturally take on water. All in all, however, the French have often assumed the strategy of using the wind to escape, moreover upon matters of the battle becoming dire of course.'

'Indeed? I had never known that, although a ship's doctor is often in his cockpit in the moments before and during battle. We never get to see a bloody thing, except its handy work.'

'So our rat, gentlemen, in my estimation, will likely prevail upon the weather gage to make good her escape.'

'Oh brilliant sir, meaning she will escape right into the lap of Agamemnon,' added McFee.

'Precisely! And should our rat turn and beat into the wind, she likely will come upon our gun at Ortac or find Cheese laid in by her side, Cheese of course by then having the weather gage,' he added, grinning at the Doctor. 'It is my greatest wish that our rat be Hasard and that her captain be gracious enough to survive, if only so he may have the honour of directly swinging from his own yard, murdering dog!'

'Captain, if I may?' Spencer boldly suggested, holding up his glass excitedly. 'It being Monday, may we drink to *"our ships at sea!".*'

'How appropriate, to our ships at sea and perhaps even one more come this time tomorrow!'

Agamemnon sat silently in wait behind an islet. The crew were now well aware they were pirate hunting and not a packet boorishly beating from one port to the next. Of all the dirty mouthed souls, hardly not a one could hold back a cheesy grin. They appeared as a bevy of bearded bandits, eyes peeled for the prize.

Cooper had much riding on the whole endeavour of course, virtually his very existence. Situated upon the masthead, young Holt at his side, he scoured the seas with his best glass, his good eye perched upon the horizon. Holt mimicked the action, his glass railing back and forth, but the only sail present was that of Cheese. It had been some hours into the day already and Cooper was almost thinking it was wishful that the French might immediately seek to come out and grab Cheese. Of course, they knew all about her, her supposed destination and her departure, the spies in Chatham most industriously dedicated to their business. It could not fail he thought, the cargo all told to be undeniably handsome. But it was a big ocean and locating a small merchantman was always a feat in itself. Nonetheless, Spencer was doing a first-rate job of dribbling along, perhaps at best three or four knots, wind spilling from his sheets in a most merchantman like manner.

Cooper laid his glass upon Ortac. What a magnificent accomplishment the fort beheld. It was most readily and most sneakily masked within the rock, a somewhat natural fortification, technically heralding the empire's newest acquisition of expansion. They even had engineered a makeshift mast, to run up the signals, albeit, able to be pulled down in a moment's notice.

'It very much reminds me of hunting with father, if you don't mind the comparison, sir?' Holt candidly offered. 'We wait upon the prey, never knowing what may come. It is all most heartily exciting, sir!'

'I gather the prey at home to be a fox or something of that nature?'

'Aye, sir, though, we have been known to bag some deer, but nothing really so big.'

'Well, we are indeed only after a squirrel today, maybe a fox tomorrow and god forbid, we really do not want a bear just yet, so let us hope Mister Shillings's report is accurate and Pompee is not venturing our way.'

'Sir, I believe I can see two sail, just barely, fine off the starboard bow?'

'Aye sir,' Eagle confirmed, overhearing Holt, which is all part of the course when bunched up in the top. 'Mister Holt is spot on, they is fine, but 'tis three sail sir, all brigs, one being our friend, Hasard.'

'Goodness, I cannot make that out just yet sir,' Holt vexed. 'Eagle must eat more carrots than a Surrey Hill's hare, such eyesight, sir!'

'Sir, signal from Cheese! Aye, they are confirming. She is changing course, looking to make her run down past Ortac.'

'Okay Mister Holt, you are now up, sir. Cheese is running for Ortac, she will manage four knots and Hasard was making at least twelve last we noted her. The French squadron is on the horizon and Ortac before us. What do you make of it?'

'Oh sir, I have already been calculating as such. Masthead is one hundred and twenty feet up, Ortac some few sea miles before us, the French on the horizon making twelve, with the wind and the current, a closure of slightly more than eight knots,' he declared, thinking aloud to himself, only to finally grimace and shake his head. 'I regret, most sorry sir, Cheese will not make it. The French squadron are sailing full and mostly before, so I have added an extra knot or two, to be sure. Aye, sir, Captain Spencer needs to make at least seven or eight knots, if he can, or they will catch up well before Ortac.'

'Bloody hell! But we most desperately need Cheese to pass Ortac. Damnation!' he further vented, thinking hard about the next move. 'Very well, Mister Holt, there is nothing else for it. We will have to take a risk and keep Agamemnon hidden. Signal to Cheese, *"Faster. Eight knots. Make all sail. Urgent."*. Make it quickly now and best let Mister Shillings in on it! Signal to Ortac, *"Silence. Beat to quarters."* and be sure to note their confirmations.'

'Aye, aye, sir! And sir, about sixty minutes, if I may.'

'What? Oh, of course. Very well, pass the word to Mister Middleton. Ask him to get the men fed and in exactly forty minutes we shall beat to quarters and we shall do it quietly if you please, that is if Cheese don't tear away every scrap of canvas in the run.'

Cannon was now being fired from the forecastle of each French brig, hopeful long shots, their chasers banging away with the utmost zeal. Mostly the shots were high, eager to tangle some rigging at the rear. They were a tidy little squadron Cooper was thinking, precisely well spaced and each vessel most proficiently well handled. Cheese was now in range, but only just. The chase had been hard, the brigs strapping on more canvas than what commonly could be considered prudent. The brigs were all in the wind, their sails quivering and shuddering, daring to shake free at any moment. It was a wonder at least one of them had not hopelessly succumbed.

'Sir, they really are crowding their sail,' reported Holt, his young eye keenly digesting the tactics of the entire scene.

'It verily seems they have something of a love affair for our Cheese.'

'Reporting sir, Cheese has just edged past Ortac. They have taken some damage to the rigging, which is likely why her way was somewhat slowed. Captain Spencer is veering course now, putting Ortac in between him and the French.'

'Finally!' Cooper returned, much to his utter relief. 'Spencer has managed that tub as if it was a frigate prancing. Goodness, what a sailor he has become!'

To the untrained eye Ortac was just a rock from which it was necessarily imperative to veer off or see your ship instantly sunk. Hardly would one conceive the existence of a battery of cannon, let alone oversized ones, especially in a time of peace. The islet looked docile enough. The only stirring upon her face presently beheld the beady little glass of Shillings, comfortably settled within the midst of the local gannet population. And oh how the birds hid him, hovering about, swooping, squawking, pecking, ever bustling in the unending pilgrimage to snatch some freshly plucked fish.

The French would never know, but of course Cooper's intended tactics for battle were now somewhat undone. He had planned upon there being one brig, had wisely considered the possible presence of maybe a second, but definitely not a third. With a third brig in the mix, a change in tact was required. Cooper immediately knew what had to be done, although now the task at hand was entirely within Spencer's privy. Those aboard Agamemnon could only but sit back and hope for the best, a most uncomfortable state of affairs for any commander.

'Good god sir!' Holt suddenly announced. 'Cheese has taken a hard hit! She has lost some sheets! She is almost dead in the water!'

'Ah,' Cooper smiled, his good eye still perched within the glass. 'It seems Captain Spencer is the man I thought him to be. Take a closer look. He has pulled the sheet as the last ball passed by.'

'Oh? I see, a ruse then, sir?'

'Indeed, a most cunning ruse. The French will come upon him directly, expecting a tidy snack. That will put Ortac handsomely abaft of our trio, point blank range in fact. And upon all accounts, the way our Mister Shillings handles a cannon, I cannot but think poor Agamemnon will likely miss out on all the fun. Of course, it is a good problem to have, but I fancy we will be watching the entire engagement from here. These Frenchies are very much done for, so I would wager. Tell me, Mister Holt, which French ship would you prefer to add to our squadron, there being three on offer? Hasard is an eighteen gun brig, the other a fourteen and the smallest a ten?'

'I would think sir, considering her intended use, we might need a faster brig and not necessarily the most heavily gunned. I would choose the ten.'

'I concur and even though it is most apparent we cannot capture them all, I am felling somewhat greedy,' he offered with a sly grin. 'Send to Ortac, *"Engage enemy. Destroy fourteen. Disable eighteen."* and send to Cheese, *"Engage enemy. Board ten. Take her a prize."*.'

'Aye, aye, sir!' smiled Holt enthusiastically.

'And there, there it is. Let us witness now the fruits of our labour! Oh and Mister Holt, ask Mister Middleton to beat to quarters and remember, insist he do so quietly. Do it now if you please.'

Cheese was drifting in the current, Ortac on one side whilst the islet hiding Agamemnon sat on the other. Captain Spencer stood tall upon the quarterdeck most carefully eyeing the presence of the oncoming French. Curiously was he garbed in the boorish drab of a merchantman's coat. His hat was floppy and covered near most of his face. Yet there was a roguish glint in his eye, one which could not be dismissed. He may have been master and commander of Cheese, no less a most docile mangy tub, but still was she a naval ship of His Majesty for all intense purposes and oh how he loved her. Presently the deck of Cheese remained mostly clear, just a working crew to man the rigging. The jacks had worked like dogs to mostly keep up the appearance of a slovenly merchantman. Now they most definitely looked the part, wildly scurrying about in the pretence of repairing the rigging. McFee eagerly popped his head out of the hatchway, the rosy cheeks of his Scottish heritage perhaps outstripping even the lustre of his lobster coat. He grinned as any pirate might, ready to take what wasn't his and be damned about thinking twice. Spencer nodded adding a wry smile, no spoken words required.

The French pirate squadron continued to bear down upon Cheese. Blood was in the water, the sparkle of a fat prize in their eye. Spencer looked to Agamemnon gauging the distance once more, handsomely taking personal note of each and every incoming signal. Their endeavour could ill afford a mistake right now, not even a small one. The oncoming action teetered on the precipice. A calm resolve, steered courageously by the steadiness of precise thought, was all but required now. Spencer was carefully summing up the situation, one which unfortunately hadn't planned upon more than two pirates. A detestable annoyance to be sure, but as a captain of the Royal Navy he would accept the hand he had been dealt. He was already addressing what he deemed the necessary amendments to his orders. It was a defining moment of course and as captain of Cheese not only was it wholly his prerogative, but it was his duty. He would sink or swim upon his next decision. How grand he thought, to witness Cooper sweating it out upon Agamemnon's weather deck and sweat the man would, waiting upon the delivery of their new strategy.

Ships of War — Murky Waters

Spencer edged Cheese toward the smallest brig, the ten gun, which in point of fact was notably proving the swiftest. Cheese had only four pounders and to that, only two per side. It was a token gesture of course, armament designed to fend off the smallest of incursion. They would not hold up against what was coming and he knew it. Long before had he wisely reloaded them with grape. He chanced a knowing glance at McFee, for it was below deck where Cheese really harboured her teeth. McFee stood fervently before his men, a complement of hardened marines readying to wildly gnaw upon the splayed innards of their foes.

'Mister Pickering, it is time,' Spencer ordered, calling upon his first officer to hoist a white flag. 'Run up a white flag, directly, if you please, but be very sure to keep our colours flying,' he confirmed explicitly. Cheese was now virtually dead in the water. The white cloth lifted above the poop and as hoped, the cannon upon the ten gun brig fell silent, the French making a direct course to lie alongside and accept their prize.

It was with some satisfaction, momentarily after, Ortac opened fire upon the rear of the French squadron. The first ball flirted with the fourteen gun brig, a monstrous splash attesting to the enormity of the cannon. Mayhem erupted upon the French ships, heads swivelling in all directions. A second shot fizzed through the air. It hit home, taking her mast entirely into the sea. A sickening crack of dismembered oak wailed within the trauma, screeching and groaning amidst the confusion of sheets haplessly plummeting. She immediately began to lose way and hopelessly turned about, untended by wind. The third ball hit home upon the quarter deck, a horribly accurate shot most likely killing every officer upon her. She broached-to and completely lost way, spinning softly now upon her beam, almost as if deserted and hopelessly set adrift. The next few moments ushered forth in absolute silence, Ortac sullen but ever watchful.

The fourteen gun brig had been reduced to shambles, listing and most likely sinking. Yet her colours remained, flapping lightly upon the breeze. It was as if Shillings had paused before the Roman emperor's personal gallery in the midst of the colosseum, waiting patiently for the thumb before bringing down the final blow. In chorus with a downward gesture, a lone distant blast echoed from Ortac. The silence broke utterly, turned heads peering desperately, as if somehow they might glimpse the speeding shot and fend off its incursion. Above Ortac a puff of smoke lingered, the islet engulfed in the wake of a laboured eruption. A thunderous clap followed, gurgling in the far distance as it resonated upon the plane of an endless sea. The whistling cries howled, gathering in intensity with every yard. The shot seemed to ever linger. The sky brooded in its wake, yet the world upon the brig remained as restful as a churchgoing day. In that, the barest of moments, all was well within the world, calm and serene. The shot fell upon the brig, unrepentant, finally disappearing into the hull with an almighty thump. The ship slowly but surely broke apart, minor explosions erupting haphazardly below deck, the cataclysmic striking of tinder reverberating within. The last report had seen the veritable beginning of the end. At least fifty men piled into the sea as the brig surrendered and splintered about them. Slowly her nose slid under, as if drawn by the devil himself. Men were calling helplessly for one another, but there was not a boat to be had. The winter's sea would see not one soul saved and as sure as the sun warmed Shillings's face, they were all doomed.

'Did you see that sir!' Pickering exclaimed, Spencer's first officer. 'She is done for! Ortac has sunk her and only four shots!'

'Very well, Lieutenant,' Spencer evenly replied, hardly able to dismiss even an ounce the scene, so horrific and damning had it proven. The carnage stood barely a cable's length from his quarterdeck and he could not only see men in the water but he could hear their pleas. There was no time and he knew it. He eyed the oncoming ten gun brig with determination and some belated interest, estimating the distance now with Holt's measuring stick. 'Mister Pickering there, strike our white flag, directly if you please. Master, hard over! Be subtle about it now and afford to have us lay aside the brig there! But let them think we are drifting, aimlessly now! All cannon, hold til you see their decks awash with men and for the love of your sweethearts, make it count! Mister McFee, ready your jollies sir!'

The tone of battle was set, dirty business afoot. The fourteen had vanished, summarily sunk right before the eyes of Hasard and her consort, most undeniably and most horribly with all hands lost.

Ships of War — Murky Waters

Immediately did the French brigs both change course, seeking to put some distance between themselves and the cannon. Though it was plainly obvious to Spencer and his crew, the French were still looking about unsure of their attacker. Stunned, scratching their heads and pointing, they were still unable to fathom from where the fire had come, lest it be some phantom. The cannon from the fort reared once more, one shot whizzing smartly through the sheets of Hasard, another shot sucking a sizeable hole in the sea beside her. Shillings it seemed now had her measure, intent upon disabling her.

The captain of Hasard appeared to be taking no chances, likely assuming there was no phantom, perhaps just a first-rate ship somehow perched in stealth on the other side of Ortac. Of course likely was it a ship of the greatest strength judging by the unusual size of the cannon. After the sudden destruction of his first consort, he was no doubt well aware that even just one ball would likely see their end. Nonetheless, Hasard headed before the wind, cleverly choosing to broad reach, so as to slant across the line of fire. What a sight to behold Spencer thought, all available canvas out running hard with cannon shot dropping perilously about her. In course, for such a prevailing wind, he was perhaps thinking they had a little too much canvas, most definitely a sign she was altogether desperate. Nonetheless her antics had sought to sour Ortac's aim somewhat, most of Shillings's balls missing, albeit narrowly.

In defiance, the ten gun brig had contrived to make a direct line for Cheese, rightly thinking the phantom to her rear might preserve her fire, so as not to inadvertently chance sinking one their own. It very much seemed to Spencer that this smaller brig in fact meant to lay alongside Cheese, her boarding parties already on deck and at the ready. This was a seasoned captain, had to be for such a bold and sensible move. The man obviously knew well his business, able to swim with sharks in a pool of bloodied water, escaping without even the slightest bite. It was daring indeed, enough even to perhaps carry the prize right out from under the phantom. And after they had boarded, Spencer knew what would come next, no doubt the rat would chance to slither off to Alderney like some hungered hound snatching stolen game. Bold and perhaps the appropriate move, but the French captain had certainly not bargained upon a hundred well-trained marines, armed to the teeth, all seething heavily below decks verily awaiting their own signal to board.

The ships collided and both sides set upon the other with their grappling irons til they were securely board and board. Grape fired over the French weather deck clearing the way and onto her McFee rushed his men. It was the start for which Spencer had hoped. Two solid minutes saw the absolute demise of everything the brig had ever beheld. McFee's jollies had stationed a strong foothold upon the forecastle, his men streaming upon her as ants to a feast. She now lay trapped, her crew terribly mauled. McFee was eager to carry the battle, for wisely he knew they would fight to the end, especially whilst they retained even an ounce of cunning. The French captain fired upon the grappling lines and rightly so, immediately breaking the brig free. In course he held firm to the helm, attempting to set her away. Cheese could only fire two cannon and presently they were loaded with grape, not shots. It seemed Spencer could do very little as the brig parted. More or less, he would be forced to simply watch the prize limp off, her captain using the gage to escape.

'Fill those sheets now, hard over if you please, let us give chase, everything she's got! Make signal to flag, *"Chasing."*, directly now!' he ordered, watching with intent the fight now unfolding upon the forecastle of the brig. McFee and barely a third of his jollies were scampering about wild as alley cats left to starve and grimly were they barely holding to their positions. It was a minor setback, but curiously the overall plan of battle was falling into place. They had sunk the fourteen with all hands and they had boarded the ten gun brig, the job presently at hand. Hasard was running, as expected, right into the lap of Agamemnon. Spencer grinned as he played the game out in his head. Hasard would not escape this time, for Agamemnon would easily run her down, nothing but sunlight and blue skies within which to hide. He would chase the ten gun prize and upon her baulking at the sixty-four, he would arrange to set the rest of McFee's jollies aboard her.

Spencer noted Agamemnon presenting herself now, slipping out from behind the islet, a slumbering bear gradually rolling from its cave. Hasard too saw her directly and oh how he wished he was a fly on the wall of Hasard's quarterdeck. Surely the French had to strike, or see themselves to a watery grave. It was then the French captain upon Hasard made his decision and Spencer gasped as he beheld Hasard changing course. He was somewhat at a loss. Inexplicable was a word which immediately came to mind. He should not have been astonished of course, for war in itself is flawed and wholly unpredictable. Having indeed taken note of Agamemnon, Hasard did not strike and she did not run, but rather she started to turn.

Hasard turned, but it was not in the direction to which Spencer had thought. She was making her course back to Cheese. Spencer wished to rub his eyes, to wash the vision away, for immediately he recognised the danger. Hasard would join the fight and assist her limping ten gun consort. It was plain and most painfully obvious, Hasard meant to board the ten gun brig, overwhelm McFee and likely scurry off like the rats they were, most definitely straying in opposite directions. At distance, barely would Cheese hazard to present any threat, no real cannon to speak of and of course, Agamemnon could not hope to chase both ships. This was a cunning rat Spencer thought, noting the depth of genius.

'Sir, they're coming back,' reported Pickering.

'Aye, signal to flag, *"Require assistance. Urgent."*,' he brusquely ordered and he swore under his breath, for he knew Agamemnon must beat into the wind to close the engagement. She would likely not make the run in time. Of course Hasard too was beating into the wind, but she very much had already secured a healthy lead and by all accounts it seemed the devil himself sought to now blow vengeance within the fury of her billowing sail.

Cannon from Agamemnon chanced a long shot at Hasard, still very much out of range. Only a raw commander might flinch and Spencer knew this one was as cunning as a rabid fox. Agamemnon fired again, but it served no purpose, the nine pound ball falling harmlessly into the sea. Spencer had to make his decision, or be left wanting. The safety of Ortac's cannon lay abaft. He could make for there and likely be successful, though he would have to chance the ship in coming about. Of course he would also damn McFee and his jollies to their fate. He winced at the thought, now calculating alternatives. Hasard and the ten gun brig were before him, but he had the gage. Hasard's broadside wouldn't be as accurate beating into the wind and if he could weather it and then somehow lay alongside, the rest of the jollies could then board. He might have to accept a broadside from the ten gun brig as well, but only if McFee's fight was waning. Even if Cheese foundered and every man, jack and officer froze to death, it seemed an outcome preferred to turning tail and leaving McFee behind. He must do his utmost. His decision was made.

Hasard was sailing very close to the wind, such beautiful lines and oh how she was bearing down now. Cheese was wearing the ship to meet her, Spencer now personally at the helm. He had to get the angle just right. It was a forgone certainty of course that Cheese would take at least one broadside, but whether the French could hit her was another question. The sixty-fours from Ortac let loose, the balls whizzing above Spencer's head, angels upon his back and oh how he admired Shillings right now. It was a gallant effort, but even Shillings's accomplished accuracy had now succumbed to the extreme range, the shots dropping harmlessly some distance before the French.

The French brigs closed the gap and once Hasard joined her consort, they would have their way with Cheese, in firepower and manoeuvrability. Spencer's only chance would be to stay afloat and live long enough for Agamemnon to enter the fight. It was a mild hope as well that, with the gage, he could press his advantage and board. It was then he humorously recalled McFee's remarks at dinner, about the cat in hell with no claws and how true for Cheese it now was. He nodded thinking about the Scot's jolly smirk and could not but help to laugh aloud, a wry grin gracing his wild visage. Pickering and the other officers were now looking uneasily at him, trying to decide if their captain was afflicted, maddened or just the bravest man they had ever known. Outmatched, outclassed and wholly surpassed in every facet, it seemed Cheese was storming the castle walls with a little more than a broken cart and a handful of rocks, readying to throw into the fray a bag full of clawless yet ferocious kittens.

Cheese was now in range and the order was given to take cover. Almost immediately, the cannon from the ten gun brig let loose, smoke pluming to envelope the entire ship. Spencer waited for the impact, fearing the worst yet hoping for the best. He waited, fearing even one ball to hit home. It was to his utmost surprise to finally realise the ten gun brig had in fact fired upon Hasard. McFee was on the quarterdeck waving more like a mad Irishman than a rabid Scot, the colours summarily struck and his jollies busying to reload her cannon.

'Damned if he didn't do it!' Spencer rejoiced as he noted Agamemnon letting go another chaser. 'McFee, you wild bloody Scot! Damned if the man could not trounce a raging bull in a locked barn! The mad bastard, I will kiss him!'

The hull splintered upon Hasard, chips flying as she weathered the broadside. Men were cast away, some even propelled overboard in the mayhem. Rapidly did she break away, changing course, her captain hard at the helm. The odds had now swung and Hasard was alone. To any seaman, she had one choice, which was to chance a run, lest she struck right there and then. It was what Spencer had expected, it was what Cooper had expected and even McFee had somewhat resigned himself.

To date, the captain of Hasard had been quite inventive in his strategies and this moment was no exception. True to form, he did not strike and he did not run. He was going to fight, his lot seemingly not yet done. Hasard headed directly in between the captured brig and Cheese, with Cheese upon her starboard beam and in tandem, the ten gun brig directly to larboard.

'Sir, she is coming right at us!' Pickering reported. 'I believe she has intentions of doubling upon Cheese and McFee!'

Hasard was edging into a perfect firing position to indeed double upon both Cheese and the brig. McFee was no sailor of course and had no idea what was coming, but Spencer however was resigned they would be soon taking a broadside. Turning now would only hazard the rear of the tub and to be raked stem to stern would see the horrible ruin of what jollies were still below. He could not do anything but admire this French captain, an officer who had outsailed and outthought them at every turn when it mattered most. Of course, the man he wholly despised, a murderer and a bloody tyrant no doubt. The broadsides finally came, a rolling wave, her cannon firing mercilessly in concert with each side of the brig. McFee stood upon the ten gun wholly defenceless, having already fired her broadside with only jollies to fumble the reload. They took the hits hard, mostly rigging and spars falling directly away. Cheese let loose with just two cannon, a cheap shot at the quarterdeck, a subtle message from one captain to the other. It was a short-lived sentiment. Poor Cheese shook and shuddered as each shot reported home, her hull horribly splintering amidst great strips of planking erupting, the aim from Hasard fiendishly true.

'The devil!' swore Spencer, immediately feeling the impact deep in the bowels of the hull, causing him to stumble. He had been around the Royal Navy long enough to know what it meant. Cheese was very much a light framed ship and even though the broadside was only one hundred and twenty-eight pounds, it was more than enough. He suspected she would likely sink now and quite quickly, lest he heave-to in order to furiously pump and repair. Even then, he was doubtful the tub could be saved. He regained his footing and as he stood looking about the damage, the tub already listing, he inwardly declared her a lost cause. Cheese was most sincerely out of the fight now and in all likelihood would go down by the head in matter of minutes.

With the state of the seas about, every man including himself was likely doomed. Hasard's boldness, once again had proven through. Agamemnon would now be painfully forced to choose. She must either chase the prize or go to the aid of Cheese. To chase would damn each and every man upon Cheese to oblivion, lest in the next few moments McFee suddenly acquitted himself in the art of repairing sail.

Hasard turned to find the weather gage, marking her escape almost directly past Agamemnon. She made way at what appeared to Holt to be nigh on fourteen knots. She came about most discourteously, the captain defiantly waving his hat at Cooper, before making good her run to sea amidst a flurry of Agamemnon's long shots. She had escaped easily once before and she most definitely

Ships of War — Murky Waters

sought to do it again, a fast rat, a dirty rodent caught mid-feast upon the galley floor slipping swiftly into the hidden cracks within the wall.

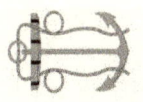

Chapter XVII
Court Martial

Cooper arrived at the dock to find the spectacle of Portsmouth's harbour bustling with officers, however there was only one officer in particular he was inclined to lay eye upon. Finally a young boy frantically grabbed his arm, begging him to follow. The boy led him to a boat, Nelson patiently waiting. Anchored beyond was their destination, His Majesty's Ship Duke, ninety-eight gun, a second-rate line of battle ship, the assigned venue for the court martial proceedings. Beside her forebodingly sat His Majesty's Ship Brunswick, seventy-four gun, a third-rate line of battle ship, presently one of the guard ships of the harbour. Upon any guilty verdicts, customarily the sentence would be carried out there, forthwith, no reprieve and no right of appeal.

'Dirty business this Captain, so it seems, dirty business indeed.'

'Sir?' quizzed Cooper.

Ships of War — Murky Waters

'Climb aboard and we shall talk as we are rowed out to Duke.'

'Surely sir, it is just a formality? Cheese may have been sunk, but Captain Spencer has acted to his utmost, perhaps if I may say, much more, indeed has he not?'

'In course, you are right, naturally. But Coops, there have been some developments and some posturing, to be sure.'

'I can hardly imagine sir, by whom and for what reason, verily?'

'Well, bloody Middleton, to put it bluntly,' Nelson angrily vexed. 'He is quite adamant that it is he who should have been afforded command of our recent prize, claiming seniority. And how did he put it, aye, it should have been him and not your particular friend, Spencer. Never mind that the ultimate decision sits with his commodore, the ignorant buffoon. Since you arrived back from sea, he has been busy writing letters to everyone and anyone who might chance to favour him. He has been most industrious and most fruitfully productive it seems.'

'What! What letters?'

'Oh, the kind which tend to cause the utmost grief,' he ominously confirmed. 'It seems he is of the belief that it was he who orchestrated the capture of the ten gun brig. Damnit, do we have a name for her yet?'

'Achilles, she is Achilles, sir.'

'Oh, indeed,' he outwardly commended, nodding his head in favour. 'How handsome and oh how fitting, for was it not Achilles who was in service to King Agamemnon and was it not Achilles who proved the most difficult son of a Greek to kill, he being so fast and slippery.'

'Quite, sir, a slayer of princes!' he smiled.

'This Middleton has made a right mess of everything, damned if he hasn't!'

'Writing letters is one thing sir, but surely Middleton doesn't believe his own fantasies, does he? What could he really write about anyway?'

'Well, for starters, he nagged on most prodigiously about his captain of course, most disparagingly, said he was offended at every turn, never once afforded his due rank as a lord, the normal griping and whining in course.'

'But that is true sir, the man insisted upon being referred to as *"My Lord"*, instead of lieutenant and I wouldn't have a bar of it of course.'

'Quite. And right you are. Never in life, not even for a bar of gold, whatever is the man thinking. But the main of it is, these proceedings have now come to the attention of a certain muster of Whigs, all of whom in course oppose the powers that be, that is, those currently wielding the Admiralty. They will seek to use this incident to their gain and to lever the political demise of Pitt and his Tory followers.'

Cooper's face melted somewhat when he heard this. A cannon ball he could accept, even a musket shot and ever should a blade be thrust his way, he was more than ready. Indeed, he was quite in tolerance of the dangers faced at sea or in battle, even accommodating the incessant pushing and pulling when it came to his career. He was so very much acquainted and ever so used to it, but he was very much a fish out of water when it came to this kind of political posturing and self-promotion. And this latest attack would be centred upon his particular friend and for what, to be proffered as some political pawn. Even worse, he now felt somewhat at fault having entertained Middleton's antics when he should have acted to remove him, or at the very least, limit the damage he might do.

'The upstart even wrote to his uncle you know, Rear Admiral Sir Charles Middleton, the very same who was third sea lord and comptroller of the navy until just recently. But don't worry about Sir Charles, as I have it on very good authority he will not be intervening. Sir Charles is quite well acquainted with our promoters in the Admiralty and is a Tory of course. And now he has some distinct distaste for his nephew. It seems Middleton had most slyly arranged his post on Agamemnon by surreptitiously using his uncle's interest. However, the only thing being, his uncle didn't know one scrap about it! Outrageous!'

'Oh, I see sir, makes perfect sense. The man is barely rated able and has the preponderance and singular ability to upset every other man within a stone's throw. He has been a most unnecessary nuisance since he arrived. I very much wish to see the back of him.'

'Well, what should have been a formality, as you say, has now verily turned into the most prodigious scrap, our poor Captain Spencer the turkey in the sandwich. I am most heartily sorry to say, but they mean to see him hanged Coops. There is this grubby fellow, Nathaniel, one of the Whigs and he has been going about the panel of captains currying favour to damn our man to the nearest noose. Dirty business indeed, but of course we know a few things too about warfare and I have arranged some *"first-rate"* assistance to our cause, which you will see soon enough. Now, let us repair aboard Duke and upon doing so, I must insist that this be the last time we speak until it is over. Trust me Coops, we will get our man out of there!'

Captain Charles Prescot Spencer, His Majesty's Ship Cheese, marched down the aisle, best dress uniform, sword at his side. Approaching the trial bench, he removed his sword and presented it by laying it officially upon the tribunal's table. Before him were thirteen officers, all post-captains, their faces grim and their demeanour most commonly unaccommodating. He looked closely for the first time and presiding, to his absolute surprise and relief, was one Captain Horatio Nelson, who managed in return a wholesome half look of reassurance. Nelson nodded as he accepted the sword, turning the tip athwart, thus signifying the trial had now commenced. Spencer's eyes hung on his sword. To be exonerated he very well knew that the hilt must be turned back to him. Should they turn the tip his way, it would signify a guilty verdict, a sentence which could vary from the triviality of just a verbal reprimand to the absolute entirety of certain death by hanging. Yet as Spencer prepared to sit, the entire gathering rose, a hush falling within the cabin. He was astounded as he turned. It was First Sea Lord, Admiral Hood. The panel of course immediately stood.

'Honoured sir,' Nelson complimented knowingly. 'May we offer the Admiral a seat?'

'Ah, Captain Nelson, thank you sir, thank you. However, in point of fact, if you do not mind, I would very much enjoy taking your seat, on the panel?'

'Sir, of course, I have no objections and in fact, would be honoured.'

'But sir, we already have thirteen?' Nathaniel interrupted. 'And this is merely just a sundry proceedings sir, simple loss of a ship to enemy fire, hardly worthy of your esteem, sir.'

Cooper noted immediately that the first shot in the battle had been fired and it was most brilliant. Thirteen captains, the maximum, had been selected for the proceedings and it was good wager Nathaniel had bolstered the tribunal with his own picks. And now the man was brazenly willing to confront the First Sea Lord of the Admiralty. What an upstart, but Cooper also had to admit, it was a good try. In course the man would be undone, for a brig cannot outmatch a first-rate. Cooper well knew Admiral Hood, had served under him and was presently serving under him in point of fact. If the Admiral wished to be on the tribunal, there was very little which could prevent it. The whole scene sniffed of Nelson he lastly thought who was outwardly quite unabashedly oblivious to the whole matter, a poker face to be admired and a master tactician whether on or off the sea.

'Captain Nelson, does this officer speak for the tribunal sir?'

'Oh no, My Lord, he does not,' Nelson confirmed sullenly, now bowing his head in apology. 'Those last comments will be struck from the record if you please,' he loudly ordered.

'Ah, very well, then you had better make room for two, Captain, the Admiral of the Fleet is making his way directly.'

'Sir, did you say Admiral of the Fleet, meaning Admiral Forbes?' quizzed Nathaniel, somewhat flabbergasted in disbelief.

'Aye, I believe he is still presently Admiral of the Fleet, last time I looked anyhow. And I suspect he is lingering upon the weather deck presently. We will both sit in and I shall preside, unless the tribunal has any objections?'

'Absolutely none sir, I yield my chair. My last act presiding will be to decide who must vacate, so, in fairness, let it be the two lowest ranking captains, whomever they may be?'

'Whomever they may be? It was laughable,' Cooper thought, inwardly grinning like a cat caught in a fish house. Of course Nelson knew who they bloody well were. Whatever deals Nathaniel had brokered were now somewhat mute. His two departing captains exited the scene more like a pair of crowned checkers hastily wiped from the board. Cooper had to physically check himself. He had so very much wagered upon there being a Nelson surgical strike, but rather more like dismissing a single chess piece one at a time. This opening salvo was too much and it sent Cooper giddy inside. He immediately compared it to watching a well-played act at the theatre, each player most handsomely discharging their lines when so required, the act playing out with nowhere else to go. His commodore's strategy, not to mention his absolute cunning, was as sharp as he had ever remembered. It was as if he had arranged two cannonades upon a helpless enemy, without even the remotest chance of a return. There was no way Hood and Forbes would ever allow Spencer to swing, not whilst they had voice on the tribunal. But the battle had only just begun and even a guilty verdict might see the end of his particular friend's naval career. To have rearranged the panel at the last moment as such was a dazzling move, no doubt taking Nathaniel by complete surprise. Short of seeing the man somehow miraculously regroup, a quick shuffling of chairs would now see the proceedings under Tory control. Spencer might now even be rightly dismissed of all charges, which is commonly the outcome of course.

'Captain Nelson, if you please, would you kindly read the report of Agamemnon, Captain Cooper commanding.'

'Aye sir, but Captain Cooper is in fact present. If it pleases, I will arrange him to read it, it being his report?'

Cooper immediately stood. It was another brilliant ploy on Nelson's behalf. Cooper's reputation preceded him and instantly all eyes focused directly upon his magnificent sword, a sword which had by all accounts cut two spies into two exact halves just with one swish. The tale of Captain Lefty had reached Portsmouth well beyond some time ago and lest one wanted to chance living out their life remainder very much learning to write and drink only with their left, one would most definitely proffer their sincerest apologies upon untowardly interacting with the captain. Even the panel of captains chanced a sly glance, marvelling at the sword's curved nature and its rather short design. Naturally they were all painfully aware about his reported friendship with The Prince William. His report would likely not be challenged, such was his current standing.

"Agamemnon, at sea, Channel Islands. It is my solemn duty to report upon our recent action which saw the unfortunate sinking of our support vessel, Cheese, four gun. Awaiting upon her arrival, her masts only just in sight, her being upon the horizon hull-down, a clear day with strong wind, she was set upon by three pirate brigs, being of eighteen, fourteen and ten gun respectively. Agamemnon, very much to leeward, immediately beat into the wind, full and by, close hauled, endeavouring to engage. It is my pleasure to report the fourteen to have been immediately sunk, regrettably with all hands lost. Cheese running full and before, under very heavy fire, closed with Agamemnon most handsomely, much to her and her captain's absolute credit. However, her being hit and by all accounts very much damaged, was unable to properly continue. Captain Spencer ordered her to instead turn and contrived to lie alongside the ten, whereby he proceeded to board, Major McFee of the marines leading. After some heavy exchanges, Cheese, four gun, did take her a prize. The eighteen gun then set upon Cheese and in course, she suffered irreparable damage from cannon and did take on water and, directly, did she most unfortunately sink. Agamemnon rendered assistance and all hands were safely taken aboard, including Captain Spencer and his officers. The eighteen, much to our absolute regret, took the opportunity to slip away, like the dog she was. Your servant, Captain Cooper."

'Like the dog she was? Very well, Captain Cooper, sir,' Nathaniel queried. 'Would you please attest that every word thus written is the truth?'

'It is the ship's log,' Admiral Hood protested vehemently. 'So of course it must be the truth or the good Captain here would be in ruin of his duty and be subject to reproach. What would you expect him to answer? Do we really need to ask that?'

Ships of War — Murky Waters

'Withdrawn, sir,' Nathaniel acquiesced, sensing some angst. 'Very well, let us turn to Mister Spencer and perhaps he might confirm to the tribunal, if it pleases, that this was in fact his first command?'

'Sir,' Nelson interrupted, pleading to Hood and very much taking away all attention that it was in fact Spencer's first command. 'The accused should be afforded his rightful rank, should he not? He was commander of Cheese and is therefore Captain Spencer and not Mister Spencer?'

'Well Captain Nathaniel, what do you say sir?'

'Apologies, sir,' he quickly complied. 'Very well, Captain Spencer, it is my duty to inform you that you have been summoned to these proceedings to answer for the loss of His Majesty's Ship Cheese, for which you were master and commander. Is it your contention that, as commander, you did your utmost to ensure your ship would prevail and that it was lost only by circumstances beyond your influence?'

'Sir,' Nelson cleverly interrupted, pleading again to Hood. 'It is my understanding that Cheese is not His Majesty's ship and, as such, I am at a loss to wonder if Captain Spencer can even legally be answerable for its loss?'

'What? Well, whose bloody ship is it then?'

'I believe the honour of its ownership falls to Captain Cooper, who had purchased it from his own funds in order to ensure supply to Agamemnon.'

'Oh, indeed, how enterprising!' he commended. 'I see, well, what the bloody hell are we all doing here then?'

'If I may sir,' Nathaniel offered. 'Agamemnon is commissioned by His Majesty and Captain Spencer is in fact one of her crew, only being made commander of Captain Cooper's private ship Cheese thereafter. Therefore, Captain Spencer is commissioned by His Majesty and remunerated by His Majesty, as such. It does not matter which ship is lost, only that he in fact, in the service of His Majesty, did preside over said lost ship. I submit that we must determine his actions and how it came to pass that his ship was lost. Furthermore, we must determine what he in fact did to prevent the loss. I concede that the loss of the ship itself is not in question, but moreover are we concerned with the honour of an officer of the Royal Navy.'

'Well, Captain Nelson, what say you sir?'

'I withdraw my question, sir.'

'Very well, let us hear from the first witness?'

'Aye, Lord Middleton, sir,' prompted Nathaniel.

'Lord Middleton?' Admiral Hood questioned, somewhat confused. 'Does His Lordship serve His Majesty in the Royal Navy? This is a military tribunal, not a common court.'

'Aye, sir, he is first officer of Agamemnon.'

'Does he have a bloody rank then?'

'Aye sir, lieutenant.'

'Then bring Lieutenant Middleton forward, if you please.'

'Your Lordship, you have heard the account from the log, sir, do you agree with it and is there anything else you might offer?'

It was the standard question of course, asked of every officer at every proceedings where a ship had been lost. In the history of most every other proceedings, it was always duly answered in course, mostly affirming the captain's account. To say anything else would only invite terror and possible reprimand, following firstly after of course a most severe probing by the tribunal. Indeed any foul answer would most heartily promote an escalated inquiry, an inquest very much broadened and hardly just confined to the accused. In times past, related officers not even charged had been known to hang, suddenly brought up to the dock from the apparent safety of the viewing area. Indeed it was well known not to play with fire on this question. Cooper knew it, Spencer knew it and every other officer present, worth their salt, most painfully knew it.

'No sir, it is not accurate and aye, I have more to offer the tribunal,' he arrogantly claimed, much to the chagrin and absolute mortification of every officer present and not just the officers of Agamemnon. More than a few lay back in their seats slumped in dismay, their faces fearfully mindful of a tsunami peaking the near horizon and their ship nowhere to go.

'Indeed, very well Your Lordship? Pray tell?'

'Firstly, I do attest and confirm that Major McFee and his marines, some of them anyway, were upon the ten gun brig fighting most rightly to take her. But plainly he did not take her. I submit that she only struck after Agamemnon had fired a warning shot upon her, the honour of the capture therefore going to Agamemnon.'

'Lieutenant, are you saying Captain Cooper has falsified his log, falsified sir, do you hear me? That is a most serious accusation!'

'Not at all, sir, but I submit he definitely was mistaken, the product of an inadvertent error, that's all. In the realm of all probabilities, it is just not possible or even plausible that Major McFee could have taken the brig. The Major, no doubt gallant, was very much outnumbered, the brig having had some eighty men.'

'But the numbers here on muster indicate almost sixty marines?' responded Nathaniel knowingly, almost feeding Middleton the answer.

'Aye, but that muster is wrong, or yet to be updated sir. Major McFee had a hundred jollies, no less and they all were aboard Cheese, but only perhaps thirty had boarded the brig, the rest being left behind due to...'

'Incompetence?'

'If you will, sir, aye,' he agreed. 'That is, of course, if you are referring to the matter upon how the brig was so easily able to break free of the grappling irons. And it would not have broken free had command been properly attended.'

'It begs me to ask Lieutenant,' Nelson probed slyly and evenly. 'Are you not senior to Captain Spencer, on the List of Lieutenants?'

'Aye, sir, I have seniority.'

'Then why is it you were not in command of Cheese?'

'I had declined, sir, affording Captain Spencer command.'

'Affording him you say? But you declined command, full well knowing Captain Spencer would be promoted. Furthermore, if you had thought Captain Spencer to be in any way inadequate, then sir, I submit you have failed your duty. If you believed any other replacement officer incompetent, you should have taken command. So, either you actually had faith in Captain Spencer or you had failed your duty?'

'Well Lieutenant?' Admiral Hood asked nonchalantly. 'Which is it now?'

'I believe, I had faith, sir. Allow me to rephrase my previous statement, in that, should I have been in command, the ropes would not have been cut away, but that is to say Captain Spencer perhaps was not to blame, only in that he did not possess the required definitive skill, that is, say, of someone like myself.'

'What I would like to know,' Admiral Hood suddenly piped. 'How is it, how is it I say, that a four gun brig managed to defeat a fourteen and a ten and here's the *"cheese"* if you will,' he grinned, chuckling at his own witticism. 'How did she do this, with her commander, as you say Lieutenant Middleton, inept or certifiably lacking the required definitive skill? I must ask you sir, how many times have you been in battle?'

'I have not yet had that privilege, sir.'

'No, you have not and yet you sit there as if you had the wisdom of Lord Rodney. No, no, no, what Captain Spencer achieved has to be a bloody marvel. Wish I bloody well had been there see it!'

'Sir, with respect, I must inform you that Cheese did not sink the fourteen. Her cannon were loaded with grape only and only four pounders at that.'

'Well it does not so much matter, sir,' Nelson interrupted, most desperately attempting to ensure the existence of Ortac Island remained hidden from public knowledge. 'If Agamemnon had fired upon her and sunk her, it is all by and by. The fact is that Captain Spencer, in charge of a virtually toothless tiger, managed somehow to lure in his prey and take her a prize. Now sir, I submit that is a feat to be lauded!'

'Indeed, indeed!' Nathaniel congratulated. 'But I am curious as to how Captain Spencer did in fact achieve said feat? It does so make me wonder?'

'Aye, I believe I can illuminate the proceedings, sir,' Middleton piped. 'I regret to report the improper use by Captain

Spencer of his colours, a breach of international law! He did knowingly and wilfully, by all accounts, raise a white flag to lure in the enemy. Upon the enemy closing, without them firing mind you, he then struck the white flag and proceeded to fight her.'

'With grape in all four cannon?' added Admiral Hood sarcastically.

'But Admiral, he raised a white flag and then fired upon the enemy!'

'Oh, I think you will find that Captain Spencer is very much entitled to raise a white flag, it not being any indication of surrender whatsoever. In fact, it merely is a request or an invitation to treat with the opposition, to have a discussion. Of course, at sea, the only method to legally surrender is to strike the colours, which by all accounts Captain Spencer never did. As long as he did not fire upon the brig whilst the white was up, he is in his exact rights! Now, it behoves me Lieutenant Middleton and you too Captain Nathaniel to think you both are very much absent of mind on this matter?'

'But sir, I protest, a white flag is a flag of surrender.'

'Captain Nathaniel, sir, that only applies to the army and last I looked, we are in the bloody navy. Sir, I believe I may have to ask you to remove yourself from this tribunal. You must acquaint yourself with the laws of the sea and know them directly, or there is no place here for you to rule over someone who apparently does. I think also we may excuse this witness, there not being so very much of use in the testimony. Aye, both of you will go.'

'But sir, Captain Cooper hid his ship behind an islet, avoiding battle, failed to properly make use of the weather gage, foolishly allowed Hasard to escape and all the while Agamemnon never hit a damned thing. I am the ranking officer and he failed to put me in command of the prize and...'

'Marines! Remove that officer! Lieutenant, get hold of yourself sir!'

'Well, I have a question,' Admiral Forbes offered, who had been most prodigiously quiet until now. 'Captain Spencer, you say Cheese was cruising to Agamemnon with supplies. What kind of supplies, sir?'

'Well sir, we were carting the marines, nothing else, from Chatham to the prearranged rendezvous, which is why Captain Cooper was moored by an islet, our tub not the swiftest cat in the alley, sir.'

'Lieutenant Middleton claims you had a hundred marines on board and curiously that included their captain, Major McFee?'

'Aye, sir?'

'And how many marines were upon Agamemnon?'

'Well, none, sir. We had taken the present complement with us.'

'I see, to guard the cargo?'

'In course, sir.'

'The cargo being new marines?'

'Aye, sir,' he nodded.

'Marines to guard marines?'

'Aye, sir.'

'I see. And after the ten gun brig cut the grappling irons, you gave chase, which is when the eighteen hammered you?'

'Aye, sir.'

'But you fired back with your cannon?'

'Aye, sir.'

'A full broadside?'

'Aye, sir, both of them.'

'Indeed, so Captain Spencer, we are to understand that Cheese, a small merchantman tub, as you put her, Captain Cooper's privately owned support ship so it has been said, was busying herself from Chatham being quite alone except for her four cannon, in order to meet at sea with Agamemnon. And suddenly in the utmost of surprise was she ruthlessly set upon by a most formidable pirate squadron? And upon your four gun tub accepting battle with these three most heavily armed brigs which boasted a sum total of forty-two gun, the sum of a heavy frigate no less, a hundred jollies which just happened to be crammed into the hold, all armed to the teeth, simply popped out as you laid her alongside the brig? Then as I understand it, upon the ten running like a frightened hare, your very much damaged tub, so Captain Cooper has attested, then miraculously found herself repaired enough and able to give chase? Thereafter the prize was taken and you proceeded to engage the eighteen, but not before you reloaded all four cannon with grapeshot?'

'Aye sir, a double load sir, of grapeshot,' he unashamedly replied.

The Admiral chuckled as he ran the scenario through his mind, the picture of the engagement quite clear now. He peered knowingly left and right, eyeing each member of the tribunal, all of them lightly nodding. It seemed apparent to any fighting captain, Tory or Whig, the entirety of the operation was hardly a coincidence and that the situation warranted the captain of Cheese be due either a hearty commendation or be directly certified into a strait waistcoat.

'Curious, very curious, indeed,' Admiral Forbes complimented. 'You sir, it seems, either have the luck of the Irish or are an exemplary officer. Let us hope it is both!' he happily added, leaning forward with a most magnanimous grin to point the handle of the sword towards Spencer.

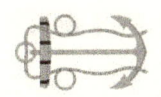

Chapter XVIII
Reckoning

Agamemnon slipped through the Channel waters once again with Ortac in her sights, her crew most happy just to be at sea once more. Of course, in point of fact, they hadn't really been anywhere else. It was true they had anchored in the harbour at Portsmouth, but not one soul was allowed on shore. With prize money due and tales of battle to tell, the captain of Agamemnon was more or less inclined to allow not even the ship's cat to leave. Much to the displeasure of every man and jack, not even the bum boats carting ladies of the night had been permitted to berth. Cooper was taking no chances and oh he knew they might despise him for it, but they were jacks and another prize would likely see them through it.

'Well Spence, your first taste of command. It was just such a tub, ol' Cheese.'

'Aye, she was not a fighting ship by any means, but she was

one which took us war nonetheless.'

'And she took the prize!'

'Aye,' Spencer smiled. 'I shan't forget her, CCPS Cheese!'

'What's that, 'ey?' asked Cooper.

'Oh, Captain Cooper's Private Ship, CCPS Cheese, sir.'

'Oh, how clever, hah!'

'Well in course, I cannot take all the credit. Did you not know it is quite the new thing as to refer to His Majesty's ships as HMS?'

'Really?' questioned Cooper dubiously.

'Aye, since eighty-nine, I heard tell of HMS in respect of Phoenix.'

'Clever, but hardly will it ever catch on, I suspect.'

'Quite, tradition is tradition.'

'Losing your first command, sunk and all that, I do hope you are not so very much put off by it all? You are a fine commander Spence.'

'No, being sunk doesn't frighten me and the thought of battle far from frightens me. In course, I am very much ashamed to say I am most wickedly more frightened of our own navy, the oars of justice, indeed. That fellow Nathaniel, what a blackguard cove he was, quite bent on putting me in the noose, the Whig dog!'

'He will get his, in course. I doubt he will ever fly his flag after that performance. Anyway, just so you know, at one stage I had verily decided upon thereafter lopping his head right off, that is should you have swung.'

'Quite, well, perhaps some kind of thank you is in order?'

'Don't worry, it won't take long to fit out Achilles and then you will command a ship with some actual cannon this time.'

'You are not offering it to Middleton?'

'The man is either grossly inept or he is a cracker short of a biscuit. I honestly cannot tell which? But Achilles will not be his, lest the world darkens beyond all known grief. Nelson won't have a bar of it either, already spoken to his uncle, in course. Did you note him at the proceedings? He was acting somewhat out of character, even for him.'

'Perhaps that was his true form sir, meaning what we firstly saw of him was some watered down version?'

'Perhaps you are right, but the way he gobbled on, it was most uncommon. He was close to hysteria, don't you think?'

'I think I was close to hysteria, if anyone was. After all, it was my neck and not Middleton's on the block, so to speak.'

'Oh come now Spence, don't be so dramatic, never was your neck on the block.'

'No?'

'Aye of course not, the Royal Navy either shoots you or hangs you, they ain't going to line you up on a block lopping heads off, oh what a god awful mess that would be. Come now, what a fellow you are.'

'Of course and so much the better for it,' he dryly grinned. 'But sir, I am not ignorant of what you and what Commodore Nelson did for me.'

'Well, who else would take command of Achilles? I think we were somewhat forced to save you.'

'Of course,' he laughed. 'Capital name sir, for our brig.'

'Aye, indeed it is. Even Commodore Nelson thought so. For such was Agamemnon a powerful Greek king, one of the most famous in fact, well known for his successful siege of Troy. Goodness, imagine going to war all because of a woman, not that Greeks need a reason of course. Worse than Scots I believe, if that is at all even possible. But it was well that Achilles fought for him, for had he not slain Hector at the gates, maybe they would not have won through. But the tact of the Trojan Horse, what capital strategy, indeed, such trickery. And it is a sentiment we shall embrace in our war with France.'

'Beware the Frenchie bearing gifts, sir?' adapted Spencer comically.

'Ha, quite, but really, when have they ever been so generous?'

'And this new lot of Jacobins, upon all accounts, seems so much tighter!'

'Thank you Mister Spencer, I believe you are next officer of the watch and I believe I just heard the bell. Now be so kind as to invite Mister Middleton to my cabin, it being the end of his watch. In reckoning, there are some bones which need to be picked!'

Ships of War — Murky Waters

'Mister Middleton, it has come to my attention that you have written a disparaging letter, sir?'

'Which, is my prerogative, Captain.'

'So you do not deny it! And your performance at the proceedings sir, I must inform you as to my utmost displeasure in what was spoken.'

'Which, is also my prerogative, Captain.'

'I would hasten to think that I am not the only one Lieutenant, who was most aghast, most mortified sir, to hear you disagree with the ship's log. Now, I am fully aware that the Admiralty has always encouraged lieutenants to report negatively upon the actions of their captain, otherwise they would not as such insist upon each and every lieutenant keeping their own log. But sir, there are very few lieutenants who would do such a thing and your failure to agree with the log can only serve to immediately disparage yourself. My bewilderment and utmost complaint of bafflement is only further promoted to the highest state of indignation by my understanding that you in fact had signed the bloody thing. Secondly, to not agree with its contents most incontestably invites and indeed opens up a *carte blanche*, free unmitigated rein of the tribunal, their powers of further scrutiny and prosecution undeniable. Now, you should not need to be told that this scrutiny will not just be limited to the accused. All you achieved was cutting off your nose to spite your face. You are damned lucky, damned lucky I say, to have come through the proceedings unscathed and free from charges.'

'Who? Me, sir? I am lucky? I rather much think it is you sir who is lucky, lucky to remain in command!'

'That is mutinous talk Lieutenant! I warn you to tread carefully.'

'If you say so, of course sir, I meant no such intent.'

'Your lack of understanding in this matter is worryingly dangerous and if you cannot still fathom how perilously close you brought the ship's officers, including yourself sir, to be damned under such unnecessary scrutiny, then you have no place as first officer here.'

'Am I not permitted my station and to report the truth?'

'I remind you sir, most emphatically, when first you came aboard you were informed of the need for the utmost secrecy, in that our commission had come directly from the King himself! And here you are in the proceedings, a very public one mind you, sprouting on, even mentioned Hasard by name. Good god man, what were you thinking!'

'Sir, I say I was most cognisant of your orders and my duty. I point out that never once did I mention Ortac, or the fort we have built there. I regret the mentioning of Hasard, it being just a slip, in the heat of it all.'

'And why is it you are so heated? Why? Is it because I, as your commissioned superior, have issued orders which don't sit well with you? Sir, this is the Royal Navy, not your private romp! Following, you have written letters to countless members of the gentry and countless members of the service, including your good uncle, who by the way is most heartily annoyed with you now. You have taken liberties sir, too many liberties above your station as first officer. One way or the other, it is going to end.'

'If you think you can disrate me sir, you had better think again.'

'Oh I can disrate you, but unfortunately that will not be happening. It seems you know too much and would pose a substantial threat to our ongoing operations here. So it has been jointly decided, you will stay on.'

'Jointly decided?'

'Good god man, do you still not comprehend? This operation sir, our commission, is very much the privy of many more than just Commodore Nelson and myself. Indeed, our immediate promoters, our commanders, include not only the First Lord of the Admiralty, the First Sea Lord, the Admiral of the bloody Fleet, but also the Prime Minister himself! They have told me, in no uncertain terms, to tell you quite clearly and quite precisely, in the form a child might understand, that should you fall out of line again, I have permission to treat you as a mutineer.'

'Preposterous! My uncle will hear of this!'

'Here sir, is a letter for you! You will note the signatories present, each and every man aforementioned a party. And please to note, the inclusion of your good uncle's signature and below that, please to note a most important signature, being George III, the King! Lieutenant, for the good sake of our country, I ask you to see reason. We are in a state of war without the formal declaration and England's naval presence is our foremost concern. I am in command, not you and I assure you, I was not picked due to seniority. If you can see your way to this reason, I will endeavour to teach you your trade. I will help you every step of the way. Promotion will come as you distinguish yourself.'

'Captain, with respect, there is very little you could ever teach me. You may or may not know, but I have seniority over you in the List of Lieutenants. As soon as you are relieved from this commission, that seniority will return.'

'Very well,' he gasped, somewhat at an end. 'But I will ask you to remember well this moment, for what happens next will now be upon your own head.'

'Oh, I'll be remembering this moment, you can count on it, sir.'

'I can see there is no dissuading you. Indeed, very well, so be it,' he sighed, shaking his head. 'Aye, so be it. Lieutenant, I must inform you officially sir, that I am most painfully aware of some operational occurrences, of which, you feature most heavily in each instance. And may I say, all of which have given me great pause.'

'I have no idea sir, what you may be talking about.'

'You do realise should anything happen to me, or should I be off ship, that you will be left in command, in command sir of some five hundred souls and solely responsible for the King's ship, which replacement cost is somewhat around fifty thousand pounds?'

'Of course, sir.'

'Very well, so it is my wish, seeing how it is an imperative matter you know your job and I say job sir, not duty, that we immediately come to an understanding.'

'How so?'

'I must be assured of your competency. Your rebellious attitude aside, these mishaps you have partaken in do not afford the greatest confidence. Aye, so solve some problems for me and should your answers be adequate, I will say no more.'

'What? Now, sir?'

'Aye Lieutenant, now, or please consider your commission forthwith to be at an end, consequences be damned. Answer competently and all is forgiven. Fail to answer competently and I shall expect to have your undertaking, your full and immediate undertaking, do you hear me? Now, shall we begin?'

'Oh, very well.'

'Let us begin with a tactical poser then. Our first question concerns your ship in high seas, in fact a storm belted sea with high wind. The ship is slipping down into the waves upon each surging roll. We are running directly before the storm and an enemy third-rate is bearing down from abaft, her chasers barking and her nine pounders now breaching our sail. You are in command, your orders, sir?'

'Oh please Captain, am I to now pass for lieutenant? I have already been through my exam, sir. What next, am I to box the compass?'

'Well, at least this time you did not protest, some progress at least. But I will have your answer sir, now!'

'Oh, very well,' he huffed. 'It is an enemy of an equal class. We must of course turn and fight.'

'I see, turn and fight you say?'

'Aye, it is our duty, to do our utmost, sir.'

'And by doing your duty, as you say, you have just killed every man aboard! Damnation man, is your interpretation of doing your utmost to ensure every scrap of sail is ripped from the yards, your command needlessly put to ruin? You cannot turn the ship Mister Middleton! You are running before the wind and you cannot turn sir, for she would immediately stall and broach-to, the swell so overwhelming that her sheets would lose wind and loosen upon the ship falling into the bottom of each lull. The ship would be taken aback, put on her beam ends and founder. Every man, jack, jolly and officer would be sent to the bottom, mind you, with absolutely no chance of rescue from our enemy, the storm preventing such kindness...'

'Let us try again. Lieutenant, the squadron is in heavy fog and has already silently beaten to quarters. A first-rate from an enemy squadron is very much known to be within reach, but you are hidden for the time being. From the quarterdeck, you suddenly see a ship, broad, three points off the larboard quarter, bearing diagonally down. You are in command, your orders, sir?'

'I would have our larboard decks fire at once. I would have the master turn the ship so they are off our beam and I would instruct them to aim low into her hull, for effect, sir. Upon firing, I would order the cannon reloaded and the master to immediately steer us clear.'

'No, no, no, sir! You cannot fire into just any ship that peeks her bowsprit out of the fog. You are part of a squadron and should the ship be indeed one of His Majesty's, you would have committed an offence punishable by death! Mister Middleton, has it escaped you that you have masts upon your ship, some two hundred feet high! Would it not be preferable to instruct the tops to search for other masts, including colours? You must identify your enemy sir! Now, further of interest is why you might be instructing your crew to aim the cannon low? I will have to assume that in your response you did in fact firstly turn the ship, or you wouldn't hit a bloody thing. Then I assume you instructed them to aim low and then gave the order to fire?'

'Aye, before, in course sir.'

'As captain, you must be exact and precise, or peril will most certainly follow. Now, assuming she was an enemy first-rate, by firing low, all you have done is poke the bear. She will still be manoeuvrable and certainly have enough cannon and men to easily capture you. Afterwards, upon being imprisoned, you will have the pleasure of drowning in the hold of your enemy's ship as she slowly succumbs to flooding. Would it not be more preferable to fire your broadside somewhat higher at the rigging or masts, thus diminishing her capacity to turn and fire and most importantly her capacity to chase? You might even direct some of the lower deck cannon to aim at the rudder? She being a vastly superior ship, a line of battle ship, it is a no-win situation of course and most rightly, you must either strike or try your luck. Should you choose the latter, you had best know your business...'

'The questions sir, if I may, are not fair. You have not presented them equally.'

'I see,' Cooper sighed. 'I would like to afford you an education in seamanship and battle tactics Mister Middleton, but we just do not have the luxury of time. In course, the reality is that we are most likely to succeed in our endeavours, which means we will take a prize, which means said prize will be taken into our squadron, which means you, you sir, will be afforded as captain of one of them. You must know your business sir, or our fleet will be undone before it even sails. I assure you that these questions are indeed simple, merely those asked upon an examination for lieutenant...'

'Very well, we can try this at a later time, to be fair. Instead, let us now directly discuss some of these mishaps to which you have been party. You will be afforded the chance of course to defend yourself, if you can. In particular, I must firstly bring to your attention said occurrences to which I wholly stand somewhat flabbergasted and most surely amazed. For example, upon our engagement with the French squadron, were you not ordered to beat to quarters?'

'Which, I did, sir?'

'Aye, but not quietly? And you were ordered to do so quietly! Mister Shillings informs me he heard us all the way over on Ortac.'

'A cowardly order sir, hardly worthy of the Royal Navy.'

'A tactical order if you please Lieutenant! You nearly gave away our position and also the element of surprise! That is unacceptable. It is also tantamount to a failure to follow orders, punishable by the Articles.'

'If you say, sir.'

'I bloody well do say Mister Middleton! Now it is also my understanding that prior, whilst I was repaired below and the ship was making her way out of the Medway, the ship did lose way, all sails taken aback and we floundered about for the next cable length, like a bloody fish flapping on the dinner table the cook having forgot to gill it? It is my understanding you were officer of the watch?'

'Aye, but a small misunderstanding sir, no damage done and the responsible reprimanded.'

'Indeed?' he remarked, his brow turned in, wondering how the man might have reprimanded himself. 'I am also of the understanding that the ship did for some part, run aground?'

'Aye, but it was just a little scraping, sir, nothing damaged.'

'A little scraping! Do you not comprehend that grounding the ship at any time is also punishable under the Articles?'

'I am not aware, sir.'

'Not bloody aware? And worse, I am further told that in the process you lost one of our anchors?'

'Aye, but sir, I did in fact retrieve it and may I say, no such shoal was present upon the chart and no call came from the top.'

'Which brings me to the next, for it is my understanding that you personally ordered Sergeant Eagle to remove his nest from the main mast?'

'Aye sir, of course, it is not regulation. I ordered Corporal Eagle to take it down and resume his duty from the masthead, per regulation.'

'Were you not aware that I had not only commended Eagle for his ingenuity and innovation, an innovation sir not ever before seen on any ship I have known, but I also rated him sergeant for his cunning and zeal and made him responsible for our new lookout brigade. Have you not noticed the feathers they proudly wear upon their uniforms? God damn it sir, did you just say Corporal Eagle? Please do not tell me you disrated the man!'

'In my defence, sir, that happened before we had come to our understanding?'

'Come to our understanding? Understanding? Be damned when I speak to an officer aboard it is an order and be damned if our understanding wasn't an order! You should have had the good sense to remedy any actions which happened prior to my order, or at least broach the subject with me, which you did neither? By removing our nest, not only did you ill afford yourself a valuable asset and not only did you very much improve the chances of running aground in the Medway, but you very much diminished our chances of finding Cheese in our first rendezvous!'

'Oh please, hardly sir.'

'Would you like to guess how much farther sir, how much farther indeed it is we can see over the horizon with the nest?'

'I imagine sir, it is much the same.'

'The same? The same! Mister Middleton, you will learn your trade or I will see the other side of you. The difference is some six thousand yards! That equates to four odd sea miles! You do realise I can have you brought up on more than one charge and not one of them will you squirm out of, not a one! Nonetheless, I will afford you one chance to redeem yourself and remedy your past errors in judgement. Forthwith will you order Eagle to restore the nest and you will inform him that he is rated sergeant and you will thereafter strike his disrating from the log.'

'I will not, sir.'

'You will not?'

'I will not, sir!'

'You will not?' quizzed Cooper again, calmly pressing his order.

'No, respectfully sir, I will not. What you ask is too much.'

'But I am not asking, I am ordering you! And there is nothing respectful about disobeying an order!'

'But it is an immoral order sir. Eagle is a man well beneath my station and any such action would only afford to diminish my honour sir, which is what you have done repeatedly since I have arrived and it is what you are doing now.'

'Lieutenant, the only thing I am doing now is exercising my command. I am not diminishing your honour sir. I am captain of a ship of war and I remind you that you are a lieutenant, not a lord, in the Royal Navy. I am affording you orders, for which you are under oath to follow. You are not entitled to pick and choose which orders to follow.'

'No, sir, you have disparaged me to the point of no return and were it not against regulation, I would ask you for satisfaction, directly.'

Cooper was stunned, astounded and very much at boiling point. The man was beyond educating, much like some old hound that just wanders off because it is too old and has lost its mind, latching onto anyone it comes upon. To put it down was not only one's duty, but some saving grace for the hound. Cooper calmly removed his hat, marched across the cabin and hung his coat.

'There, sir, I have taken off my hat and coat. I am no longer your captain. Now, I see you are wearing your sword, as am I.' He shoved the table wildly to the side before returning directly afore Middleton. 'I accept your challenge. You have your chance sir, one chance, to restore your honour, or never bring this up again!'

Middleton's eyes bled, infuriated and very much incensed. Frothing as a maddened dog he drew his cutlass, the offer seemingly accepted. About him hung a muted dullness, a blank toneless gaze Cooper had before witnessed many times. Rage had finally beset the man, furious anger now commanding a compulsive seething beast. Absent all sanity, his mind bereft of all reason, indignation fuelled Middleton's hatred, the utmost limits of his annoyance long past repair. He would fight and like most before him, he would fight without reason, without care. With a sudden cry he charged at his captain, fed with a wrath only the devil might instil. The tip of the cutlass was surprisingly well aimed and though driven in wild craze, it was nonetheless fashioned directly at his captain's heart.

Cooper maintained a calmness one might not expect, his breathing even and easy. He had the experience of twenty duels, twenty-one if he were to count Pendleton. In the last war he had been a party to multiple boarding actions and even his swordplay practice with Hiro was hardly for the fainthearted. Middleton was no warrior, just a man who had boiled his efforts into a thundering attack. But the man had undeniably committed himself, moving upon Cooper without hesitation, a courageous act if anything. Yet, it was his commitment Cooper was counting on. Middleton could not now easily dodge nor retreat, not without some concerted effort. Cooper adjusted his stance, moving ever so slightly, his hands already poised upon grip and sheath. The katana came alive, proclaiming its arrival with a distinct ring, no less the quality of the eastern steel singing as it departed the sheath. It was an action he had practised thousands of times, a quick downwards twist of the sheath, a sudden lift of the blade, his hip powering its swiftness until the handle was lifted above his eye line. It was never a direct move of course, the masterful circling of the blade, the subtle dragging upon the tip, the edge precisely planed, all creating a desired rapidity with which to surprise an opponent. The cabin height was limited, but from just above his head the katana continued, circling downwards whistling upon Middleton's cutlass, ever so smoothly all in one continuous action. The blade was aptly designed for such strikes, the tip much thinner allowing fast slicing, whilst the much sturdier middle supported an irrepressible strength. Well handled, it would verily cut through and by almost anything and hardly require sharpening thereafter.

Middleton's chances splintered as his cutlass cracked upon impact, two distinct pieces woefully dispatched as litter upon the planking. A quick glance confirmed his undoing but the attack continued, such was his ire, pathetically insisting to thrust the stunted remains. Cooper deftly twisted his sword, using the blunt hardened back to knock Middleton directly upon the top of his head. It was a strong blow. Had he used the sharpened edge, the man would be stone dead. Blood poured and Middleton stumbled to one knee. Cooper's boot thereafter found the brunt of his face, Middleton now squared up upon his back. Sprawled upon the planking, blood was spooling from his mouth and nose. A prize fight in the sixty-fifth round could not have proven more gruesome.

Middleton rolled about somewhat dazed, but nonetheless sought to sit up, finding purchase upon the nearby cannon. Somewhat bewildered, he peered at Cooper who was now leering above him. Middleton was perhaps even wondering if the bout had properly started, the end seemingly now before him. The tip of Cooper's katana forebodingly poked the softness of his gullet and a sudden realisation surfaced. Cooper had every right to finish the duel and Middleton winced as he expected the very end. He squiggled in an effort to rear back, turning his head, squinting as he strained to urge himself away from certain death. In a sudden flash, the katana came to life. In a blink had it set to rights the end of the bout, impolitely nicking Middleton twice upon the cheek, even more blood spooling to freshen what was already festering. Middleton flinched, no choice but to accept the slashing. Somewhat satisfied, Cooper casually sheathed his blade and strolled across the cabin to return his coat and his hat to the command of his shoulders and head.

'Thank you, Lieutenant. If I am to understand the rules of gallantry and honour, yours I believe is now restored? However, for what you have done, calling out your captain sir, in addition to the other charges, I also believe I can have you hanged, directly. Unfortunately for you, it seems the whole endeavour was most handsomely witnessed by Mister Fredricks here, who had his tubby little nose poking around the door. Should you give me even the slightest reason, you will hang. And I will even pull you up the yard myself, do you hear?' he warned forebodingly, only to have his attention distracted by the door belting open. McFee sprawled into the cabin, immediately beholding Middleton's blood-ridden body, an image which threw him in absolute astonishment, or perhaps was it horror. He held out his arm to stay the two armed jollies, both of whom already had their muskets out not sure as to who they should be aiming. Their faces joined McFee's in muted shock. 'However, Lieutenant, contrary to your popular impression of me, I assure you that I consider myself to be an officer who is also a gentleman. I am willing to forgive your insolence, but I will not forget, no sir. As I said, should you take it upon yourself to fall into your old ways, I will bring you up on charges, hang you from the main and indeed no court martial in the land would sniff twice at me. Ah and here is Major McFee. Please to consider yourself confined, to quarters, directly if you please. Mister Fredricks will help you there and clean you up. I recommend you take your time Lieutenant, for whilst this will allow you to ponder upon this matter, it will also afford me suitable pause as to reason upon what further use on board I have for you, if any?'

Middleton groped the cannon as he started to pull himself up, levering upon the cascabel in order to gouge himself from the humiliation of the bloodied floor. His hands fumbled, very much missing the iron, still in a state of absolute grogginess. His grip slipped, clawing upon the tackle ropes.

'Belay that sir!' ordered Cooper frantically, but before anyone could arrest Middleton's efforts, the tackles were undone and the cannon fell dangerously loose. Some two thousand pounds jumped free, like a wild stallion at the gates. It rolled most horribly over his arm, Middleton screeching like a wild banshee.

'You men, lend a hand! Major, the Doctor, immediately!' Cooper hastily ordered, urgently bending to pull the cannon from Middleton's arm. 'Do not move sir, the Doctor will be here directly.'

Cooper examined the wound and immediately he grimaced. It was one he had unfortunately seen many times before, mostly from many a jack and from many a ship. Only just recently had he witnessed the remains of the first ship's doctor, having been completely crushed by a lower deck cannon. The hand was mostly flattened, flopping about without any real bone to speak of, but the wrist seemed very much intact. Blane was aghast of course, but agreed with Cooper's diagnosis. With a last grim look at his captain, he ferried Middleton out of the cabin to his cockpit.

'Captain, I will have one of my loblolly lads carry the report to you directly, once I am sure. But for now, all I can say is, he will likely live.'

Drums rolled and following, an awful ruckus boiled upon the weather deck, the clatter of frantic steps pounding in every direction. Cooper immediately straightened, for he very well knew in that moment the ship had beaten to quarters. Swiftly he navigated his way to the quarterdeck, pistols now gracing his belt, his katana swinging by his hip.

'Sir, French seventy-four sighted,' reported Spencer, standing the officer's watch upon the quarterdeck. He found his captain barely a few paces before Holt. The other officers attended in course, most hurriedly, glasses at the ready, a sea of heads swivelling to spot the French.

'Where away?'

'Sir, she has just come out from behind that islet. We couldn't see her sir, not until now, very sorry. It's Pompee, sir.'

Ships of War — Murky Waters

'Blast, she is right upon us, what is that, a thousand yards?'

'Nine hundred and seventy-five, sir,' confirmed Holt, holding up his range stick, one eye squinting in the process of checking the distance.

Cooper grabbed his glass and immediately laid it upon the French ship of the line. It was a most magnificent beast, turning handsomely and not so sluggishly either he considered, not like some of the older ones. He was annoyed to be sure, Agamemnon caught with her britches down and most forthrightly. Damn that Middleton he silently lamented, for Eagle perhaps may well have spotted her masts over the islet had he been in the nest, the man able to eye a skulking rat sniffing cheese at five hundred yards.

Pompee was most definitely changing course, wearing ship to intercept and she had the weather gage. Their way was conceived with thought and executed with precision, a commendable commander no less. Cooper was of course in silent admiration, for hiding behind the islet had been one of his ploys. He was now beating himself that he hadn't issued standing orders to account for these strange islets. Agamemnon would need to run, he knew this and thankfully Ortac was not so very far away. Should he somehow manage to slip away, Ortac's sixty-fours and Shillings's propensity to hardly miss would likely have Pompee dished. However, he would have to get his ship there first and upon this matter he was far from convinced. The calculations, the variables together with Agamemnon's rate of turn and handling at first glance seemed to prove insufficient. Would there be time enough he pondered, especially if Pompee increased her way directly with all her sail pressed. As swift as Agamemnon was, never would she fill enough wind in such a short distance. At best, all he would offer the French is an easy target, deadwood barely moving, if at all, perhaps even his stern. He poured his good eye over Pompee, searching, eyeing, desperate to discern anything that might procure some advantage.

'Mister Spencer, spring her luff!'

'Slow her down sir?'

'Aye, helm-a-lee, slow her down. Bring us closer to the wind.'

'Sir, you will have us pass directly by her?' he worriedly accounted.

'Aye, but not one man is to open one cannon door, not til the order is given. Not upon pain of death, do you hear me! Arrange the men on deck to stand in divisions, at attention. Mister McFee, if you please, your marines to larboard, line the side. Mister Holt, fly the colours sir and have the drum and fife report to larboard.'

'Drum and fife it is, sir,' he confirmed, looking somewhat blank.

'Tell me Mister Holt,' Cooper added calmly. 'Do they know the French Royal Fife and Drum Medley?'

'Sir?'

'Mister Holt, if we are to render honours to a French ship of war, it is usually best we know their tune, is it not?'

'Render honours sir? To Pompee, sir? Aye, aye, sir!'

The seventy-four bore down, straightening to match an opposite course. She was a beast of a ship, not greatly longer than Agamemnon, but very much heavier and her broadside all the more weighted. However, she had very much eased now, her sails spilling and the heaving of the bow much lessened. The quarterdeck remained silent, mortally stiffened in horror by the entire ordeal. Barely were they breathing, the consternation of a French broadside virtually at boarding range sick in their minds.

'Tell me Mister Holt,' Cooper casually remarked, his demeanour relaxed, unperturbed, his tone perhaps more in tune with just passing some time. 'In tonnage, how does she out rate us?'

'Five hundred pounds more, sir.'

'Come now Mister Holt, exactly if you please?'

'Five hundred and eighteen, sir.'

'And men?'

'One hundred and forty more, sir.'

'And her broadside?' he added, now noting a smidge of Holt's nervousness starting to play havoc with his silent counting. 'Come now man, out with it.'

'Two hundred and thirty-two pounds more, sir.'

'That much, 'ey?' he returned, rather in admiration. 'Now Mister Holt, let us say we are doing eighteen knots and they are doing twelve knots, which they ain't, but let us say, then how fast would we approach each other?'

'That's thirty knots to close, which is, fifty-one feet per second sir, or seventeen yards per second.'

'Seventeen yards each second! That is handsomely fast, ain't it? And...?'

'And she is exactly two hundred yards, bow to quarterdeck, sir,' he added holding up his measuring stick, 'Ah, eleven seconds sir.'

'But in point of fact, I reckon we are doing three knots and she about the same. Quickly, what is it man?'

'Aye sir, six knots to close, which is ten feet per second and she was at a distance of six hundred feet a few seconds ago,' he calculated aloud. 'Say sixty seconds taking off a few seconds, sir!'

'And a lot can happen in a minute,' he lazily remarked, hardly perturbed. 'I believe I am starting to see how you calculate your adjustments so quickly.'

'Sir?'

'Well, take your last calculation for example. Because you already know the first factor, being the speed in feet per second and its relative difference, you can jump to the answer of sixty seconds directly. Specifically, if the speed difference was fifty-one feet per second to ten feet per second, it's a simple difference of five times. Therefore, if the first answer is eleven seconds, simply times that by five to equate just less than sixty seconds.'

'Aye sir, quite, it's definitely one method I utilise.'

'Ah, hear that?'

'Why sir, that is Heart of Oak, is it not?'

'Indeed, it seems they are rendering us honours, as I had supposed. Prepare to render honours in return. Now be sure we fire out of starboard Mister Holt, starboard sir. Please to play the French Royal Fife and Drum Medley.'

The two ships were close now and should each of their cannon suddenly be run out, a man of balance might walk from one ship to the other. The French quarterdeck was so very much taller, but to Cooper's surprise, her captain was politely standing on the gangway to the quarterdeck. It was a gesture of peace which made perfect sense, the gangway the official place on the ship for receiving honoured guests and officers. They were soon eye to eye and the French captain it seemed was taking no chances, a white flag in his hand, only a tiny one, perhaps a scarf and he was waving it in the required fashion. Cooper had barely the space of a half second to make his decision, now feeling remorseful as to how he had earlier taunted Holt under pressure. He exchanged salutes, nodded his head and pointed leeward, to the base of a rather large islet.

'Come about Mister Spencer, follow the seventy-four if you please.'

When Agamemnon arrived, Pompee had already moored most efficiently along the islet, the rockery masking her from almost every direction. The French captain was perched in his boat, officers in company, rowing to the rendezvous.

'Well, it seems we have guests. Mister Holt, please to arrange Mister Fredricks to make his best croissant. Be sure to inform him it will be tested most thoroughly by the utmost of experts. I leave the rest of the dinner to his imaginative discretion. Spence, do we have some of that French wine, the good stuff from Achilles?'

'Sir, I will get it hauled over directly, it will cool nicely in time.'

'Not too deep now, the French enjoy their wine served at room temperature and I don't want any bloody sharks snacking on our prize. Gentlemen, best you get your dress coats. Senior officers to the gangway and dinner directly after, if you please. And Spence, how is your French?'

'What? God sir, you know it's bloody awful, of course.'

'Perfect, that is what I thought.'

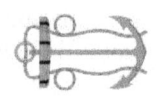

Chapter XIX
Pompee

Acting first officer, Lieutenant Charles Prescot Spencer, stood upon the quarterdeck, Blane's loblolly boy in approach. The lad hastily made his knuckle before shooting away and back to the Doctor's cockpit. Spencer opened the note directly, a remnant of half dried blood speckling the parchment. He winced as he read it, but it had not ventured to tell him anything he didn't already know. News of Middleton, as such, was already rifling through the ship.

'Sir, I beg to report on the first officer. If I may, it has been conveyed that Mister Middleton did directly lose his forearm, cut off by the Doctor. I have the official note here for the record. However, prior, I did have cause to converse with the Doctor and I have to say, the discussion was all somewhat cloudy, sir.'

'What do you mean?'

'Well, Blane contends that the man is quite mad, sir.'

'Mad? Aye, we know this already, insufferably livid to the point of no return I would say, a complete wretch, not a good thing to say about anyone or anything.'

'No, sir. I mean he is dicked in the nob, touched, unhinged, loopy. The Doctor wishes to put him into a strait waistcoat, to prevent self-harm.'

'What? His is mad, mad?'

'Aye, sir. It seems upon examination Blane had subsequently found an old wound, upon his head, he having been previously shot, part of the lead still wedged in there. Nasty business sir, as it was not removed in the first instance, so verily he cannot now remove it, for fear to kill him instantly. I am told the lead has slowly been seeping into his brain.'

'Causing these wild acts of ignorance and stupidity?'

'Aye sir, so the Doctor has since explained. And now with the recent surgery and the concoctions so administered, Middleton's mind has completely slipped. He is as done as a mad dog.'

'By the heavens, no wonder the man has no reason. First he elicits his uncle's displeasure with what can only be described as the most dishonourable act of self-felicitation, installing his presence here under the gravest of false pretences. Then he has the ignobility to undermine every man, jack and officer aboard, including me! His singular recklessness at the hearing was an act begging the need for self-harm. But his attack on my person was beyond the last straw. I really should have put him down for his own good it seems, the man being willing. But is there nothing else we can do?'

'Well, presently the Doctor has him a little more than cut right now sir, perhaps in measure, a little past a drop in the eye. Well actually, to be frank, he is quite corned.'

'That drunk 'ey?'

'As drunk as David's sow.'

'So, the Doctor took his forearm you say. I assume there was absolutely no chance to save it?'

'None sir, the thing wasn't even fit for the sharks. And sir, the whole ship already knows, but you ain't going to like it?'

'What? What's that?'

'Well, seeing how Fredricks had his nose stuck in the great

cabin and as such was privy to the whole ruckus, the whole ship now knows Middleton tried to fight you. They are thinking it a mutinous act of course, they not having much love for him. They all heard he lost his arm, sir,' Spencer paused, waiting for his captain to grasp the meaning. 'Lost his arm, being his right arm, sir, if you get my meaning?'

'Good god, they think I lopped it off?'

'They won't hear it any other way sir. You know how the jacks are.'

It was quite a sight to see, the French officers making their way up the side, the bosun piping them aboard, hats off, immediate nods offered, officers of each ship handsomely lined directly opposite the other. All and every courtesy was afforded, seemingly dished out like it was the latest Parisian fashion.

Spencer offered what arguably could be considered history's worst attempt at the French language possible. Cooper could only grimace as each word jumbled out, a most horrific southern English accent adding salt to the already deepened wound. Poor Holt had not a clue, only that he was to remain perfectly quiet and speak only the King's English. Duty of course demanded the repression of any overwhelming smirks. To the very limits did poor Holt struggle, barely able to contain himself, very much attempting to belay every urge forced upon him. To his relief, eventually he managed a most solemn yet serious and unperturbed look, a demeanour of some forced acknowledgement and grace. The French were less successful, their manners only so wilful and most openly were they unable to resist looks of utter disgust or uncontrollable mirth. They whispered in French amongst themselves, as if it were Sunday, they being at the enclosure of a local zoo, bar all the expected pointing of course.

'My god, he is, constipated?' whispered one French officer,

looking curiously at the contortions gracing Spencer's face as he wrangled with the wording.

'Oh, far worse, poor English,' added another.

'Poor him? It is poor us my friends, my god, my ears.'

'Their tongues are not so fit it seems?'

'So all their women say too,' added another to receive quite a barrage of suppressed giggling.

'These English, but hardly can they speak even their own language you know.'

'Captain,' one whispered directly. 'I must protest, we should not be here. This is a mistake. If any Jacobins learn of this, we will be shot.'

'We serve the King, not those dogs.'

'But the English, what can they do to help? Nothing, but of course, not even one of them here can appreciate our language?'

'Lieutenant Spencer,' the French captain suddenly announced in English. 'Allow me to introduce myself, sir. I am Captain Poulain and if it is acceptable, we can converse in the tongue of your king?'

'Oh, thank god sir, I most sincerely apologise for my lack of finesse with your most elegant language. I really was at a loss.'

'It is quite alright sir, every officer here before you speaks perfect English.'

'In that case, sir, may I present Captain Cooper.'

The introductions proceeded with somewhat more success and Cooper was thinking his ploy to use Spencer's French may have in fact had its desired effect. To his satisfaction, English had now been established as the common thread, his hope all along. Now only if he could catch them disclosing some important slip whilst they bantered in French. He had Holt stationed on the far side, so if anything was offered, one of them would likely hear it.

Cooper reasoned the French definitely were up to something, they had to be, for he knew Pompee was a pirate. Shillings had confirmed this first-hand only some short time ago. By rights, he was almost of a mind to simply shackle Poulain directly and be done with it. There was little the seventy-four could do either, for they had no idea they had just moored under the comfort of Ortac. He could just imagine Shillings skulking about the ramparts, taking dead aim with a handful of the greatest land cannon known to man. It would only take one shot and the man had many more than one at the ready, never missing at such range. Indeed, he could just take Pompee a prize and no one would dispute it. However, it was curious. If Poulain was a pirate, what was his game, why would he step even one foot upon Agamemnon and surely these pirates talk to each other? Surely Poulain knew everything Hasard knew? Cooper posed his strategies, never ceasing to roll the likely outcomes around in his mind. He well knew curiosity had caused certain grief to many a cat, though he grinned as he also considered the furry little buggers had nine lives. He would stay his course for now and see what might come.

'Sir?' Spencer whispered worriedly. 'Do you see that?' he furthered nodded, aiming his gaze past the French officers.

'Good god!' whispered Cooper silently.

Middleton appeared sheepishly out of the hatchway. It was with absolute regret Cooper eyed the man, a man who with one yelp would likely sway the balance of trust, especially considering the delicate nature of the decorum which had just been established. Sneaking his head out, Middleton swivelled it about like an escaped convict testing the darkened night. He was armed to the teeth in fact, two pistols under his belt with another in his left being now his only hand, a musket slung upon his back and a dirty old cutlass slipped upon his hip. The pistol in his hand suddenly ignited. He surged onto the weather deck like a crazed mutt hurled into the midst of a fat herd of its unknowing prey.

'The French have boarded! Open fire! I say open fire there below!' he bellowed. 'Aim at her masts!' he called and he pulled out his blade. 'Major, take those officers into custody immediately. Do you hear me men, I am taking command, lawfully and wilfully!' he shouted, now running down to the French officers. What a wild sight he was, bandaged around the head, the stump of his arm flaying around in a bloodied sling, a feral glazed look washed over his eyes. With the sword in his left, he mindlessly attempted to pull a pistol with his right, only to suddenly realise in fact he had no hand. In frustration, he immediately threw down the sword, frantically struggling to lever the pistol from his belt. Standing firm, he slowly brought the barrel up towards his eye, readying to fire into the French.

'Hiro!' Cooper ordered, addressing him urgently in his language. 'Quickly now, put that man down!'

Hiro flew across the deck, but the entirety of the crew had barely budged. They knew a right and proper lunatic when they saw one and not only that, but this one being their mutinous first officer, they had little care. The man was absolutely past drunk and in point of fact could hardly stand, let alone aim a pistol some thirty feet across the weather deck. They could only giggle and chortle as they noticed the Doctor sneaking up behind, strait waistcoat at the ready, no less than an avid hunter stalking his wild prey. Hiro being no stranger to action moved upon Middleton with the speed of an ape ascending, much to the amazement of every jack aboard. Happily he knocked Middleton on the head, quite directly, the entire crew cheering whilst the Doctor swooped in with his waistcoat.

'For the love of god!' vexed Cooper.

'Take that man away!' ordered Spencer.

'Doctor, if you please, secure him directly and make sure of it this time. Captain Poulain, my sincerest apologies sir. You have my absolute word that none of your officers are anything but our friends here and will not be molested in any way. You are under the protection of a white flag and are our honoured guests, sir. But if I may explain, in mitigation, that man has been incensed with madness, poor devil.'

'Ah, it is quite alright Captain, for in France it is not so much different, many men now incensed with madness, except there they wear no straight waistcoat. It seems we upon Pompee are quite used to it by now. You need not apologise.'

'Thank you, that is most graciously accommodating and now sir, honoured to meet with you.'

'And you, a pleasure Captain, indeed. I presume of course you are the very same Captain Hayden Reginald Cooper, out of Chatham?'

'You are quite right,' he curiously confirmed, some wonderment creeping his visage, thinking the spies of Chatham must be thicker than originally thought.

Ships of War — Murky Waters

'Well then Captain, it is my duty to arrest you, for the murder of Chevalier Yves Maurice Rocques du Motier de Lafayette, our once most famous *Champion de France*, better known to you as Lord Pendleton.'

'I beg your pardon, sir, what did you just say?' questioned Cooper, somewhat bewildered. The entire gathering stiffened and Poulain quite unashamedly peered blankly back. Cooper was about to contest this of course, McFee was all but ready to call his marines and Eagle having returned to sergeant was of a mind to leap from the masthead head first knife in teeth, whilst Spencer was in the correct process of a step forth in protest when the French captain suddenly clarified himself.

'Ah, but it is a duty I will not be performing Captain, not any time soon I should think.'

'Indeed, then if it pleases, let us repair below and we can perhaps discuss the matter at hand and perhaps why you are here? Do you like a good French red, sir?'

The dinner had been quite a success, the officers of each ship most respectfully enjoying each other's company. To their surprise, they had found they were not very much unlike one another. Apart from their uniforms, they laughed similarly in jest, they afforded respect and courtesy much the same and they very much spoke of home and their families with love and devotion. Had it not been for the fact they were upon two heavily armed opposing ships of war, cannon lined forebodingly upon the other, they might verily all be great friends. The discourse had been, to this point, very much limited. Not much of real importance had been floated, dessert still yet to be served. It was what Cooper had expected. It was the tradition naturally, whichever navy one might serve. But there were many items on his agenda to which his curiosity had continued to make demands. Nonetheless he would be patient, or so he had decided, the presence of the French captain very much a gift horse to which he would not be looking in the mouth. With the ongoing piracy and the tensions brewing within Europe, he would wait and soon enough he would hear, right from this horse's mouth, as it were. No need to spook them. Some good wine, some good food, together with some naval camaraderie and he would see the other side of dinner much the wiser. Naturally, the French were not here out of charity. They too had an agenda, but oh how grand it might be should Cooper reach some accommodation. All he needed now was dessert.

Dessert appeared most impressively. By consensus, Fredricks surpassed even his best dish to date, the man seemingly a culinary vision, if but nothing else his entire life. Fluffy croissants filled the table, still warm, the butter and jam melting directly. And had these not suitably enthralled, a most impressive pudding was placed before each and every member.

'Ah Fredricks, what do we have here?'

'Sir, I believe you know it as fish eyes and why that is sir, I will never understand. However, for our esteemed guests, may I describe it as a version of tapioca pudding. May I impart, this tapioca starch has been extracted from cassava root, *"Manihot Esculenta"*, a particular species native to the northeast region of Brazil. Even though it is a tropical somewhat perennial shrub, I have successfully managed to maintain it, especially being that cassava thrives in the poorest of soil. Sir, I can affirm that the dish is most sweet, constructed with my best tapioca and an auxiliary of coconut milk together with some other undisclosed, yet most secret ingredients. As you may be aware, sir, the dish may vary equally in style depending upon the culture, or lack thereof, of the land. Sir, I have chosen, for your consideration, a consistency rather leaning to a fine shallowness, very much on account of the splendour of our guests.'

'Ha, fish eyes it is! Do you know, gentlemen, English schoolchildren have since nicknamed the dish, frog spawn?'

'Only due to its appearance Captain,' added Holt, who himself had only just recently departed school.

The pudding proved absolutely sweeter than ever thought possible, each serving a delight to melt the mouth. Wine glasses were filled, a beautiful Burgundy from seventy-eight and high were they held as Cooper proposed the Loyal Toast.

'To His Most Christian Majesty, the King of France, Louis XVI!' posed Cooper, who was now curiously glancing at Poulain. If the French captain was royalist of old, or a republican to be, it would now be obvious. Poulain it seemed was quite cognisant of Cooper's sly undertakings, nodding back in appreciation.

'His Christian Majesty, the King!' returned Poulain, confirming his allegiance.

'The King!' they all replied and they drank again.

'Thank you Captain,' he commended, standing to return the toast. 'In case it had crossed your mind and you were perhaps wondering, especially considering the state of my country, we of Pompee are all indeed loyal followers of our king, as no doubt are you. But it has not always been that way, which is a matter of later discussing. For now, let us please toast to His Majesty, the King, George III.'

'His Majesty, the King,' returned Cooper.

'The King!' they all replied.

'To both kings, may they ever reign!' Cooper suddenly proposed. 'To George III and *Louis XVI, par la grâce de Dieu, roi de France et de Navarre*,' returned Cooper, most correctly, much to the astonishment of the French. 'That being Louis XVI, by the Grace of God, King of France and of Navarre, that is, for the benefit of our English officers.'

'Oh Captain, such beautiful French, sir and ah, I see you have somewhat played on us a small ruse. I do hope this now means we are truly friends? Naturally, I commend you sir, a wise precaution. I believe your Parisian perhaps even more perfect than the royal court itself,' he happily commended, now choosing to sniff his croissant and eye his wine. 'Are you sure you are English sir,' he jested. 'Such poetry in one's voice and but of course, such wondrous croissants!'

'Alas, I do not get to practice so often, for hardly do the English venture the seas of other languages, its own being already so difficult. It would be nice sometimes to have someone aboard with which to converse. So it is, I am very happy to have you here sir.'

'My god, what splendid wine sir!' Poulain complimented, admiring the texture. 'I know this one, but of course, sponsored by the Academy of Dijon, a most sought after Burgundy. Pray tell, where did you come by it?'

'Ah, indeed, perhaps that is a matter for later discussing.'

'It seems we will have an interesting discussion later Captain,' he added knowingly. 'But I must tell you something strange, something we Frenchmen have heard. We are told that upon British ships of war, toasts are always made with empty glasses? Of course it did not seem plausible to me, in fact some kind of madness perhaps? I am glad to see this notion is not true.'

'But you are quite right. I must admit that it had been suggested to the King once, who rejected the notion quite out of hand. For the main part, the practice of drinking the Loyal Toast in an empty glass was firstly suggested in order to defend an officer's pocket from the pain of penury. It never took shape of course, but we can hardly now halt the telling of old wives' tales, can we?'

'Oh splendid, a joy to hear Captain, for we French cannot bear the thought of an empty wine glass, except but to fill it once more. But, Captain, you say, *"wives' tales"?*'

'An expression sir,' he explained. 'Very similar, I guess, to *"scuttlebutt"*. But the former, wives' tales, was brought about in 1611 when the King James Bible was published, there being a translation of the Apostle Paul to his young protégé Timothy, *"But refuse profane and old wives' fables and exercise thyself unto godliness."*.'

'Scuttlebutt?'

'Aye, a naval slang term, for gossiping.'

'Ah.'

'It should be explained it originally came about because the water on a ship of war was usually stored in a scuttled butt, that is, a butt being a cask which had since been scuttled, that is, by fashioning a hole so the water may be withdrawn. And since sailors have a propensity to exchange gossip upon gathering at the scuttlebutt, that is to take a drink of water, the term scuttlebutt thereafter became an unofficial navy term for the act of gossiping.'

It was noticeable that some of the French officers were now whispering in Breton, something that had not escaped the ears of Cooper or Holt. The revelation that Cooper had all along been able to speak French indeed had some effect and inside he was swilling, all told the result going exactly as planned. He noted the two now chatting, a harmless discussion, but one veiled nonetheless.

'Is that French?' asked Holt, playing the young heart.

'It is Breton, Lieutenant, for many of Pompee are from Brittany.'

'Ah, then let us toast again?' Cooper offered, taking the attention quickly away from the discussion. He paused, damning himself, finally an awkward glance at Spencer returning him the required answer as to which day of the week it was. 'Ah, it being Saturday and as tradition dictates in the Royal Navy, let us please drink to *"our sweethearts and our wives..."*,' he happily posed, looking slyly about the table as he all but held back a beaming grin.

'... *"may they never meet!"*,' Poulain added, correctly completing the toast, a jovial jest received to the mirth of all. 'Captain, I am afraid to say sir, it seems you are now a marked man in France. They have put a reward on your head for the murdering of Chevalier Lafayette. It has most wildly incensed them, I assure you.'

'Preposterous, Chevalier Lafayette was posing as Lord Pendleton, a spy no less and should he be dead, even by my hand, it would be just. But I must tell you sir, he is far from dead. Oh no, he lives, only to rot in a prison hulk.'

'What? But we have it on good account that you had cut him down and another man, cut them into two with just one swish of your most magnificent blade!' he added, now mimicking the swish.

'By all accounts, I too have heard that one. But I assure you sir, I was quite within my rights to set upon him, the first man having called me out to duel and the Chevalier thereafter seeking to murder the King's son, if you can believe it?'

'It would not surprise me Captain, such are the new ways in France, ways we do not agree with. So, you did not strike him down?'

'Oh, the Captain never said that sir,' McFee snappily answered, happy to promote the idea his captain was a professed wild duellist with little less remorse than even the devil. 'Oh, he indeed struck him down, took his right arm completely off, saw that with my own eye, more fearsome than any highlander ruckus I've ever been a witness, his second dismembering of the morning. Had he not done so, the King's son, The Prince William, would very much be dead.'

'Animals, Captain, animals! To attack the sovereign is but to attack god. It is not just or fitting. They are pigs these Jacobins, a scourge upon the lands of France. We are not unhappy you have acted as such. But alas, now all of France is searching for the one they call *Le Capitaine de la Gauche*.'

'Ah,' he lamented, shaking his head, translating to the silent mirth of all. 'Captain Lefty.'

'Yes and now at least we know why you are called as such, ha, ha! And Captain, your first officer maddened upon the deck, I noticed he was missing his right arm too? A recent wound perhaps, a sword wound, yes?'

'Aye sir, it was, a minor incident, most unfortunate.'

'Only a minor incident?' Poulain admired, grinning. 'I see. Discipline is enforced strictly upon your ship. But do not worry Captain, we are at your service in this matter of the Chevalier. I must say, for you to best Lafayette, you must be a swordsman of some singular skill. No one in the games has ever defeated Lafayette, not in many, many years of trying. He is a most dangerous prospect, heartless too if I may add. It would be wise though, should you venture upon shore, any shore sir, to take all necessary precautions, for my countrymen will want the prize.'

'Indeed, well, Hiro is almost always in company.'

'Hiro?'

'Aye, Kensei Hiro sir, the man that struck down Mister Middleton.'

'The Orient? I see, he was most impressive, but what is his position?'

'Oh, well, he has been serving unofficially as my coxswain, but officially let us just say moreover is he a *master of arms*.'

'He was impressive, but he is so small Captain. I really believe you will be set upon. France has her spies, as does England, almost everywhere. They will wish to scoop you up.'

'Hiro may be small, but he is also my personal tutor in matters of the blade. His skill far exceeds my own, I assure you.'

'That sir, is an incredible statement, for have you not bested Lafayette and surely he was already undeniable. Now you say this small Orient easily bests you? My god, it is incomprehensible.'

'May I offer that *"Kensei"*, in the tongue of his land, translates as *"master swordsman"*, though it literally means *"sword saint"* and sir, is there not always a better swordsman?'

'Indeed, how prophetic Captain and how true. You say it of course to apply to any situation of war?'

'Aye, sir, no matter our skill, we must choose our battles wisely, lest we one day depart this world in ignorance. But, is it not time? Let us repair to a private setting so we may now have our discussion? My officers will entertain yours.'

Poulain drew a parchment from his jacket and proffered it to Cooper. It was plainly obvious upon sighting the seal and though it was in French, even at distance he of course easily read every word.

'This, sir, is a Letter of Marque or should I say a *Lettre de Marque* or *Lettre de Course*?' declared Cooper, somewhat amazed.

'Please Captain, let us speak in French. And you are quite correct, but it is not mine. It belongs to the previous captain of Pompee. I assure you, I was witness to the many acts upon your merchant vessels. Indeed did he prey and for quite some time, procuring much wealth and fortune for himself and much praise from his superiors.'

'This is an act of war, you realise this of course? It has been granted by the King! Why would you show me this? I am duty bound to report it!'

'No, sir, nothing is granted by the King anymore. He may sign documents, but he is not afforded the right to read them. The Jacobins are in control and they can do most anything, I assure you.

The King is as powerless as a mouse nibbling a lion.'

'And now you are captain?'

'I was originally captain of Pompee, but I would not act upon such immoral orders and so was I removed. We are not at war and from all accounts it is no less than piracy. And whether some court determines its legality or not is irrelevant. I have another list here Captain, of every merchant vessel so captured by Pompee. You may take the list and do what you will with it, with my gratitude.'

'But this is evidence of war upon my king. Sir, this may throw us at odds here, should our countries go to war!'

'We will never be at odds, as I will explain. And if it pleases your king, I have the man responsible confined in irons.'

'Imprisoned?'

'Yes, ready to be transported to your ship directly. Do with him what you will. He is but a pirate, Letter of Marque or not, a pirate and a dog!'

'I see. And if he refutes this claim, is there other evidence available?'

'You will not need it. You will see. He is a mad dog and he will not refute it. He will not mention the Letter of Marque either, such is his devotion to the idea of this new republic, the dog.'

'I see and, as such, my king will now have his pound of flesh, war very much averted, for now anyway.'

'Yes Captain, as you say, for now anyway.'

'I will think on this matter and have an answer for you before you depart Agamemnon. And now, sir, I must inform you that we have recently been in battle with some pirates, French pirates, in fact a squadron of very fast brigs.'

'Ah, your spoils of war from Burgundy, but I know this squadron, La Hasard's is it not, her being the flag? They are very fast Captain, I know this, much too fast for us poor ships which form the line of battle.'

'Of course you are right,' he openly lied.

'But you must have caught one of the dogs, did you not? Your French wine is quite rare of course. It did not escape me that the only way to procure such magnificence, would be to take it?'

'Quite, we did capture a small ten gun brig, after having destroyed and sunk a fourteen.'

Ships of War — Murky Waters

'Two ships? You have done well Captain, for are these brigs not little rats of the sea? They slink around stealing whatever they can, scurrying off as soon as they have been seen, worse than rabid dogs.'

Cooper grinned, for he and Poulain were of the same heart and the talk of rats soon brought about the memory of Cheese, a tub of a ship, but nonetheless one of his own, sunk at the paws of these very rats.

'Regretfully, in course, our support ship was sunk by Hasard. And though she escaped, we nonetheless hold the captain of the other brig, in England. However, he has not given up his squadron commander and nor is he seeking to rely upon any Letter of Marque.'

'Then, he will hang?'

'Aye, but the Admiralty is doing its best to firstly glean him for information. He may yet crack.'

'They are extremists Captain, a scourge upon mother France. He will not crack, as you say. But if you need the evidence, I can help you, for I have been aboard this little rat and I know her secrets. Do you still have access to her?'

'Aye, she is Achilles now and Lieutenant Spencer here will eventually take command, assigned to my squadron.'

'He is a good officer, I can see that, though should he dare to utter French out loud in Paris, they might lop his head directly, so poor it was, ha, ha! He will find the Letter of Marque on board her. The captain would not have thrown it to the sea, in case he most definitely required it later. There is a loose board, hard to discern, in the captain's berth,' he explained, now drawing a small diagram of the location. 'This will offer to your king the required evidence and perhaps it may be of some use diplomatically? Though, it would be wise to hang that captain before it is found. Once the Letter of Marque is presented, he will escape such justice and legal or not, no captain should act as such in peacetime, lest he be rated pirate.'

'I will see it done.'

'Captain, I truly hope we have come to an understanding today. It is my proposal to support my king. To support my king, I must fight against his enemy, the Jacobins. It seems England is already an enemy of these Jacobins, moreover opposed to the idea of a French republic, is it not?'

'Aye of course, I fully understand. The enemy of my enemy...'

'...is my friend,' he finished for him. 'Yes, an ancient proverb of course. I was not aware the English knew of it. Interesting, maybe in time we will become true friends. Please convey these wishes to your Admiralty. Pompee is not the only ship either. The royalist count is every three in four ships, with all her men, all sailors of Brittany, who will never fall under the hoof of this republic. They are loyalists Captain and would much rather die first.'

'And should war break out?'

'If Louis is not king, you have our pledge, to ally with England.'

Cooper sat back, astonished. Upon Poulain boarding Agamemnon, he was very much thinking the man would be leaving in shackles. Now, he was being offered three quarters of Brittany's French navy to fight against France and her newfound madness. The Admiralty must hear of this, but naturally sceptical they will be. Poulain was genuine, no doubt, but there must be something more or the Admiralty would never believe it.

'I see.'

'Soon Captain, Louis and Marie Antoinette will seek to escape Paris. We can only hope they will be successful. We had already, most elaborately, arranged the publicised death of their son, our Dauphin. It was all a ruse, in order to secretly send him away. We had planned this for long, but tragically upon his exodus was he discovered. It seems he did not escape, our plot foiled and now we fear his death for real this time.'

'Sir, I need some faith here from you, in order to trust your offer. I assure you my king will require it. So, it is my wish for you to tell me the destination of your king's exodus?'

'But Captain, it is folly to disclose such a secret. Surely you must understand?'

'But you must sir,' he sincerely pleaded. 'What if I told you the Dauphin is alive and well, my being in his presence, in England, this I swear upon my honour?'

'Really?' he considered. 'Well, Captain, can you tell me which vessel the Dauphin travelled upon?'

'Of course, His Majesty's Ship Resignation.'

'My god, is it true, he lives?'

'Firstly sir, tell me about Louis?'

'Very well,' he agreed. 'It is Varennes, they have left for Varennes.'

'Sir, you and I both know that is not the final destination?'

'I see,' he finally admitted, now understanding Cooper in fact already knew. 'Montmédy, it is Montmédy. It is our intent to get them safely to the Austrian border, Marie's homeland. Please do not ask me to say more, please Captain.'

'But I already know more. The Dauphin has told me and by my estimation, they should have already left and be safely on their way.'

'Then, it is true! So, you spoke with him? Is he well?'

'He is well, but it was close. Resignation went down in the mouth of the Thames, exploded utterly after heavy fighting with your rat, La Hasard. All hands were lost, succumbing to a most despicable broadside deliberately abaft the ship.'

'My god!'

'Quite. But the Dauphin was already in a boat, unknown to Hasard and we rescued him from the water just in time. Upon returning to Chatham, it was Lafayette who did set upon him. The King's son, The Prince William stood before him and the boy. Lafayette meant to murder the Prince and then the Dauphin. I was fortunate in the order of things, very fortunate and so did the day prevail.'

'Ah, so that is where you lopped him, 'ey? But please, not in half?'

'No sir, not in half, only his arm, in half.'

'Then it is *half* true, this story,' he remarked, now grinning. 'If you do not mind, I will tell of the other version, where you lop him in half, it being much more a better story. So much more frightening and perhaps more useful to our cause, ha, ha! Captain, you have saved our future king! I can only hope France one day will thank and honour you.'

'The Dauphin is in hiding, with a good family, but I think he will never be king. I fear the events have soured his taste for the throne. I think he will stay where he is, live out his life in comfort, the world very much believing he died of consumption some two years ago in eighty-nine, in fact two years ago this very month.'

'We shall see, but upon leaving Agamemnon, it will be my honour to seek out all friends of the King. We shall be ready when war presents itself and it will, it is certain. In the meantime, it is my hope we may well be of some use to you. Shall we keep in contact through your fort here on Ortac?'

'What! Captain, you know about our fort?'

'Ah, you are a sneaky one indeed, from the very first instance we met in fact. I would not ever enjoy the prospect of fighting you Captain. Tell me, for I must know. Upon our approach, with Pompee bearing right at you, how did you know we would not fire upon you? Surely you cannot know who is a pirate and who is not?'

'You had opened your cannon doors to the far side sir, an act usually reserved for rendering honours. I saw drum and fife upon your decks and you had slowed your ship to barely three knots. We are not at war, not yet and so nonetheless I was compelled to take a risk. After all, your brilliant strategy had me very much at your pleasure sir, having the weather gage and having come into sight only nine hundred and seventy-five yards away.'

'I see. You are right of course. But if I was as cunning as you Captain, perhaps I may have posted the drum and fife, opened the opposite side doors and slowed down just to trick you? Thereafter, my seventy-four firing point blank into your much smaller ship?'

'It did give me pause sir, but we must live and breathe upon the weight of our earliest conduct, for later we are sometimes committed nonetheless. And earlier I did err, for I had not accounted the islets, though I should have. In short, later, I had no choice. The battle would have been yours, won by your zeal and very much lost by my lack of forethought. But please, you know of Ortac?'

'Indeed, I know of your fort. But it is only I who verily knows of it. None of my officers are cognisant of its being. I do not know who I can trust upon Pompee. We have sailed past many times and I had noticed some debris, some flotsam washing within the sea. I laid my glass upon her and for a moment I thought I saw a post with flags upon it. Upon looking closer, so very much closer, I discerned some unnatural formations in the rockery. When I heard of a sixty-four patrolling so close to Alderney, I had supposed as much. One night Pompee was moored just south-east of Ortac, upon another islet in fact, so I rowed out in the dead of night and sat listening. I heard your men Captain, to be sure. I understand why you firstly motioned for Pompee to moor here, for if we were indeed your enemy, the cannon upon Ortac would have served to sink Pompee directly?'

A new appreciation for this French captain came over Cooper. His cards, so to speak, were all laid upon the table now, a most handsome strategy, a strategy barely ever proffered by either side, the absolute undeniable truth.

'Captain, you are right in course and I am grateful. I will take your prisoner directly sir and I assure you that your sailors of Brittany will be welcomed by King George, should war break. In the meantime, I suggest you procure a small yacht for Pompee and perhaps use this to sail upon Ortac in secrecy, delivering what messages and notes you deem fit. Agamemnon and Achilles will continue to scour the Channel for these republican pirates. Any assistance will be greatly appreciated. Do you have any message sir for the Dauphin? I would be most happy to convey it?'

The French officers were preparing to leave. Poulain shook Cooper's hand and nodded knowingly with a genuine smile. Holt stood directly before his captain, his face begging permission to report.

'What is it Mister Holt?'

'Sir, a private discussion is required, immediately. Captain Poulain will need to be in company, sir. It is about what you asked me do, at dinner sir, after you and the Captain left, sir.'

Cooper knew immediately to what he was alluding. He had

ordered Holt to entertain the French officers and keep his ear out. His ploy it seemed had worked. They had let their guard down and even if they had some slight suspicions, barely would they believe young Holt any threat. After all, only Cooper had been speaking French at dinner, under the misconception they were all now friends, no one else coming forth to converse.

'Captain Poulain, sir,' Holt started in complete and perfect Breton. 'It is my duty to inform you that two of your officers, sir, are very much plotting against you. Sir, you are in the gravest of danger.'

'Lieutenant, you speak Breton?'

'And French and Parisian, sir, my nanny being from Brittany sir, a beautiful girl she was and she taught me every day in the tongue of Breton.'

'Most perfectly, almost as good as your captain. If only we could all grow older with such beautiful girls, there would be no war. I see you are most careful Captain, another ruse and one I am sure to commend. But one thing I most undeniably see, now we are most definitely friends. Your forethought has won through on this occasion, the ruse well played and Lieutenant, you have caught a rat?'

'Out with it Mister Holt.'

'Two rats, sir, they are Jacobins. I heard them discussing, in Breton, plans to overthrow Captain Poulain here. It seems, as soon as you return to Pompee sir, they will seek to create an *"accident"*. They mean to restore the previous Captain, who I am to understand is locked up?'

'Captain Poulain, I commend you. You were most wise sir to moor under Ortac. You cannot be overthrown whilst we protect you. It seems we are not the only ones here with some forethought. Well done Mister Holt. Now go grab Major McFee and put together a boarding party. Run up the signals to Shillings upon Ortac, *"Quietly. Beat to quarters."* and pray tell, what is the signal to hold fire until we fire first?'

'One red flag, sir.'

'Very well, make it so.'

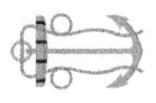

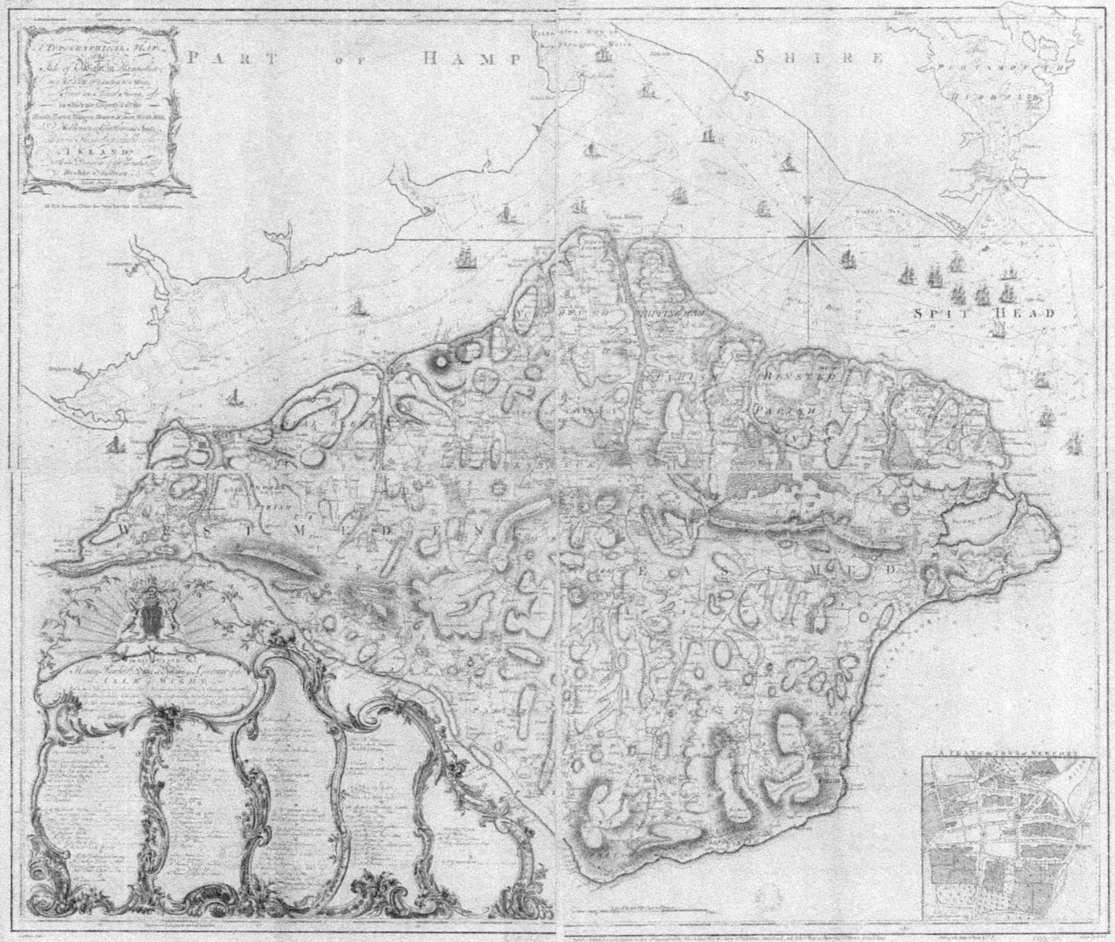

Chapter XX
Brading Harbour

Agamemnon stood in to harbour, the eyes of her crew wide open, most curious to discern what business the ship might have in such a deserted abject location. To everyone's surprise, a litter of brigs loomed into sight, scattered somewhat about the far side of the haven. On approach, it became all apparent. The brigs were quite familiar. French naval vessels in fact, all prizes taken by Agamemnon, the industry of many a painstaking month spent deviously hunting and gloriously fighting. Whispers aboard quickly whistled through the ship, the scuttlebutt insisting Agamemnon was now about Brading Harbour. Humorously some jacks had to in fact ask where that was, embarrassingly trying not to look absent of mind. Yet those who had already crewed the prizes well knew what waters washed about them.

On all accounts and from the speckled conjecture aboard, the ship now rife with furious debate, the consensus had Brading Harbour relegated as some lost ancient corner of England, a place not so worthy of their presence. It seemed hardly a soul had ever been to the Isle of Wight, let alone to one of its harbours. Nelson had delicately described it to Cooper as a somewhat decayed place, almost dejected, half ruinous with a history of no great distinction meriting its honour. Considering the Isle of Wight was hopelessly separated from the mainland, accessible only by decent seafaring vessels, it was not surprising guests upon her shores were very much limited, not that anyone was planning to call. Apart from the honour of being the largest island in England, there was not much worthy of note. The local populace was sparse and countrified, barely cognisant of what year it was, albeit quite content with the idea no one from the mainland might chance them a second thought. Naturally, this was exactly what Nelson was hoping. Cooper, in all his life, had honestly never ventured the harbour and of course how incredulous this now seemed, considering the frequency with which he had verily sailed past. After all, its mouth was only a few miles from Portsmouth, the home of the entire English fleet, the lands barely separated by the waters of Spithead.

'How curious?' thought Cooper, admiring the shape and the august size of the harbour. It seemed to be entirely protected from the ravages of wind and sea, perhaps somewhat shallow in parts, but there was a tidy little river feeding the heart of the island. Overall, he was strategizing it to be quite a defensible place.

'Sir?' Holt remarked. 'Our prizes?'

'Indeed there they are Mister Holt, moored here for safe keeping,' he added with a victorious smile.

Cooper continued to admire the extent of his handiwork, the product of almost twelve months of cruising and oh how enterprising Agamemnon and Achilles had been. The last time an English captain had secured such a smorgasbord was perchance only during the last war, or perhaps the one before. At a quarter share each, he and Nelson would undeniably be stinking rich and they well knew it. Perhaps they could just retire to the countryside right there and then, a mundane life of peace and tranquillity verily awaiting. Naturally, he and Nelson would rather be clapped in irons and keel hauled about Agamemnon in the shark infested islet of Ortac. No, they were of a different breed and ever would they fight tooth and nail, likely suffering to return much of their prize money back into to the operations of their squadron. War was coming, if not this year, then most definitely the next and so was it time for the men of England to stand tall.

In stature had Nelson and Cooper greatly risen, promoting the private war against France with the utmost endeavour. Such was their zeal for king and country had they already voluntarily agreed to send one eighth of the prize money to the Admirals. Hood, Howe and Forbes would enjoy such a feast and in course, ever would they loyally serve to protect their cubs. One eighth to ensure endearing fidelity was a small price, a bargain to which Nelson and Cooper had happily compensated from their personal portions. Their command, the squadron's very existence, was always going to rely upon such necessities, anything to ensure balance and harmony and the continuity of their world. In testament, it was how poor Spencer had unfortunately learned this lesson, as such at the court martial, thankfully the weight of interest levering his side.

Within his quiet moments of late, Cooper was often rapt in contemplation. He gazed upon each and every French brig. Ever mindful he resolutely became as he reflected upon of the concept of prize money and its absolute necessity. Not only he, but every single crew member would partake, even tubby Fredricks who was now very much rethinking his detestation for the navy. The enormity of the prizes had served mightily to clench tight the fist of the squadron. Oh the jacks would always delight in haplessly chasing down French ships, letting loose, banging away their cannon and boarding the enemy in fits of blissful rage. But ultimately it was the joyous thought that after ransacking, pillaging and thieving every item aboard, it could all be sold, the resulting coin legally thrust back into their pockets. With his officers partaking a quarter share and every other crew member the final quarter, the struggle to continually foster a happy ship soon became obsolete. The officers, all who lived in a perpetual state of immobilising penury, would now uncharacteristically find themselves in funds for some time to come, if not for the remainder of their natural lives. Oh how they would meticulously rub each and every coin to the utmost of their unending disbelief. On the other hand, the crew, men who could barely envisage the sun setting on the morrow, let alone in a week or a year to come, would no doubt already be inventing new ingenious ways to wastefully spend every single penny. Either way, Cooper was thinking the squadron would mostly continue to manage and run itself, a virtual life of its own. He just had to keep the prizes coming.

'Mister Holt, inform Hiro that myself and the officers will be going ashore, directly, if you please and to prepare my boat. Make same in signal to Achilles.'

It had been almost twelve months since Poulain's Pompee had first graced their presence at Ortac and a little over a year since Cooper had the honour of first assuming command. Never had a captain served so independently and so successfully in so little time with such a measure of fullness and activity, not that anyone in England might know. Cooper likened it to a lifetime of sailing, now thinking his preceding years somewhat insignificant and tedious. Three personal duels and twenty-six fat pirate prizes all coupled with multiple acts of dismemberment very much had seen Captain Cooper walk the weather deck of Agamemnon with unqualified reverence. Jacks respected a fighting captain, mostly because it meant prizes in return. But a captain who actually took to his sword, chancing to bleed by their side, now that was a captain like no other. It was an absolute added bonus of course that Cooper had also proven a cunning captain, one who knew his business and wasn't afraid of it. They would do most anything for such a man, a long lost father they had never known.

In short time had Agamemnon and Achilles formed an undeniable squadron, a crew battle hardened even beyond that of any wartime ship. Cannon accuracy had been refined to a measure beyond Cooper's wildest thoughts, all very much a product of the mathematic brilliance of their second officer, Acting Lieutenant Jarvis Thomas Holt. The science behind the young officer's distance stick had every jack making a knuckle, reverently referring to him out of earshot as the *"Little Lord"*. Acting first officer Smythe, for Middleton was still under the Doctor's perpetual care mad as a wet cat, had the cannon outrageously firing three successive balls in just on four minutes, the gun crews sniggering and grinning crooked as drunken pirates upon a ranting feast. Eagle and his detachment had every ship dished miles before they were ever aware, allowing Agamemnon to gain the gage and bore down upon them before they could twice blink. And in the thick of it, his sharp shooters at fifty yards were able to clip the wing off a March Brown Mayfly. Of McFee, his boarding marines had sought to make a mockery of the French in every instance of close quarter combat, the Scotsman and Hiro having combined to instil a savagery within the jollies perhaps more worthy of tribal Maoris.

Cooper had refined his method of capture to an absolute art, each new success happily bringing the ship's company a step closer to unqualified perfection. And to his satisfaction, each prize seemingly all but assured unending discipline upon deck. Oh how a prize made a happy jack and a happy jack drove the ship beyond what any wind could ever achieve. Of course, they were yet to fall upon anything heavier than a brig, but of these little brig rats, there had been oh so many. To Cooper's glee, he had discovered that a small ten gun, such as Achilles, very much presented quite the cheese for these rats of the Channel. He was thinking every ship of war should have one, standard issue for the act of clandestine peacetime piracy. Of course it had been of tremendous benefit to know where these rats preferred to feast, Captain Poulain of Pompee and the spying of Shillings upon Ortac very much filling that gap.

'On deck, sail!'

'Strike me blind!' remarked Cooper, lowering his glass to fully inspect the sails with the naked eye. Slowly the sails rounded the mouth of Brading Harbour, a majestic sight beholding to their absolute monstrosity.

'It's a first-rate sir, a big one!' confirmed Smythe anxiously.

'Sir, the price on your head?' reminded Holt.

'So, you suppose the French have come to snatch me?'

'They wouldn't dare, would they, sir?' added Smythe.

'With that much gold on the Captain's head, who is to say it is just the French coming for him? I fear many may dare, as you say.'

'Aye, it is a lot of gold,' Blane added, a sly grin about him. 'And if the Captain had not been hatched from a devil's spawn and had an actual mother, she might even dare come for him too, ha, ha!'

Ships of War — Murky Waters

Cooper indeed had no doubt in his mind about the French daring and their propensity for villainous acts. It was English waters of course, but once they had swooped in, seized their prisoner and whisked safely away to Paris, there was little anyone could do. A once joyous stint of contemplation quickly reverted to madly strategizing chances of survival. His head swivelled around the haven. Only one way out, but that was directly past the first-rate. He quickly thought about running Agamemnon inland, up the small river, but he knew not its exact depths and any chart was hardly able to be trusted. The haven was shallow in parts, which could afford him a chance to pass where larger ships could not. Once out into the waters of Spithead it was a short cruise to Portsmouth. Perhaps the obvious was to repair to the safety of the small forts upon shore, hide under the range of the cannon. To make the forts in time he would have to move off swiftly. But once there he would be trapped, open to small boarding parties and a first-rate would boast over a thousand men. The first-rate slipped fully into view, her colours now showing, a cannon firing to leeward.

'That's Queen Charlotte!' exclaimed Cooper.

'Aye sir, thank god!' confirmed Smythe.

'Her pennant sir!' Holt added who, now a year older since first boarding, still had the only eyes upon the ship to rival Eagle and his nest. 'Aye, sir, pennant in sight and confirmed, it's the flag sir, Admiral of the Fleet!'

Queen Charlotte made her turn, most handsomely and fell into the harbour, her sheets brought to a luff. Cooper could only stare in admiration as he noted the efficiency of her crew. He had not expected her presence, but at least this behemoth was English. With the horror of such monstrous sails rounding the mouth he was half expecting her to be Royal Louis, traditionally the largest ship in the French Royal Navy, perhaps come to retrieve their fleet of brigs and the English pirate captain who had taken them. Either that or Dauphin Royal, displacing some five thousand tonnes, a new ship which he knew had been laid down in Toulon and launched only last July, this notably being about the same time he had ventured out with Agamemnon. And if it was not the French, come for his hide, perhaps it was some jumped up admiral seeking to halt every ship afloat and fleece whatever they could. To his utter relief it was definitely Queen Charlotte, none other than the flag of the entire Royal Navy carrying no less than Admiral of the Fleet, the Honourable John Forbes, his squadron's immediate benefactor. It was a good wager he wasn't alone. No doubt Commodore Nelson was aboard and most likely so was Admiral Howe, considering Queen Charlotte was in fact his ship. Perhaps even Admiral Hood might be present, they all being thicker than a den of thieving wolves.

'Confirmed sir, she is falling off now, readying to drop anchor.'

'Well, well, well,' Cooper remarked. 'What has prompted this honour? Mister Holt, beat the ship to quarters, quietly now and thereafter, wait upon the signals if you please. I suspect we will not be going ashore. Signal to Achilles, *"Close formation. Wait. Quietly. Beat to quarters."*. Let us plan for all contingencies. Mister Smythe, be so good as to render the appropriate honours, Admiral of the Fleet.'

'Twenty-one, sir?'

'Goodness, no Mister Smythe,' he frowned. 'That honour rests with the King, it being the Royal Salute.'

'Mister Holt, what say you sir?'

'Well, it cannot be of an even number Mister Smythe, that being unlucky of course. And it cannot be all of them, as we are not entering a foreign port, they being so frightened they will sink us at the first inadvertent sneeze.'

'Aye, good point,' Cooper commended. 'For the custom there is to show the ship is defenceless, all her cannon dispensed and commonly, unable to reload for the next five minutes as she sails into range.'

'In course, sir,' Smythe offered. 'Better to have more than less? Perhaps nineteen?'

'Mister Holt?' tested Cooper.

'I am dished sir, having to look it up to be sure, but I would suggest maybe seventeen, it being two steps below? I am thinking there might be some others of higher importance above a Fleet Admiral?'

'Very good Mister Holt, dished or not, you have it. Now Mister Smythe, tell me sir, if Agamemnon had her pennant, being a flagship, how many then?'

'Oh sir, I know this. It is two less, being fifteen.'

'Very good,' he commended. 'And Mister Holt, how many will Admiral Forbes return to us?'

'For flag officers it is two less in return and for captains, it will be four less, sir. I am not certain about commanders though, maybe six less?'

'Ah, there, you see, quite simple after all?' he teased. 'Make our salute seventeen gun, if you please Mister Smythe. Now, whilst we wait upon our friend, Mister Holt, might you regale the officers on deck of our Queen Charlotte here?'

'Happy, sir,' he accepted, another gauntlet thrown down by his captain to attest his absolute knowledge of the Royal Navy, Cooper hovering intensely about like a mother cat coaxing her kitten. The other officers grinned knowingly, some side wagers discreetly taken. 'Queen Charlotte sir, named after Her Majesty The Queen, Sophia Charlotte, Charlotte of Mecklenburg-Strelitz, one hundred gun first-rate ship of the line, built to the draught or class of Royal George, launched April 1790 at Chatham. Designed by Sir Edward Hunt, though with a modified armament, she is a monster sir, one hundred and ninety feet of gun deck supporting thirty cannon of thirty-two pound, twenty-eight cannon of twenty-four pound, thirty cannon of eighteen pound, there being an additional ten cannon of twelve pound upon the quarterdeck and two cannon of twelve pound upon the forecastle. That's a broadside of one thousand one hundred and fifty-eight pound and she carries eight hundred and fifty men, sir.'

'Mister Holt, are you of the opinion we can take her?' he jested.

'Well,' he paused, very much thinking about it, much to the murmuring mirth of every officer present. It was of course a rhetorical question, for no sane officer aboard would endeavour to imagine Agamemnon would do anything except be blown to tiny bits in the first broadside. Very much was Cooper surprised to hear his second officer's most genuine response. 'Sir, I know this might sound far-fetched, but there is in fact a small mathematical chance, albeit very slim and the strategy most singular. It would require a muster of speed only Agamemnon could boast sir, for fear she would be blown to tinder otherwise. Nonetheless, I expect most captains might well be aware of the ploy and as such, easily repel the advance. In course sir, I would recommend caution, to our utmost.'

'Sir, if I may?' Smythe candidly interrupted. 'I would recommend speeding away, to our utmost.'

'Of course gentlemen, to our utmost, we must always do to our utmost, but which one, 'ey?'

Cooper had his eye on the signals. Naturally he was aware of the prearranged meeting with Nelson, but usually the Commodore chose to arrive discreetly on some swift sloop, privately owned, alleviating suspicions. The appearance of Queen Charlotte was most curious. Perhaps it made some sense though. With each new prize snatched up, it had only furthered to inflate a growing problematic situation. It seemed Cooper had captured so many brigs, it behoved the Admiralty as to where they might put them. It was another good problem to have he was happily thinking. They couldn't all be sailed and paraded about in Portsmouth in such regularity, or certainly the proposition of unwanted questions would surely arise.

With the promise of funds pending from the prize courts, the solution to their conundrum had been bought, so to speak. That is, they had bought the favour of Brading Harbour and her local town, a purchase that was proving to be most conveniently profitable. As depositories go, the Isle of Wight, some eighty miles almost directly north of Ortac, was proving a prime location, quite handy in fact. Achilles had happily found herself escorting prizes and ferrying the crews directly back to Agamemnon's station all within the same day. Brading harbour was well protected from the worst weather and the prizes lay safely under a tremendous array of cannon, all courtesy of Nelson. And of course Portsmouth was only a handful of miles to the north, the convenience of His Majesty's most powerful ships readily at hand. It seemed Agamemnon and Achilles could cruise the Channel at extreme range with absolute impunity, utilising Hood's signal array to confirm the identity of virtually every French ship that might pass. It was a net the French could barely escape. Upon each capture could they then easily sail the prize here and there, no one being much the wiser, especially

Ships of War — Murky Waters

the French who must now be at some considerable loss to know what the hell was going on out there.

The Isle of Wight could possibly just be the perfect place Cooper needed to rest his crew from time to time. It was barely one hundred and fifty square miles, but there were a handful of charming villages and absolutely no way to leave the island. It wasn't paradise, but it certainly appeared comfortable and homely. He could ill afford letting even one soul upon the mainland of course, for fear they would run away or be drunk ten minutes thereafter, their operations suddenly exposed to every spy south of Chatham. Indeed, this island and this harbour might at last afford the opportunity to safely rotate the men upon Ortac, their morale and the squadron's secrecy assured. He could also alleviate the Doctor's burden of Lieutenant Middleton's care, for the madness of the man convalescing upon this desolate island could never chance to damage their operations.

'Charlotte signalling sir,' Holt announced, not waiting for the signal officer to translate. 'Sir? She wishes to challenge?'

'Ah, I smell Nelson's hand in this. Very well! It seems they wish to see what we have got!' he gleefully acknowledged, turning himself to the weather deck. 'Men,' he boomed, addressing the crew, already at quarters. 'Charlotte sits out there, flag of the fleet by god! It seems they have need of a challenge, to test her crew! That's right, men, it's a game of war! So, let's give them one they never will forget!' he wildly announced, the entire crew cheering as if they had just been roused at the colosseum of Rome. 'They may have a hundred gun first-rate, but we have Agamemnon! They are slow and haven't seen a real cannon shot for years. They wish to test their steel, but they are only going to test ours! And we will show them steel!' he shouted, pulling his katana to point it skyward, an act which always stirred the jacks, their toothless grins beaming. 'Mister Holt, signal to Achilles, *"Game of war. Attack. Formation three."*, if you please. And Mister Holt, you had some inclination we might take her? Well, here's your chance, take the ship in. Let's see what you've got?'

'Aye sir!' he grinned, turning to the master. 'Mister Thornton, signal to Achilles, *"Attack. Correction. Formation six."*. And shake a leg there now!'

Bradley John

Cooper was piped aboard Queen Charlotte, Captain Hugh Cloberry Christian waiting in greet. In fact, the entire ship's company had been called to divisions awaiting their arrival. Cooper politely smiled as he pulled himself aboard, though he was met with a reception somewhat less than what he might consider cordial. Christian appeared rather grim, stern and unwavering, his eyes dwindling under the weight of an enormous brow. Perhaps it was the usual visage, a captain's prerogative to appear eternally damned or perhaps the hostile lines upon his face were pending his decision upon what to make of the junior captain before him, a captain not yet even post. Cooper was now thinking he had given young Holt too much leeway in the game of war, apparently to the penance of a most frosty reception. All the officers were quite numb, not a soul stirred in fact, not for a good moment, Cooper thinking he may have just boarded a French first-rate by mistake.

'Captain Christian, honour, indeed,' he energetically announced, perhaps endeavouring to alleviate the tension. 'No need to formerly introduce yourself sir, for I am well aware who you are. Indeed, very much aware of your endeavours upon Suffolk and at the Battle of Grenada. I am Cooper.'

'Do you always cheat sir?' Christian abruptly challenged, now eyeing Cooper as a freshly cut fillet, medium rare. The man was his senior, but the comment did however meet with Cooper's disapproving eye. 'Well, let me rephrase, for honour's sake, bend the rules then, 'ey? Well, sir?'

Cooper cringed, his stomach sinking, he had most definitely offended Queen Charlotte and her captain. He should never have let Holt take the command so far, for in essence, it was just a game and in reality, he needed the ongoing favour of such officers. Agamemnon had indeed made an uncommon mockery of the games, a product of Holt's most unorthodox manoeuvres. The cheating was true of course. He knew it and his officers well knew

Ships of War — Murky Waters

it, a distinct liberty about the rules very much taken.

'Sir, whatever do you mean?'

'So you deny it? I see, well there's only one thing for it,' he replied and he motioned to his captain of marines. The marines immediately stepped forth, muskets in hand, led by a burly officer. 'Colonel, if you please, take the good Captain here, scour him in cramp rings if he dares resist and present him directly before the crew, for punishment,' he gruffly ordered, the Colonel now grimly prompting Cooper to step forth and be recognised. Cooper looked about and nary was there any sign of Nelson or Howe or Hood. Surely the Admiral of the Fleet had to be aboard, his pennant still fluttering, but nary a sign of him there was either.

'If you please Captain, to stand here, whilst the proceedings commence,' insisted the Colonel, now looking to Christian for instructions.

'Well, get on with it Colonel, we haven't got all day. Nice and loud, if you please? Huzza for Captain Cooper!' he happily ordered and the crew of Queen Charlotte wildly cheered three times. Cooper was very much relieved to find Christian stepping forth to offer his hand, now grinning. 'Well done sir, bloody well done! It's not every day one gets to see a sixty-four sink the flagship of the Royal Navy! But I would have much preferred to be upon the sixty-four when it happened. By god, if you didn't sink us! I should be most upset at you, most upset, the impudence, the absolute impudence! Never in life have I ever struck sir, never. What an upstart you are, 'ey? I didn't know whether to shoot you or to promote you, such is my amazement. And we did have such an argument on board here too, with our impartial adjudicator, who I verily did think of shooting directly. Next time I'll just get an adjudicator who's a little more partial, ha, ha!'

'Sir, I do sincerely apologise for our actions within the game.'

'Hogwash, sir! You were unfairly matched, hardly just and with a little English zeal and ingenuity, a little bending of the rules, 'ey, you have won against all odds. No complaints here, but my first officer is wholly beside himself of course, he having been given command to show his stuff, ha, ha! Once Forbes is finished with him, he'll be lucky to rate able by the end of our cruise, poor sod.'

'In course sir, I was quite expecting a fiery death, to our utmost. Our stratagem was in fact quite a long shot. Albeit, it was all we had, short of striking before we even started. And it was moreover my second who had the necessary zeal to insist upon the chosen manoeuvres, the honour being all his.'

'Your second, sir?' he remarked, somewhat surprised.

'Aye, sir, for we have been engaged quite regularly with the French over the last many months. He is young and so I very much wished him to get a taste of it, so to speak. He was also cheeky enough to state at the outset there was a minute mathematical chance we could prevail, much to everyone's mirth of course.'

'Ah, well, who's laughing now, 'ey? Which one is he then?' he insisted, eyeing each officer as if the next man selected would hang directly from the yard and be fed feet first to a shark.

'Sir, may I present Lieutenant Jarvis Thomas Holt.'

'Sir, if I may, Acting Lieutenant,' added Holt politely.

'Good god, only a midshipman!' Christian vexed. 'Captain, this is not how you glean the best slice of duck from my table sir, ha, ha! I take it this is Lord Holt's lad then?'

'Aye, sir, you are well informed.'

'Well, at least we wasn't beat so *commonly*, ha! Well done, well done Your Lordship. You shall have the honour to sit right next to me at dinner and I will insist you tell me blow by blow how the bloody hell you went about it! By god, have we ever seen the likes!'

Christian had been captain aboard Lord Howe's flagship during the Spanish Armament, Cooper quite cognisant the man was no fool. He was now perhaps regretting his endeavour to impress the Admirals, of course at the destruction of Captain Christian's reputation. But dinner and some deference would perhaps heal such wounds. Cooper was most happy to finally see his commodore and all three admirals present, their grins smirking beyond all prudent society.

'Most happy I am to see you all again sirs. I was in expectation of it upon sighting Charlotte, though doubtful when I did not behold any admiral's coat upon the weather deck.'

'Oh, don't mind them,' Admiral Forbes answered directly. 'They were just licking their wounds, a might annoyed at being sunk by your midshipman and of course the dull prospect of having to swim home across Spithead. I'm quite sure not all of them can swim you know, hence their penchant for being assigned to a first-rate,' he jested, his sense of humour, as always, somewhat dry and to the point. Nonetheless the mirth brought the entire table to a roar of unimpeachable laughter. 'It was mightily well done Captain, indeed, they are all talking about it. And they have all remarked the incredulity of speed made way by your ship, sir. Speculation is rife, if I may. In fact, they are taking wagers upon it now, as to how many knots she made, I do hope you had recorded it?'

Unimpeachable laughter indeed there was, the delight of such an undeniable feat enjoyed by both ships, the Charlottes' embarrassment of being sunk very much set adrift now, such was their camaraderie and such was their respect for the twenty-six prizes which lay moored yonder. Above all, Nelson was very much enjoying the whole scene. It was he of course who had suggested the challenge, to sharpen up his man for something bigger than a brig. He was hoping Cooper would acquit himself handsomely and not be sunk too swiftly, an opportunity to show his grit. Never had he in his wildest dreams believed he could take Charlotte a prize. In course, the Admiralty had some important news for Cooper and before they were to discuss it, they very much desired a show of skill on his part. The news was from France, not the regular correspondence one might imagine either. The foreboding nature of it most definitely had Nelson and the Admirals all agreeing Cooper could definitely use a *first-rate* challenge, as they comically put it.

Dinner was the usual extravaganza one might expect, that is, should the host be Admiral of Fleet. The usual toasts prevailed and out of playful interest Admiral Forbes soon had Cooper dicing fruit with his katana. They had all heard the rumours of Captain Lefty and his magnificent sword. Some were even told the blade might serve a small boat in half, others perhaps dubious of such scuttlebutt, insisting they at least see some decent sized fruit spliced first. Forbes, Howe and Hood already had the advantage of witnessing Cooper's skill first-hand, long ago at the Admiralty. Soon enough the trio had any officer daring enough employed in a wager against Cooper. And oh how proficient the Admirals were at hooking their fish, cleverly insisting they would only win their side in the event Cooper remained undefeated in each and every challenge so presented. Immediately Spencer got silently into the action on the Admirals' side, prevailing upon young Holt as his innocent mule. Spencer hardly needed to see his particular friend in action to know he had a sure bet. He also noted the Admiral's sneaky wording of the wager, which specified the word *"undefeated"*. To those sharp of mind, Cooper could remain undefeated even if a match was drawn. In effect, to lose any coin, Cooper had to be beaten.

The first few challenges started simply, Cooper slicing up different fruits, all of them sitting most still, easy targets. The challenger from Charlotte would swing first, Cooper matching his trick directly thereafter. Soon enough they suddenly realised that a draw result was not good enough to take the pot. The challenging cartel was at pains to come up with anything Cooper couldn't do, even upon the presentation of their best man. To the finale, the Admiral had Cooper matched against the first officer of Charlotte, a grudge match of course, the poor man keen to avenge the sinking of the King's flagship and return his honour. With a sideways grin, Cooper perched a baguette high upon a long pole.

'How's your rapidity Lieutenant?' Cooper encouraged. His opponent nodded back, a pool of sweat swimming his brow. The comment brought a hush from the room, some extra side bets placed. 'I will strike first, so you may know the trick,' he announced. The baguette sat high on the pole. 'Please to watch carefully,' he insisted. He had the baguette sliced nicely in two, the force of the strike sending the lopped half immediately from its perch. He eyed it carefully as it fell, swiftly slicing it again in mid-air as it plummeted to the planking, a pure flash of the blade.

'What was that, sir?' Charlotte's first officer comically remarked, knowing the trick could not be matched of course. 'I didn't quite catch it. Please to see it again?'

It was good hearted humour, the Charlotte officers feeling a might less man handled in the game of war after coming to know the Captain more intimately. The last comment immediately opened up a side bet with the Admirals, insisting that Cooper should in fact do it a second time, exactly as the first, the sliced pieces thereafter to be measured in accuracy of the wager.

Ships of War — Murky Waters

'By god Captain, I sit here amazed, utterly,' Admiral Forbes complimented. 'You have won sir, against all odds, again ha, ha! But Captain, these tricks and whatnot, as amazing as they are, short of chopping up a midshipman or two, surely is there not something truly more you could show us, a grand finale?'

Cooper glanced sideways around the room, his eye falling upon a scarf. He strolled about the cabin as perhaps might a magician plotting to saw his assistant in half, verily stalking the entirety of his routine, no less a sly glint secured in his watchful eye. He halted and grinned, nodding to the Admiral, much to the appreciation of the entire cabin.

'Admiral, if it pleases sir, would you do me the honour of lending a coin? Please to excuse, but I only ask, sir, in consideration that no other officer here has but two pieces to rub together, they all being very much fleeced to a state wholly beyond what even the barest sheep in England might enjoy,' he jested, much to the approval of the room. 'I assure you it will be returned,' he promised, the entire room now murmuring. They had no idea what he was going to do, only that there was no way they would dare miss it. 'And sir, may I use your candlestick?' he politely asked. Upon gathering his items, he placed the candlestick before him. Upon the melting wick he hovered the coin, a gold one in fact much to his hidden mirth. He applied a small portion of wax, affixing it to the coin and curiously, he pressed the coin to the overhead, the wax now holding it in place.

'Sir, that coin will not hold there for long?' warned Holt.

Cooper kneeled upon the planking and tied the scarf around his eyes, completely blindfolded, appearing as the condemned awaiting the final barrage of musket. 'I must insist, sirs and gentlemen, absolute silence thank you and god forbid, nobody move an inch,' he politely insisted. The room indeed fell silent and immobile. The outside world offered just a splattering of an odd wave, gurgling upon the hull. Within the cabin, here and there an odd creaking strained the ageing lumber. The only other discernible noise was the Admiral's nostrils, slowing heaving amidst absolute silence. Cooper had his hands upon sheath and grip, at the ready to draw. His eyes remained covered, his ears now stretching to discern any movement of the coin. Time passed, almost half a minute, but every officer attested their discipline, remaining absolutely quiet. The quivering in expectation, the excitement of the feat all but ensured their silence. Yet in point of fact, the Admiral had also foreshadowed a nasty keel hauling to their absolute and utmost peril.

Still affixed above their heads to the aging plank, the coin finally started to tremble, the wax spent and no longer able to hold its weight. With a small shudder, perhaps only the slightest resonance, it tinkled from its perch. Cooper appeared lethargically asleep as the coin suddenly dropped, tumbling as it plummeted upon its journey to the cabin floor. His katana suddenly railed out and barely a few feet from the planking his blade sang in the still of the deadened air, chirping as the edge spliced the gold. The coin sat on the planking, neatly spliced in two, an astonishing feat.

'Your coins sir, returned as promised,' offered Cooper humorously, the entire gathering chortling.

'By god Captain, I thought I was utterly amazed, but now I am well past that,' Admiral Forbes complimented, congratulating him as the officers all continued to roar. 'Had I known what you were doing, I might have offered a penny though!' he jested, now patting Cooper on the back. 'This man has been out twenty-one times you know? Can one conceive what kind of idiot would go out with him?'

'Well, sir, I regret, in course...'

'What?' he blubbered. 'Not twenty-two, now?'

'Aye sir,' he sheepishly accounted. 'Regretfully, there was a most unfortunate incident with my first officer.'

'Oh, of course. I am much surprised you did not hang him, directly.'

'It was later determined he was ill sir, in the head and in any case he had been relieved of his right arm, punishment enough.'

The entire cabin called for a toast to Captain Lefty, much to Cooper's silent indignation, they all mistaking he had in fact lopped off another arm, in lieu of hanging. McFee of course was fuelling the idea, the legend of Agamemnon growing with every breath the Scot could muster.

'You have done wonders with young Holt here Captain, a true example of English zeal. May we hear from him, his strategy today, with your permission sir?'

'Oh sir,' Holt modestly started as he eyed his Captain ensuring the permission to report had naturally been granted. He found Cooper's wince in return, a subtle message to keep it respectful. 'Very happy as it really was a long shot. In course it was not such a fair fight, as you all well know, it being our two ships against only one,' he comically started, receiving a rising cheer from the table. 'We had our little ten gun brig Achilles purposefully positioned, our intent for her to use the gage sir. We were very much of the considered opinion that a ship such as Queen Charlotte would rightly choose to ignore her. Achilles is quite a runner sir, ever since the Captain had her bottom refitted with copper.'

'You mean to say that little brig has a copper bottom?'

'Outrageous! There it is!' confirmed Christian, feeling vindicated.

'Aye sir, she is fast, can make fifteen knots standing on her head, more if we push her. So I ordered Captain Spencer, most politely if I may, he being my absolute superior and I having such regard for him, to steer a predetermined course, which I calculated would eventually prove abaft Queen Charlotte. Upon Agamemnon, it was our immediate desire to manoeuvre away from the slanting gun of Queen Charlotte, so much that the great ship would be forced to wheel on the spot and turn. Upon turning, she would show her stern to Achilles, her *heel* sir if you will excuse my mirth, allowing our brig to run down directly, hopefully unscathed. Achilles in course was always in the sights of cannon and even the quarterdeck cannon of a first-rate could quickly sink her. Our ultimate hope, our wish was that Queen Charlotte would not waste shots upon her, reserving her fire for Agamemnon. Agamemnon, sir, if I may, is quite the runner as well. Agamemnon's game was to continue to push past the bow of Queen Charlotte, thus escaping her every effort to turn for the broadside. At that time only the forecastle chasers could bear upon her. She, for the moment would remain relatively safe, awaiting Achilles to present herself at the stern.'

'I see, to arrive upon our Achilles heel, as it were!' he laughed. 'And I take it this is when you contrived Captain Spencer to cheekily moor his ten gun brig to my rudder sir?'

'Aye sir, upon our signal, a system being the most excellent concoction of Admiral Lord Howe, Achilles made her run and she did most cheekily attach the entirety of her weight to Queen Charlotte's rudder. Of course, she being so small and now completely attached to the rear itself...'

'Yes, yes, we know, our gun couldn't lever down to take aim and we couldn't turn our bloody ship to fight Agamemnon, fish in a bloody barrel! And to our utter surprise, upon our utmost effort to board Achilles and relieve our rudder, a hundred jollies led by a wild Scot simply popped out of her decks screaming and yahooing like banshees in the night, but not before a load of grapeshot was fired down our arse, killing every man and jack lower aft.'

'Exactly sir, aye, with Agamemnon almost in the sights of your broadside, I ordered Achilles to heave hard, a counter weight so to speak. Whilst Queen Charlotte was fouled and unable to turn, Agamemnon luffed her sheets handsomely bringing her to and as she did bear, presented a rolling broadside directly down the snout. To her credit, I believe Queen Charlotte's twelves upon her forecastle did hit us directly, according to our adjudicator, Agamemnon taking damage to her sail.'

'Which I am sure you figured to directly repair with your share of the prize money afforded from King George's flag!' Christian humorously added. 'Aye our great ship being wholly impeded, a turtle on its bloody back unable to turn, Agamemnon was afforded free gunnery upon us. Good god Captain Cooper, three broadsides sir in less than four minutes, outrageous, absolutely outrageous!'

'Capital fighting, absolutely capital. But I must say to you Mister Holt, sir, who the devil said you could mount those damned thirty-six pounder carronades on your brig's quarterdeck? Blazes, whoever puts such a beast on a ten gun brig!'

'And at such range sir, Achilles, if I may, had Queen Charlotte dished. If she had not struck, Achilles would have continued shot after shot into your hull, two thirty-six pound balls a time, reloading until she might go down by the stern.'

'And was Major McFee here really going to board us? My first tells me he had them ready and lined up like locusts, willing to fly into the lower levels. I mean, we have eight hundred and fifty souls aboard. That is heavy work!'

'Sir, if I may, I believe Major McFee would verily storm the walls of York with no more than a wheelbarrow and a blunt pitchfork, if you would let him!'

McFee hardly minded such a distinction. He played upon its hopelessness, assuring every officer there that young Holt might look small, but moreover was a giant cat upon the waves of England, with claws to match. And when he is promoted admiral, perhaps sometime before the end of the dinner, he would be most honoured to serve under him.

'Well gentlemen, I think we know why the harbour is, as such, filled with twenty-six prizes. By god's wings, twenty-six prizes and Captain Cooper here, when pressed with just one lowly first-rate of course felt we were only good enough for his second officer to take the helm, a midshipman! Ha, ha! By god, will I ever live this down!'

'Sir, in earnest, I feel it would be appropriate to keep Mister Holt's manoeuvre very much a secret? We might have cause to use it again and its main flaw relies upon the cat not being concerned with the rat.'

'Indeed, sir,' Nelson concurred. 'Let us and no man aboard ever divulge Holt's rat, lest we soon be at war and the rats aware.'

'Well, well, well, that is very handsome of you all. I can bloody live with that!' Captain Christian happily agreed. 'Let us toast to His Lordship's rat catcher, to Holt's Achilles Heel!'

'To the Lord of the Rats!' they all cheered together.

With dinner dished and serious matters to discuss, it was with interest and yet some moderated concern that Cooper and Spencer called upon their superiors. They were correctly guessing the flag of the Royal Navy had not ventured from Portsmouth merely just to congratulate Agamemnon or to have their finest pork sampled. Grave had matters recently become, England now ostensibly engaged with the revolutionary regime of France in what could only be described as an unspoken state of war.

'Gentlemen, much in Europe it seems has come to pass, indeed,' Admiral Forbes roughly announced. 'Let us catch up first for those who have been busy at sea, as such, those not afforded the liberty to gorge upon the current affairs. Admiral Howe will fill us in to start.'

The Admiral was of course referring to Cooper and Spencer. Although in point of fact Cooper was already well aware of every action, issue or item of news. He most likely had the information in hand well before the Admiralty. From France had he the courtesy of Captain Poulain and from Chatham had he a grand network of spies, a web which very much had grown with the benefit of excess coin. His friends had all fed him most handsomely and more often than not. Verily was he a pig rolling in a barn of muck having happily gorged upon each and every morsel.

'Gentlemen,' Admiral Howe started. 'It was only mid last year we all sat very much stunned, June of ninety-one to be precise, in particular upon hearing the fate of Louis and Marie Antoinette. I refer of course to their most unsuccessful attempt to flee Paris, they being hopelessly caught part way upon their journey to Montmédy. Regretfully were they arrested, escaping only as far as the small town of Varennes. Hopelessly recognised upon stopping, most foolishly from all accounts at Sainte-Menehould, immediately were they taken back to Paris. The monarchy of France, since then, has officially been an outright sham.'

'And may I add,' Admiral Forbes interrupted. 'As such, only a month later, we saw Marie Antoinette's brother, Leopold II of Austria, instigate the Padua Circular. Now, we all knew in advance he was planning this, an open invitation to England, Prussia, Russia, Spain and Sweden to collaborate against France and perhaps reinstall the monarchy. With the shambles at Varennes, his sister very much a powerless figurehead and both her and Louis now in the most horrible jeopardy, he followed in late August with this damned Declaration of Pillnitz, it being an agreement between he and Frederick William II of Prussia. Whilst he sought to serve a rallying cry and save his sister, in France it moreover just poked the bear.'

'Aye,' Admiral Howe confirmed, continuing. 'Leopold had no desire for war of course, the bluff being immediately called, so to speak. Now, not everyone may have heard the latest, quite shocking in fact, but I regret to inform that Leopold is now dead. Indeed, died suddenly last month.'

'Good god sir, they killed him?' cried Cooper.

'Undetermined, but I guess we can all draw our own conclusions. Curiously, just this week, Louis attended a session of the Legislative Assembly. It was reported he sat mildly, mostly unconcerned through one speech after the other, all calls for pre-emptive war. It seems the death of Leopold has empowered the Girondin ministry to seize the moment and oh how they have been agitating for war. Well, by all accounts, Louis abruptly rose and formally was war declared against Austria and Prussia that being the twentieth of April in the year of our Lord, 1792. No mention of England of course.'

'And it doesn't take the smarts of a homeless rat catcher to comprehend that the man has just declared war upon his wife's homeland,' Admiral Forbes brusquely added. 'We realise of course Louis has not a scrap of power. So it is likely he has either been coerced to declare, or perhaps he has some wild hope a combined Austrian and Prussian force might expel these damned revolutionaries and restore what is left of his monarchy.'

It was exactly as Cooper had firstly been told, war was coming and England had to bolster its position, no different to pieces upon a board in a gentleman's game. Yet he also comprehended, all too well, that any conflict with revolutionary France would verily be like no other war England had ever known. Wars between the monarchies, whilst brutal to the core, had traditionally been conducted with at least some modicum of moderated civility. It would be hard to imagine any conflict without at least some standard of grace or regard, for did not each monarch have much to lose. Military decorum all but insisted upon such standards, it always had, an unspoken reverence disposed from one king to the other, very much serving to recall either side from the precipice of completely obliterating the other. But to fight the mobs of France would be to fight the common man, a wretched beast who had very little for which to live. It seemed a frightening prospect, a wholly unknown quantity to which Cooper could only shudder. To what extremes these mobs might aspire, to what laws they might ignore and to what might become of England was a little bit more than just a sobering thought. And he had already seen the emergence of such sentiments in the French, their undeniable hatred, their immutable disposition. La Hasard, the spies at Chatham and the bloodthirsty privateers of twenty-six pirate brigs were all prime examples of what was rallying across the Channel, their minds washed tooth and nail with political grandeur and wild aspirations of maddening dominance. Perhaps it had been patriotic rage or perhaps it had been mob lunacy. He wasn't sure which, but whatever it was it was frightfully alarming, to him and any man upon the shores of England.

It was to this very end that Cooper had toiled over almost a year of cruising, all to ensure the efficiency of his crew and construct a healthy network of unassailable spies. He would need more than just English zeal to rid the waters of the French scourge. His success too had been noted, English shipping now taking a stronger foothold to secure commerce. But time was short. War was coming and the privateers still sought to menace England, piling upon the English backs their absolute damnedest, indeed everything short of declaring war. And still there remained one matter which had dared to elude. Oh how it hung as a thorn in Cooper's side, the complete and utter failure of course to capture the one pirate that mattered most.

Hasard was still out there, a rabid dog skulking the woods, but long had it been since any soul chanced to spot her. It was Cooper's pound of flesh, the horrid memory of Resignation's vile end forever vivid within his mind. Many a sleepless night had been served. It was a recurring nightmare forever endured, the blatant murder of his countrymen, the stern of Hasard cruising into a gloomy horizon and he unable to reach out and grab her. Of course, Hasard may well have already succumbed, or her captain forcibly retired. Shillings was of the considered opinion she had likely been sunk, to which even Poulain concurred, the ship's whereabouts very much at a loss even to the royalists. Outwardly Cooper rejoiced at the possibility Hasard had met her demise. But in his heart, he very much wished her to suddenly appear, the collection of his pound of flesh the only tonic for his malady.

If Hasard was about, her time would come he considered. Eventually her crimes would be answered. After all, she was a rat and no rat can ever be denied their cheese. But of late had there been many a rat loose in the pantry and so if Cooper couldn't have the pack rat, he would have the pack, setting about the destruction of every other brig the French had sent to sea. They had all been pirates, rats of the Channel and now, their ships were his.

The Admirals had only mirth and joy to gather as to how Cooper had snared his prizes. To hear the royalists of Brittany had come to the industry of his venture was a sweet surprise, pleasant indeed. And how they gurgled upon hearing he had constructed an impregnable fort upon Ortac, a barrage of sixty-four pound cannon audaciously stationed barely three miles from France herself. To set Spencer adrift in Achilles, a duck on the pond with its wing clipped, all after garnering information from Poulain and Shillings was truly a testament to his powers of deception. Oh how they all wished they were there as Agamemnon swooped upon each pirate with speed undeniable, the advantage of a nest affording the extended sight of many more sea miles than reasonably thought possible.

'Well, Captain Cooper, here it is, straight from the French packet,' Admiral Forbes roughly announced, holding up a sealed parchment. 'No doubt it is in French of course. No one here has read it, or even had the chance to read it. Even if we could, notwithstanding, it is addressed to you. But firstly, if I may, it is the second such dispatch so received, which is why we have arranged our august gathering here at Brading. I am sure you will be interested to hear the contents of the first dispatch, received three weeks ago?' The Admiral started, pausing only as he perused the words before him. It was admirals and captains only, closed doors so to speak and most of them sat blankly as if they already knew the contents of the letter.

"To Admiral of the Fleet, Admiral John Forbes, Whitehall, London. It is France's most earnest intent to declare war upon your king, His Majesty King George III, unless our most sincere and humble demand be directly met. We assure you of our sincerity in this matter and request your response in the immediate. We

will send in exactly three weeks by sea to Spithead our said demand and should His Majesty graciously look amenable to peace, our ship will meet in your waters and afford such magnanimous request. To find no ship waiting affords your response in the negative, war most assuredly following. His Most Christian Majesty, the King of France, Louis XVI."

'They are insane of course,' Admiral Forbes remarked. 'But most curious it is that this dispatch was written before the declaration of war against Austria and Prussia. It behoves us to think they would wish England to join against them? Insanity, as I have already attested. Nonetheless, we met with their flag at Spithead, Royal Louis, great oversized beast it was. And now here we are with the second dispatch, their *demand*, at hand, so it seems. Captain Cooper, if you wouldn't mind sir?' he requested, handing him the second dispatch. 'Please to inform us sir, what lunacy this new note now entails?'

"To Captain Hayden Reginald Cooper, His Majesty's Ship Agamemnon of Chatham. It is publicly recorded that you alone perpetrated a vile act, most cowardly and most unfairly, in murder of our citizen of France, Chevalier Yves Maurice Rocques du Motier de Lafayette, Champion of France. It has further been attested and since, your guilt tried and convicted in our great courts. In addition, the court finds you have also acted in piracy and murder upon the seas of France, having sought to prey upon what can only be described as innocent shipping. Satisfaction immediate in nature is now demanded of your person, forthwith, or never will such smite upon the honour of France be in remedy. You will bring your ship, Agamemnon, upon the fullness of October's moon, to the harbour of Brest and present yourself. To restore the honour of France, our ship will meet and may God have such mercies upon you. Failing such, forthwith is war immediately declared upon His Majesty George III and any such ally seeing fit to declare allegiance. Captain Lafayette, by proxy, His Most Christian Majesty, the King of France, Louis XVI."

'Innocent shipping they say!' remarked Admiral Howe.

'Outrageous!' declared Admiral Forbes immediately.

'And satisfaction?' posed Spencer, somewhat dumbfounded.

'Are they serious sir?' enquired Cooper calmly.

Ships of War — Murky Waters

Admiral Forbes looked to his adjutant, who they all assumed was merely the Admiral's man servant, or his doctor, he being dressed as a civilian. They were shortly to discover he was in fact the head of the Admiralty's secret association of information gathering agents, a spy no less.

'Pratt?' nodded Admiral Forbes.

'Ah, this letter is from Chevalier Lafayette's brother, so we have been informed, most reliably it seems. And may I point out that among those recently calling for war, of prominence in Paris was the Marquis de Lafayette. I can assure you he is most definitely the elder cousin of both Chevalier Lafayette and this Captain Lafayette. And to add spice to the pudding, it seems you have met Captain Lafayette already Captain Cooper.'

'I assure you sir, I have not.'

'He is captain of La Hasard, until recently commodore. But seeing how you have sunk, burnt or taken every ship under his command, he is now just plain old ordinary Captain Lafayette, having not even a tub to add to his squadron. I suspect you may not have seen him of late?'

'No sir, a point of vexation, to be sure.'

'He has been in hiding. The new regime has not taken kindly to the loss of its privateer fleet. This ultimatum is his way back of course, his cousin in Paris arranging this little note from Louis. He intends to bring your hide into Brest and declare his reputation mended.'

'I see.'

'However, in the grand scheme of things, we are to understand Captain Lafayette was only in command of the southern fleet. Whilst you have seen fit to destroy it, almost completely, I assure you the French in the north have been most productive in their piracy, most productive. Apparently, they possess mostly fast frigates and be damned if we have been able to catch even one. We were about to request you relocate your operation as such, so as to weed them out, but then this all arrived of course and here we are. As far as Captain Lafayette is concerned, apart from the utter destruction of his squadron, we think him a might annoyed at you, personally of course, the issue with the loss of his younger brother in Chatham?'

'Come now, the only loss was the man's arm. I had left him very much alive, not that it would matter either way, for he was a spy and deserved much worse. So, sir, the letter is a fake?'

'Oh no, Louis himself signed it, our man saw it in fact. They mean to declare war. It is our opinion they will do so in any case, it is just a matter of when. However, should we meet the demand before us, the declaration may not be so immediate and either way we would be afforded a stay until at least the end of October. Winter will soon follow, so it is thereafter likely nothing further would happen til the thaw in the new year. England is still barely ready Captain. If we can glean another nine months of preparation, perhaps hold out until the spring of ninety-three, it may make all the difference in the end.'

'Said he means to meet? Something about satisfaction?' pointed out Spencer frowning.

'No less a duel, I assume?' confirmed Cooper most correctly.

'Ha, called out with a ship of the line!' Admiral Howe chortled. 'Now we have seen everything, surely!'

'Good god Cooper, this will be twenty-three!' exclaimed Admiral Forbes.

'Sir, in fairness, I am not entirely sure this counts?'

'Come now Captain, of course it counts. Be damned, twenty-three!'

'Of course it is some kind of trap,' Pratt candidly offered. 'Hardly is there an honest word upon that parchment. They mean to ambush Agamemnon and no doubt our good Captain Cooper here will end up in Paris, prey to this new contraption they have invented, which apparently lops off one's head most efficiently.'

'What?' cried Cooper, his widened eyes worriedly raising his brow.

'Aye, it is called a guillotine, after its inventor, physician Joseph Ignace Guillotin.'

'Ah sir,' Spencer interrupted. 'If I may, I believe that rumour not to be true.'

'Indeed, well I am sure Captain Cooper would consider that good news, if that is in fact the case?'

'Indeed sir, for I have it on good account from our own information gathering behemoth that the inventor is actually not Doctor Guillotin.'

'Huh,' brandied Cooper.

'Oh no, it seems the invention has been swinging around different countries for centuries, not exactly as it stands now of course. Everyone agrees the good doctor was indeed the proposer of such a contraption, a few years ago now in fact. Aye, but he was never the architect. It seems the thing was designed by one Antoine Louis, physician to the French King in fact. There was some Strasbourg fellow who helped him with it and they had a German engineer build it. Apparently it is quite distinct from its predecessors by the nature of the angled blade, seems the others all had nice curved ones.'

'Oh, oh, is this thing similar to the louisette by any chance?' enquired Admiral Howe knowingly.

'Louis 'ey?' Admiral Forbes muttered. 'Any relation by chance?'

'The Louisette and the guillotine are the one and same in fact, sir!' Spencer returned proudly. 'They have since had the name changed to guillotine, as well as the truth of its origin it seems.'

'Well, I bloody well never heard of either of 'em!' sprouted Forbes.

'Well,' Pratt conceded, waiting for the dust of the discussion to settle. 'It is an apparatus, most efficient from all accounts, designed to execute by beheading. It is a construction of a tall upright frame in which a blade is raised to its top, waiting to be released upon the condemned. The condemned is always secured with stocks at the bottom, one's neck verily awaiting the dropping of the blade. Upon such, with a single and supposedly clean pass, the head falls off into a basket below.'

'A basket?'

'Supposedly,' Pratt coldly estimated, his face immutably pondering said outcome with the emotional penance of a parliamentarian asked for coin. 'Well, I can say the first use of this thing was only this week in fact, twenty-fifth April, upon some highwayman, one Nicolas Jacques Pelletier. And if we are informed correctly, it should have all happened at *Place de L'Hôtel de Ville*, but we haven't heard yet how it went. But we imagine the science is sound, especially with the oblique style blade.'

'Barbaric!' cried Admiral Forbes.

'Well, in point of fact,' Pratt defended. 'It is actually a somewhat more humane method, considering the previous method of the wheel.'

'The wheel?' sounded Cooper, concern now bringing his brow down to squint upon his eyes.

'Aye, the Breaking Wheel or Catherine Wheel,' Pratt confirmed. 'It being the French method of torture for public execution most preferred in the past. They had been using the bloody thing since antiquity. Not much science in that one I'm afraid. Quite the thing though, quite the thing, breaks the bones of the condemned whilst bludgeoning them to a long and painful death, moreover a form of deterrence by agonising execution.'

'Ah, I know this method,' Spencer announced, happily explaining the niceties to Cooper. 'The poor sod is most often dragged to a public stage and so there would they tie them down. The wheel itself was typically of a large wooden spoked frame, very much the same as our carts and carriages. Many of them actually boasted a purposely built rectangular iron thrust attachment, a blade extending from the rim. There were many facets to the act, all most gruesome. The first it seemed entailed the agonising mutilation of the body, so as not to cause death. For example, commonly would the executioner commence with breaking just bones, usually legs and arms. He would drop the wheel on say, the shinbone before slowly working his way up to the arms.'

'Grief!' cried Cooper.

'Indeed and any number of beatings were prescribed, sometimes it was just purely the absurd number of spokes on the wheel. For full effect and try to imagine this, sharp edged timbers were often placed under the joints of the condemned thus enhancing each strike. I have also heard of certain devices, in which the condemned could be harnessed. It would be some act of kindness, though hardly commonplace, whereby the executioner finished the deed right there and then, a *coup de grace*, I believe is how they say it. Upon continuing the saga and I wish you all to imagine verily the exact state of the scene. The executioner would go about physically braiding the body, like knitting, into a secondary spoked wheel, only made possible by the severity of broken limbs,' Spencer embellished, now flopping his arms about as if they had no bones. 'Aye, so much, that the executioner simply tied the condemned into the wheel. The wheel soon became a crucifix, very much like a mast on a ship. Oh, then the fun would begin! With so many choices prevailed upon the executioner, it was hard to know what might come next. Decapitation, hanging, garrotting, or sometimes a fire was kindled under the wheel and if they couldn't be bothered they just had the condemned thrust into a waiting blaze.'

'For the bloody love of god!' wailed Cooper.

'Not sure the heathens have a god,' snorted Admiral Howe.

'Well, Captain Spencer, I thank you, a most apt rendition of my forthcoming demise at the hands of the French.'

'Oh nonsense,' Admiral Forbes sharply added. 'They will never do such a thing, never in life. Goodness me, please Captain Cooper, you just heard our man Pratt here. They are since very much preferring to guillotine you, the wheel having since been discarded.'

'Of course, sir, apologies,' he politely afforded. 'And Spence, may I say perhaps that was the best pronunciation of French I have ever heard you utter. Perchance could it be the only words verily known to you, though such a fountain of knowledge you are.'

'The French always have been somewhat ghoulish,' added Admiral Howe.

'That wheel is beyond ghoulish,' Admiral Forbes agreed. 'How the devil do they even arrive to conjure such a thing? Makes a man wonder it does?'

'Aye, sir,' Spencer continued. 'It is overall a gruesome event, may I say the condemned lasting longer than ever thought possible, some accounts ranging from four to even nine days, the latter having been kept alive with a strong drink.'

'Well, there you go Cooper,' Admiral Forbes happily added. 'If you get caught, insist upon the drink and we will have up to nine days to rescue you.'

'I will endeavour to my utmost, of course, sir.'

'And after they are done,' Spencer added, still not finished. 'Having not been rescued in course, the carcass remains on the wheel, left to scavengers. The thinking being that this would hinder the transition from death to resurrection. Curiously though, if the condemned ever slipped from the wheel, it was interpreted as an intervention by god, the condemned directly released.'

'Good to know,' thanked Cooper.

'Good god!' remarked Admiral Hood, who had remained somewhat subdued til now. 'I had heard of the Scottish Maiden and the Halifax Gibbet, these contraptions intent to crush the neck or simply use a blunt force repeatedly until it removes the head. But the wheel far surpasses those, absolutely brutal.'

'Well, if Captain Cooper was to go, on the mission that is,' Nelson vexed. 'He should not go alone, like any duel, he should have a second. We should at least park a squadron of first-rates at distance, in case of any shenanigans.'

'It would only incite that which we wish to avoid, sir,' Pratt replied. 'All those ships of war in the water together, cannon at the ready, tensions high, no, only a bloodbath would come of it.'

'But they mean to murder him, most horribly!'

A silence paraded the cabin, no obvious happy solution presenting itself. With a price on Cooper's head and any resulting loss meaning his certain horrific death, not even Forbes was of a mind to insist he go. The cards had been laid before Cooper. He knew the odds and the stakes. Contemplation for him was over long ago.

'I will meet him!' Cooper announced boldly. 'Alone.'

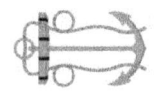

Chapter XXI
La Vénus

With the departure of Queen Charlotte and Admiral of the Fleet, the tension wringing the officer corps finally tapered off. This change in mood unfortunately had resonated through the lower ranks to a point of notable concern. A slack jack was a useless jack and so Cooper and Spencer took it upon themselves to remedy the situation. Oh how they enjoyed haphazardly storming the weather deck and for that matter any deck that randomly presented itself. They set about ruthlessly terrorising every jack, man and jolly to within an inch of their lives. Randomly did they inspect equipment, call the crews to quarters and sometimes to divisions, even adding the odd impromptu challenge between stations. In short time did it have the required effect. The fighting spirit of the crew soon resurfaced. Rather than a dog's body of flea bitten toss pots, they now mimicked a professional crew somewhere in between a crack legion of legalised ark ruffians and a gang of wild rogues. Indeed was it most promising and in kind did Cooper afford the crew the pleasures of the island.

Bradley John

After even just a short stint of island life Cooper was ultimately convinced that Brading Harbour was just the thing. Apart from bestowing the most excellent stores of water he had ever seen, the usual peskiness suffered by a ship's captain now very much lay dormant. There was no fighting, no stealing, no accidents or injuries, the ship's livestock happily roamed unmolested and the docks remained clear, quite bereft of spies. Neither did he or Spencer suffer the usual pesky barrage of beached officers clambering the gunwales in search of employment. Much to each's utter relief, nor had any gentry chanced to find the ship, unable to proffer their sons as midshipmen. This was most pleasing, for such refusals often led to the customary threat of personal damnation and the usual promises of demise by political interest. And by far the greatest outcome was the total absence of the ever shifting sands of the Admiralty's insanity, Brading Harbour far removed from veritable cannon shot.

It was of immense comfort to Cooper that his men might convalesce safely upon the island, knowing full well not even the wiliest jack could chance an escape. Even the most reckless could enjoy drunkenness to their heart's content quite unconcerned with the danger of loose lips irreparably sinking the entire squadron. The sight of twenty-six prizes yonder to leeward proved a sullen reminder of their duty, not to mention their wealth to be. The timing could not be better either, the middle of summer providing an idyllic relaxing tonic.

The crews of Achilles and Agamemnon had also chanced to enjoy the inner shore. Oh they created some havoc as expected, not that the locals really minded, the coin thus tended dulling most irritations. Cooper had even ventured as far as Saint Catherines, the far side of the island of course. It seemed Nelson was intent on rebuilding the lighthouse there, although he had only partly managed to reconstruct it, the propensity of surrounding fog perhaps dissuading him. All in all, the entire area was proving to be a grand training ground for the surplus jacks and jollies, of which there now were many. They would need them though. With war barely around the corner, Nelson would likely be afforded a ship and the scarcest resource was always well-trained men.

It was with great pleasure Spencer and Cooper sat in the local tavern of Brading, affording themselves a homemade pie, washed haplessly down with some fresh ale.

'Your pie looks particularly inviting, sir?' admired Spencer.

'Oh, indeed, you must partake this version upon your next visit. I had the baker make this one specially, from one of Nelson's favourites.'

'Sir, are those onions there, in the mix?'

'Indeed, for our Nelson is such an advocate of the thing,' Cooper confirmed, adding a sly glance as he chewed in between each word. 'A vegetable like no other he says and in kind promotes the well-being of a sailor's soul, like no other. These are local, if you can believe it. Our commodore had a whole garden installed just yonder. I see your pie has a modest complement as well?'

'Quite,' Spencer confirmed, happily mincing the pastry. 'Well, sir, isn't this a far cry from the regular stuff we get on board.'

'Only when Fredricks falls short of provisions, which isn't so bad and anyway, what's wrong with a bit of boiled corned beef or salted pork, 'ey? Let us not forget the heavenly aroma of a nice batch of lobscouse, or a sea pie or even some sauerkraut, 'ey? You know, I am actually quite fond of pease pudding and some plum duff.'

'Sauerkraut, ugh, not quite the King's dish now is it? The jacks are not fond of it. But, sir, I must agree on the lobcourse, the version Fredricks presents in any case, quite passable indeed.'

'Well Spence, we both know there are so many incarnations of that particular stew. It can be such a beast of course and it really does depend upon who is making it. Our man Fredricks is a heavenly prodigy, to be sure. But either way, at least it is meat and at least it is hearty. The men are quite partial I believe and it is our commodore's wish that we officers eat in equality with the men. I think you will find in the Nelson version the thing ever littered with onion, ha!'

'At least it is a diversion from salt, a welcome reprieve.'

'Quite.'

It was good to be away from the ship, a small respite and so was it with empty distaste they noticed Blane hailing them as he broached the tavern door.

'Sir, may I beg to interrupt you and Captain Spencer? I have something astounding to report, if I may?'

'Of course Doctor, you sir are most welcome any time. Please, sit and have and soothing ale with us. Try this pie, it is extraordinarily alluring.'

'It is about Lieutenant Middleton, sir.'

'Oh?'

'Upon our stay here at Brading Harbour, I very much feared the worst for him, his condition having degraded. As you know, I had him moved into town and very handsomely has he been set up, a credit to the generosity of coin you had donated. In course, fearing his imminent death and very much upon my own volition, I decided to operate.'

'But you said it was an inoperable condition, for fear to kill him?'

'Aye, but failure would mean a quick painless death, much better than a life of mindless haze I suspect. I considered the man, sir and thought he would have wished us to try.'

'Ah, then he is dead?'

'Oh no, quite the contrary, sir,' he happily announced. 'I am heartily amazed to report that not only is he alive, but he is quite cognisant and progressing, mostly.'

'Goodness, then, he is not dead?' vexed Cooper, fearing the obvious consequences, now trading a worrying glance with Spencer.

'Upon removing the lead from his brain, it has served to immediately remedy his affliction. He seems somewhat normal, almost. I dare say he might even eventually resume his duties.'

'His duties?'

'He does have bouts of random madness, but only when plied with tincture or alcohol it seems. But yes, he might resume his duties, only with your permission naturally.'

'With my permission?'

'Aye, resume his duty as one of the officers, sir? In course, that would be at your discretion and I would leave it to you to decide.'

'Have you not gone mad, sir?' he snapped.

'Doctor, with respect,' Spencer interrupted. 'It must be explained to you that Mister Middleton's duty and position is not at

Captain Cooper's discretion. He has been commissioned by the King. Were he to be cleared by you as fit for duty, his seniority would immediately relegate him to first officer upon Agamemnon, with or without Captain Cooper's approval.'

'First officer?'

'Aye, Doctor,' he intoned. 'No less, a heartbeat away from complete command.'

'Oh dear.'

'Aye, Doctor,' Cooper added. 'And please to note that I would not approve, no sir! I ask you to consider that our ship, a ship which is about to fight to the death at Brest, has performed handsomely to date and all without the bungling antics of our Mister Middleton. And may I say Doctor and let me make this abundantly clear, you sir will be there at Brest fighting with us. And unless you have discovered a cure for being frozen and forever drowned in the icy fathoms of the Channel, you will enjoy in the fate of the ship with the rest of us.'

'I see,' he responded somewhat taken aback, his gaze falling oddly upon Spencer who now curiously appeared to be silently holding his breath, as if drowning. Spencer's mouth gaped open and shut, reminiscent of a fish out of water, mimicking efforts to unsuccessfully draw air, the colour in his face almost draining. Blane paused to consider what he had done. Oh how he wished he had thought about it before operating. Naturally he only wished to see Middleton repaired to good health, a noble act perpetrated with the best intentions. He had no wish to see the man restored to the post of first officer, not if he was incompetent and not if his captain wholly disapproved. He cringed to think this one act of charity could conceivably result in the end of his ship, sunk by Middleton's crazed ineptitude in the throes of a fiery battle. He had heard all the stories of course and not a one of them at all reassuring. He had no inclination to see the ruination of his captain, a man he very much respected. In fact, he very much wished to see his captain live out his days fat and rich in the meadows of lower England. But on the other hand, he owed a sacred oath in his duty to his patient, by all accounts, to the denunciation of all other matters. 'Oh dear,' he further lamented.

'And Doctor, did not the man try to murder me, verily whilst in command of my own ship and verily, in my own cabin, or do you not comprehend this?'

'Yes, but, he was mad?'

'No, no, no, good Doctor. It matters not, we cannot allow this, for only would his presence as first officer seek to condemn every man aboard, including yourself. If you persist with your official determination on his medical status, I assure you, he will be reinstated as first. And upon that moment, I will be forced to bring him up on charges. I cannot let him resume one foot on the quarterdeck, not one and he will swing Doctor, there being only one penalty available under the Articles of War.'

'Surely, sir?'

'Do not test me upon this, for one crazed lunatic swinging from the yard, albeit one of the gentry, is a cheap price to pay for the hundreds of souls he would no doubt damn. Not only that, but England and her king are counting upon Agamemnon to do her duty. There is much at stake, most of which you are not yet privy. I am most sorry Doctor, but I think the way forward is clear, abundantly.'

'Doctor, it is not my place to say sir,' Spencer softly added. 'But are you sure, certain of your diagnosis? Perhaps you might consider a further examination of the patient?'

'Albeit, Doctor, that would be your prerogative and your decision alone,' added Cooper respectfully.

'Captain, I am not in the habit of second guessing myself or making mistakes in the first instance,' he protested, his gaze now fixed upon Cooper's blank muted eyes, a visage more befitting an executioner of the Tower. Spencer similarly offered no respite either, now somewhat blue after holding his breath again. 'Well sirs, perhaps. What if I was to suggest and that is, suggest mind you, that perchance Mister Middleton may possibly be fit for duty only upon shore? Of course, that is only applicable where a further examination reveals something tangible.'

'Is that possible sir, without afflicting your honour or your profession's oath?'

'In course, my preliminary examination is not yet logged, but Captain, I would have to find reason sir, or my conscience would not be at rest.'

'Of course, then let us pray for such a reason.'

'Sir,' Spencer suggested. 'If I may, even without the honour of your extensive knowledge, ponder immediately did I the question as to the negative effects of incessant rolling and endless rocking to which a sea affords upon a ship. Of course, I expect you may have pondered this as well? Perhaps, if I may be so bold and suggest that any preliminary examination may not yet in fact reveal such effects, being that Middleton is yet to return to said ship? Perhaps, who knows of course, but perhaps it may bear out that duty upon a ship will not be so ideal for our Mister Middleton? I am not a man of such knowledge or esteem, but it seems to me this kind of consideration might logically come some time during say, a second examination, on board?'

'Well,' he carefully deliberated, trying to find some way out, conceding that the welfare of the entire crew was his charge. 'It is true I have no cure for the imposition of immediate drowning by a near frozen sea. But, for other reasons, I must concur. It is likely Mister Middleton's condition would not be amenable to ship duty.'

'Likely?' pressed Cooper, his brow bearing down upon the good doctor, not unlike a first-rate holding the gage at her back, probing for a definitive striking of the colours.

'Ah, well, probable.'

'Probable?'

'Definitely?' offered the Doctor, sheepishly.

'Aye, very well,' Cooper nodded. 'Then in course, if you are certain, that sir would be agreeable. And I am sure the King himself might knight you for your service here. And sane or not, Doctor, I find the man too much of a risk to let loose upon shore, even upon the far reaches of Brading. However, I could station him upon Ortac of course, under Shillings. Sir, would that be acceptable?'

It was with some anticipation that Agamemnon met well with Pompee, Captain Poulain very much aware of the recent ultimatum delivered upon his ally and friend, Captain Hayden Reginald Cooper. It was as Cooper had thought, duplicity awaiting him at Brest.

'Captain, they are talking about you as if you had already been captured, tied as a hog and brought before the ministry on its spit. Already have they commenced construction of the stand for execution, the trial as you know already concluded. I am not privy to the fullness of their plans of course, but I know enough to believe the meeting at Brest will only serve to see you in irons. They have no honour, these pigs. The war now with Austria has them unchecked of course. The scum are in power and they are rounding up anyone who sneezes, executing them in the guise of spies. It is not permitted to breathe so heavily without Girondin accord. There is much terror now in Paris, the mob ruling the streets. Only just recently they lopped off a man's head, this thing called a guillotine. My god, what has become of my country! But, I have come of course not to lament upon my lot, but to help you my friend. There is an opportunity here, Captain, to save yourself.'

'Indeed, from what, pray tell?'

'It is a trap Captain, a sham. They mean to lure you to Brest and take you and your ships. It will not be a fair match. Captain Lafayette means to meet you with La Solitaire.'

'Solitaire, you say?'

'Yes.'

'Not, His Majesty's Ship Solitaire?'

'The very same.'

'But that is not a French ship sir, not anymore.'

'It is true, but once she was a French ship, handsomely designed by Antoine Groignard you know. Launched at Brest in seventy-four and she was in fact lead ship of her class, a very well-known vessel. And you are right, being captured in eighty-two, King George bought her into his service of course, such a fine ship. But Captain, she is French again, for was she not sold out of your navy only some two years ago? You did not know this? Gold has no sovereignty but its own, even to the English. This ship, she was bought and paid for by the Jacobins and now have they given her to Captain Lafayette.'

'A sixty-four is she not?'

'Yes?'

'Then, is it not a fair match?'

'Well, fair enough, however, Captain Lafayette has sent for the commander of the northern privateer contingent. He means to have La Vénus assist, she being a forty gun heavy frigate!'

'Oh, but I know this ship,' Cooper casually remarked. 'Thirty-eight gun Hébé class? In eighty-two I believe she operated as a transport between Rochefort and Île de Ré, serving in Martinique during the American War. But, as I understand it, was she not wrecked in eighty-eight?'

'Wrecked, yes and given up for good by the navy. But later, she was salvaged unaware, by these privateer dogs. And Captain, this Lafayette dog, he means to also have La Hasard nipping at your heels. With such a force, you cannot hope to withstand, not even with every ounce of your skill sir. And he very much knows you will present yourself alone with just Agamemnon and Achilles, for your honour so demands it. Of course, if you dare present with a larger fleet, he will cry foul and make his case to the ministry. However, upon destroying you, he will seek to murder every man in your squadron, for this is how he will hide his duplicity. He is a clever one. He has thought it through most thoroughly. In the next day will Captain de Rossily and La Vénus come, his journey to Brest already under way. Upon arriving, he will take part in the action against Agamemnon and assist your capture.'

'On his way, you say?'

'Yes Captain, he will come because I had been ordered to fetch and safely instruct him upon his course. We are but only one day ahead of him.'

'But how can you be sure of his intended course?'

'But I am senior and know these waters, whilst he does not. He must follow where I order and I have made his course already, if you understand?'

'Aye sir, I believe I do,' Cooper grinned. 'Am I to understand Venus is to cruise past Ortac?'

'But of course, unless you have some other indestructible fort sneakily hidden about these waters? Maybe, you have some island fort hidden in the harbour of Brest, Captain?'

'Ha, very well sir, very well.'

'Although Captain, one thing, we are not at war. You know this. If you attack him without cause, he can have you hanged.'

'Hanged is it, or guillotined? Those are my choices? And what grand choices! Oh, let us not worry about small details just now Captain. But I assure you, the very presence of peace is exactly the detail I wish to rely upon.'

'Captain Cooper, sir, I know you are most cunning of course, but please be careful. One wrong move will see our countries at war and many awkward questions presented upon my person, ones I cannot hope to escape. I do not wish to be dragged like that poor sod into the square of Paris and my head lopped into some cheap basket.'

'Fear not my friend, for never will I allow that.'

'Perhaps it is better to retire to the safety of your shores and just wait for war?'

'Captain, war is coming sooner than you think. Now, am I correct in assuming you have not yet had the honour of actually standing upon our fort at Ortac? Perhaps, sir, it is time we extended an invitation?' Cooper grinned. 'Now tell me my friend, are you very much afraid of sharks sir?'

Venus presented herself upon the horizon, Eagle's nest spotting her tops as the early morning sparked. She was indeed a heavy frigate, now forty gun. It was of course the latest thinking in wartime strategy, promoting fast ships with eighteen pounders instead of the traditional twelves. She was sailing large it seemed but Agamemnon had the advantage of some four sea miles before Venus could chance to spot her and then, only with the sharpest of

French eye. Holt was quick to suggest Hébé class frigates were likely to make ten or twelve knots, the ensuing calculations buzzing though his head.

'Twenty minutes then Mister Holt, is it?'

'Captain, you beat me sir? I was going to say a tad more, but mainly because the masthead on a frigate is somewhat lower, making our standard four mile advantage slightly more. I heartily agree that with a small safety buffer, it should be no less than twenty minutes before Venus will spot us, providing of course we do not move towards her. It is most likely we will get a bit more though.'

'Very well, twenty minutes it is, just to be sure. Now, Mister Smythe?'

'Aye, sir?'

'Prepare to set the ship on fire, if you please.'

'Aye sir, set the ship on fire,' he confirmed. 'Sir! What?' he frantically responded.

'Have you never set a ship on fire sir?'

'Only once sir, but I must point out that it was in fact an American frigate and I had the pleasure of not being aboard her at the time.'

'Mister Smythe, I believe the Captain wishes you to make smoke and lots of it, so as we take on the appearance of being on fire.'

'Oh, I see,' he confirmed, much relieved. 'Aye sir, setting a forecastle fire, ablaze and dark smoke it is!'

Agamemnon limped into the strait between Ortac and Alderney. Blackened smoke billowed from the weather deck and the forecastle came alive with flame. The jacks were hard at it, brewing lard and whale fat in a great many number of tubs. The foremast lay bereft of sail and the jacks hauled the mains, ragged, fluttering haplessly as a wounded duck. The entire ship appeared very much weathered and ill formed. Boats were launched, buzzing haphazardly about the hull, floundering as if they had spotted a fat whale.

'Fire one cannon to leeward, if you please Mister Smythe.'

'That has done it, she has seen us sir!'

'Very well, when she is almost in range, fire all cannon, low into the water, if you please.'

'Sir?'

'We wish to show them we are defenceless. Now be sure not to accidentally hull them as they approach. I would have to insist upon becoming furious if you do. Thereafter ensure all the ports are shut, but be quick smart about reloading. And have the helm put us under the gun at Ortac, subtle now, as if we are drifting.'

'Sir, Venus making for us. She has her ports open and cannon run out. I think she means to fire?'

'It's just French precaution Mister Smythe, do not fret now.'

'Ah, aye sir, they are dropping boats. Aye, two boats on their way.'

Whilst his men waited in the boats, Captain de Rossily made his way upon Agamemnon, welcomed in the usual fashion for a visiting captain. A number of officers clambered over the gunwale, anxiously looking to the fire.

'Captain, welcome, I am Spencer, Captain Spencer, but I am somewhat surprised sir to find you here on my deck?'

'But I have come with men, to offer assistance to your ship.'

'Assistance, sir?'

'She is on fire, no?'

'No, sir, she is not on fire. We have recently purchased a horsepiece from a whaler. Presently we have a number of books in some makeshift tryworks up there on the forecastle. Moreover, sir, we are in the process of boiling blubber, to make oil.'

'Then you do not need assistance? But your ship is wailing about in the sea, your boats are in the water and you fired your cannon?'

'It is Sunday sir, the men are afforded a day of leisure, swimming, cooking and skylarking. Surely, is it not so dissimilar in your navy?'

'Well Captain, yes, in fact it is. We do not allow such behaviour, nor do we boil oil on a ship of war. Very well, we will repair to our ship and leave you to your skylarking.'

'A word first, sir, in the great cabin if you please?' Spencer politely requested. 'It is a matter of some delicate importance, so perhaps it might serve for you to attend alone with perhaps just one senior officer?' he suggested. Captain de Rossily entered the great cabin and to his great surprise he found Cooper slouching lazily before him, a half drunken bottle of rum assisting the nearest glass. Cooper looked at them in bewilderment, visibly straining his gaze in a most prolonged gawk and most undeniably, did he continue to stare. 'Admiral, sir, I say Admiral Cooper, sir,' Spencer intoned, raising his voice as if the man was a tad deaf. 'I present Captain de Rossily of the French Navy frigate Venus, forty gun.'

'Admiral? This ship has an admiral?' de Rossily openly quizzed, somewhat amazed. 'But, sir, I think I recognise you, Captain Hayden Reginald Cooper of Chatham, of Agamemnon, are you not?'

'Aye, sir,' Spencer immediately answered for him. 'The very same, although now he is Sir Hayden Reginald Cooper, Knights Companion of the Order of the Tub, recently knighted by King George himself.'

'Knighted?'

'Aye and promoted admiral, Admiral of the Purple.'

'Purple?'

'And this ship?'

'His Majesty's Ship, Agamemnon.'

'What? But is this ship not *"Game"*, for your stern was so marked?'

'Oh, we are in the process of washing the name and remarking her.'

'What? This is Agamemnon!'

'Very good, very good,' Cooper abruptly asserted. 'Now Captain Spencer, where are your manners? Please to offer our good Captain some rum?'

'Admiral? But it is barely an hour past the sun rising sir?'

'Oh, I see, perhaps some wine then?'

'Admiral, sir, if I may,' Spencer interrupted. 'Captain de Rossily here has just kindly surrendered.'

'What?' de Rossily immediately protested. 'I have done no such thing! What outrageousness! What impudence!'

'So, Captain,' Cooper immediately challenged, now picking up his rum to fully fill his glass, a penetrating gaze slyly laid amidships. 'Am I to understand you have not surrendered?'

'Of course not!'

'Captain Spencer, please to inform directly sir, did Captain de Rossily row here under a white flag?'

'No, sir, he did not.'

'So, Captain de Rossily, no white flag sir?'

'No? But of course no white flag, why would we need a white flag?'

'To afford your protection sir, otherwise you may be struck down of course, quite legally I am afraid,' he casually cautioned, his fingers now plainly tapping the hilt of his katana.

'Struck down? But sir, we are not at war! We came here to offer assistance, not to be subject to this abject attempt at English piracy!'

'Not at war? Not at war, you say! Oh dear, sir, oh dear indeed. Captain, I am very much afraid that our two countries are most heartily at war, declared only last evening. But do not fret, for you are not the only ship to be caught unaware. Please to cast an eye out the stern light sir? There, that is the nose of Pompee, anchored about the rocks of Ortac there. I have her commander, Captain Poulain, secured upon Ortac, shackled safely in my fort there.'

'Shackled? You have an officer shackled!'

'He did not comply sir, nothing else for it.'

'Did you say fort? What fort?' he cried, now straining to discern Ortac. 'You cannot build a fort on French soil!'

'Of course not, which is why we have built it here and I assure you we are well over the three mile stipulation from Alderley, at least by about two hundred yards, measured shore to shore.'

'But you did not build this fort just last night, surely you had it built some days or even weeks ago, such is its complexity! And you say war was only declared last evening, sir?'

'Oh small details, small details, let us not quibble over such things. Here, take my glass, you will see a barrage of sixty-fours awaiting, there, sitting upon the rockery, all pointed at Venus naturally. Our man up there, Lord Shillings, well, he can hit a sloop at five hundred yards and your frigate, as magnificent as she is, perhaps lies barely a hundred yards? Duck on the pond sir, duck on the pond!'

'Admiral, I must protest and I fear sir, you are not yourself?

Ships of War — Murky Waters

Perhaps it is the rum?'

'I did have the same conversation with Captain Poulain of course. Nasty man, very nasty and well, let us say he did not come to reason upon the matter.'

'Admiral, I say again, I protest. We are not at war and even if we were, your honour would afford the opportunity to allow Venus to sail to port, under parole, for we have not yet been informed of the declaration. Upon my honour, you have my parole.'

'Oh, no, no, no, my dear Captain,' Cooper angrily differed. 'We are well past that, you refusing my rum and all. You now have but two choices before you. I rather care not if you accept the truth that we are at war, for it does not alter your predicament. Venus will strike sir, or you will see her sunk, directly,' he adamantly insisted now motioning to Spencer, who nodded and every so casually opened the stern light and waved his scarf. A moment later, an almighty roar broke the silence. They could hear the whizzing of a lone ball flying past, met with an uproar of wildness upon the deck of Venus. 'A warning shot sir! And might I advise that Agamemnon, whilst presently not in a position to fire upon Venus, is very much able to slip her cable sir, quite swiftly. Our cannon is already reloaded and should Venus not sink fast enough from the weight of a few more sixty-fours, our eventual broadside will ensure every revolutionary aboard will not be afforded the chance to drown!' he gruffly warned, the end of the game very much afoot. Captain de Rossily remained quiet, his head down in obvious contemplation. Cooper looked to Spencer. 'Very well, Captain Spencer, signal to Ortac to fire upon Venus. Slip the cable and I suppose we must beat to quarters now, although Lord Shillings will likely have this over in a moment.'

'Aye, aye, sir!'

'Very well Admiral,' agreed de Rossily abruptly, now offering his sword.

'Colonel McFee, please to take Captain de Rossily's officers to the prison. In the meantime, blindfold Captain de Rossily and transfer him to Ortac so we might continue our little chat.'

Bradley John

The lower chambers of Ortac were dank and dark, the sounds of a howling madman echoing faintly through the hollows. Much to his disdain, the French captain was escorted into what barely could be called a cell. Before him a man was slumped, moaning and blubbering as might a crazed lunatic, gingerly cradling the stump of a missing arm. It was Middleton of course, not making any sense, the look of homeless rat catcher gracing his visage. In the other corner sat Captain Poulain, of Pompee, quite contrite and sullen, his clothing tattered and damp.

'Poulain, my friend, what is this place? Who is this English dog?'

'We are prisoners of a madman, I assure you. You know our ship, *Le Triomphant*, eighty gun?'

'But of course, out of Brest, she took part in the Battle of Martinique with the Comte de Guichen's fleet.'

'She would not strike of course and this madman sank her, right before my eyes as I stood helplessly upon Pompee.'

'What!'

'His cannon upon this rock, they are sixty-fours and did the deed with just one barrage. I am afraid she exploded wholly to bits. I of course had to strike and here I am, a rat in a hole, as now are you.'

'He will hang, for we are not at war, not yet!'

'Ah, but it is war my friend. I received a dispatch, but this madman snatched me up before I had chanced to read it.'

'Then it is true?'

'It is true, I am afraid. There will be no *duel* at Brest now, not with such hostilities under way. Lafayette's honour will have to come to him by other means.'

'But what is it this madman wants? If we are at war, why are we locked up? It is not civilised of course and my god, who is this, this blubbering fool over there?'

Ships of War — Murky Waters

'Oh, that is Captain Lord Middleton, one of the Admiral's officers.'

'A captain? And he is mad?'

'Not at first, but then they took him away and when he returned his arm was gone. Can you imagine what they did? And to a captain! Whatever semblance of sanity there was, surely is now all gone. I cannot get much from him, but it seems he had displeased his Admiral.'

'This madman, he dismembers his own officers, this one even a lord as well? What kind of lunatic is he?' he cried, now gingerly approaching Middleton. 'Hey English, what did you do?' he whispered.

'He wouldn't call me Lord,' he blubbered, obviously inebriated.

'What?'

'Captain Lefty,' he replied somewhat drifting in and out. 'God damn my arm. No! No, the shark....'

'Mad as a Parisian skunk?'

'Yes, but it seems they do have a shark, a big one,' Poulain warned most earnestly. 'I have not seen it, but I think this officer's arm was fed to it?'

'But, that is madness!'

'This Admiral, he will test us soon. Already has he asked about the fortifications along our harbours, the number of our ships, the location of our stores and our armaments.'

'Surely he does not expect us to tell him anything? We must look to our honour and so never can we tell of course. But you are right. We should not incite him so, lest we are fed to some shark. Perhaps we can play a ruse, insist we are ignorant and unimportant and have no such knowledge of these matters?'

'To play dumb, this will not work, not unless we offer something up. As mad as he is, he is not so stupid I fear.'

'Perhaps, but we must not offer anything that will matter.'

'Agreed.'

'Wait, be quiet now, they come for us.'

Bradley John

Captain de Rossily was escorted into the sunlight, his eyes squinting indignantly within the harshness of the midday zenith. Slyly he ventured to glance about. Poulain had disappeared and Venus was nowhere to be found, perhaps moored the other side of Ortac and very much out of view. Soon enough he found himself upon Pompee, a pair of ropes ominously hanging from each side of the yard. It was there he found his comrade and very much to his utter shock was poor Poulain dangling, struggling and wriggling as they lowered him towards the sea.

'Ah Captain de Rossily, just in time!' welcomed Cooper.

'Please Admiral,' Poulain shouted from afar. 'I do not know anything! I cannot tell you what I do not know!'

'Come now Captain, if that is true then I have no real need of you, do I?' Cooper resentfully bellowed, now turning to idly chat with de Rossily. 'Your friend Captain Poulain is quite resilient,' he grinned. 'I am almost in belief that he knows nothing. But, alas, if he doesn't give me something, anything, I will feed him to Lefty.'

'Lefty?'

'Oh, that is what the jacks are calling my shark. He's a big one too, lives here at Ortac. Loves an arm or a leg, sometimes she just swoops up and takes it all. Oh how the crew enjoys watching her go at it. But you will see her soon enough, once the good Captain is a bit lower.'

'Admiral!' Poulain pleaded as he dangled from the yard. 'I have done nothing to merit this treatment. By rights, you cannot proceed, for I have acted in accordance with all honour! Please Admiral!'

'But come now Captain Poulain,' he insisted quite convincingly. 'Come now, you sir are a pirate! We have proof! Do you deny Pompee has preyed upon our shipping? And all of these deeds perpetrated well before the declaration mind you! So, you see, I am quite in my rights to hang you! Or in this case, hang you and feed you to my shark, ha, ha!'

'But Admiral,' Poulain cried again. 'Pompee was a privateer, not a pirate. Sir, with respect, you cannot legally do this!'

'Privateer?' he barked. 'Who says, 'ey? Why would I believe such nonsense? Mister Smythe, lower the good Captain down to sea level, he is of more use to Lefty than to us.'

'Admiral, I can prove it sir, please!'

'Oh very well,' Cooper huffed. 'Belay there, Mister Smythe. Be so good as to bring him and Captain de Rossily to Pompee's great cabin,' he reluctantly ordered, storming off. Poulain appeared very much maddened with fright. McFee dragged him into the cabin and threw him to the planking. 'Now Captain Poulain, it would very much honour me if you would tell me sir about your operations before the war, as a private ship of war, you say?'

'As a privateer, yes Admiral. But please do not be mistaken sir, we had authority, credentials, otherwise it would be piracy of course.'

'Well, I might beg to differ and would offer that I very much might prefer to see you hanged. However, I must unfortunately agree, if you can prove such a claim, I cannot hang you. If you indeed have your Letter of Marque, I will deem you personally blameless and as such will not hold you to account. But, let me make this very clear, your ship will still be forfeit either way. And Captain de Rossily, sir, I have the pleasure to inform that you are next. I have irrefutable information about the operations and piracy of Venus, in the north,' Cooper rightly accused, now handing him a list of the ships that actually had been taken. 'Venus is a pirate, as are you and please do not insult me by denying it sir. Now, gentlemen, it seems you are both in the same boat, ha, ha! Well, maybe different ships, but most definitely the same boat, ha, ha, ha!'

'We must not say anything Poulain,' de Rossily warned, now speaking in French, unaware Cooper had his ear. 'We may save our necks from the English as privateers, but we will lose our heads as traitors when we return home. You know this and in any case, he is bluffing. He will not execute us as pirates, no. There is no proof.'

'But he has proof of our fleet actions, much proof. Without our authority, without our Letter, to him we are nothing but pirates and rightly so. If we say nothing then our war is over my friend, over. We will not be fighting the English in what is yet to come. This privateering is of no consequence now, none, being that we are presently at war. What can it matter?' he whispered in French, now switching back to English. 'They can do nothing to us as legal privateers and hardly can they now complain to our government. Time for that has since passed. Why be hanged or fed to a shark? And the good Admiral will be compelled to trade us if we cooperate.'

'Indeed, if you are to inform me correctly of your operations as a privateer, present your Letter of Marque, then it is my duty to see you are not hanged as pirates. And you are quite right Captain Poulain, I will be compelled, albeit unhappily, to trade you for one of our captains, once the opportunity arises.'

'But Admiral, we must make it clear we cannot inform you of operations crucial to our country's war effort. If we are to offer up our evidence, will you give us your assurance that we will be treated correctly as prisoners of war thereafter?'

'It is fair enough. I must get something from you and this will suit. I can use the evidence for reparations of course, after the war has ended. French privateers have preyed upon English commerce for some time now, all during the peace. The King will very much thank me once he finds out and so will he sue for his lost ships, once we have beaten France. All in all, this suits me, but to be frank, I think my crew would very much rather hang you for Lefty's dinner. Nonetheless, you have my oath upon my honour and I will even return your swords, 'ey, good enough?'

'On your honour?'

'On my honour, Captain, but I will need some evidence first. Hardly is the word of a pirate going to hold up now is it?'

'As you wish Captain,' Poulain offered, now looking to de Rossily for approval, but it was not so forthcoming. 'In the hull behind you is a loosened board. You will find the document there.'

'No Poulain, he is bluffing!'

'I see,' Cooper replied, levering back the board to reveal a tidy hiding hole. 'Well, well, well, unfortunately Captain, there is no document here?'

'What? But it was there!'

'Mister Smythe, take him away!' he angrily ordered. Cooper continued to eye de Rossily, the disbelieving visage of the French captain mocking every moment. A grand cheer roaring atop broke the stalemate of silence. Cooper grinned and he motioned through the stern light, a capital spot to discern the lowering of Poulain into the sea. It was with shock de Rossily witnessed a monstrous shark leaping from the depths, snatching whole its meal, tumbling and twisting as it struggled with its prey. The French captain's uniform fell shredded, left to float in the swirling wash of the Ortac swell.

'My god!' de Rossily cried. 'This is madness sir! You cannot feed naval officers to sharks, even if we are at war!'

'But I just did? I assure you Captain it is no less than the madness sweeping Paris, except our guillotine swims in the sea, 'ey and goes up not down, ha, ha! Nonetheless, on my honour, you will be afforded every luxury of your rank and ever will I uphold our agreement, provided your Letter of Marque is somewhat more tangible than that of poor Captain Poulain's.'

'Very well, it is as Poulain said, it is of no consequence and once I am returned to service, I will enjoy very much our next meeting. So there it is, I agree Admiral. You will have my Letter of Marque, what verily does it matter now anyway.'

What verily does it matter. Cooper was thinking a noose around his neck for abject piracy on the high seas might definitely matter, at least to him. Without a good and proper reason to take Venus, that would be the only likely outcome. Yet now Cooper could breathe easily. His elaborate ruse had won through. He had Venus, legally now.

'Very well Captain, then you have my word and will be treated with dignity and deference to someone befitting your rank. And I will arrange to have your sword returned sir, on the promise of your parole of course. Now, whilst we are waiting for it to be fetched and seeing how we are now friends, I would verily be interested to know something, something I am sure you will agree is no longer a state secret?'

'But of course Admiral.'

'And I only ask now, because of course you have proven to be an honourable officer, only following orders. And what would our seas be, without the honour esteemed of our rank and privilege. Therefore, in turn, I would be honoured if you might regale me with a step by step blow, as to how you and Captain Lafayette were plotting to capture Agamemnon, in our little duel at Brest? I only wish to know of course out of the mildest of curiosity. I am sure it will amuse.'

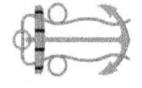

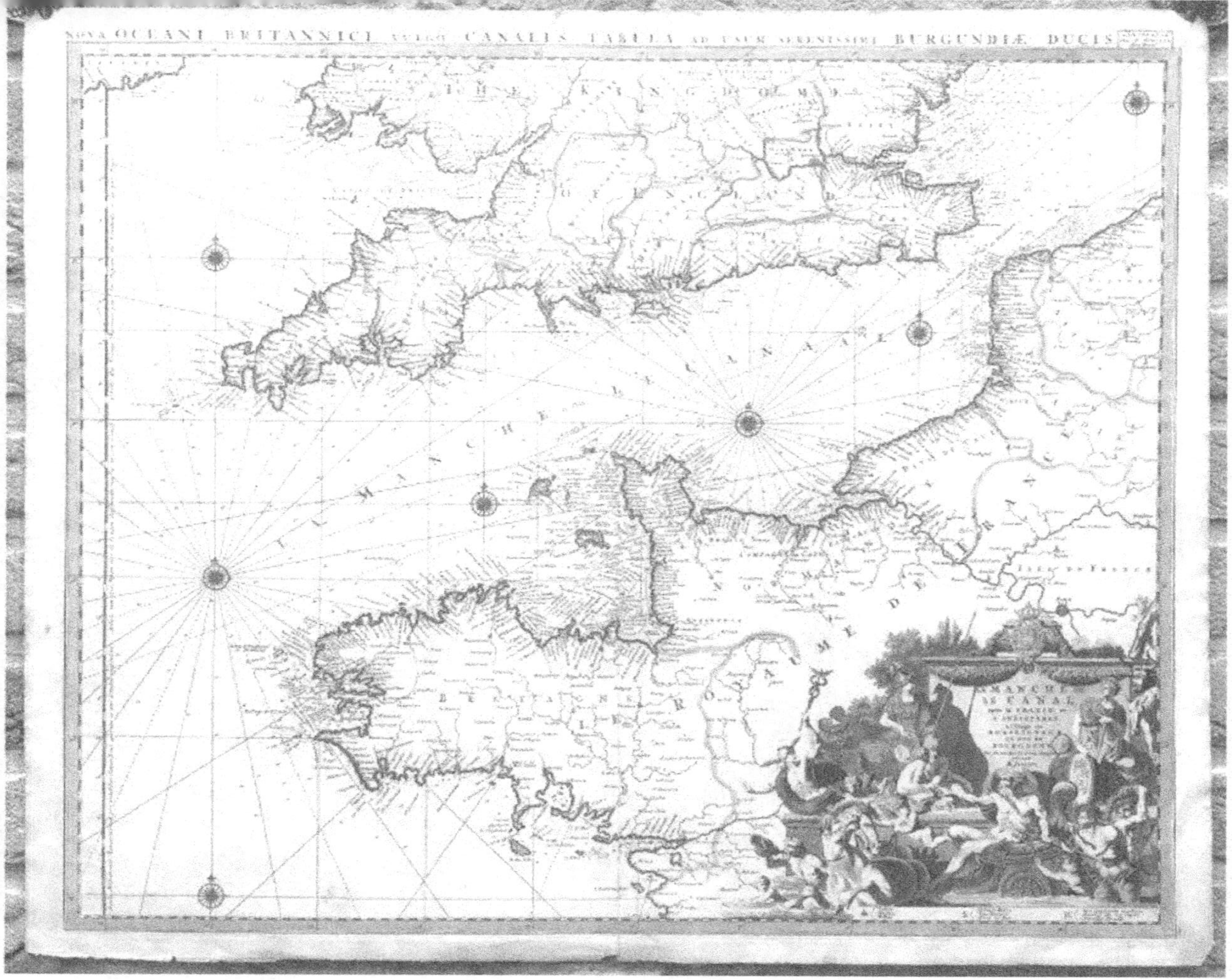

Chapter XXII
La Solitaire

Agamemnon headed south by west, her course laid in for Brest. It was with some dignity that all officers were present upon the quarterdeck, including Doctor Blane, Major McFee and even Captain Poulain. Agamemnon had taken many ships, but never a frigate and never without even firing a shot. They were licking their chops at the prospect of another and the hope of more prize money. Yet especially prevalent was the gratifying thought of Solitaire soon to be helplessly striking to the dogged cunning of their illustrious captain. It was interesting that the alternative, being the notion of their ultimate and complete destruction, had never once surfaced. Perhaps it would only have obliged to offer some kind of betrayal and most assuredly, to their minds, the battle had already been played out and the prize since divided up.

It warmed the hearts of all to know Achilles was presently cruising a good handful of sea miles further south, which is to say forward of Agamemnon's position off her larboard bow. Of course no one on the quarterdeck could see her, Captain Spencer ensuring her sails peeked just over the horizon. Industriously was Spencer hugging the shores of Brittany, keeping the French coastline broad upon his larboard beam. And verily with Venus some miles further to the west, which is to say forward of Agamemnon off her starboard beam, the eyes of Cooper's squadron now spanned well beyond the natural horizons.

For many bells had Cooper maintained himself upon the quarterdeck, a sight which very much sought to calm the crew. He held his usual place, to leeward, segregated from the others. But very much was he comforted by the thought of his consorts and his man Eagle sitting atop. Nothing could hope to come upon him, not without some great forewarning. Outwardly he was as stone, as well he should be, carefully monitoring the progress of Agamemnon, taking note of every detail before him. Yet inwardly he stood fierce and determined, a raging lion upon the sea, deeply aware of his every obligation, his utmost duty. It had not escaped him, not even for the barest of moments that his ship would be entertaining battle upon the rise of the next day's sun, the appointed day. To win would merely be to do his duty, but to lose would see him fall hopelessly from grace, nothing less than the fiery pits of bubbling hell water verily awaiting. Agamemnon could well be food for the fish by the zenith of the morrow's midday, just another insignificant speck of history ultimately lost in time to the tyranny of French cannon.

Cooper was well aware, surely as it was so glaringly obvious, that this would be the first real engagement for his squadron, their first real test. Oh, they had taken brigs and of course they had pretended to fence with Queen Charlotte, but the task of taking Solitaire would be a matter of the greatest consequence. And no less would he be pitted against one of France's acclaimed revolutionary heroes. Lafayette was a seasoned pirate, an esteemed commodore who had furtively fought his ship for some two years. He would be a most dangerous adversary and Cooper knew it, all too well. The man's reputation upon the sea of course preceded him. Likely brilliant he was of course, albeit somewhat certifiable. And it was this, of all things, Cooper feared most.

Hasard's engagement with Resignation, the strategy undertaken, the wild manoeuvring, the gruesome sinking and the heartless murder of almost every man aboard had definitely given Cooper some pause. Of further concern was no doubt Lafayette's distinct lack of regard even for his own crew. A man so maddened was as a rabid dog cornered, the only remedy but to put it down. And Poulain had already foreshadowed that to lose would mean the likely death of everyone aboard. Good god Cooper thought, would this lunatic even murder the boys? If there had been doubt, there was none now. Never could the honour of this Frenchman be trusted or held to parole. It was all or nothing, no middle ground. Lafayette had already plotted to cheat upon the terms. To insist Venus secretly attend the duel, no doubt easily swaying the battle, was an effrontery to the honour of every respectable Frenchman, let alone to the entire Royal Navy. It was all no surprise of course. However, it begged Cooper to consider what else the villain might have in store. What other dastardly tricks would he have up his sleeve? He recalled Lafayette's brother, the Chevalier. They had duelled at the Lion, only a simple game of cards, but oh even there how the man had dared to cheat, a family trait perhaps. Contemplation sought to engage Cooper's every waking moment. Upon it, the very lives of every man aboard depended. It dogged him as a storm hounding a flock, maddened gulls desperately fleeing the tempest. It was not until Poulain approached that he chanced to break from his trance.

'Captain Cooper, I believe you owe me a new coat sir?'

'Of course,' he smiled, the thought of Poulain's best coat shredded by shark all but forcing a humble grin. 'I heartily regret the loss of your fine coat sir. My acting first officer, Mister Holt, will no doubt loan you his.'

'Your acting first officer? The lad, he, he has a captain's coat?'

'Indeed,' he posed, as if it were normal practice.

'Is not Mister Holt still rated midshipman?'

'But of course,' he stoically teased, silently implying there was nothing untoward about a fifteen year old lord afforded the right almighty as it were to take the helm of a Royal Navy sixty-four gun ship of war.

'And he has a captain's coat?'

'And more,' he grinned. 'From where did you think I acquired the Admiral's coat? It seems his father, the honourable Lord Holt, is very much the optimist. The lad has not yet even passed for lieutenant and his father insisted upon packing them, just in case I am told. At least His Lordship had the good sense to make them a tad bigger, in expectation of the lad's growth. Oh, here he comes now, I believe with your new coat sir. The lad is something of a psychic you will find.'

'Captain Poulain, might I offer you the loan of a coat sir? And sir, may I congratulate you on your splendid performance.'

'I assure you Mister Holt, the fear I felt dangling from the yard was no performance. I could see that dark monster circling underneath you know. My god, it must have been some twenty feet long?'

'Twenty-three feet, in course, sir.'

'That big! My god, I was in definite wonderment as to how high the thing might be able to leap.'

'They are told to leap most prodigiously,' added Holt.

'Are they?' Cooper blankly teased, copiously playing dumb, much to the immediate horror of Poulain. 'It was well played nonetheless,' he praised. 'You have my personal gratitude. And now our pirate friend, Captain de Rossily, is headed for an English prison!'

'And you have Venus!' commended Poulain.

'Captain de Rossily was somewhat furious to discover that war had not yet been declared,' Holt smirked. 'And he was banging on about how you fed Captain Poulain to the shark. The port authorities very much think him a madman, sir. But Fredricks, I fear, is somewhat beside himself, after we had fed his best beef to Lefty!'

'We must all sacrifice in our endeavour to do our utmost Mister Holt.'

'But Captain,' Poulain worriedly posed. 'Had Captain de Rossily not presented his Letter of Marque, I struggle to know what you might have done sir? Without such damning evidence, you had nothing to establish the taking of his ship, except piracy. No doubt, a noose could have been placed about your neck?'

'A calculated risk, sir.'

'My god,' he vexed. 'A bluff?'

'Such is war. We cannot verily know every outcome, only our chances and I deemed my chances with Captain de Rossily were better than good. We have taken our first frigate, without even firing a shot and now she is part of our squadron. We shall have to insist some works be performed upon her of course, she is much too sluggish and unkempt. And I am also thinking a more appropriate name is in order, especially considering His Majesty already has a Venus.'

'A new name? Indeed, sir!' Holt enthusiastically remarked. 'And so it seems, in history's pages, here ends the voyages and tales of La Vénus?'

'I have no doubt, considering the indelicate manner in which we took her, the history books of France will likely reflect she did in fact remain wrecked, back in eighty-eight. Which reminds me, Mister Holt, where away is our Venus?'

'Sir, by now Captain Smythe has her some miles to our west, all upon the prearranged course to Ushant, of which Captain Poulain had originally laid out. With the prevailing winds at this time of year, she will likely enter the battle from the guise of the local islands, with the gage no doubt, just as Captain Lafayette had instructed.'

'And Captain, may I say how handsome it was for Captain de Rossily to convey the details of Captain Lafayette's plan of battle, in full it seems. I congratulate you sir.'

'Indeed and if he was wholly truthful, which I unreservedly believe he was, then we will not be as surprised as Captain Lafayette thinks. Good god, a rogue heavy frigate bearing down upon us with the gage at their back! It's quite brilliant of course. Even with Venus now commandeered, we are still outgunned, our Achilles not quite in match with Hasard, but with our extra carronades and McFee's jollies upon her, it should even the bout somewhat. Captain Spencer has his orders and no doubt will do his utmost. I trust no other man with what I have asked.'

'But Captain, you say you are outgunned? Am I to understand you will not entertain using Venus?' Poulain remarked with some qualified amazement. 'You know, of course, it would be over quite smartly.'

'It is a duel, not war and our honour demands it, even though our counterpart, the dog, has none as such to speak of. I will not use Venus.'

'Of this, you are sure, sir?'

'Of course I am sure, there is not a skerrick of doubt he is an honourless dog,' he blankly returned, holding back the driest of grimace, much to the mirth of all in earshot. Captain Poulain could not help but heartily grin, very much in admiration of the pre-battle levity displayed by this young English captain.

'Sir, four bells in the first *dog* watch,' interrupted Holt, timing his candour precisely, the mirth of the quarterdeck now forming the foam of a tumultuous wave of laughter.

'Very well, make it so and *roll over* the glass,' Cooper cheekily added, a playful squint in his eye. 'Gentlemen, let us all repair to the great cabin with a promise of good company and of course a succulent lamb. Fredricks has been sulking of course, but I have every hope our fare will be magnificent, as always. My apologies, in that our beef had been *hung* out and is now somewhat a loss. I do believe lamb is in the offing. Nonetheless, so shall we enjoy our dinner tonight, as brothers in arms, for tomorrow so shall we fight.'

Stormy seas awaited Agamemnon at Ushant, murky waters spawned within a darkened sky. It was no less a chilling reminder of what was yet to come. The sun had risen. But still there remained a bleak silhouette ever gracing the eastern horizon, a dull dome serving to surround the last remnants of the Channel. With Brittany looming, the Iroise Sea now beckoned and with Ushant behind them, there was definitely no turning back. It was with some gratification that Cooper accepted the conditions. The Iroise Sea was well known for her violence, all told beholding a temperament more befitting a maddened wild beast. In the offing, high seas threatened, a cold outlook promised. Nonetheless did

Eagle manage to maintain an unrestricted view to the horizon, the regular call of *"all's well"* constantly reassuring the ship. Upon rounding Ushant the great ship spread her wings, sailing large, the wind swirling about her back til she bore directly south.

'Captain, it seems the seas have built even more since we rounded Ushant,' Blane nervously vexed. 'Could they become any more monstrous?'

'I assure you Doctor, with some degree of exactness, these seas can form even monstrously bigger, given leave to do so.'

'Egad. But is not the ship already shuddering somewhat horribly at the stern? Is there no cause for concern? The quarterdeck is as calm as Brading Tavern on Sunday, almost as if I had prescribed them a tincture of my finest laudanum?'

'But it is just Agamemnon pooping Doctor,' reassured Cooper.

'Pooping? Well, yes that makes sense, but I very much rather it is I who is in danger of *pooping*, such is my distress.'

'What? Oh? Indeed, ha, ha!'

'I could be wrong of course, just a simple doctor, but is not the ship shuddering perhaps to the point she soon might break up?'

'It grieves me to inform you sir that you are indeed wrong, on both counts.'

'Both counts?'

'Aye, come now sir. Firstly, you are no simple doctor and I think you know this. And secondly, that shudder you discern is merely the resultant shock from the prosecution of high and heavy seas, the hull scudding and trembling as the ship is belted somewhat upon its quarter. It is most common for her to scud before the wind within such a tempest. And good sir, it is called pooping.'

'Oh? Well, yes of course, that pooping.'

'If you are unwell Doctor, I give you leave to repair below. We can only expect such savagery to continue I am afraid.'

'It is true Doctor,' Holt sympathised. 'Upon rounding *Ouessant*, or Ushant as we say, so did we leave behind the last remnants of the Channel and with it the sanity of her seas. Now we have the honour of finding ourselves upon the Iroise Sea, in particular the *Passage de l'Iroise*. And Doctor if I may, you will find the natural differences in depth between here and the

Channel, which runs adjacent of course, prodigiously considerable. These differences, in distinct point of fact, chance to create the strong currents affecting the very seas we now toil and suffer.'

'Very good Mister Holt and in course, if I may, low tides in the Channel accordingly serve to bring about tremendously untold south-westerly currents here. We are in fact experiencing such a current right now, which is why together with the wind at our back we are easily making way at some ludicrous rate.'

'Ludicrous?' questioned Blane.

'Oh, certifiable is likely more apt. And Doctor, I dare not ask how fast we make. Oh no, that would never do, for I am certain that should I hear of it hardly will I ever come to believe it. And presently to what end but mere vanity might it serve? Scarcely could I ever hope to boast the truth of such a feat at such establishments as the Lion. Nay, for immediately would I be accused a liar or set upon by men in white coats.'

'Naturally,' conceded Blane.

'Strike me though, is it not undeniable, she really is running! Perhaps, Mister Holt, you might be disposed to inform me later,' he grinned. 'In case I change my mind.'

'Of course, sir.'

'And Mister Holt, please to note, these currents will naturally reverse at high tide. You will see soon enough for yourself, but they can reach outrageously high speeds even as far as the Raz de Sein to the south or even the Goulet de Brest.'

'It hasn't seemed to deter the French navy though, having maintained a base at Brest for over a hundred and fifty years now.'

'And how fitting a sea is she named, Iroise, of course meaning *"angry"*, referring no doubt to the eternally rough seas.'

'Indeed, does it Captain? I have not yet had the honour of stumbling upon that meaning?'

'Ah Mister Holt, but it is an abject perhaps dubious adjective of Old French. And to the point, moreover the word commonly refers to the Irish of course, which makes perfect sense being they are mostly known to be eternally stormy, rough and somewhat livid, ha, ha! Also, may I offer that in Breton, the word supplies to mean, as such, or to depict rather, something that is *"deep"*. It is apt, a name which serves to oppose the shallowness of the Channel I suspect.'

It was with some bewilderment that the officers began to silently ponder the course maintained by their captain. The winds continued to howl southward, a true northerly zephyr. Agamemnon had every scrap of it directly at her back now. In consequence she was flying, her timbers moaning, the sheets shaking. But every mile directly south only put her farther away from the shores of Brittany and farther away from their intended destination. Cooper as yet had not disclosed his plan to the crew and that even included the officers. However, their journey and its purpose was no secret and upon embarking even the ship's cat was aware of the intended destination. Murmurs grew as Brittany slipped further away, speculation running ripe.

The considered opinion scattered upon the quarterdeck was most undeniably singular in mind. They wholly expected to approach Brest by rounding Ushant, which they had done. Yet next, they naturally conceived that standing into Brest would only be served by continuing east by south through the Passage de l'Iroise. This was yet to come. But when it did, every man and jack would know, as it would require the ship to wear, to turn somewhat to larboard from their southerly route. It would have to be timed perfectly, lest the ship would be pressed within wind and tide, floundering forever southwards. Presently, the helm remained, steadfast. The murmur of silent whisperings had begun. The officers edged uneasily. They would need to turn soon, very soon, if they were to have any chance of rounding Pointe Saint-Mathieu. Such a course would handsomely see them nigh upon the seas washing Brest, the Goulet and their destination rightly set happily before them.

Considering how treacherous the sea about Brest and the Goulet purported to be, the officers had all been of a mind to immediately rejoice upon learning the wind was somewhat holding to favour Agamemnon's back. And following, they all very much supposed that battle would be healthily accepted with the holiest of advantages, the weather gage. It stood their captain in great stead. Yet much to their dismay, very much to their mounting hysteria, mysteriously the ship continued directly south.

There was not even a hint she might turn. It was a matter which now purported to weigh indecently upon their thoughts.

'Captain?' Poulain delicately whispered. 'If I may sir, we are some sea miles south of *Ouessant* now. It is not my place of course, but I am curious. Is it your intention to turn the ship east, to come upon Brest? Captain, I only ask because very soon, if we do not turn, we will very much find ourselves south of Brest. Upon that circumstance, we begrudgingly would be forced to beat back into the wind, from all accounts, most laboriously.'

'Firstly, you may sir,' Cooper grinned. 'And secondly, let me say I have every intention to most definitely beat the ship back to Brest. It is my belief that Lafayette will be holding somewhere in the vicinity of Pointe Saint-Mathieu, lying in wait behind the headland as it were, very much expecting us to emerge from the Passage de l'Iroise. It is there he has planned to surprise us, able to initiate battle to his immediate advantage, a trap.'

'That is all very well, but, if you do this Captain, you will not have the weather gage when you come upon Solitaire.'

'That, sir, is precisely correct,' he grinned.

It was with sullen anonymity that the officers performed their duty, all in the absolute knowledge that Agamemnon had now in fact sailed well south of Brest, perhaps even as far as to soon make Raz de Sein. Finally the order came to bring the ship about. It should have been a relief, but being so far south now, she was, as feared, forced to beat into the wind. There was no longer any speculation, the gage had been lost. It begged many questions of course, questions only a captain might answer at a court martial. Yet upon the quarterdeck, only one officer might ever dare question his captain. That honour and privilege remained with the first lieutenant. Presently, acting first officer Lieutenant Jarvis Thomas Holt was hardly thinking such a privilege much of an honour. To incorrectly question his captain would be to tread the lion's tail whilst it was napping. He was definitely not of a mind to be so inclined, as naturally was the case with many first officers.

Amidst the sulking and glum faces, Holt was also forced to weather the customary glances to which junior officers afforded their protests to be silently registered. Like most nautical protests, so were they summarily waved off with a practised nod, Holt also biting down hard on his bottom lip for effect. Nonetheless, he conversed repeatedly with his captain, biding his time. Yet curiously, each and every discussion only ever entailed the likely calculations, moreover the factored probability of Agamemnon's speed, all in her endeavour to beat back to Brest. Holt didn't need to make any exact calculations either. It was always going to be slow going, the tide and wind hammering terribly every inch of the ship's effort to make way. Even his best wild guess was not going to be too far off.

Holt trusted his captain implicitly. Moreover though, throughout it all, he found it curious his orders had made quite a point upon the preciseness and the timing of their navigation. They had checked and double checked every tack along the way, measuring the progress of the tide at every opportunity. Cooper had been most adamant about a great many things, forever looking to the ship's timepiece, his good eye perched upon the dogvane. Finally a call came from Eagle, muffled within the height of the gale. Yet Cooper knew all too well it could only be one thing.

'Sails ho!' repeated Eagle, now cupping his mouth and leaning over the nest to direct the great force of his lungs towards the quarterdeck.

'Very well,' Cooper accepted, his eyes now turning to focus upon the ship's glass. The grains of sand were mostly depleted and soon it would have to be turned. 'Mister Holt, it seems we have been hauling the wind most handsomely, so handsomely I feel we are pointed almost to the wind's eye.'

'Aye sir, as close hauled as you might ever have her,' he admired.

'But it simply will not do.'

'Oh? Sir?' he vexed.

'No, Mister Holt, it seems we are early.'

'Early? Captain, I was unaware.'

'We must spill some wind, if you please. Slow us down, just a tad, any way you deem fit.'

'Slow us down? Aye, sir, luff and touch her it is.'

Solitaire and Hasard were indeed beating back and forth, waiting as expected under the protection of the headland at Pointe Saint-Mathieu. It was a devilish trap, one Cooper could only admire. No doubt, French eyes were rather fixed to the north-west, upon the Passage de l'Iroise. In no uncertain terms would they have ever expected Agamemnon to approach from the south, not in this gust and never with the brewing swell of the Iroise Sea seeking to drain every ounce of a ship's speed. Even so, strategically it made little sense. In course, any ship approaching Brest from the south would not procure the advantage of the weather gage, a custom very much preferred by every English captain. Conversely, it was true that French captains almost exclusively preferred to attack from leeward. However, that was only so they could use the gage to expedite their escape, if need be. Lafayette was no such man. He had no inclination to escape, not this time, no matter what transpired. He would seek to use the gage to promote every advantage of attack. This duel was to the very end as far as Lafayette was concerned and if there was going to be an end for someone, he was very much preferring it to be Cooper's.

Cooper found it tactically interesting that Lafayette had been hiding under the headland at Pointe Saint-Mathieu, most cleverly it seemed. The plan was simple enough, to remain out of sight whilst Agamemnon blundered by on her run, a very fast run, from Ushant to Brest. By the time Agamemnon realised the enemy was afoot, they would have already slipped by, putting themselves well to leeward. Solitaire would instantly have the immediate advantage, able to press battle with the gage. Lafayette could just slip upon the gage's back and run directly down, easily wearing ship as need be, making way at twice his opponent's speed. To bring her cannon to bear, Agamemnon would be forced to languish in tack, to beat into the wind, a duck on the pond. Lafayette's cannon would present with preferred angles of attack, letting go almost at will, whilst Agamemnon would have to stage her broadsides most carefully, all but waiting for her chance to line up their enemy. Cunning indeed and even should luck not be on Lafayette's side, soon enough would he be joined by Venus, a heavy frigate. Short of a typhoon suddenly engulfing his squadron, the Frenchman could not hope to lose. Poor Agamemnon would be forced to strike or flee, albeit with nowhere in particular to go. Most likely, she would be destroyed.

The entire plan was shrewd indeed Cooper concluded. He admired it, for it was exactly what he might have concocted. Yet knowing the particulars in advance now offered some leeway to accommodate it, to commandeer it so to speak and so bring this Frenchman to account. He had pondered many a different tact, but in the end decided upon a course completely diverse and unexpected.

Agamemnon would approach in the guise of normal shipping, from the far south. This would still afford Lafayette the weather gage, however there were other discerning factors at play this day. For one, the rough weather in particular was foremost in his calculations. For another, Agamemnon would be afforded ample time upon its run, able to exactly identify Solitaire's station and ultimately choose the preferred leeward angle of attack. It was a mighty gamble of course, but who better to lay odds than the gambler himself he considered. Agamemnon was totally committed now, there being no other course. She would accept battle, offering Lafayette the gage. Cooper could only imagine how the French might rejoice at suddenly finding their foe languishing to leeward. At first they likely would not believe their luck. Would it make them wonder he thought, or would they accept it as just another English blunder?

It took some time for the French to comprehend that the sails beating towards them from the south were in fact English, those of the long awaited Agamemnon. It was as Cooper thought, they could not conceive such absurdity and why should they. They were well acquainted with Agamemnon's movements. They well knew she would hail from Ortac and they well knew English captains would hold to attack with the gage. To do that, Agamemnon must approach from the north, rounding Ushant verily making the Passage. What Frenchman in their right mind would believe sails to the south to be English? It was a facet upon which Cooper was hoping to rely. It was his utmost wish, very much a wholly preferred part of his plan, that the French would fail to take action until Agamemnon was so much the closer. Without Achilles in tow to give them away, it was a good wager the French might be fooled.

Naturally the French lookout was aware, but for some

considerable time had Solitaire continued to beat up and down under the protection of the headland. Cooper had gambled. So far it seemed he had won, Agamemnon plying closer and closer. With great thought he tacked Agamemnon nicely into what he deemed the most advantageous point for attack. He had taken into account the wind, the run of the water, the nature of the rough seas, as well as the beckoning shore yonder. Not that the French realised it, but he very much wished to fight within the confines of the headland. He would seek to limit their sea room as much as possible, very well knowing his ship would turn and make way at a faster rate. He was ready, as ready as he was ever going to be. Yet the French were so docile he was thinking he might have to fly his colours or even fire a gun to wake them up.

In fact, Cooper eventually did both. Having been called out with a lone shot to leeward, the French noted his colours. Finally did they break from their perpetual round of tacking. Both Hasard and Solitaire turned to bear upon Agamemnon, dogs scuttling after the rabbit, as well they should. They had found her alone, Achilles nowhere to be seen. It would be two against one, holding the gage at their back. The entire scenario was too good to be true, a dinner dished with every accompaniment. With Venus secretly leaping from the north, Lafayette likely accounted Agamemnon was already as good as his.

A red rocket suddenly lit the deadened sky, propelled from the tops of Solitaire, her call to beckon Venus. Soon it would be three against one. The battle was still yet to commence, but it was very much well and truly over as far as Lafayette was concerned. Agamemnon would be their prize directly, an unknowing Cooper delivered up, his head soon to adorn a proverbial, if not, literal platter. In that moment would Lafayette's vengeance of his poor brother be all but complete and the man's reputation, rank and privilege be summarily restored.

'Mister Holt, how long sir til we are met in battle? That is, say, to arrive at a distance of five hundred yards to be precise?'

'Oh sir, with Solitaire bearing down, a good fifteen minutes I would think. We are hardly making way of course, so it verily depends upon them.'

'And Mister Holt, how long to high tide, that is, in the

Channel?'

'Sir? Sorry sir, what's that, the English Channel?' he questioned.

'Aye, Lieutenant, the English Channel, or *la Manche*, or *Mor Breizh*, the Narrow Seas, aye the strip of water between northern France and southern England, high tide if you please, quickly now young sir?'

'Aye sir, I would guess it turned some fifteen minutes ago?' he returned, clicking his fingers at the nearest officers. In haste they reported with the log, to which Holt quickly poured over his stumpy boyish fingers. 'Sir, there it is, high tide turned exactly seventeen minutes ago. Is there some reason, sir, you wish to know? Or were you just testing me once more, to pass the time. I was only off by a minute or two?'

'A prodigious mind you possess Mister Holt, no doubt, no doubt. Now let me add to your well of knowledge. If you would be so good, perhaps might you now impart upon us the exact direction of the current, in about thirteen minutes or so?'

'Good god sir!' he cried after thinking about it for a solid moment. 'Aye, thirty minutes of rest for the slack and as the tide turns, she will be flowing north-east and if I may say, at quite a rate too sir, especially in the Goulet!'

'And?'

'And that means Solitaire will be battling against it directly, considering whereupon you have now stationed Agamemnon. Sir, we will have the direct favour of the tide, as you say, in about thirteen minutes!'

'And we will not come upon Solitaire until at least fifteen minutes.'

'Indeed sir.'

'And the wind?'

'Well, it will still be somewhat against us, but as we close in on the headland, I must admit that it will be much reduced.'

'And what do you think, should you be standing on the quarterdeck of our prize over there, our Solitaire, in say the next thirteen minutes?'

'Well sir, considering, especially once the tide turns against them, it very well might be backs to the wall for Solitaire, the current seeking to bring them to a lee shore. But surely the prevailing wind will not fail them?'

'We will soon find out, Mister Holt. Now let us see if we can make signal to Achilles. She is hiding beyond the headland to the north. I deem we may still have line of sight, although the day is most dreary. Send to her to beat to quarters, if you please, we have a rather large rat to catch!'

'Aye sir,' Holt grinned. 'And one dirty mouse!'

Agamemnon made her way most comfortably. She was sailing close hauled, full and by as handsomely as any ship might ever manage. She might have even sailed a point or two slighter better, but it was a prudent strategy considering the tricky swell. All in all, to sail as such allowed a polite margin of error so as not to be taken aback. Cooper could also not risk arriving early before the tide turned. He was in no extra hurry, timing his run perfectly.

The ship had beaten to quarters, this time without the usual insistence and bluff. The jacks all knew what that meant, very much implying the ship was to simply go about its business, to steadily get on with the job. At this early stage Cooper was adamant to avoid any undue strain or urgency. It was good too, for throughout their voyage had the seas remained rough. There was perhaps only a minute now before battle would be joined. As predicted the tide had turned most cruelly, its flow now surging in kind to assist Agamemnon. It was apparent Solitaire's way had been substantially reduced. Lafayette would still have the gage, for what it was worth, an advantage Cooper now judged somewhat diminished.

Considering the unexpected position of Agamemnon, Lafayette would soon be forced to ponder strategic alternatives, much to Cooper's pleasure. The only remaining question begged which path Lafayette might now take. Cooper was of a mind to almost not care. He was past ready, having himself pondered long enough. Yet it did give him pause. The extremes as to how far this Frenchman might venture would always remain an unknown quantity. Lafayette may not even alter his tactics, the significance of the belting tide perhaps a factor not so greatly concerning. He, after all, had complete and utter reliance upon the incoming support of a forty gun frigate. The man had slyly sought to hedge this encounter, as well he should. In the thick of battle would he do his utmost, of course, but should Agamemnon prove too much of an annoyance, he would simply stall and wait upon the irrepressible firepower of Venus.

'Mister Holt there, inform the gun captains to fire on the upward roll of each wave. That is, upward roll, if you please, just as we had practised.'

'Aye, sir, upward roll it is.'

'Ensure they understand, for they are many of them old salts and will prefer to fire on the downward, to capitalise the damage to our enemy's hull. Oh how they love to see a good ship splintered and holed. But I mean to take her, not sink her and they must comprehend we are to be fighting the ship from leeward.'

'Aye sir, I believe I understand. Am I to assume our cannon will be caused naturally to point higher, seeing how the ship is heeled over with the wind?'

'In course Mister Holt, yes. As such, we are more likely to hit her spars and sails, which is precisely my wish. But Mister Holt, take care with the helm. The more we careen, the more our lower sides and our bottom will precariously be shown. You know this I assume? As heeled as I intend to make us, we cannot afford to take even one shot low under the waterline.'

'Understood, sir.'

'To be hulled between wind and water will see the end of us. Have the helm approach as such and please to minimise our time afforded before the eyes of their cannon.'

'Aye, aye, sir!'

'It is my most fervent hope these French remember they are French.'

'Sir?'

'French are favoured to fire on the upward roll. Should they do

Ships of War — Murky Waters

this, our exposed hull will be of less consequence, meaning they will be more likely hit spars and sail,' he further explained. 'Ah, almost in range, see how Solitaire is turning to line up her broadside. Get the helm prepared Mister Holt! We shall drop a few points off her and let her wildly reach, the wind abeam!'

'Aye, sir, a soldier's wind it is. Oh sir, look!' he pointed, very much excited. 'Solitaire's lower gun ports!'

'Aye, they are awash in the high sea!' Cooper confirmed, grinning worse than a maddened March Hare. He rejoiced as he beheld first-hand his plan coming to fruition. The French were frantically heaving cables to retract their cannon, unable to shut the hatches, whilst the murky water of the Iroise Sea washed wildly within. It was a capital blunder, one he earnestly had not expected an experienced captain to make. Cooper was almost thinking she might bear away, before the ship was rightly swamped. It was a wishful greedy thought, one which might see Agamemnon afforded a complete broadside, without even the slightest fear of return. 'High seas are not the gage's friend Mister Holt. She cannot risk being swamped. They must secure the gun ports, or see themselves founder. Of course, we experience no such malady as both decks of our cannon sit on our windward side, suitably raised by the heeling of the ship,' he rightly submitted, a knowing triumphant glare attesting. It was a look which finally offered Holt and Poulain the long awaited rationale in remedy of their captain's apparent tactical lunacy. 'And it was in 1545 when Mary Rose, no less than the pride of England's fleet of course, sank completely and utterly as the ship heeled over to starboard in such a sea as we verily see right before us. The sea swiftly flooded her gunports, the crew unable to rectify in time. However, back then, Mary Rose had only just been refitted with much heavier cannon, making her dangerously top heavy. And may I point out that in eighty, Admiral Rodney, upon noting the inclement weather and roughness of the seas, ordered his ships to attack the Spanish from leeward, all in the most despicable stormy weather, the victorious Battle of Cape Saint Vincent. But, if you please Mister Holt, Admiral Rodney hardly expected the Spanish fleet to miraculously sink before him, nary a shot fired? How is it, do you think, he exactly expected to profit?'

'Oh, sir!' he excitedly exclaimed. 'Of course sir, of course, only their upper deck cannon will now be presented!'

'Indeed Mister Holt. In consequence, they will only have half the weight of broadside upon the first exchange, perhaps even upon the second. What a blunder. Let us not waste it! Now stand tall sir and courage there, all of you!'

But courage was hardly needed, not just yet, Lafayette forced to bear away or be swamped. Some of the lower gun ports had been successfully secured, but never enough. She was taking on water and even a maddened rabid dog knew when it was hopelessly being bitten.

'She is bearing away Captain,' Holt reported, his glass still fixed upon his good eye. 'They are in some bother it seems.'

'Masts, spars and tackles now, Mister Holt,' Cooper ordered, his eyes silently fixed upon his first officer to exaggerate its importance. 'As she is turning from us, fire as we bear, a rolling broadside if you please. And Mister Holt, although your place is here beside me, you are to personally captain the last three cannon. See if she might present her stern long enough for you to take on her rudder?'

'Indeed! Oh Joy!' he rejoiced excitedly. 'Aye sir, but I'll be better chanced if I am permitted to use the lower deck cannon, considering the pitching of the sea. However, sir, I must point out, they are twenty-fours and we may inadvertently hull her below the waterline?'

'Oh, I am sure Captain Lafayette will have her pumped sufficiently til we are ready to take possession,' he jested. 'It's only a few balls, do your best then.'

The barking thumps of exploding cannon paraded forth one by one, lower and upper decks letting go as their intended targets bore upon them. Solitaire had indeed turned her back, offering Agamemnon free reign with six hundred and seventy-eight pounds of weight itching to be thrown. The crew roared as they beheld the product of their past diligence and training, spars and sail cruelly stripped from Solitaire, the invigoration of battle wildly washing within.

Holt waited patiently as the stern chanced to present itself. It would be the barest of moments, if any, hardly a prospect at all offering only the slightest of margins. Considering how swift Lafayette had cleverly organised his tack, it would be pure luck to hit the rudder. Holt was further thinking that to even hit the stern would be some kind of miraculous feat. All three cannon would have to be fired simultaneously he considered and the timing would have to be absolutely perfect. Upon checking and rechecking his yardage stick, the ropes were finally adjusted. Each cannon lay ready, Holt's nose lining down the snouts, a final check. His crew stood back, excited but quietly confident. They nodded in approval, beholding the meticulous proficiency of their young master, the Little Lord. They knew what he was about. They were loyally of a mind to fire into the gates of hell should the lad so order it. They had served up the best of their balls too, methodically rounded to perfection after much painstaking chipping and rubbing. They well knew that to hit the rudder would mean the prize. They grinned as hungry dogs awaiting the bowl, their chops smacking, their tails wagging, all in full expectation of a tasty treat. Holt waited upon the downward roll of each wave. If he was to miss, he well knew it would be to miss low.

'Fire!' he yelled, all three lanyards simultaneously yanked. The balls flew true, barely skimming the surging sea. Hovering in unison, they hung low, a small flock of devil fowls spiralling from hell. At first, they were quite visible, Holt and his entire crew admiring the lines of smoke trailing their course. Solitaire lay a few hundred yards beyond, a short wait, although ever did it seem to drag in time. Eyes were ever watchful, but as the ship moved off, the smoke vexed to grip her. Blowing back most indignantly to shroud their feat, the final impact of each ball disappeared, verily eluding them. Eventually they could hear splinters flying, the distant cracking of oak drowned within the roars of the crew above. Immediately Holt scurried to the quarterdeck, puffing as he arrived, hopeful he had achieved the impossible. 'Captain?' he anxiously called.

'It seems you have missed, but not by much,' Cooper pridefully nodded. Holt was now eyeing Solitaire with his glass, but she had already made her turn and the smoke was yet to fully clear. 'I can assure you that two of the shots hit home very close to the rudder housing, high upon the upper deck. I am thinking

Captain Lafayette will not anytime soon be hosting dinner parties within his great cabin. A horrible mess, most horrible, most likely a complete and utter shambles, but no rudder, alas. I did not see it, but Hiro thinks the third ball hit home quite low, perhaps below the waterline. It may have knocked some of the rudder, but we cannot know of course, not until we perceive Solitaire upon her next few turns.'

'A capital piece of gunnery young sir,' McFee complimented, the roughness of his grin bearing through the bushiness of his handsomely trimmed Scottish beard. 'Most capital indeed, a shot unimaginable I would hazard to say, worthy of wild rabid Highlander!'

Smoke puffed from Solitaire, her stern cannon firing upon Agamemnon. It was a futile attempt, perhaps only a wicked gesture of their fighting spirit, for it could not have chanced to achieve any proportion of useful damage. The balls whistled upon the quarterdeck, just over the heads of the officers, finally splashing into the sea barely beyond, but close enough so that each and every one of them tasted the salt of the spray.

'Sir, I do believe that dog meant to fire upon our quarterdeck!' McFee angrily protested. 'The cad, I'll have his pirate's gizzards for stew and his guts for garters, mark my words!'

'My god, garters?' Poulain whispered to Holt, somewhat stricken in French bewilderment. 'Is that, indeed, how shall I put it? Is that a thing? You know, a thing that is actually done?'

'Aye, the bastard!' McFee loudly cursed. 'I'll butter my knife in him!'

'Captain Poulain,' Holt whispered back in French, his tone even and most serious. 'I would not fear to wager against, not on my life, having come to well know the ferocity of such highland men as our major. And I regret to inform that now I very much cannot shake from my mind the vision of our maddened Scot savagely taking his butter knife to poor Lafayette and accommodating his thighs with said garters.'

'It seems we have aroused our French captain,' Cooper dryly quipped. 'It is only fair and reasonable of course that he indecently try to murder us upon our own quarterdeck. After all, let us not forget, our young Lord here has likely just slain his entire collection of fine wines,' he added with a victorious smirk. The officers were now gurgling. McFee was further insisting that the unmolested state of the French wardroom would instead be most accommodating. It would provide the necessary wine in accompaniment, that is, as he served up Lafayette's gizzards for the evening's stew. Poulain's eyebrows were suitably raised as he noted the last comment, now wondering if said stew was indeed also a done thing. 'It is a fine sentiment! Let us return the gesture, shall we? Mister Holt, bring the ship immediately about.'

'Aye sir, coming about!' he confirmed loudly, only to enquire with a ratifying whisper. 'Sir, might I respectfully request we boxhaul her?'

'Have you ever performed this manoeuvre Mister Holt?'

'In course, no sir.'

'You are quite right of course. The weather being so rough, it is the suggested course in order to tack a large square-rigged vessel such as ours, short round. But think about it, whilst holding the helm hard to weather, the sails must firstly be luffed and backed to take off our way. The ship will cause to go astern, that is until the eye of the wind catches the other side. Sails must then be handled around to the new tack, split timing required from our jacks. Oh, I know they can do it and I know it is a much preferred method in these seas. It had crossed my mind Lieutenant, but I fear we might lose too much time, waiting upon the wind.'

'Sir, then you are sure, tacking as such in this sea?'

'Nothing is ever certain of course,' Cooper returned, hardly bothered by the challenge. In contrast, he heartily remained in awe of his young first officer, performing his duty with nothing but good faith and cheer in his soul. 'But I believe the crew will handle it, for they must if we are to prevail in an oncoming campaign against France and perhaps Spain. We have a chance here to see Lafayette enjoy a second broadside, all without fear of return. It is true, this rough sea mishandled might verily see us broach-to. And Lafayette will be counting the minutes of our cannon reloading. However, of course, we have two sides of a ship we can fight. I deem they will not be ready for this and we must ensure chaos reigns upon each and every one of their decks.'

It was with satisfaction that Agamemnon fired a second

broadside, sneaking upon the head and bow of Solitaire, the French hopelessly unable to complete their turn in time. The broadside let go all at once, the ship utterly shrouded in heavy smoke, the distant sound of ripping sheets and cracking spars afar a joy to the English ears of all.

'Mister Holt, I believe her consort Hasard is sneaking upon our stern. They mean to utilise their speed upon the gage to rake us. Quickly now, keep us in the smoke, make our turn, sharply there and then bring us close to the wind. See her turn on her heel if you please, most abruptly, whilst the smoke still chances to veil us. I am thinking the French will see what we are about, but perhaps all too late. Let us then maximise our way, so we might dash out of the smoke very much in surprise. Thereafter, it is my wish you put us directly between Solitaire and Hasard!'

'In between, sir?' confirmed Holt nervously.

'Have you not noticed, but we have cannon on both sides of the ship. In course, we shall set ourselves between them, for I deem they will not expect it. Would you not agree?'

Holt immediately grasped that the French of course would not expect it, because only a certifiable madman recently since escaped might ever chance such a bold manoeuvre in such wild seas. It was not a thought any officer would relish, the enemy crowding both sides of the ship, hammering relentlessly with nowhere to hide, no room to manoeuvre and thereafter be totally defenceless waiting upon the long minutes to reload. It had been done before many times, usually by senior captains maddened by notoriously never tasting defeat. It was always a gamble. It could verily see the end of the engagement should the French gunnery skills line up upon a weakened spot. To maintain faith in his captain was his solemn duty, but this was a stretch. There had to be a reason, a good one, not that he could presently discern it. Inwardly he winced at the decision, now understanding that the captain of a ship of war wore very much the hat of a maddened soul.

'Aye, very happy, of course, sir! Doubling upon them it is!'

'Oh, brilliant!' Poulain whispered excitedly to McFee. 'This will allow us to openly fire both sides of the ship. And, in return, should the product of my countrymen's aim prove a little high, inadvertently overshooting Agamemnon, they may indeed accidentally hit their consort. Of course, we may very well be blown to bits, being the down side. However, it also begs thereafter that both French ships must move off in different directions, their choice of escape verily limited by the crowding of ships. This will afford Captain Cooper a chance, a magnificent chance, to chase after one and should he reserve some cannon, he may very well chance to rake them, fore and aft Major, stem to stern!'

Cooper had Solitaire's movement engrained in his mind's eye. With the lack of sea room and the headland yonder, there were few choices for Lafayette. It would be an easy wager as to which way each French vessel might head. His decision would have to be swiftly made though. The smoke poured over the quarterdeck, the outside world slowly disappearing. In course, Cooper not only welcomed it, but he wished for more. He urged the plumes to grow, a small volcano billowing from the murky depths of the Iroise Sea, rising up as a great leviathan to finally swallow her whole. All captains knew that fighting from leeward, into the wind, invariably occasioned such envelopment. And for long had English captains moreover used this to their advantage, their enemy trapped within, unable to properly discern the movements of battle or see the enemy in order to properly aim and fire. Lafayette would hardly believe it to be anything but a gift from the gods. Yet Cooper would seek to make him rue that thought as Agamemnon vanished within.

Agamemnon's bowsprit emerged from the smoke, breaking through the veil as a wild beast bearing upon its prey, fully intending to slip between the two French ships. Thus far had Solitaire been twice mauled, her cannon still cold and silent. They definitely were about to receive a third broadside, but they raised their fists as they beheld their first chance to unleash in return. They of course could not fathom Agamemnon presenting herself in such fashion, so perilously between their ships, except that perhaps she had blundered being somewhat turned about in the smoke. Nonetheless, ever were they hungry to see the English finally accept French iron and oh how they begged Cooper to foolishly advance.

The ships glided deliberately towards each other. The tension stalking the prevailing moments very much the eye of a great storm, silent and surreal, no real hint of the tumultuous disaster readying to befall. The seas surged as wild horses lunging under each ship, bucking and rolling with no real harmony or assurance. Agamemnon again beheld Solitaire to windward, the French still afforded only one deck of cannon. Yet Hasard was now cleverly scurrying to leeward full well knowing that similarly would Agamemnon have only one deck of cannon upon her, if any. In the prevailing seas she would present quite a small target and she knew this. Yet should even a few balls catch her, jeopardy would very much find the brig. Many aboard Agamemnon were thinking payback had come, their minds harking back to poor Resignation and the total loss of all hands and oh how they now beckoned Hasard with both fists.

Agamemnon had at first approached in apparent haste, but now with both ships almost upon her flanks, she sought to slyly creep towards her prey, wind spilling cleverly from her sails. As each of the enemy ships came abeam, the sheets let go and wind abruptly filled her canvas, speedily bringing her back to life, much like a stalled stallion suddenly heeled in the side. She surged forth, her pace very much a surprise. The cannon upon Agamemnon commenced, a rolling broadside as each barrel lined upon the other. Solitaire was almost caught unaware, the suddenness of Agamemnon's ability to make way causing havoc with their aim. Hastily the French struggled, desperate to properly time their linstocks to the touch holes, for they had not flintlocks. Finally the French unleashed their iron, all in one cruel moment, a total broadside.

Holt beheld the incoming broadside standing tall upon the quarterdeck. In the first moments he regarded the undeniable sight of smoke instantly puffing from the ships yonder, silently though, for the sound had not yet fully travelled. He was thereafter borne of a singular mind, assuredly a mind to which all familiarity with the outside world now fell lost. It certified within him a suffering never before deemed imaginable. It was a hostility he would soon not forget, such was his boyhood innocence. Noted instantly were a great many astonishing sounds, all racing to rupture the virtue of his lobes, an overall resonance seemingly strange and without a doubt wholly outlandish. Having never been on the receiving end of such a broadside, it openly gave him pause. The whistling tunes aloft seared the sky and oh how they chanced to inflict the gravest of thoughts, the wind of the enemy's shots whizzing as they trespassed upon the ship. The scene descended upon him most abruptly, the horrendous tearing of sails overhead, the ripping of canvas crying aloud as the weight of spars sought to claw them down. Splinters upon bulwark and gunwale haphazardly flew, mimicking a violent winter's storm, more furious than even a hundred wood choppers madly serving their axes. All about the planking, indeed immersed within the depths of the structure, Agamemnon shuddered and trembled, the penance of each shot hurried from the ship. The roaring of cannon reverberated within his chest, almost as if he were in fact somehow the barrel itself, the hum of each shot grabbing wickedly at his heart. The deafening turmoil within sought to impose a hideous most disturbed feeling and immediately he felt inclined to be uncontrollably ill, the vile gurgling about his abdomen finally seeping the sanctity of his throat.

    Commonly could Holt discern explosions from all parts of the ship, the ensuing chaos distinctly mingled in the distance with the thumping bang of yonder French cannon. Here and there could he hear shots striking the sides, the ricochet of the balls within as they forced their way through the oak, ever refusing to resist. Within the smoke, beneath the hail of iron, it was as if the ship had been levied by a thunderous tempest lighting its fury upon her, randomly strewing the fallen into weeping pools of its bloodied wrath. It was a scene which very much sought to arrest his entire being, the chaste adolescence beholden within him now very much befallen, the eyes of a young soul ever youthful no more. He attended his duty nonetheless, an indescribable confusion surging about the decks as he found himself giving orders as if he was the only body still standing. A jack not thirty feet before him stood attending his gun, only a moment later to instantly disappear with nothing apparent striking him. Another jack stumbling had lost his leg, hopelessly fumbling to tie off the stump with a handkerchief. The hand of god breached the ship and oh how every man prayed as the carnage fell haplessly upon them. Yet in the next moment, within the despair, unexpectedly and seemingly all at once, almost without warning, indeed without the slightest prejudice as it is with all great storms, was Agamemnon engulfed in compelling silence. Shots on both sides had been spent and the race to reload began. Only the cries of the wounded and the sporadic squawking of some ragged gulls served to remind Holt that he was still the first officer aboard a ship of war and not some spirit haplessly wandering the afterlife.

Cooper's immediate attention found his ship in good stead. Sailing between the French had definitely taken a toll, a price paid, but now he was of a mind to collect. Agamemnon had taken some damage to her sails, but nothing so serious as to prevent her way, unlike the French. She had also taken hits to the hull, the report pending. It seemed much of the fire had been relegated to the weather deck and her men. The wounded were quickly ferried to the Doctor's cockpit, many a foreboding bloodstained dye left prevalent upon the planking.

It would take some minutes to reload and Cooper was now curiously looking to the damage so inflicted upon Hasard and Solitaire. He had savaged Solitaire most cruelly once more, the ship visibly limping as she turned into the wind to retain the gage. Hasard joined her fate, limping away after having lost a mast, her way somewhat reduced. The damage could well have been more he considered, but both French ships had cleverly fired everything they had, all at once, allowing them in mitigation to quickly turn away.

The engagement had seen Agamemnon charge both French ships head on, a standard method of accepting battle. Yet as soon as the broadsides had been thrown, the French turned into the wind, both heading back towards the headland to the north. It was exactly what Cooper expected. They were rightly attempting to clear Agamemnon, position themselves upwind once more and afford the gage on their backs for the next attack. This was correct thinking, naturally, but it now provided the very opening for which he had so fervently hoped. To such experienced sailors as Cooper and Poulain, the next move was as clear as the freshness of Ortac's bay on a windless summer's day. Agamemnon had paid dearly for

Ships of War — Murky Waters

it as well, a sickly butcher's bill reckoned in good men lost and injured.

'You have my esteem Captain,' Poulain congratulated. 'Three broadsides to Lafayette's one and you have winged his mutt in the process. The doubling, it was a bold manoeuvre, one which has paid off!'

'The ducks have been clipped, it is true, but we must labour still to see them to our dinner table,' insisted Cooper solemnly.

'Is that caution I detect sir?' Poulain commended. 'So, you are a captain who is not only bold, but prudently wise. Very good, it seems I am on the right ship. You will chase down Hasard now I assume?'

Cooper eyed Hasard with the vigilance of a hungered hawk, for in the exchange had she used the gage to pass by to leeward, downwind of Agamemnon. Her new course was already made. She had turned, sharply into the wind, following Solitaire. Cooper grinned, beholding both French ships making the same tack, close hauled, desperately driving every inch of their wrecked canvas to somehow put themselves upwind. Should they continue, they would be afforded the gage and some mild comfort. It was expected of course, but he instantly knew Agamemnon could now outsail them both. His canvas was mostly intact and already was his ship more of a runner. It was the moment for which he had so patiently waited. Happily the time had now finally arrived. He immediately issued the order, the order he had so longingly wished to give ever since he first concocted his plan of battle.

'Our minds are as one my friend,' Cooper confirmed. 'Had they continued south with the wind upon their backs, they would have made it difficult for us to close so quickly, even as winged as they presently are. But instead they are beating into the wind, slow going at best. They will not put so much sea room between us now. Once we turn and chase, it will be a race. The headland will be directly afore all of us, thus neatly trapping them. We will seek to cut Hasard off and force battle.'

'A battle they cannot hope to win!' grinned Poulain.

Agamemnon started her turn. She would come about, serving to follow exactly the same path as the French. If he poured on the canvas, with a little luck, he estimated Agamemnon might come up directly behind the brig. It was no small manoeuvre, a healthy margin of error inherently attached. It would prove to be a large swooping turn, coming about some two hundred and seventy degrees. It may have been a gamble, but in entirety was Cooper certain. In fact, he was more certain than anything before in his life ever gambled, so much he was not even of a mind to insist upon the mathematical scrutiny of young Holt. He played the scenario out in his mind. He would turn and turn and finally bring his cannon right up behind Hasard, a hound chasing the rabbit. With no rabbit hole in sight, soon would he be snapping at her tail. Indeed, handsomely would he find himself abeam, a perfect firing position, just a tad to windward.

The manoeuvre of course supposed that Hasard would choose to run, instead of turning. So far, they were running. Once they were aware, it would be too late. They could not turn larboard to west, for there Agamemnon would eagerly be waiting, any easy broadside. And they could not turn starboard to east, for precariously would their stern be exposed. Agamemnon would easily rake her, firing shots by her stern and out the bow. The damage would be catastrophic. The French captain would see both of these scenarios of course. The broadside he might risk, but never would he chance a raking, as even one good shot would see her sunk. Directly ahead, north, lay the shores of the headland, jagged rocks looming with every new breath that chanced to fill each sail. It seemed clear now, Hasard would be forced to sail into the wind, unable to turn, her only option to outrun her foe, or to strike. To outrun Agamemnon would be some feat and Cooper was very much wagering that the French brig would soon find herself hopelessly cut off. It would come down to a race and rarely did the pawn outrun the horse.

Agamemnon's run doubling between the French had been bold, culminating in firing everything she had on both sides of the ship. Yet with the leeward ports awash, she had not been afforded the opportunity to fire her lower deck. How fitting Cooper thought, that these cannon would now be facing Hasard during the course of his swooping turn. In glee he watched as Holt chanced a few long shots, harassing all sides of the tiny ship. The jacks roused as one shot removed their pennant, fluttering indignantly in tatters finally to rest peacefully upon the darkened wash.

Agamemnon steadily continued to creep up, soon to lay alongside Hasard. Yet even with one mast awash the brig was running faster than expected. Perhaps it might take a moment or two longer than first thought. It hardly weighed upon Cooper's mind. With the headland looming directly before her, she could not hope to hold forever. Once Agamemnon overtook and held beside her, the entirety of reloaded cannon could be thrown. Hasard could not hope to withstand even a portion of such a broadside. Alternatively, she could not hope to turn either, less she be mortally raked. She must strike.

Amongst the chase, Cooper periodically took note of Solitaire. Like Hasard, she had turned into the wind, heading directly for the headland attempting to retain the gage. Curiously all three ships were now on the same tack and course. They were lined up, ducks in a row, a Sunday afternoon yachting race, the rocky shores of the headland the finish line. Cooper happily deemed the overall control his, holding the outside windward lane as it were, shaping the engagement. Solitaire was uselessly positioned well beyond both ships. Hasard was dangerously hogging the middle, hopelessly wedged between the two great sixty-fours, a place she never intended to venture. And nary could Solitaire chance any shots at Agamemnon, not without venturing to inadvertently destroy Hasard. The race was on, the headland loomed and Cooper all but waited for his opponent to blink.

It was with some satisfaction that Achilles suddenly bore into sight, doubling the headland to the north almost at the exact appointed time. To everyone's mirth, Venus was running abaft chasing her with French colours flying, the wind on her quarter broad reaching. She was most diligently firing her forecastle chasers, a complete façade of course, each shot hopelessly amiss.

A French rocket whistled from Solitaire, Cooper quite correctly deeming that this was perhaps the prearranged signal for Venus to break off and intervene. Cooper knew he had the advantage and this all but confirmed Solitaire to be in bad shape. After three thundering broadsides, he had seen his foe diminish from a racing stallion to a lame limping nag, perhaps ready for the final musket. Hasard fired a gun as well, no doubt emphasising its predicament, not that anyone could do anything except behold the monstrous sixty-four gun ship of the line bearing down upon their tiny rear.

A barrage of cheers roared from the English ships as Venus suddenly struck. She hauled down her French colours, a white flag hoisted in its stead, the official surrender to Achilles. Lafayette was at a loss, but he well knew he was now very much on his own. Cooper immediately realised this would usher in the most perilous stage of the engagement, a rabid maddened dog so hopelessly cornered no less metamorphosed into a wild unpredictable bruiser with nothing left to lose.

Hasard, as mauled as she was, had no choice but to pour on her remaining canvas, her course shaped to hopefully escape by way of the headland. She couldn't turn, not now, not with Agamemnon nipping her heels. The brig leapt through the rough seas, the bow over and over smashing the surf. It was quite possible she might broach-to, but she had no other course now that Venus had struck. Solitaire could not hope to assist either, not without significantly losing way and they surely couldn't fire without likely hitting Hasard. No, Hasard was most definitely left to her own devices. Never in life had they imagined Agamemnon could ever catch her up. The sixty-four had made such a grand turn, but should have been far away abaft. Yet, there she was, close upon their heels, gaining way with every lunge and every breath, the ship pitching wildly. Agamemnon's forecastle cannon began to let go, nine pounders, seeking to harass the brig and perhaps bring them to their senses.

'Good god!' Cooper swore, admiring the flight of the shots hurrying from the nines. 'What grand chasers! Ha, ha, what virgins, freshly plucked! I shall have to compliment Mister Shaw and Captain Spencer upon their diligence. Never in life, god be praised, look at them fly!'

It was as Cooper had verily imagined, a most satisfying scene indeed. They, all three ships, were now pressing on in the same direction, a point or two north-west, but more or less towards the headland. Achilles and Venus were in sight converging to corral them. Hasard was the proverbial meat in Cooper's sandwich and soon would he have her, swallowed whole. He held his glass upon his good eye one more time, examining Solitaire, making sure of his calculations. He could see Lafayette helplessly eyeing him and for a small instant he felt some mild sorrow for the man, much the same as a fleeting thought just before an executioner's blade drops. Yet Cooper rightly reminded himself of Resignation and the poor souls who had unfairly perished. He surmised the scene one more time. For Solitaire to even hope to fire, she would have to come about. To come about would likely see even more sea room put between them. By then, Hasard would be gone, sunk or struck. Cooper grinned in this comfort. It was just a matter of time and so ludicrously did each ship stay the course, waiting upon the other. It was a grand stalemate, but in Cooper's mind, patience would see Agamemnon win through, finally.

'Mister Holt, if you please, it appears we are no longer gaining upon Hasard? What do you make of it?'

'I doubt very much she has increased her way, sir,' he correctly offered, snapping his fingers again at the junior officers next to him. He added a knowing nod and sent a midshipman running off into the bowels of the ship. 'I have a theory sir, but I wish not to offer it, for you will not like it.'

'Will not like it!'

'Aye, sir.'

'What theory?' Cooper insisted. 'Come now, out with it!'

'Well, sir, I may be wrong, but I get the feeling it is we who have slowed somewhat,' he timidly suggested, waiting upon the wrath of his captain to erupt. They both ventured to peer over the side, attempting to visually judge the pace of the water beneath. Holt was about to order the log to be heaved out when he was confronted by the ship's master, Thornton, standing anxiously before him, a puffing midshipman leashed by his side. The conversation at first was somewhat abrupt. 'Good god sir! You had better hear this!'

'Captain, sir,' Thornton started, his hat respectfully in his hand. 'I regret to inform, but we have been hulled. We are very sorry sir, seeing how we didn't see it at first. It was in a spot well-hidden I am fearful to say. But the heart of the matter is that we are taking on a goodly amount of water, enough to slow our way. And may I say sir, if we do not attend it soon, it will be enough to see us founder.'

'Sink, Mister Thornton? Did you just say sink! Damnation!' Cooper vexed. 'You have men pumping the hold I assume?'

'Aye, sir, but there are two holes I fear.'

'I see. And I take it that because we are now heeled on the opposite tack, the water is coming in?'

'In course, sir, aye,' Thornton agreed. 'Sir, we must change our tack, to allow the water to shift so we can move in and repair the holes.'

'What? What! You cannot be serious. Look out there man, look at where we are! We are about to take Hasard! Perhaps we are only barely moments from sinking her or seeing her strike! Is there no other way?'

'Well, sir, all we can do is pump and pray it be enough. I can offer you no more than five minutes sir, before I cannot guarantee the safety of the ship. But, may I say, it would very much help of course should we take Hasard directly and allow us to change our tack. I do not have to tell you sir that should we take on too much more, we will just end up a duck on the pond.'

'No Mister Thornton, you do not, of course,' he returned, in any case now thinking that the Master had in point of fact just told him outright in no uncertain terms and perhaps rightly so. Cooper vexed at his situation. They were barely moments from finishing Hasard and Solitaire was far away to starboard limping like a stuck pig. He could always bear away, let Hasard go. Perhaps Achilles might take her, but in his heart he very well knew she would scurry off, never to be seen again. The jacks would not forgive him, not this time. They had their hunger set upon their pound of Hasard flesh and no hulling of the ship would hope to ever explain it away. It was one of those moments in battle Cooper very much dreaded, a split moment at best afforded to make a decision which would see them victorious or forever ruined. At least this time he had some five minutes to decide.

'Sir, may I request a favour?' expressed Holt, quite formerly.

'Of course, Mister Holt,' Cooper returned somewhat curious, perhaps inviting a moment of respite. 'It seems we are at an impasse for now, for at least some minutes, in any case. Pray what is it?'

'Sir, may I be afforded three shots, lower deck cannon?'

'In course, I have no objection, though presently there is nothing to aim at, not unless you have concocted an innovation to turn our cannon sideways through the hull?'

'No sir, I have not,' he genuinely answered. 'But before you agree, sir, I must inform you I am likely to waste each shot, they being something of a long shot? Meaning, I will not be aiming at Hasard.'

Cooper was all but intrigued and was now of a mind to agree, if only to satisfy his building curiosity. With the entire engagement about to fall to shambles, his curiosity could definitely afford a few cannon balls. Agamemnon was now holding pace with Hasard, perhaps even losing some way, the headland maybe some eight minutes to make. It didn't matter of course, for Agamemnon would likely founder and sink well before that, unless he broke away. There was no sign of Hasard striking either and some jacks were starting to think the French might choose to wreck themselves rather than surrender. It made complete sense of course, better to risk drowning and likely escape to shore, rather than hang directly from Agamemnon's yard.

It was with a happy surprise that shortly thereafter one cannon under the quarterdeck let go. The ball trailed high into the sky, very high, smoke pouring from it. It flew completely over Hasard, very much abaft her which incidentally had the entire French crew roaring in laughter.

'What is the lad's game there Captain?' quizzed a baffled McFee.

'Whatever it is, I think I want in on it!' Cooper returned, perhaps now half guessing the ploy, his good eye fixed inside his glass. Another flew, followed by another. 'By the devil!' he suddenly exclaimed, now finding Holt running back to the quarterdeck, much akin to one's favourite hound returning successfully with the pheasant. 'I cannot believe it!' he blankly offered, the entire quarterdeck now eyeing Solitaire with their personal glasses. McFee was at a loss as to what had happened, when Eagle called from the nest.

'One hit home! True, amidships!'

'It seems Mister Holt has just annoyed our Captain Lafayette somewhat. His shot has indeed hit Solitaire, much to their utmost displeasure I would think!'

'Good god sir, that must be...'

'One thousand, three hundred and ten yards Major,' answered Holt.

'Astounding!'

'The first two balls I wasted on purpose, to gauge the distance, they straddling each side of her. In truth, the third was aimed for the sails, they being a much larger target.'

'Of course, Mister Holt,' Cooper sternly reprimanded. 'And for blatantly missing and hitting the hull, I will see your wine at dinner withheld from you sir, one round only, in recognition of the disgrace and your utter incompetence.'

'But sir, Mister Holt does not partake wine just yet,' reminded McFee.

'Oh?' Cooper returned knowingly. 'Well, all the more for us, 'ey?'

It was with mirth that the crew of Agamemnon noted a complete broadside returned from Solitaire. Perhaps it was in anger or perhaps the French had held to some modicum of levity, no one could be sure. The jacks could eye the puffs in the distance, the sound not making the ship until some seconds later. The old salts were quick enough to count the seconds of the interval, to assess the relative distance, just as youngsters might excitably check upon the thunder and lightning of a faraway storm.

'They are striking sir!' informed Holt excitedly.

'What? From one lone thousand yard ball! Preposterous!'

'No sir, it is Hasard who has struck!' he rightly pointed out, the entire quarterdeck now cheering as the French colours were run down. 'It is Solitaire, sir, her shot has fallen short and may I say sir, one has hit Hasard and taken out her mainsail!'

'Oh, indeed? Ha, ha, ha! What a grand shot! Proof Mister Holt that there indeed is a god, an English one, ha, ha! Thank you, thank you! And we must remember to thank our French commodore, just before we string him up! Very well, signal to Achilles! Secure the prize! Oh and Mister Holt, inform Mister Thornton we are coming about, directly!'

Agamemnon made her turn to starboard, shaping her course east with the headland broad on her larboard beam. Cooper had informed the crew they were going straight at her, much to the pleasure of their tempered wildness. With Hasard struck, it was now ship to ship, a fair fight and every jack was teeming with giddiness as they eyed the prize. Their captain had fought hard and to their mind had not only outsailed the French, but he had outwitted them at every stage. This was a man for which they would fight tooth and nail, a man they would follow blindly into the fiery pits of hell and brimstone, wholly expecting the devil himself to instantly strike under the press of their captain's wild advance.

As Agamemnon approached, swiftly closing the thousand yards, it was curious Solitaire had failed to yet turn. She was heading directly north into the headland, the shore looming. With less wind prevailing much closer to the rocks, protected as it were, the rough seas and the customary flow would no doubt soon present a lee shore. Every officer on the quarterdeck eyed the situation with wonderment, many a plausible explanation wilfully offered. A young boy sheepishly presented himself to Holt, a note clinging to his hand.

'Sir, Captain!' Holt called. 'One of the monkeys has a note here from Eagle atop. He believes Solitaire has lost her rudder!'

'Well, well, well, it seems your first long shot upon her has paid off.'

'Perhaps sir, may have hit close by, the stress of sailing her into the wind likely being too much in the end.'

'Then she is dished sir!' McFee declared excitedly. 'With your permission, I'll go get my butter knife!' he added evenly, Poulain immediately seen to be bewilderedly whispering to Holt once more.

'Mister Holt, let us monitor the situation most carefully. I fear what Lafayette may yet do, to be frank. He is quite mad, I am most sure of it. Now my orders sir, we are to make our way with all haste, all haste and let us take the wind from that madman before he wrecks our prize upon the rocks!'

'Oh and Major, permission granted!'

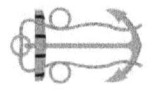

Chapter XXIII
Vive La France

It was the considered opinion of every officer aboard Agamemnon that the fight was now all but over. It was also the considered opinion that Lafayette was a maddened dog and would perhaps see his ship wrecked and his entire crew drowned like rats, rather than surrender. Short of war being declared, nothing short of a musket ball to the head would save him from being taken a pirate and shown the noose. It was also their considered opinion that they may well be stripped of their prize, robbed so to speak. Most sullen had they become, sulking uncommonly which in course had now even spread to the jacks.

As Agamemnon near arrived, a completely diverse scene presented itself, an enigma now accompanying Solitaire. She indeed had been stripped of her rudder, the men still frantically working their gear, quite visible, but the ship had most definitely been moored. She was rather close to shore, but she was not listing. There were no jagged rocks protruding her hull and she pitched healthily in the surge of the oncoming breakwater hardly perplexed and seemingly out of danger. The entire ship, apart from the savagery of many an English shot, remained quite intact. Perhaps she was intending to strike. It made sense, the crew might be spared and Lafayette could chance his escape to shore, a perilous chance, but a good boat with experienced hands might see it done.

'Belay there!' Cooper ordered. 'Give her a wide berth, keep our distance Mister Holt, quickly see it done!' he frantically added, now examining Solitaire through his glass. It very much appeared she was waiting in a prepared state ready to fight. Indeed the ship had been moored, but curiously it hung in the shoreline more like a castle edged into the rockery of a great cliff. Cooper immediately noted the cables running athwart, as did Poulain who had already politely whispered the finding in his ear. The cables ran from each end of the ship, no doubt to anchors lurking some hundreds of feet distant. Cooper intently studied the scene, rightly thinking Lafayette's madness was far from done. The sly dog may have had no rudder, but now he had run cables out to anchors, springs already in place. His ship lay abeam the shoreline, which is to say parallel, easily afforded the ability to veer and point his cannon, all in quite a wide arc too. No longer needing to sail the ship, he possessed a surplus of fighting men and the cannon need only be manned from one side. Even though many had been killed or wounded, Lafayette now perhaps boasted more productive fighting men than Agamemnon, all chomping at the bit. It was true quite a number would be standing by to haul the cables, but once the ship had been properly veered, they could very much take up the fight. It was a good wager that every cannon was healthily crewed and well stocked, perhaps even with a modest measure of reserves. And as battle progressed, damaged cannon might easily be bolstered by those sitting unmolested upon the opposite side. The tops had become somewhat crowded too, an industry of swarming muskets gleaming amidst the rigging. 'Be ready men, she has not struck, not yet and this madman means to fight on!'

Cooper beheld the industry of Lafayette's labour and as he mulled each detail over in his mind, only could he admire it. The French captain had given his ship one more fighting chance, a good one. The fight was far from over and he was now postulating that if all French naval officers fought as such, any oncoming war would likely last for decades. With the sight of Solitaire intact and safely moored the jacks now sparked somewhat, the prize in their eye. It was fortunate, because not much can ever be done with a sulking jack and whether or not there was a fight to be had, Agamemnon still remained perilously close to a hazardous lee shore.

'Sir, we are steadily making way at two knots. We will likely be able to make our broadside and still remain on this tack, if it pleases.'

'I see, very well and thank you Mister Holt. Well, plenty of time then,' Cooper started, addressing his senior staff. 'Gentlemen, it is my intention to take Solitaire, rather than see her destroyed. But if we must destroy her, we will of course. It appears Lafayette may have set up a tidy position in amongst the rocks there, it being a bold shore,' he confidently added, his good eye examining the steep coast afore them and the deep colour within its surrounding water, all good indicators which might permit the close approach of a sizeable ship. 'And had you not yet noticed, he has afforded himself the ability to veer the ship in a handsome arc. I believe it is very much his intention to fight the ship anchored, but we still have a way in. It is going to be dirty work, very dirty, but the prize awaits us. Mister Holt, we will present ourselves abeam and we will see three broadsides sir, in five minutes or less if you please. Thereafter, will you personally see our nines and eighteens afforded with grape. Men, we mean to take her, not hull her, nor rip any more of her canvas. Solitaire is moored as you can all see. She is not going anywhere, lest Lafayette hole her himself. We must indicate to them our intent to slug it out rather than to board, our strategy to rely upon our superior reloading time, all of it a ruse of course. In course, they must at some stage tire and be reduced. At some point, they must expend their cannon. That will be our chance. We will approach quickly whilst they fumble to reload. We will fire our twenty-fours into her upper and lower decks and our eighteens and nines will see grape sprayed across her weather deck and rigging. We will lay Agamemnon beside her. Mister McFee, you will see to her being promptly boarded. Put your sharpshooters in the tops of course, for we will be rightly close. It will be a battle of attrition and in this venture they cannot hope to prevail. But as with any drowning man we must verily ensure he does not take us down with him.'

'Sir, sorry to interrupt, but Eagle has reported. She is flying a white flag and they have a boat in the water?'

'Good grief! A parlay?' guessed Cooper rightly.

'Sir, no, don't do it,' McFee pleaded. 'You cannot trust that dog!'

'Aye sir,' Holt added. 'Remember what he did to Resignation?'

'He means to murder you sir. I am sure of it!' warned McFee.

It was with some trepidation that Cooper stood within his boat, Hiro, McFee and Holt by his side. They would not otherwise agree to let him go, the Doctor insisting upon the immediate certification of a declaration of sudden illness should he resist. They pulled towards the French boat. It appeared to be a parlay. Cooper wished it to be true, but he was too well acquainted with Lafayette's ploys and hardly was trust factored into his thinking. McFee had brought his best scrappers too, though they looked as mangy jacks slumped lazily upon their oars. Yet they had brought enough firepower to engage a small brig and they were as wild boars seething to let go.

Lafayette in contrast stood tall, handsomely, hand on hip, patiently awaiting Cooper. If he was intending to fight, he would be an easy mark. The sea surged slowly as it lapped leisurely about the boats, the inlet providing some much needed respite from the prevailing roughness of the Iroise Sea.

'Captain Cooper, I presume!' Lafayette started, almost honourably it seemed. 'My congratulations, your skill thus far has added quite a flavour to our little duel,' he commended openly, now taking his hat in hand to bow. 'I am glad you have come. It is only fitting.'

'Captain Lafayette, my officers very much believe you have arranged this parlay if only to kill me. But I have assured them, no man in such a position as yours would do such a thing, lest he forever molest his good name, even after death. And why would you of course?'

'Indeed, my officers believe that of me too and have begged me not to contemplate such a thing. But please rest assured, I have not come under the white flag to kill you Captain. No, no, no, of course not. But, if I did, I deem you would deserve it, no less for the crime of murdering my good brother, the Chevalier.'

'Ah, we come to it and without waste. It is fair enough, but Captain, was your brother not a spy, surely he was and you know this?'

'It is of no consequence, he was a Chevalier and not some commoner to be butchered or hanged.'

'Very well, you are right of course, but I say to you wholeheartedly that you have been sorely misinformed. I cannot answer as to being butchered, but your brother is very much alive, albeit in prison.'

'Oh come now, please Captain, do not offer such falsehoods, not now, for we are both far past such indignations. I have come only to meet you, a small offer for your consideration, something in measure before we commence to finish our business here this day. And of course, I am open to explain, should you wish, the reasons as to why I have hunted you from the outset, though it be obvious.'

'A small offer you say, intriguing,' Cooper returned, now speaking in perfect Parisian. 'But I attest, indeed do I attest that your brother, sir, is alive. He should be dead of course, for if you did not know, he very much attempted to kill the King's son with his fine blade. And you, you of all Frenchmen should verily appreciate his undeniable skill. Can you imagine what would have followed, had he murdered The Prince William? Our two great countries would immediately be thrust into war. I could only consider it the act of a madman. As such, we did fight, very true. And I count myself fortunate to have prevailed. Indeed I count it fortunate for both our countries. But I say in all sincerity, upon my honour, only his arm did he lose, not his life.'

'Upon your honour?'

'Sir, I swear it.'

'Alive, but, how can that be?'

'Oh, I presume you allude to the trusted information gathered by your ring of Chatham spies? I assure you, what I say is most true. Perhaps your spies have confused the death of his accomplice, for I verily carved up that crud swifter than a turkey at thanksgiving. A most regrettable man and let us not forget, it turns out he was in fact English, a traitor and mine to do with as I please. But let me now make it abundantly clear, so you may gauge my meaning. None of this, not a scrap matters squat to me, for you sir are a pirate, a murderer and you have no honour. You have against all dignity and rationale murdered every soul aboard Resignation and we have more reports of your operations acting as commodore of a renegade pirate squadron. Even with a Letter of Marque, you cannot explain away the sinking of Resignation in such a manner. And to add to your effrontery, you dare challenge me with the ink of your good king, only to thereafter completely seek to cheat upon the terms!'

'Ah, La Vénus, but of course,' he conceded. 'I do not know how you came to take her, but it was well played. You may think otherwise, but please Captain, she was only a precaution should the duel go ill, should you perhaps chance to lay some of your notorious English trickery upon us. I was never going to call upon her, please do not assume. Your comments of course offend. Nonetheless, you have fought with honour thus far. I will remember that at the end.'

'Sir, I thank you for this chance to acquaint with each other, but I have come here for one reason alone, to offer terms. You will surrender and you will be afforded a trial, which is perhaps the appropriate forum for any further discussion. And of your remaining crew, I say all will be spared. You will see your brother again, should you agree.'

'You would do this?' he considered. 'You would not seek to just hang me from your yard and be done with me?'

'No Captain, do not do it!' shouted one of the French sailors, angrily pleading with Lafayette, much to the surprise of the English, for no jack would ever challenge their superior as such, even in good faith. It was clear now how a revolutionary France was emerging. The monarchy would fail, men refusing to be governed, anarchy all but readying to emerge. And yet the world lay ignorant, still to behold the full impact of the ideals of this dogged uprising. The man continued arguing quite vehemently, almost embarrassingly. He was rabid, a frothing mongrel quite out of control. Hastily a pistol emerged, the barrel forebodingly raised.

Ships of War — Murky Waters

'I will kill this English dog for you!' he lastly declared, steadying his aim.

It was with interest that Lafayette had been swift enough to present his own pistol as well. In fact many pistols had been drawn. It was as if a lone pheasant had finally emerged after hours of a fruitless vacant hunt, every hunter parched with a maddened thirst to be first, frantically setting upon it in wild hysteria. Many pistols had been drawn indeed, but none able to match the speed of McFee, who had sent his ball directly between the man's eyes. The shot was received in sudden shock, the officer stiffening as his gaze fell blank. He slumped, finally slipping over the side forever disappearing into the murky waters. Lafayette spat into the water after him, thereafter looking upon the English boat.

'A fine shot sir!' Lafayette casually applauded. 'You have my apologies Captain, sincerely. Alas, such is the mind of men in France these days,' he sincerely offered, casually returning his pistol to his belt.

'Come now Captain Lafayette, you must consider my terms. If you do not, we will storm your ship or see her sunk, surely as rain falls daily in London.'

'Is that a threat, sir, really?'

'Oh please, no, no, no, it is no threat. It is a fact, for the rain always falls daily in London.'

'Ha, of course,' he smiled, now perhaps understanding his counterpart somewhat more. 'It is curious I come to believe you, that my brother still draws breath. But I regret, Captain, I cannot accept your terms. I beg you to try and take my ship. My small offer to you, my reason for coming is singular. Should we meet upon my quarterdeck, let our conversation not be so civil and so shall we soon behold who is the real Champion of France. You should know, my brother, although competent, hardly wielded the finest blade in our family. Perhaps if this interests you, we will see, maybe? I bid you farewell Captain, *Vive la France!*'

'I believe, sir, the dog just invited you to the kennel,' McFee quite correctly pointed out. They rowed back to Agamemnon and it seemed their world had just been turned upside down. French captains refusing to strike, French seamen pulling pistols under flags of truce and hardly did Lafayette blink upon his man's unruliness and sudden execution. 'I think he means to offer you his sword, upon our storming his ship, sir?'

'Ha, well put Major. One way or the other, I will be in acceptance.'

'*Vive la France*?' Holt questioned. 'Captain, I am at a loss. What does it mean?'

'Oh I know, the translation doesn't make any real sense of course. When I first heard it, it gave me pause too. Of course the word *"vive"* is derived from the irregular verb *"vivre"*, which in essence means *"to live"*. Suffice to say, it is an expression, a new one of course, offered to show patriotism, to laud France. It hails actually from the taking of *La Bastille* back in eighty-nine when all the trouble began. You see, by capturing the historic structure, the mobs of France no doubt sought to announce that the power to rule the country was now theirs. And Lafayette is definitely one of these revolutionaries, probably knocked down the Bastille door himself. I fear, Mister Holt, this is an expression we will hear much more, perhaps many times before our lifetimes are at an end.'

Solitaire bobbed as a floating fortress, her cannon busying as Agamemnon glided abeam. The fight had turned into a slugging contest, the grind of most weight thrown likely determining the victor. It would come at a cost no less, for the strategy of tide and wind was long lost. Courage and good aim would see through the fight and oh how Agamemnon went about her work, toiling upon each and every shot.

Upon the third pass, Solitaire's cannon had started to dwindle, a product of attrition. One might suggest the aim of the English somewhat superior, but Cooper knew a duck on the pond when he saw one. It was a wonder she still had not struck. In contrast,

Ships of War — Murky Waters

Agamemnon leapt back and forth varying her range at every approach. The French cannon barely had reported a decent shot, a fast ranging target with a clever helmsman thwarting every effort. Nonetheless, Solitaire's ensign remained, flapping indignantly in the prevailing wind, albeit reduced and somewhat tattered. Cooper was indeed starting to wonder if there were even any French still left alive upon the poop, able to haul it down. Upon the last broadside, the ship started to visibly break, awash with flying splinters and great chunks. Cooper surveyed the decks of Solitaire most carefully, finally deeming that it was now time, the final assault.

'Mister Holt! Now, if you please!'

'Helm-a-lee!' ordered Holt and the great ship spun towards the French, going straight at them.

'Bring us board and board! And be at the ready to claw off there, should we need to! Fall not off helmsman!' Cooper ordered sternly, cognisant he had just enjoined his ship to approach the breakwater of what could well turn out to be a lee shore. The wind favoured their escape but of course the tide was sending the flow heavily upon the rocks. It was not exactly clear which would prevail, but in they went nonetheless. 'Let the tide take her. Edge her in now, handsomely! Mister McFee, ready your jollies sir!' he finally grinned, turning back to Holt. 'Mister Holt, you have command of the ship!'

'What?' he spluttered, very much taken by surprise. 'Of course sir, but I must protest. Surely you cannot lead the boarding party. You are much too valuable and cannot be risked.'

'I can, I must and I will. You will see Agamemnon safely secured to the prize and you will see her decks awash with grape and you will see to it that any borders so bold are sufficiently repelled. And Mister Holt, do not allow them to shot us whilst we are board and board.'

'But sir,' lamented Holt, the water in his eye betraying his youth, the thought of never seeing his captain again ringing hard within.

'My place is with the jacks. I cannot in good conscience send them upon Lafayette's quarterdeck, for he would likely cut them down. Please do not distress my lad,' he added with a whisper.

Nodding with a smile, his hand reassuringly found the lad's shoulder. 'Hiro will be by my side,' he lastly offered. Beside him Hiro wildly grinned, the sneer of the devil in his eye and lastly he nodded as he eagerly tapped the hilt of his katana. 'Look at him. There is not a Frenchman alive who might chance to best him. With god's grace, I will return.'

Each ship sat eye to eye and apart from raised areas such as the quarterdeck and the forecastle, the usual advantage of expected elevation lay mute, for Solitaire was no brig. It was upon these areas Holt first maintained firing his grapeshot. He would clear the decks and ensure the French cannon could not work upon the boarding parties. He had already issued muskets to every jack below decks, marking any Frenchman who came within a shadow of their cannon. McFee's shooters held true in the tops, already banging away, fencing with their counterparts. And in the masthead, now looking somewhat like a converted fort, Eagle had half a dozen muskets at hand, his aim true enough to afford a crew of young lads. They laboured much like powder monkeys, all dedicated to reloading as fast as they could possibly muster. McFee and his jollies poured over the side as did Cooper and his jacks, wild and furious, bawling louder than banshees stealing away in the night.

For the first moments the melee upon the weather deck was brutal, waves of men crashing as breakwater upon the rocks, neither side giving way. McFee's jollies proved particularly ruinous in close quarters, their training with Hiro decidedly proving through. The French could not hope to hold, as valiant as they stood. Some minutes later Cooper had worked his way to the quarterdeck, Hiro holding loyally by his side as the brunt of the French summoned the necessary courage to fall directly upon them. It was notable how inaccurate the pistol shots were proving, on both sides in fact, the stress of battle perhaps touching the steadiness of aim. Yet the blade was a weapon to behold and nary could a large group hope to overwhelm a duo who very much knew what they were about. Cooper and Hiro thrashed through the ranks akin to a great whale upon its krill. They had spaced themselves nicely, ever moving forth, their steel scything a widened arc before them. With McFee wildly hovering their

Ships of War — Murky Waters

flanks, bolstered by his very best, the French could only hope to approach in a frontal challenge. And those that dared were quickly carved up. By the time Cooper arrived on the quarterdeck, Lafayette had already arranged himself, his pistols laid down, only a lone blade gracing his hand. The trailing deck fell littered with the slumped bodies of many a poor soul. Yet the ensign remained, Lafayette still arrogantly refusing to strike.

'Have you not gone mad, sir! The battle is beyond lost and still you have not struck. You have needlessly wasted your men Captain!' Cooper angrily challenged, laying his eye cruelly upon him. 'Wasted them and for what, for your pride, your arrogance? It is fitting that no matter what happens next, you will no longer be a captain of men, for I declare, you are not fit to adorn even the gutters of hell! This is your last chance to strike, though seeing how you have already led your men to total damnation, I very much now wish you to stay your hand.'

The time for small talk was well and truly past, Lafayette choosing not to return the gesture except but to offer a wry grin. The entirety of the ship gradually dwindled, falling to an odd silence, much the same as a wood fire spitting and crackling in defiance of its extinguishment. It was a sign that the end had come, for the French anyway. Lafayette could have escaped, his boat readied, the shore and his homeland barely a hundred yards yonder. Yet upon Cooper his blade served to point, his face grim, his eyes fired, his steps beneath now stalking, purposeful and exact.

'The flag you seek is verily before you, sir,' he offered, goading Cooper to come and strike it. '*C'est la vie*, Captain Cooper, *Vive la France!*'

It seemed the entire product of Cooper's existence had now culminated to this instant, to this minute point in time, a moment which would decide all. The toil of his every labour, the suffering of his longstanding patience, his every breath was now very much awaiting the outcome. Would his life be awash, wrecked upon a lee shore or in the next few moments would he emerge with the prize? It would only take one swish and either way it would be over. One blunder albeit slight would see his ruination, his entire being wasted, his legacy lost forever sunk in the obscurity of all time. No quarter would be given, he knew this, the man before him rotten to the core, more rancid than any rabid dog ever imagined. It was his charge now, perhaps even his sacred duty to rid the world of Lafayette, to see such tyranny to the other side. Such is life Lafayette had mocked and how true Cooper now thought this might prove. He pondered it momentarily, for when had life ever deferred to arbitrarily judge the good above the wicked, the jury upon a ship of war deliberating only upon the skill of the swiftest blade.

Lafayette suddenly edged forth, a fake motion, sharply testing Cooper's reaction. Cooper held true solidly maintaining his position and balance, scarcely startled, his reflexes not quite willing to betray. He grinned knowingly, eyes locked, the two circling as wild cats readying to pounce. He bore his usual mind, preferring to gauge his opponent before wholly committing. Yet perhaps this time it was a risk, a luxury which might actually see his end before he even started. His heart thumped, a drum banging within the desolation of his warring soul. Upon Lafayette his gaze fell directly, keenly eyeing the grip, the footing, the posture, even the hinging of the hip.

Cooper most carefully studied the one-handed western rapier poised before him, much the same as the Chevalier's smallsword. It was the simplest of swords, but oh how he imagined the speed it might afford, a distinct advantage with thrusts and stabs promoted down the centre, although it could just as well slash. Many times had he and Hiro played with such strategies, toiling as wild cats stalking its prey, forever testing such limits. He knew his katana had more power and likely an advantage upon the flanks, the blade styled for large circular motions. Upon the flanks would he hover, never allowing himself to be found in proximity to Lafayette's stabbing strikes, especially whilst the man had free reign.

Lafayette's first attack came swiftly, direct and straight, lightning sparking over and over from an ominous cloud, unrelenting. Oh how each strike howled, crying in tune with the shuffle of short brisk steps, a grand symphony from which usually there is no escape. Three magnificent thrusts followed two wild slashes. Cooper's steel barely matched as he wheeled back. His good eye remained, searching for any tell or trait. Lafayette was as a muted devil, his eyes glazed and his expression blank.

It was not lost on Cooper that the attack came just as he had chanced to blink. It was likely no coincidence, a masterful tact and inwardly he applauded it. Rhythm would lead to his immediate downfall, a malady he immediately sought to correct. He had a strong inclination now of his opponent, a true swordsman, a vicious combatant harbouring the empathy of a hungered cat. Cooper gathered his breath, reining in the irrepressible surge that the first strikes of battle impose. As he pondered the fortune of surviving the first onslaught, he could scarcely imagine how many souls this man had cut down.

Lafayette seemed somewhat satisfied with himself and idly did he stroll back towards the poop. The French ensign dangled before him and even for a moment he arrogantly turned his back. Perhaps he thought he was at the games in Paris and not upon a ship of war fighting to the death. It was obvious he had somewhat summed up his opponent already, much like a master of any gentleman's game surveying the first few moves. His conceit was meant to rile, offered in indignation and in course, he sought to dredge the well of Cooper's anger. To incite emotion was a good ploy. Rage never mixed well, depleting one's speed, diminishing one's mind and Cooper knew it. Hiro often professed that an angered blade was a blade rarely blunted. The insult had hit the mark, but this was hardly the games in Paris, Cooper's mind as stone, a seasoned veteran. Lafayette's ploy had not gone unnoticed. Yet inwardly did it please Cooper, perhaps now suspecting some overconfidence, a trait which often accompanied the gravest consequences.

Within the mix Cooper had his own ruses to play, subtle offerings meant to confuse. He continued to adjust his grip for no apparent reason. Curiously he randomly moved about his feet, purporting to some hidden devilry. From time to time he even grinned stupidly, another childish distraction of course. Yet masked within the subterfuge had he offered one true ploy. During his defence had he feigned to hold one or two of his parries a little tight. Lafayette would instantly discern it. It was a simple ruse, yet he was thinking the offer of some technical deficiency might provide the necessary encouragement. It may have been the pretence of a subtle error, but it was one which would see a defending blade less reactive, more open to manipulation. A seasoned master might utilise this to great advantage. Indeed, a swordsman such as Lafayette knew only the truest grip might hope to control the measured weight of steel as each blow met. This was the real cheese for his rat. Should Lafayette take the bait Cooper might have him, for normally his hands were softer even more than what Hiro could muster. Oh how he wished to see the Frenchman challenge him on this point and oh how he yearned to see the rapier thereafter indignantly fly from his grip.

A stalemate had emerged, each watching the other intensely. It was temporarily broken as Lafayette shuffled slightly. Immediately Cooper lunged, striking heavily at the blade. In course, he never aimed at the blade, only the man. It was with note that the weight of Lafayette's sword fell easily aside. Cooper chanced the attack again, this time adding a secondary strike, moving swiftly, venturing high upon the throat. It was a masterly attempt. Yet the onslaught fell thwarted, aptly met, Lafayette proving quite able. Indeed the man proved quite swift, a natural zeal to parry and counter. They continued back and forth, hardly acquiescing, yet ever searching, probing, feeling for the slightest opportunity.

The seconds transpired to minutes, the performance nothing short of exact perfection. Sweat beaded upon their brows, their gaze diligent yet subtly telling. It seemed a hopeless void. The barrages were terrible and swift, yet each set gently aside as pebbles thrown against a great fort. Hardly could it last Cooper rightly considered. Of such an impasse, a man such as Lafayette would surely tire, his eyes betraying his impatience. Cooper could grasp the way forward now. Tolerance, coupled with the absolution of unbending patience, his long road to victory. Of this had Hiro schooled him mercilessly. He had even suffered to stand with his sword poised an entire morning in the beating sun, sweat beading and muscles aching, with an hour added for every inadvertent move made. And hardly was that the worst his master had piled within his cunning. Every lesson by design had wreaked of some subtle hardship, fashioned to illicit the utmost steel within the fortress of his mind. More now than ever, it was apparent, such lessons had proved a life-saving enlightenment.

Ships of War — Murky Waters

Cooper wasn't as such a deeply religious man, but you can be sure he was now praying hard for the absolute evisceration of the man before him. It was his will against Lafayette's and never would he fail. He would subtly adjust, continuing to fence with less risk, maintain the stalemate as long as necessary and perchance would he goad his opponent to finally err. Patiently would he wait, a cat upon the mouse.

It took some minutes thereafter, a virtual lifetime in any bout. You can be sure McFee was already thinking to simply shoot the French Captain and be done with it, a row of sharpshooters at his every beck and call. Poor Holt in like mind was nervously mulling whether to let Eagle take him down, short of personally standing by the swivel cannon and letting fly a small pounder at the man's head. But finally it came and it came in a flurry. Lafayette risked a determined attack, a wondrous combination of blows. His efforts were rewarded, the tip of his blade ultimately slipping by to nick Cooper's shirt. It was an upward slash of some qualified proportion. It seemed the Frenchman had indeed tired of the back and forth slogging. He had hazarded a spinning approach, a strike not once before shown. Barely an inch farther and the fight would have been over. Nonetheless, first blood had graced the tip of his rapier.

Cooper was immediately attuned to the sudden sting. The gash oozed dying dark his white shirt, the rounded claw mark of a great cat seized upon his chest. In silence the entire gathering fell, shock upon horror extorting every ounce of breath. Even Hiro instinctively reacted, immediately clutching the hilt of his sword. Their captain had fought valiantly, the exchanges of the duel indescribable, those honoured to be present very much in awe. But Lafayette took the honour, his spinning upper slash undeniable and hardly had he even begun. The upper slash was but only the first swing of his ultimate combination. The Frenchman continued, spinning now in an opposite tack, bringing his blade swiftly to Cooper's neck in a heavy downward slash. They were the moves of a great swordsman, a hidden combination so to speak, perhaps only played upon the greatest of opponent. It was the highest compliment of course, a testament to Cooper's great skill, not that the dead might ever chance to return the gesture.

The two slashes flashed and nary had a soul ever expected such brilliance, such strikes, such cunning. In fairness, Cooper knew something was coming. He wasn't exactly sure what, but the differing balance upon Lafayette's feet had all but announced it. In readiness had he wisely slipped his weight slightly back, only a few inches mind you, though in retrospect he had perhaps required just one extra inch. Nonetheless, his life remained. Distance was always a fine balance. Moving too far back would forgo his counter and not moving far enough would see his instant death. He knew a good swordsman could not win from afar. Risks at some point verily had to be taken and this was indeed one of those times. His shirt was torn, bloodied, his flesh deeply nicked, but thankfully for now that was all.

The second part of Lafayette's combination fell, a spinning heavy downward strike to the neck, the finale. Yet as the combination played out, Cooper unexpectedly lunged wildly forth. He held his steel high, catching the attack early in the spin, ultimately holding firm Lafayette's rapier in a strong block. Nullified, the blades met, the combatants very much shoulder to shoulder. There the steel held to each other, locked, pushing against one another, tips skyward, hilt to hilt, each fighter now virtually face to face. Whoever flinched, whoever fell away first would fall. For a good many moments they held strong weighing each other's blade, ensuring there was no room to pull away and strike. They pushed and pulled, testing each other's resolve, testing each other's strength. Yet Cooper had two hands upon his hilt to Lafayette's one. If the Frenchman was to prevail, he would need to bolster his sword with his free hand. It was the correct choice naturally, but instead he was verily thinking to draw his knife. It was a risk, but should he succeed, he would finish Cooper in short time.

For Holt looking on, his heart was somewhat now in his mouth. His captain had been struck and was bleeding. Now they appeared to be in some clinch, some kind of strange dance, not quite a waltz, but close enough. Naturally he could never appreciate the dynamics or the strategy involved. Why were they so close? Why had they not chanced to strike yet? Why did they continue to hold, face to face as such, prancing in some crazy saunter upon the deck? Holt could not fathom it, the jacks could not fathom it, the officers could not fathom it, but Hiro knew. And all at once Hiro's hand slipped away from his hilt, a shrewd smile emerging to wipe away the natural sternness he ever so enjoyed. Lafayette now had both hands upon his hilt, the shoving action against him so overwhelming. His thoughts to grab the knife dissipated, the greater risk before him pressing. Cooper searched for his footing upon the planks, wriggling his hips in amongst Lafayette, pushing and pulling, ever subtly positioning, just as Hiro had taught him. Hiro began to wildly grin.

'Bravo Captain Cooper!' Lafayette complimented, still struggling to match the weight of his blade being rammed. 'You are the first ever to have survived that move. You have survived, have you not? I do see you are now bleeding? Perhaps I have spoken too soon?' he teased, wholly unaware of the absolute peril before him, no less a deer grazing before the hunter's bow.

'It was well done Captain Lafayette, I commend you, but in the end have you blundered. I do not mind to tell you, for I see our bout at an end. You cannot now escape.'

'Surely sir, you jest! This is a simple respite amongst two great fighters. Indeed you jest. Let us return to our mark and restart?'

'No sir, I think not, for had you not noticed, our steel slides upon one another and our hilts are thus trapped together. Yet mine has the honour of sitting very much below yours. You may note that mine is of a wholly different nature. Have you not noticed its girth and design and the nature of the guard? Not even the best swordsman in the world can escape what befalls you next.'

'Best in the world, you say? High praise indeed Captain, I am honoured, but it will not change the outcome.'

'No Captain, I refer to Kensei, Hiro, that small Orient standing yonder. I imagine he is grinning right about now. He never grins. For he is the best swordsman I have ever known and from this predicament, never in our play has he once escaped.'

Cooper waited upon the rhythm of Lafayette's blink, suddenly allowing the pushing power of the Frenchman to surge forth and unbalance the dance. Cooper's hilt was now tucked well under Lafayette's and easily he forced it high, thrusting it upward. Lafayette beheld his sword levered hopelessly above his head, unable to retrieve it. His eyes widened, suddenly realising his plight. He was now completely open to attack, Cooper's blade very much below his. The katana had free rein and down and across it came, slashing its razored tip through the abdomen. Lafayette stiffened, immediately losing all way, his sword falling harmlessly. Cooper had struck smoothly yet deeply, a long slash through the length of the body. He continued to drop into a spin, now half slashing each calf. Lafayette fell to his knees, pain unimaginable gripping his every being. Cooper's spin reversed and so did he strike cleanly upon the outstretched wrist, the right wrist in fact much to the irrepressible pleasure of the jacks. Lafayette held to his stump, agonising within the excruciating agony.

Cooper eyed the man with some mortified level of disdain, an overwhelming feeling of hatred he never imagined possible. Lafayette had murdered countless souls, horribly, remorselessly, the prejudice of an immutable unthinking beast. The memory of poor Resignation now evoked within Cooper a loathing most undeniable. Lifting the tip of his katana, Cooper held the point before Lafayette. Without so much as a pause, steadily he ushered it through and by the base of the throat. He eyed with curiosity the sudden shock upon Lafayette's face as it railed silently out the other side, the man's mouth gaping but no sound afforded. Blood piled about the steel, gurgling in the suffocation of the last moments, a fitting end with no last words. Cooper's boot finally found the man's chest, levering out the blade.

It may have been curiosity or perhaps just contemplation. Yet over Lafayette's lifeless body did Cooper ultimately perch, the wind belting his lungs now gently subsiding. For the first time upon his chest did he lay his hand, feeling for the wound. It was deeper than he first thought and upon first touch immediately did it sting, though indifferently he remained. The blood was oozing, thick, still warm to the touch, an accompanying ache ever mounting in unison with every moment of his apparent idleness. His gaze remained fixed, still eyeing the Frenchman as if the man might suddenly rise and somehow indignantly strike him down. But there was no mistake, Lafayette had most definitely departed the world.

Ships of War — Murky Waters

In eventual realisation, a sullen contemplation sought to trespass upon his fleeting thoughts. With some qualified reservation he eventually took a much needed moment of respite. He had won. It was over. He was alive. The madman was dead. Vengeance had been delivered and so once again might the world be at peace, that is, until the next Lafayette happened along. Curiously he regarded his deed for one last time, almost wondering what next he should do. It irked him somewhat, for he was no stranger to war, to death, yet in this one moment he held his place, almost dumbfounded. Gradually could he feel a semblance of order returning and soon hopefully he thought sanity might follow.

All was well with Cooper's world. The battle had been won, the prize would now be secured and at the point of his katana had the devil himself been sent back to the pits of hell. The scene remained somewhat surreal, yet the throes of Cooper's contemplation were soon awoken. Before him a loud shriek broke, followed by a wild scream, both verily serving to wake the dead. It was a dragging moment in time, a beguiling consternation striking heavily upon his bewildered soul. The sight sought to arrest his very being. He gasped, shocked, looking up to behold the barrel of a pistol being levelled his way. The young French officer continued to charge, emerging violently from the poop with a sword in one hand and a pistol in the other. Behind him the absolute legitimacy of the French ensign fluttered indignantly, for the ship had not yet struck. The man was entitled and upon Cooper did he riotously descend sprinting madly, fixated with one deed in mind, the hounds of hell urging his utmost. The pistol took dead aim. He would not miss, not from such proximity and Cooper readied for the inevitable, recalling Lafayette's last words, *"such is life"*.

The shot rang loudly and ever did it cause Cooper to stiffen, such was his ultimate shock beholden to the anguish of its report. The entire boarding party stood silent, mostly in gutted astonishment, hardly knowing what to do. The shot was true, rendering its mark directly between the eyes, a certain death blow. The planking echoed as it reported a horrid thumping upon its timbers, the sound of a lifeless body plummeting. It was the sudden thump one knew when the fallen was already well and truly quite lifeless. For what it was worth, the entire boarding party now had their pistols drawn and pointed, yet it was a moment in time much too late.

McFee strolled sullenly about the scene, his pistol still drawn though he held his good eye upon his captain. He chanced to glance skyward. Yet it was not despair which drove him, but pure curiosity and he nodded as he beheld Eagle atop the main mast, a hundred and twenty feet in the air, the smoke from a musket still hounding the masthead. It seemed every soul present was now looking to Eagle, their eyes filled in astonishment beyond any worldly comprehension. McFee prodded the French officer with his boot, but he well knew the man was dead, outrageously shot between the eyes by perhaps the best musket man in the entire Royal Navy. It was fitting the young French officer lay next to Lafayette, the fate of their lunacy intertwined.

'Good god!' McFee softly cried, looking back at Eagle, who was now visibly gleaning the barrel of his musket with a cloth. 'For the love of Mary, by all that is bloody holy, good god!'

'Indeed, I think he is, in part at least perhaps,' agreed Cooper prophetically, somewhat dazed by it all, once more physically checking that somehow his body still entertained the mortal world and was not some lingering spirit wandering aimlessly about.

'What a god damned shot!' remarked McFee.

'Praise that man to have many children!' added Holt.

'Captain Cooper, sir?' McFee offered, motioning to the wound upon his chest. 'Are you alright sir? Perhaps it might be best the Doctor is called, may I?'

'Indeed you may!' Cooper agreed, finally realising that he was very much alive and it was the charging French officer who lay dead, struck by Eagle's musket. He looked upon Lafayette one last time. *'Vive la France!'* he bade, ceremoniously flicking the blood from his blade.

'Captain?' Hiro offered, coming to his side, a repressed look of indignation haunting him. Poor Cooper stood there bedraggled and spent, bleeding, but content to see his friend. Yet sternly Hiro eyed him, a mocking disdain, not unlike the loathing of a dispassionate Shogun looking down upon a peasant who had failed to bow, a hastened repressed look of absolute annoyance gracing his every grimace. Softly he shook his head, taking a deep breath. 'Twenty-three!' he scowled in admonishment, eventually smiling, unable to now hold back his mirth.

'But I almost lost Hiro, almost.'

'Never,' he disagreed, now checking the wound, not unlike a qualified expert. 'And you will live. You played the bout as you should. You have prevailed, not because you are lucky, not because you are a good student, but because you are the better. But should you have lost, rest assured, Kensei Hiro would have taken his head for you, for such is my duty and my affection.'

'Indeed, I see. Well, in course, I am sure I would have thanked you.'

'Sails ho!'

The call was somewhat more frantic than the usual call, Cooper and Holt immediately fearing something was afoot. They could see Eagle scrambling to the nest to confirm the lookout's call.

'It's Royal Louis!' confirmed Eagle.

'The devil, Captain!' Holt vexed. 'Their flagship, one hundred and ten gun with a deck of forty-eight pounders! Sir, we are dished.'

'By all that is holy, must you always be right Mister Holt! Take down that ensign, at once!' Cooper ordered, pointing to Solitaire's flag. 'Hoist the jack! This ship is now ours! Beat Agamemnon back to quarters and have all hands report to stations!'

'Sir, your wound?'

'Have the Doctor report to the sovereign's parade. He can stitch me up there, perhaps just in time to see us blown to kingdom come by this behemoth! Good god, forty-eights!'

'Are we not running, sir?' questioned McFee.

'Even a hare cannot run in a barn Mister McFee,' returned Cooper.

'We are tucked in here tight sir, almost a lee shore,' Holt quickly explained. 'But, Captain, we could definitely boxhaul her and make our way, perhaps almost in time. We are not anchored, so there is no need to cut and run, meaning we can just run, sir. We would have to leave the prize though.'

'But can we hope to make sufficient way?' Cooper doubted. 'For we have taken much damage to our canvas and did we not take two shots in our hull?'

'You are right of course, sir, no, I fear not.'

'Hoist our jack so they can see her!' Cooper commenced. 'Drop the bloody anchor. We are not going anywhere. The victor does not run and we have their king's permission to be here. To run would only invite destruction.'

Royal Louis loomed into sight, her cannon visibly in the action of being run out. Agamemnon was unable to move, not in time and she was hardly able to fight, let alone prevail against a ship in the first class of the line of battle. The ensign upon Agamemnon held true, but if it came to it, Cooper was of a mind he would be the one to haul it down. His heart sank as he eyed the great cannon protruding the French ports. Royal Louis glided into range, his mind already assigned to take the short walk to the poop and strike.

'Here they come, sir!' Holt reported. 'Sir, they are firing!'

It was perhaps the sweetest sight Cooper had ever seen, albeit one of the strangest. He would accept it of course with all happiness and candour, for never before had he been so dished, excepting maybe when Pompee leapt from the islet. Royal Louis was firing every shot she had on every deck, both sides of the ship. Oh what a fortune it must have cost her captain and oh what a handsome gesture.

'Aye, but not at us,' Cooper happily confirmed. 'It is a gesture, Mister Holt, a gesture of goodwill. They mean to approach and they wish us not to fire upon them.'

'Sir? Fire upon them?'

'What? No!' Cooper quickly relayed. 'Good god, no. Belay

Ships of War — Murky Waters

quarters and close the gunports, if you please. Have the drum and fife assembled. Send a crew to secure the prize. Have the remaining French crew ready to be transferred. Officers to present themselves in their best dress uniform. And if the French are to change their mind, at least we will be blown to bits in grandeur and style.'

'Aye, aye!'

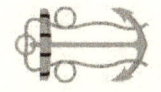

Chapter XXIV
To Our Utmost

It was an absolute indulgence, but Cooper was thinking not only he, but the entire crew had verily earned it. As Agamemnon limped her way back to Ortac, in course had he ordered every member of the drum and fife to practice their best tunes upon the sanctity of the weather deck. That was how he had cunningly put it, considering it was otherwise against regulations. And he added that they should continue to practice their best tunes, even the French ones, until he was bloody well satisfied they knew them, which he assured wasn't going to be anytime soon. It raised a few eyebrows from the old hands who knew the indulgence of music was not permitted on a ship of war. Ultimately they grinned from one ear to the other, boasting how their captain had again most cleverly navigated his way around some bothersome rule. They were of a mind Captain Lefty could do almost anything and in due course later legally justify it in some handsome way. After all, he had built an English fort on a French islet and there it still remained. He had captured a French forty gun frigate, no less than by way of absolute piracy and the Admiralty were even about to pay her off. He happily had a lord locked away in the ship's asylum for a whole year and not a peep from anyone and that was even after he had lopped off the man's arm. And he had dismembered more members of the English and French gentry than humanly thought possible, all without a how do you do from the powers that be. He may only be a lieutenant in command, but this was a fighting man of great cunning and one they would follow into the next war and beyond. The entire crew were all now stinking rich too of course, which naturally within their hearts held a little more than a modicum of sentimental favour.

Cooper was cognisant of the men's feelings towards him, but they were still men who needed to be governed. It was almost of scientific interest, perhaps most worthy of some further study, as to how keenly they now acted upon his orders, any order in fact, even the most unpopular commands. And all it took was to lop off a few arms and perhaps a head here and there. He was rightly guessing the way in which he had coldly skewered Lafayette had laid the icing of discipline to his cake of command. Even the known slackers snapped to when he was about. The men had indeed become hearty dogs of war with almost thirty engagements under his command and oh how in turn he had come to love them. But he must keep them strong, that is, to keep them safe. His sanctuary upon the quarterdeck proved a godsend, a place to steer clear of the crew, keep them guessing. He feared it would be the absolute end should they come to somehow personally know him. He was determined to remain aloof and at the same time allow them some measure of uninhibited space. Yet he was not so bereft of company as to have no other with which to share his quarterdeck. Presently he enjoyed the companionship of Captain Poulain and Captain Spencer, most gratefully in fact.

'I must thank you again Captain Poulain, your friend upon Royal Louis was so very accommodating.'

'I agree,' Spencer happily added. 'What a fellow, who would have thought he might tow our prize out from the breakwater, what a fellow!'

'He is a royalist, of course,' grinned Poulain.

'Well,' remarked Cooper. 'I very much thought he was going to royally blow us to kingdom come.'

'Perhaps if we had been Lafayette he may well have, for I must say, my friend has been quite incensed of late.'

'Indeed?'

'There is even a rumour the Girondins will rename Royal Louis. They propose to call her *Républicain*. Can you believe it, the pigs?'

'Oh, I see and his position?'

'Likely promoted, which is to say, replaced.'

'Ah, of course.'

'He wishes war to break tomorrow, you know, so he can properly fight against these revolutionists, with the English. His entire ship is loyal.'

'This is food for thought André, indeed food for thought.'

From his sanctuary, Cooper eyed Hasard in the near distance with some distinct satisfaction. Eventually his gaze fell upon the other prizes. What additions they were to the squadron he thought, a sixty-four, a forty and of course finally Hasard, eighteen. Venus and Solitaire were handsome ships, to be sure, but he was already thinking the names would have to be changed, provided the Admiralty permitted their retention. That was the arrangement of course, but who can ever tell with the Admiralty. For all he knew, they may very well say thank you and show him the beach, installing a new captain with somewhat more interest. No matter what would befall and whatever was to become of his career, he was content. He had done his duty, to his utmost. The last eighteen months had seen hard work prevail. He clung to hope, for that was all he had, nothing being certain.

One thing was sure, a grand entrance to Ortac was soon in the making, not that anyone would see it. He was thinking he would remember this moment all his days, his first ship to ship action of equal strength. Oh how he wished Nelson could see the squadron now. He thought well of his commodore, always zeal ringing within his heart, always endless hope. And oh how the man enjoyed a good prize, not that he might need the coin anymore. But at the very least, the surplus men languishing upon Wight might now be called to arms, immediately installed within the squadron. Together, hopefully now with Nelson, oh what a force they might present.

'Sir?' Holt interrupted, presenting himself before his captain.

Ships of War — Murky Waters

'Very sorry sir, I know you are convalescing, but I must report. Sir, Eagle has sighted Achilles. And sir, for some reason, she is heading back to us, at some pace too I might add?'

'Oh?'

'Aye, I had sent her ahead with Mister Pickering in command, to Ortac, to scout. Something must be amiss, if I may.'

It was with absolute mortification that the head of Shillings popped over the gunwale of Achilles, the man readying to make his way aboard Agamemnon. Eagle was first to see him, immediately tooting a secret note upon his whistle. Nobody of course knew what it meant, except Holt. The lad stormed to the side of the ship faster than a March Hare on heat.

'Sir,' he yelled, trying to overpower the wind and ocean. 'I say Lieutenant Shillings there, sir, belay, if you please! We have just had the sides ripped apart in our last action. It ain't safe, not safe at all.'

'Are you sure? It looks fine? But I must see the Captain, most urgent, most confidential.'

'Of course, sir, may I beg you to wait aboard Achilles, momentarily.'

'Good god, is that Shillings?' Spencer vexed, now standing beside Holt. 'The Captain will be suicidal. You aren't going to allow him on board, are you? And the Captain is in no state to be clambering down to Achilles. Doctor just stitched him up.'

'I have a plan, sir. If you could arrange for the Captain to attend the lower deck stern cabin, I have something that might just do the trick. Though I am afraid we shall have to completely heave-to.'

Captain Cooper stood within the state room peering through the stern lights as Achilles came to be moored to the very rear of Agamemnon. Shillings looked sheepishly from his own deck, patiently waiting upon the two ships to close, readying himself to leap aboard.

'Oh that's close enough Mister Shillings, no need to trouble yourself risking to board now. Please do tell, what it is?'

'Well sir, I don't rightly know how to explain,' he fumbled in agitation. 'But the short of it, well, it's Mister Middleton, sir.'

'Aye, I see, what now?'

'Well sir, he is dead.'

'What?' Cooper quizzed, the news slowly sinking in. 'What!'

'Aye sir, it seems I have killed him, dead.'

'Get a hold man, you cannot kill someone dead. What did you do, c'mon, out with it, I'll not judge.'

'Shot him sir, stone dead I am afraid. And the shark ate him, well not all of him.'

'What the blazes, which is it, was he eaten by shark or shot?'

'Both I'm afraid, sir.'

'What? Come now, in what order? Look, bloody hell, what a mess, I am coming over. We must discuss this forthrightly. Now, you will repair to the captain's berth and I'll meet you there.'

Cooper, Poulain, Spencer, Holt, McFee and Blane all assembled upon Achilles, very much at the extremes of their curiosity. They had heard Middleton was dead, not that they held any love for the man, but this could be trouble. The man may have been a lunatic and a never-ending bothersome pain, but he was also a lord, not to mention nephew to a most powerful admiral. As they felt the planking of Achilles beneath their feet, they exchanged sombre looks with each other. A gang of ruffians with the noose already about them, ready to swing, could not have matched such glumness. To share any vessel with Shillings perhaps conjured within a myriad of wild trepidation, fears hardly matched by even the thought of a slowly foundering ship hopelessly engulfed by the frozen waters of the North Sea. One by one they entered the captain's berth, quite a confined space in fact, only to find poor Shillings cowering, very much trembling in his plight and hardly able to solidly eye even one of his fellow officers.

'Mind you, this is in no way whatsoever a trial Mister Shillings, but please tell us what happened. You say Mister Middleton is dead? Tell the truth of the matter now and everything will be okay.'

'Of course sir, my absolute intention,' Shillings returned, now finding some courage. 'Well, sir, everything was going fine, with Mister Middleton that is. He was...'

'Sorry sir,' Pickering suddenly interrupted, bursting through the berth's door. 'Begging your pardon, but we are unable to get under way, rudder is suddenly off. It is the damnedest thing, most inexplicable, sir,' he reported, much to the morose receipt of a roomful of knowing yet horrified faces.

'Very well Mister Pickering, as long as we ain't sinking!' Cooper barked, now deeming his stay upon any ship with Shillings an act of wanton foolhardy recklessness. 'We ain't sinking? Tell me we ain't sinking, are we? Very well, please to continue Mister Shillings.'

'Well sir, he was fine, seemed a right normal chap from the outset. Was handy with the cannon too, most handy and didn't mind deferring to me in any way as his commander.'

'And...?' prompted Cooper, handing the man a small brandy, the entire gathering gawking about him, patiently expectant.

'And today sir, thank you, it all went wrong. I wished to check upon the cannon, that is, from the sea sir, as I usually might. So we got into the boat,' he nodded, sipping his brandy, the room at once swapping a flurry of wry knowing looks.

'A boat? Together?' Cooper vexed. 'Same boat? What, upon the water!'

'Aye, he insisted he come, lend a hand so to speak and assist in the review. To be frank, I normally do it myself, mostly being that the men are much too frightened to go out in the boat of course, you know sir, on account of Lefty.'

'Well Mister Shillings, you cannot blame them in course. It is a rather monstrous hazard,' he added, hardly referring to the shark of course.

'But the shark never bothers me, don't know why. Oh I see him from time to time, but what can he really do if I'm in the boat, right sir? Sir, I cannot lie, Mister Middleton was a bloody good officer, right up til then.'

'Indeed, so what happened?'

'Well, we rowed about Ortac, just us sir, no others and after some time he started to look strange, act strange too. Had that look sir, that wild look, you know the one. Then he started to ask me weird questions and insisted I call him *"My Lord"*. Indeed he got most upset when of course I point blank refused.'

'Bloody hell and what questions?'

'Well, he wanted to know from what part of France the Shillings family hailed? How long had I been in England? My family is from Sussex, sir, fourth generation. It was all very weird sir, most unsettling and then he suddenly drew his cutlass, ordered me into the water, to swim back.'

'Which you obviously refused, drawing your pistol and may I say, if that is how it happened, rightly so?'

'Aye, Captain, I wasn't too concerned at first, the man having only one arm of course. But then he took a good swing at me, took some flesh, see?' he accounted, peeling back his jacket to show a fresh wound, neatly stitched. 'Aye that was when the pistol went off and he fell slumped sir, dead as stone I reckon, before he even hit the planking. His arm, the good one, lay in the water and a moment later that bloody great behemoth snatched it clean off! Never in life sir, never did I wish to kill him and never in life have I been so bloody afraid, that shark circling the boat lying on its side with one eye poking out, 'twas the devil's eye it was sir.'

'Say nothing of this, do you hear me, say nothing of this to a soul.'

'Aye, aye, sir.'

'Very well,' Cooper nodded, a moment of silence pending his decision upon what to do next. He weighed his thoughts, gently eyeing the bedraggled man before him. 'Alright Mister Shillings, better get Mister Pickering to arrange a rope,' Cooper sullenly announced, much to the astonishment of all and mostly to the rigid shock of poor Shillings, who now stood there mouth gaping in mortified silence.

'Sir, really, must Mister Shillings fetch his own noose?' protested Blane politely, feeling the man's angst, a few nods in support.

'What? Oh good god no! We need the rope to get back aboard Agamemnon. Never in life will I see the man before us hanged, a man who has done his utmost, a man who can shoot a sixty-four and knock the legs of a dragonfly at five hundred yards. Now Mister Shillings, do not misunderstand, go on deck, get some fresh air and act as if you have done nothing wrong, nothing, do you hear me, nothing!' he insistently ordered, thereafter waiting for Shillings to clear the cabin. Silently he shook his head until he couldn't take it anymore, gazing at each and every face present. 'Upon my soul! Bell, book and bloody candle, the devil! Good grief, Doctor, what do you make of it?' he gasped, the entire gathering very much speechless, confounded in sullen silence.

'Oh sir, of it, I make a lot actually. Captain, I have a suspicion, but I will have to examine poor Mister Middleton, who had on all accounts obviously regressed. I believe Mister Shillings had his remains put aboard. May I suggest you all repair to the safety, er, comfort of Agamemnon. I will remain and hopefully, god willing, you will have my findings upon our fall at Ortac, that is, short of the brig broaching-to and suddenly drowning us all.'

'Oh please Doctor, goodness, ha, ha!' Cooper cheerily corrected. 'Oh please do not be ridiculous. You cannot be serious, drowning, come now. What a fellow you are. I am quite certain you would freeze to death long before you might drown.'

'If I may, Captain,' Holt insisted, ready to offer his import as first officer. 'Well, sir, I would wager it is unlikely Mister Shillings murdered the man.'

'Indeed, how so?' Cooper entertained, somewhat intrigued. 'After all, it is just a story he has told so far, one with facts we are yet to bear out. He could have just now told us anything.'

'Perhaps, but most likely in that case, only the smaller details might be altered. He cannot lie about rowing around Ortac, too many a soul bearing witness. He also cannot lie about being alone in the boat with Mister Middleton, but the deed itself was in fact perpetrated without a soul to bear witness. It stands to reason that a shrewd cove could have easily disposed of the body, an alternative accusation, or alibi, only a splash away.'

'You speak of the shark.'

'Aye, would have been very easy to say the shark leapt and took Mister Middleton, the shot fired into the shark thereafter. The shark would nicely clean up any evidence of a musket to the head.

Curiously though, Mister Shillings instead comes to you sir, verily begging his life bereft any solid evidence, all in the faint hope you might believe him.'

'Sir, Eagle reports Ortac on the horizon,' announced Holt.

'How the devil does he distinguish one islet from the other?'

'Well sir, in this instance he is pretty sure it is Ortac, considering there is a great bloody first-rate moored next to her.'

'What?'

'Aye, sir.'

'Is it ours?' he anxiously vexed. 'And what of Achilles, sent ahead? Do we see her anywhere?'

The joyous report of Ortac looming on the horizon was quickly doused by the sighting of a line of battle ship moored monstrously beside her. The rumour mills of the ship started to grind. To date had they been most fortunate with the French, firstly with Pompee leaping out behind an islet and then with Royal Louis at Brest, in both instances the French able to completely dish Agamemnon. It had been a blessing both ships were not yet part of the revolutionist forces of France, otherwise Cooper might have awkwardly found himself in the main square of Paris eyeing the newest French contraption. The captain in Cooper quickly postulated, firstly considering that in point of fact the fort may have been lost. He was further agonising that Achilles had been sunk or taken. Whichever way he worked it, it did not look good. He may possess an armada of ships presently, more than enough to take on one first-rate, but Agamemnon was limping and the others barely had enough hands to sail, let alone to crew cannon. Any bold presentation of his squadron at Ortac would be little more than a bluff, a bluff he figured might easily be called.

'We are not yet sure, sir. The sails have only just come into view. But it's a forgone conclusion they already know we are here,

Ships of War — Murky Waters

all of us. And sir, very sorry, no sign of Achilles, though she may be moored the other side of Ortac?'

'Aye, or sunk already. Damn. Well, hardly can we run, not in the state we are in, so let us push on,' Cooper reluctantly ordered. He detested these situations, ones in which he really had no choice. However, in the throes of his estimation, if he had to wager, he was of the first opinion that Ortac could not have likely been taken, not even by a first-rate. The fort was much too defensible. But it was worrying they could not see Achilles, for she should have easily made Ortac some time ago. It did cross his mind that the French may have chanced to trick the garrison there somehow, which is the exact strategy he would have undertaken. However, all in all, if the first-rate was in fact moored, it could only mean two things. Either it was guarding its prize or in some wild fantastic alternative world it verily was a prize, the latter a conceited consideration of course. 'Thank you Mister Holt, I am sure Eagle will have his report directly and any decision can wait til then.'

Indeed and if the report confirmed it was a French first-rate, Cooper may as well decide to just throw himself overboard and let the sharks have their way. It seemed a cruel blow in the twists of fate. Finally had he bested Captain Lafayette, a painstaking pilgrimage to say the least and finally had he taken not one, but two worthy prizes. To see it all undone was far too much for any sane man to suffer. The men had gone through fighting hell and hardly could he stand idly by as it was all about to unravel.

'Sails ho! Queen Charlotte! Achilles!'

'Thank the gods!' vented Cooper, much relieved.

'And sir?' added Holt.

'Yes, yes, I heard it is Charlotte, of course. And let me guess, Admiral of the Fleet in company, come to see if I remain unkilled by the French revolutionist heathens no doubt?' he added derisively, thinking he did not require the keenness of Eagle's nest to attribute the pennant which was likely flying.

'Sir, actually I have a curious report from Eagle,' Holt informed. 'Aye sir, Admiral of the Fleet in course, but it seems there is more.'

'More?'

'It very much appears we will be in immediate need of twenty-one good cannon, to properly render honours.'

'What? The King? Good god, the bloody King is out here!'

'It is his pennant flying sir, highest mast upon Charlotte. And I checked it twice. Also, The Prince William is in company, his pennant flying just below.'

'Now Mister Holt, you are doubly sure it is not a French first-rate, is it?' suggested Cooper, not entirely certain which ship he might rather now prefer, weighing the merits of each.

Agamemnon's cannon boomed one after the other, rendering the Royal Salute, twenty-one gun. In return, Queen Charlotte commenced to return the honour.

'Fourteen, fifteen, sixteen, seventeen!' Holt excitedly counted aloud as the entire quarterdeck of Agamemnon stood attentively proud. Not one officer ever had experienced a Royal Salute and sullen pride all but gripped them. 'Well, that is mighty handsome ain't it sir, even if they got it wrong?'

'What's that, Mister Holt?'

'Seventeen, sir, they have fired too many. They have fired four less than we fired, being the number reserved for post-captains, not commanders.'

'Quite, well when we repair aboard, please don't go about correcting the Admiral now. I just got used to having you as my first officer and one word about it and Admiral Forbes will surely have you scrubbing the bilge from his pet dog, lordship or not.'

'Understood sir, mum is the word.'

It was with some trepidation Cooper and his officers repaired aboard the flag. All in all, it was a magnificent ceremony, played out to absolute perfection. As Cooper finally pulled himself up the side he fell into complete disarray, at once noticing Shillings. Immediately he wondered what the bloody hell he was doing aboard and secondly what madman had let him. A sideways glance at his other officers confirmed their angst. Standing next to Prince William he then happily beheld the Doctor, though the man's face grim and blank. Dark thoughts already sought to envelope Cooper and further now did he digress upon recognising who was also in company. There stood Middleton's uncle, Rear Admiral Sir Charles Middleton, retired as he understood it, but very much in full dress uniform. Next to him surprisingly stood Lord Thomas Holt to which Cooper could only rejoice, happily turning to confirm that at least this man's son would soon be presented, very much alive, unscathed and wholly intact. He wished the same could be said of Middleton, an awkward moment no doubt pending.

First to greet Cooper was Nelson, looking splendidly august in his commodore's dress uniform. They shook hands and with satisfaction did Cooper immediately note the promotion.

'Why sir, may I give you joy of your promotion, commodore first class!'

'Thank ye Coops. Now come and meet George,' he whispered. 'We have it on good account that you were successful, more than bloody successful judging from the prizes I see about. The good doctor, Blane, has filled in some gaps, nothing of great detail of course, that honour remaining yours. And it is in stone now too, His Majesty is affording us the privilege of retaining the sixty-four and the forty! But for now, not a word.'

Upon the quarterdeck a small throne sat, such an indulgence and one Cooper was thinking he might verily enjoy installing upon Agamemnon. He had not the honour or privilege ever bestowed upon him to have met the King of England, but the ceremony seemed somewhat all the more relaxed, especially now he was happily joined by the bubbling presence of a familiar face, Prince William.

'Captain Cooper, allow me to personally thank you for saving William in Chatham. I am in your debt sir, such a gallant and noble feat. All of England, sir, is in your debt.'

'Honoured, Your Majesty. Just doing my duty of course.'

'Indeed and it seems you do a lot of this duty, so I am informed. But I regret we have breached some protocol, upon returning honours to you.'

'Sir?'

'Apparently, William tells me we fired too many cannon? I must believe him as he is an admiral of course. Apparently, four less is wholly unacceptable, such an honour reserved for a post-captain. Goodness, how do you fellows ever remember all these little rules and regulations? William is most displeased I am afraid and I cannot in good conscience allow him to suffer one moment more. So it is my solemn duty to now rectify the error. We cannot of course retrieve the shots, the horses having bolted. Instead I must inform you sir that you must forthwith be promoted to the rank of post-captain, with said effect to be officially recorded upon the seventeenth cannon so fired this day. And there will be no waiting, the Admiralty are here now and have already confirmed it, such accommodating fellows,' he added with a wry smile. Cooper's face immediately drained of all colour, his ears in absolute disbelief and had it been anyone other than the King, he would have dismissed it out of hand as disingenuous poppycock. The words sank in, he had been made. The King may have been casually flippant about the entire saga, but for a lowly lieutenant it was no small thing. Cooper's career was now assured. He would sit on the Captains' List of seniority and no one could deny his eventual promotion to admiral one day, except of course the devil and the deep blue sea. Even if war did not break and even if he was not already stinking rich, he would be afforded a lifestyle of guaranteed pay. His place upon any ship was assured in kind, never relegated to anything other than the honour of command. 'There William, does that suffice?' the King boorishly enquired, now seeking approval from his son. 'And Captain Cooper, now that you have distinguished yourself, very publicly of course, I wish to remedy my previous promise. I think the act of capturing almost thirty French ships of piracy might warrant some reward. Kneel sir and so shall you arise, Sir Hayden.'

Post-Captain Sir Hayden Reginald Cooper arose and the King retired, a savage mad glint in his eye. From all accounts, it seemed the man had not enjoyed himself so much for so very long a time, for never had they allowed him the privilege of ever cruising about on his great ships of war. Even with the King's departure, the quarterdeck remained littered with more dignitaries than the court at

Saint James's Palace. Cooper one by one shook the hand of each, the standard congratulatory procession. Nonetheless the painful duty of confronting Sir Charles verily awaited and for once, Cooper was most unsure.

'Good show Captain, good show!' complimented Admiral Forbes.

'You have done you duty indeed,' added Admiral Howe happily.

'Especially thanks to your invention sir, the signals have been of the greatest import to the success of our operations. We have made some handsome modifications, awaiting your approval of course.'

'That is most kind,' Admiral Howe returned. 'Admiral Hood would be most pleased about all this I imagine, most pleased. After all, he was your promotor, was he not. You must forgive his absence, some dirty business afoot back at Portsmouth, mutineers in fact.'

'Indeed sir? Mutineers, in peacetime? That is outrageous.'

'Quite, but I suspect you already know something of it, all that business with Bligh and Bounty,' he casually added. 'It seems our Captain Edwards, dispatched upon Pandora, had been mostly successful in finding the blighters, enough anyway to make a show of it. Well, all told he snatched fourteen of them! Should be quite the spectacle I would imagine.'

'Aye, Pandora, twenty-four gun porcupine class, sixth-rate, but sir, I had heard she was lost, foundered and wrecked upon the Great Barrier Reef?'

'Aye, true,' Admiral Howe confirmed. 'But a company ship picked them up and brought what was left of them to Cape Town, whereupon Gorgon did the rest, recently arriving most handsomely in Portsmouth. They are being tried aboard Duke of course, a ship you may recall all too well, our Admiral Hood presiding.'

'Well Sir Hayden, I guess you are wondering what comes next, of course?' Admiral Forbes remarked, bringing the conversation to heel. 'Being that you have now amassed a tidy squadron, which didn't cost one English penny, we will handsomely arrange for it to be bought into service. It was what we had promised and we find it terribly difficult to do anything but what was promised.'

'Especially since we share one eighth of the prize,' Admiral Howe added with a devilish smirk. 'All thanks to such a handsome gesture from the Captain here.'

'Ha, indeed and now it seems his generosity has paid off, so as to speak. It is only now we understand the cunning depths of his enterprise. But I regret sir, with such an endeavour proposed, a commodore will now be required. It cannot yet be Nelson either, too soon. So it is our intent to install a commodore, second class mind you, to see over the operations of the new squadron. We will discuss the details later, over dinner of course.'

Cooper's elation instantly sank. It was as if he had just captured the entire harbour at Brest only to have each and every prize directly sink verily before his eyes. It was half expected naturally. He wondered if Nelson even knew about it, the man likely thinking he would be the one to go to sea and take command. It was a blow to be sure, as it was every day to serve one's life in the Royal Navy. But oh how the report of these blows seemed especially more, so it proved, when in cannon shot of the Admiralty. Short of offering himself in sacrifice to Lefty, the displeasure of such news had Cooper unhappily divining different ways in which he might immediately kill himself and be done with it. He peered back, inwardly distressed, the wealth of his disappointment ever growing. Tonight's celebratory dinner would see his squadron command officially at an end.

'Of course, sir, very happy.'

Upon his next handshake, scarcely he could harbour anything but an innocuous grin, taking the hand of his first officer's father. He had very much been curious about Lord Holt, not sure on all accounts if the man was a tad absurd or just a great judge of his son's character.

'Sir Hayden, pleasure sir, absolute pleasure,' Lord Holt thanked. 'I have enjoyed reading about your exploits with my son, not that he alluded to all the juicy details, but I got the gist. It is all so hush, hush. Even George wouldn't tell me a thing, the barbarian. Oh the things you all must be doing out here, sneaking around like old harry with the French. Jarvis is quite adamant you are the finest captain in the entire Royal Navy.'

'Too kind and thank you, Lord Holt, perhaps just the exuberance of youth no doubt. But may I say, never in life have I seen a midshipman so skilled. Young Lord Holt is destined for greatness, I am sure of it. Already has he been promoted to acting first officer, a genuine feat for his young age.'

'I see, but only acting?'

'Oh, sir, he is Agamemnon's first officer, I assure you, but his official rank as midshipman cannot afford to have him described as anything beyond *"acting"*. It is a curious whim within the regulations, that's all, just as I was acting captain until just some minutes ago.'

'Oh, indeed? Well, I will not forget what you are doing for my boy Sir Hayden, may the grace of god keep you safe sir. Goodness, what the bloody hell was that?' he cried, looking about to the stern. The crew were frantically skulking about, wild as kitchen mice scattered by a rogue cat. A loud crack reverberated through Cooper's ear and immediately he guessed what had transpired. The great ship was visibly moving now, edging itself dangerously towards Ortac. The bosun's whistle was tweeting hard. 'Have we been fired upon?' he begged of Captain Christian, now anxiously passing by.

'Lord Holt, sir, no, one of the anchors just let go, most inexplicable. We just had the ropes bloody well checked too! Damn, very sorry sir and please to beg my pardon.'

'Lieutenant Holt!' Cooper cried, wheeling around to locate his first officer. 'Please to see Lieutenant Shillings from the flag, immediately. Have him report to the fort upon Ortac. His orders are to visibly check the berth of Queen Charlotte and thereafter watch keenly for the French. The King's life must be preserved.'

'Amen,' added McFee under his breath nearby, somewhat relieved.

'Do you think we are in danger Sir Hayden?' posed Lord Holt.

'Oh, not any more, I am sure any hazard will soon be alleviated.'

If it was not one thing, Cooper thought, it was the other. And now the other moment had verily come. In all the commotion Cooper now found Sir Charles standing before him. This man could arrange his very end, knighthood or not. Again, it was one of those moments to which Cooper wholly dreaded, unable to do anything except ride the broadside still yet to come.

'Sir Hayden, do not fret in any way sir,' Sir Charles begged. 'I have already been informed about my nephew and his sudden departure from the world. I know he had turned stark raving mad of course, certifiable, but all they have told me is that he suffered some act whilst he was performing his duty about the fort?'

'Ah, then you have not been privy to the details? Please sir, allow me to introduce our doctor, a most eminent physician,' he motioned, affording Blane to enter the conversation. This was it, another gamble, for he had not yet found time to further discuss the matter. Shillings's entire career, in fact his very life now depended upon the judgement of Blane, a wholly honest and unwavering man. And should Shillings be brought up on charges for murder, surely such proceedings would include the newest knight in England, the man who had verily sought to elevate him to command. The Doctor had a good heart naturally, but in these matters he stood somewhat naïve.

'Very sorry sir, very sorry, your nephew succumbed to shark.'

The dining room of Queen Charlotte was in fact fit for the Queen herself. It was an absolute joy for the officers of Agamemnon to return so soon. It would be the first time however that they had ever partaken in the Royal Toast with the sovereign but a few seats away. It was with absolute interest that Cooper had been afforded the seat of honour next to the King. They toasted long and hard, Cooper very much preserving himself with just a practiced sip each time.

Cooper was altogether pleased. He had been made and he had been knighted, a most unexpected bonus. But he couldn't shake the undeniable prospect of losing his command. It often happened upon a successful campaign, a parting gesture from the Admiralty

Ships of War — Murky Waters

dishing out what they considered nothing less than a handsome reward. But to a fighting man, it was a fate worse than death, a slow dreary existence upon shore. He would be happy to retain command of any one of the ships of course, but his very life would thereafter rely upon the new commodore. There was very little assurance it would ever be a man of worth. And what of his officers and the dogs of war he commanded. It did not sit well, not well at all.

'Sir Hayden, you have done your duty sir, to the utmost and more,' Admiral Forbes complimented. 'And upon that note, may I now officially announce the Admiralty's plans for the squadron!' he further asserted, grinning. Cooper unhappily noted the words specifically uttered, being that the Admiral referred to *"the"* squadron and not *"your"* squadron. 'The squadron will retain the services of the captured sixty-four, the captured forty and the captured ten, Achilles. Gentlemen, we are not yet at war, but we have it on good account we soon will be, most likely at the turn of ninety-three. I call upon Admiral Howe to give us the unhappy news from France...'

'Indeed,' Admiral Howe vexed. 'At first, things were looking bright. As you may know, France had issued an ultimatum demanding that the Habsburg Monarchy of Austria renounce any hostile alliances and withdraw its troops from the French border. Their reply, it seems, was interpreted as somewhat evasive and as such the French Assembly voted for war against Austria and Prussia, this April just passed. The foreign minister, one Charles François Dumouriez on all accounts then prepared an immediate invasion of the Austrian Netherlands. There was some qualified expectation that the local population might rise against its Austrian rule. However, the revolution had seen to thoroughly disorganise the French army, the forces said to be raised proving wholly insufficient for such an incursion. What a debacle and we are told, most accurately, French soldiers deserted en masse, even saw to the murder of their general, Théobald Dillonnews...'

'To take advantage and promote their cause, a Prussian army under Charles William Ferdinand, Duke of Brunswick, assembled at Koblenz on the Rhine, the revolutionary government of France still in disarray to raise fresh troops. The Duke then issued a proclamation called the Brunswick Manifesto, which curiously was in point of fact drafted by the French King's cousin, Louis Joseph de Bourbon, Prince de Condé. The proclamation declared their intent to restore Louis to his full powers, anyone found in opposition to be earmarked a rebel and condemned to death. Unfortunately, this only served to strengthen the resolve of the French revolutionary army. So it was, upon the tenth of August, a crowd sought to storm Tuileries Palace, whereby Louis and his family were seized. Thereafter, Brunswick's army thus invaded. They easily took the fortresses of Longwy and Verdun...'

'In England we eagerly awaited the logical end to the French revolution, the writing on the wall, so as to speak. In Brunswick's attempt to march on Paris, they were then met at Valmy, only some weeks ago in fact. The whole thing came unstuck, whereupon he found his army pitted against Dumouriez and Kellermann, who cleverly held the high ground. It seems the professionalism of the French artillery very much distinguished itself and the Prussians turned tail to the sound of brood cheering and the bloody *"La Marseillaise"*. It is bewildering to say the least, some eighty thousand soldiers upon the field and only something less than a couple of hundred casualties on each side. It is suspected the cost and the expectation of their campaign running into winter were the determining factors...'

'Unfortunately for England, the very next day, the French monarchy was formally abolished and the First Republic of France was declared. That was on the twenty-first of September, just passed. And to rub salt into the wounds, our spies have it on good account that the French are now wildly marching upon the Austrian Netherlands, even though winter is coming...'

'Gentlemen,' Admiral Forbes summed, 'No doubt, this madness will be ours to manage come spring next year. That is the considered opinion of all the brightest minds. We do have some time to prepare of course, albeit through winter.'

Not a man amongst the gathering could honestly have wished for more. Without war, they all of them would be beached on half pay or less. They would be scrounging for employment, their lives boorishly filled with petitioning whatever interest they had left in favour, forever stalking the rooms of the Admiralty. And the ad-

Ships of War — Murky Waters

mirals themselves would be faced with a changing of the guard, the likely result from a political shift away from the Tories.

'For now, it is our wish that the squadron heave-to for the time being, a small matter of resting the officers and men. Soon thereafter will they be afforded to cruise, hunting pirates in the happy protection of our merchant shipping. It is with regret we cannot instantly afford Commodore Nelson the public arena of command. However, nonetheless, he will immediately be afforded a handsome ship and to his squadron will also the eighteen gun brig Hasard be offered.'

'Wasp, if I may sir, that being her intended name.'

This was news indeed to the welcoming ears of Cooper, who was now immediately conjuring some scheme to somehow whisk his way into his commodore's fleet. It would be a step down from a sixty-four of course, but a command under Nelson would be worth it. He passed a knowing glance to his commodore and to his satisfaction did he note a warring glint return to the man's eye.

'Now, gentlemen, it is my honour to announce our plans for our newest captain of the fleet. Sir Hayden, before me I have your orders and I would be most happy if you might read them aloud.' And with that Forbes thrust within his palm the parchment and so did Cooper sheepishly begin to recite them aloud:

*To Captain **Hayden Reginald Cooper** hereby appointed **Commodore, 2ⁿᵈ Class**, of His Majesty's Ship **Menelaus**, in Company with His Majesty's Ship **Helen** and His Majesty's Ship **Achilles**.*

*By Virtue of the Power and Authority to us given We do hereby constitute and appoint you **Commander** of His Majesty's Ship **Menelaus** willing and requiring you forthwith to go on board and take upon you the Charge and Command of **Commander** in her accordingly strictly Charging and Commanding all the Officers and Company belonging to the said ship to behave* *themselves jointly and severally in their respective Employments with all due Respect and Obedience unto you their said* **Commander** *and you likewise to observe and execute as well the General Printed Instructions and such Orders and Directions you shall from time to time receive from us, from* **Commodore, 1ˢᵗ Class, Horatio Nelson**, *or your superior Officers for His Majesty's Service hereof nor you nor any of you may fail as you will answer the contrary at your peril. And for so doing this shall be your Warrant.*

Given under our hands and the Seal of Office of Admiralty, October 1792.
By Command of Their Lordships.

The entire gathering applauded and held their glasses high, but Cooper was somewhat at a loss as to what it all meant. He had no idea what ship Menelaus was, or Helen for that matter, never heard of them. To be promoted commodore was always an acting role of course, returning to the rank of captain as soon as new orders were beseeched. And in course, the whole thing could only mean his squadron would now be detached from Nelson's, a most disappointing state of affairs.

'Captain, you looked as dished as a roast on Sunday sir,' Admiral Howe smirked. 'Let me prevail upon you the meaning of said orders. You are to take Menelaus as soon as is practicable and form your squadron, prepare for war.'

'Aye, sir, but forgive me, where is she?'

'Why, she is moored, oh, let me think, I guess she is perhaps some hundred feet away. You know her well Captain, indeed, for you had just fought tooth and nail against her. She is Solitaire. That's right sir and all the cannon you had laid upon her must now by your hand be fixed.'

'Ha, ha, ha! It is only fitting of course,' Admiral Forbes added.

'After all, you bloody well captured her, you can bloody well fix her.'

'And Sir Hayden, please to note that your squadron will ultimately remain under the flag of Commodore Nelson, who will in turn have his own squadron. Commodore Nelson will afford your orders, very much like a rear admiral. But, let me make it clear, as commodore, you alone will command your squadron.'

'I sit amazed sir, thoroughly and heartily amazed,' he genuinely offered, now postulating the joy whelming within. Solitaire had been quite a runner, not as fast as Agamemnon, but she could turn handsomely on her heel. With the funds pending from the prizes, a copper bottom would see her turning the brow of more than one old jack. 'What a curious name, Menelaus?'

'Indeed, Sir Hayden,' Nelson happily proffered, all but waiting for the chance to explain, his grin searing through the candlelight. 'For did you not know that Agamemnon had a brother, Menelaus. And so it was in Greek mythology that Menelaus was in fact King of Sparta. He also had the honour of being the younger son of Atreus, King of Mycenae. What a happy band,' he hinted, the face upon Cooper suddenly showing signs of understanding. 'And it was of course only the tragic abduction of his wife, Helen, which verily led to the infamous Trojan War. Please to note that Menelaus did honourably serve under his elder brother Agamemnon, who was for want of no better words I can perhaps conjure, the *commodore* in chief of the Greek forces!'

'Oh, cracking sir,' Cooper celebrated, finally comprehending. 'Am I to understand they have given you Agamemnon? And we are to be Greek pirates!' he jested. And with that last quip the King suddenly burst, spitting his wine forth.

'Ha, ha,' King George rejoiced. 'What a joy to be away from the boorishness of the bloody palace, oh to be amongst the true warriors of the Empire and her true sons! And you are bloody right Sir Hayden. Nelson may not have captured her, but he has all but bloody well paid for her. And so shall he have Agamemnon to rule the bloody seas, Greek style!'

'Quite, Your Majesty. And may I further regale our gathering,' Nelson continued, 'For it bears upon your squadron, Commodore Cooper, second class. Helen of Troy, also known as Helen of

Sparta, was told to have been the most beautiful woman in the world. She of course was married to King Menelaus, but suffered notably to be abducted by a mischievous Paris, ha, ha, Paris! They did of course fight for her and so was she returned safely to Menelaus. It is of significant note that the etymology of Helen's name continues to be a source of annoyance for our scholars. It has been suggested that her name is very much connected with the root of Venus.'

'Venus? La Vénus!'

'Aye Commodore, unto your squadron will you take His Majesty's Ship Helen, formerly known as Venus. And so shall you both have Achilles to nip at the heels of your enemy.'

'Bravo!'

'Captain, some happy news if I may,' Admiral Forbes added, if that was not enough. 'With your promotion to commodore, second class, it begs that you will have command of a squadron. As such, the King has contrived to afford you the honour of promoting one officer to post and another to lieutenant. But let me make it clear that the latter promotion is subject to the officer successfully sitting the examination for lieutenant. Naturally, you may choose anyone, without the standard time restriction applying.'

'Oh sir, how handsome,' Cooper immediately thanked. 'I need no respite to mull it of course. I shall choose in course Mister Spencer and Mister Holt.'

'If I may sir,' McFee candidly suggested. 'I am verily sure young Mister Holt would happily agree to being made post as would Lord Holt no doubt, but I hazard to guess Mister Spencer hardly wishes to be made lieutenant, again, a drop in seniority it seems?'

'Ha, ha!' the King burst. 'Bloody Scots!' he swore and he encouraged the gathering to toast to the bloody Scots, may they reign with us forever. Of course, it begged to be explained later to Lord Holt that his son was in fact to be favoured only for lieutenant, not captain.

With permission, young Holt excused himself only to return shortly, curiously hugging a jacket or two. He stood behind his commodore begging permission of an immediate exchange.

'Sir, for you, my commodore's coat,' he politely offered and splendidly a moment later did it adorn Cooper's shoulders. Cooper grinned as he beheld Holt now standing behind Spencer. 'And Captain Spencer, for you sir only the best, please accept my post-captain's coat.'

'What a resourceful young officer,' complimented the King, quite astounded.

'Ha, ha!' McFee gurgled. 'Enjoy it whilst you can Captain Spencer, no doubt the lad will be wanting it back upon his next promotion. The way he is going it might very well be before we even dock!'

'Indeed, Lieutenant Holt,' Admiral Forbes added. 'Are we to understand that as a former midshipman, you chanced to have these delicacies just lying about?'

'And more sir,' Cooper teased. 'Should you find yourself in need of a jacket, I am sure Mister Holt will afford you the honour of lending his admiral's coat.'

'Ha, ha!' the King gurgled. 'Oh, that is too much, too much sir! I can see you have chosen your promotion wisely Sir Hayden.'

'Now Mister Holt,' Spencer insisted, standing to enact his own form of retribution. 'I am sure you have one lying about, but please to take my lieutenant's coat. I have no compunction in thinking anything else but your successful testing for lieutenant is all but assured. If I may, I am sure no one will mind, just for tonight?'

A sudden knock at the door saw Lieutenant Shillings politely seeking entry. Within his grasp he had such a glorious bunch of fresh bananas, a gift for the gathering of course. Holt was first to notice and immediately did he thrust his knowing glare upon Cooper, the standard nudging of a subtle nod towards Shillings. Cooper instantly recognised the gesture, the one most commonly used by his first officer in said events purporting imminent destruction. Cooper immediately stood, his eyes as wide as a rabid hound and quickly did he intercede to block the door.

'Oh welcome Lieutenant Shillings, it is good you have come as soon as your watch ended, most diligent,' he announced aloud, whilst next under a whispered breath he offered the sternest of reprimand. 'What the blazes sir? You cannot for the life of the King bring bananas on board, let alone to his state room dinner. Quickly, away with them before a soul dares to see them.'

'Very sorry sir, is he allergic?'

'What? No! It is considered very bad luck Mister Shillings, to the extreme sir, in case you had not known. It is of the worst luck to have bananas upon any ship upon any sea. What a fellow, I say what a fellow you are to not know this!'

It was with honour that the King chose to make his stroll about the ship accompanied by the realm's newest knight. The prospect of his intended journey back to England a joyous respite for one so endlessly petitioned. Cooper too was enjoying the lull, for his duty weighed as a ravenous hound ever commanding him. In short time had he chanced to understand the King a little better now, the man endlessly beseeched on all sides, the irons of society very much corralling his every move. Cooper was thinking how relieved he was to just be a sailor, the wind at his back, the prize in his eye.

'Sir Hayden, I am told that there is a great shark in residence to our fort yonder?' the King queried, pointing to the small wash about the rocks. 'I must say, it is a brilliant stratagem of course, for no Frenchie might try to furtively swim over in the dead of night.'

'Aye, sir, he is a big one, some twenty-three feet.'

'I see and Sir Hayden, am I to understand that this is where the shark ate your previous doctor, a few random crewmen, a French pirate and one of your officers, a lord in fact I believe?'

Cooper smiled unable to dismiss the absurdity of such claims. Of course the previous doctor was crushed by cannon, the French pirate was actually a slab of beef and Middleton was shot point blank right between the eyes by Shillings. Yet the rumour mill of England served to grind its own purpose in the standing of war and who was he to stand in the way. He might verily object and try to correct the truth of the matter, but with the ever expanding weight of incredulous claims so regularly set against him, he was of a

Ships of War — Murky Waters

mind to no longer bother. After all, had he not severed two men into exact halves with just one swish of his blade? He very much wished to remain honest and forthright, at least with his king, his honour demanded it perhaps.

'Aye, sir,' he confirmed, regaling the legend of Lefty, very much surrendering to another curious whim of the Royal Navy. 'In course, right about there.'

'Oh I see. But surely we could train it, don't you think, to entertain itself on perhaps just the French?'

'Sir, ever shall I do my utmost.'

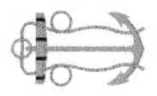

Epilogue
Of the Chevalier...

Cooper lingered upon the hulk's deck, a drift of snow lightly collecting the heights of his boots. For the moment his good eye was persuaded by the far distance, his interest somewhat piqued. Upon the docks, ferried across the harbour, a faint echo barely drifted. It was hardly an affront to the sullen calm, but a noise out of place nonetheless. Straining to discern the din he tilted his head, angling to adjust his acuity. Then it found him, falling lightly upon his good ear. It was not quite the sudden eruption of battle. Nonetheless, within the blanket of fog there it was, the unmistakable levity of wanton drunkenness. About six fellows he guessed, stumbling about too. With a wry grin and an indignant huff he nodded knowingly, just the fleeting annoyance of a minor disturbance, hardly worth his attention.

The hullabaloo trailed into the distance, the mob hapless in its efforts to randomly meander the dusky streets. Strange it was to hear so clearly such drunken sods from so far abreast and not lay even one lazy eye upon them. It was not unlike the stalking of a ship action, a hush upon the decks bar the jingle of some loose chain, the lapping of some rogue wave upon the bow or the inadvertent flapping of taut sheets untended. It was with mild interest Cooper proceeded to ponder the range, the nautical distance to target, immediately noting how easily he had so quickly come to pinpoint the fracas. It was not unlike a good lookout cleverly noting the splash of a misplaced oar beholden to an approaching vanguard. The disturbance lay buried within the murk, but if he was to guess, they were hovering perhaps around the mark of eight hundred yards. Instinctively he tilted the small cannon before him, eyeing the line down the sight. It was an old school guess, but he was an old school sailor. Of course he had Holt's range stick presently squared away in the depths of his jacket. Goodness, he thought, what would the young prodigy ever do without his range stick? It amused him to picture poor Holt mayhap stumbling to offer a decent guess without the aid of his contraption, experience no substitute within a harbour's settling mist. Oh what a shame the lad was not here, but Cooper grinned suitably as the semblance of a plan started to hatch. Would it not be grand to test Holt at the first opportune moment. He would have to wager on it with Spencer of course, or what fun would it be. And Holt would have to risk some punishment as it were, or indeed what fun would it really be.

About eight hundred yards indeed he considered and he played out the required elevation upon of the ship's gun before him. His gaze wheeled slowly about the harbour, gauging the seas before him. The water was calmer than a priest kneeling on Sunday. An easy shot he granted, so much so, even tubby Fredricks could not miss, provided the maths was sound. Yet hardly did it matter, the perpetrators no more sinister than a bothersome band of Merry Andrews, the entire vicinity hopelessly distracted within the initial throes of the upcoming Bonfire Night festivities.

It verily occurred to Cooper that Bonfire Night was fast becoming more and more the harbinger of unmitigated lunacy, every passing year the surpassing benchmark for bolder and wilder acts. What a bunch of mad toms and jingle brains he thought, the whole lot totally off the hooks. Oh how he wished the press was in force, sort them out quick smart. Such a comeuppance could come none too soon either. The doodles, as he liked to call them, seemed to venture out almost religiously, surfacing like clockwork whether it rain, hail or shine, or in this case whether the sleeting frost of winter fell literally upon them. For now it seemed this band was the only one about, nonetheless his keen eye continued to survey the outskirts.

All in all the harbour appeared still, mostly settled and commonly bereft of even the barest of movement. The surrounding dock too lay very much vacated, the normal bustle oddly absent. He had been eyeing it now for at least half a bell. It positively seemed the biting cold had successfully seen the back of every able bodied man. Not a skerrick was stirring. Not a soul showed, not a woman, not a child, not a mangy hound, not even a homeless beggar. Perhaps some semblance of sanity had prevailed, for even the staunchest Bonfire Night fanatic was somehow dissuaded from their annual wanton madness. He grinned as he imagined them hunched morbidly in front of a warm hearth, naturally whining to each other as they fumbled to further plot their rebellious acts. He would never have believed the district to be so quiet. The serenity of a calm sea was all that remained. It was a translucent scene, the silhouette of a deserted harbour deepening as it found itself hopelessly shackled within the light touch of an ever mounting mist.

Cooper was however thinking it would be a soup of unmanageable fog in the next bell. One by one the moorings slowly disappeared from sight, some within the shadows, others consumed within the accumulation of frost and the waning hour. The harbour sank slowly into obscurity, the devil and the deep blue seeking to devour whole its prey. For once it was a satisfying scene, one upon which he wished to linger. It was a simple sailor's pleasure, moreover the chance to enjoy the expenditure of a quiet moment. To be deficient of all and any intrusion was a rarity seldom afforded a ship's captain. To be at peace, real peace, even if it were for just a fleeting instant, would be to count the joy of one's eternal blessings. To take in the next breath would be to consume whole the blessings of the world, yet it was a world for him which had now most definitely shifted.

Cooper's penchant for preponderance presently had his gaze firmly enslaved. Finally his eyes dragged and a sullen calm washed warmly over the breadth of his being. It was a fine moment indeed, yet the starkness of reality was but only a single breath away. His face suddenly screwed, his nose twitching. Pressed upon his senses the squalid arrival of a latent draft brought with it a stiffening realisation. Oh what a horrid pong, the brunt of the offence falling directly upon him. It was a dank lingering aroma, undeniable, no less the oozing stench of some four hundred or more poor wretches, all crammed of course into just a handful of withering decks.

At once he contemplated the old failing ship, the weathered planks aching under his feet. Barely could he escape the despicable state of the rotted timbers or the painful incessant groan throttling his lobes, no less the cry of a wounded beast. Never again would she let fly upon the open sea, ever condemned to attend His Majesty's service as no more than a lowly prison hulk. She was once a fine ship, a line of battle third-rate. He had seen her in action too, long ago in the war, but now she languished timeworn and rotted, a decayed fiend. Sadly her duty upon the sea was well and truly over, her lot no better than the unfortunate wretches she so faithfully harboured. It was a cruel fate, one he would not wish upon any ship, or for that matter, any man.

'Good afternoon Commodore, a cloth, sir?'

'Oh, 'ey?' queried Cooper, looking upon the officer before him with mild curiosity. At first he could not contrive anything but pity for the lad, a prison hulk hardly duty befitting any ambitious young officer. His thoughts soon harkened to his own lot. Only two years previous had he himself been hopelessly beached. It was a stark reminder. To be bereft of vocation was to be shackled, deprived of life's breath, destitution barely a small step away. A man struggling to properly feed oneself beheld little less than a man broiling within a sea of squalid desperation, a man perhaps staring blankly into the abyss. He shuddered at the thought. No, no, no, he rightly considered. Employment was employment and suddenly he found himself admiring the zeal of this young officer.

'It's clean sir, for your face. The hulk is rife, you know, with disease and all that. I beg you take it, if not for yours but perhaps for my well-being?'

'Of course, thank you Lieutenant,' he nodded. 'Lieutenant...?'

'Oh, Cummings, sir, pleasure,' he smiled. 'Won't be long sir, they are looking for him now. That is, unless he has gone off to

Peg Trantum's. But I am guessing he's still alive, lest he croaked last night or this morning. We haven't checked the berths this afternoon, not yet, still a might early. Don't worry, I have asked for your man to be moved to the upper deck, too cold to bring him up here. They don't really have clothes you see. I hope this agrees with you, sir? In course, I cannot now have a commodore going below. Goodness no, oh my lord, you might never venture back up you know. The Admiralty would boil me alive.'

'Oh, come now, I hardly think so.'

'Really sir?'

'Aye, I am quite certain they would hang you first. Anyway, you would probably get away with a stint in the basket or maybe run the gauntlet,' he added with a reassuring grin. 'At least we are not in France where it would be the wheel, 'ey!'

'I am not sure any of that helps, sir.'

'Said measures naturally would be most annoying, an unwelcome, unwanted and wholly unfortunate turn of events to be sure, not just for you but also for me. Well, probably more for you,' he smiled and he stroked the cannon with the affection afforded a smutty ginger cat.

'Eight hundred and ten yards, sir, if I may,' confirmed Cummings.

'I believe this is a French cannon?'

'Aye sir, you have a keen eye. And if I may sir, you have a keen aim. That level of tilt should see off those larrikins upon the dock.'

'Indeed?' tested Cooper, immediately realising the young officer before him was no slouch with the cannon.

'Oh most definitely sir, a capital piece of gunnery, more especially since the dock is not yet even in view and let us not forget, it is only a French cannon after all.'

'You only have one?'

'Oh sir, it is just for salutes and it hasn't been used for some time now. We don't even have any powder or shot for that matter. One report and the whole bloody ship would disintegrate beneath us. And sir, if I was to let you below, the first thing you might do upon returning would be to set the thing off, a quick and fitting end for the poor sods we harbour.'

Ships of War — Murky Waters

'Indeed?'

'Sir, will your friend be accompanying you? It's just that I am not supposed to allow civilians access of course.'

'My friend?'

'Aye sir,' he politely motioned with a gentle smile. 'That distinguished gentleman sir, the one milling around just behind you?'

'Oh, of course, you are quite right,' Cooper acknowledged, having temporarily forgotten about his guest. 'Fret not though Lieutenant, my friend in fact holds the distinguished rank of general, albeit presently retired. Will that suffice?'

'Commodore Cooper, sir, I believe you have just lied to that young officer.'

'Marquis, please, whatever do you mean sir? Oh, what a thing to say? Are you not a general, albeit retired?'

'Retirement was hardly my choice.'

'In fact, come to think of it, are you not a major general? That is my understanding of the situation? It is quite correct, is it not?'

'Ah, but that was under the American revolutionary forces.'

'Your point, sir?'

'The American forces? Which at the time was your enemy?'

'Yes, yes, yes, I see. But in France, were you not commander-in-chief of the National Guard and if I may, a man holding the rank of general?'

'Yes, in fact a lieutenant general.'

'Well, even higher, there we have it, you are a general. So they can pick and choose whichever country they wish to honour, 'ey?'

'In course, you are right,' he begrudgingly agreed. 'But I am not sure being a general of an army which had directly opposed your king is quite what the good Lieutenant was asking?'

'Oh details, small details, let us not trifle or concern ourselves as such. I am sure, yes, quite sure it is verily alright,' he nonchalantly gestured, once again proving slyly economical with the truth. 'Come now Marquis, let us find your cousin. Let us pray he has not succumbed to this wretched place.'

'Indeed Sir Hayden. And may I offer my thanks either way. Your prevailing generosity in this matter is most assuredly far past any reasonable expectation.'

Before them upon the planking a man lay writhing, huddled within the darkened shadows. He held gingerly to the stump upon his arm, desperately clawing for the nearby gloom, perhaps searching for some haven within which to hide. It struck Cooper at once. He recognised the man, or at least he thought he did. He continued to study the wretch, mesmerised, somewhat unconvinced. Surely it was the Chevalier, or at least what was left of him.

The prisoner was dirty, unkempt and quite reduced. His hair was long and bedraggled, strangling what little left could still be seen of his face. A fuzz of some proportion dangled prodigiously, chancing almost the length of his chest, wiry whiskers worthy of a rancid pirate. His right arm was bereft of its hand, the product of a clean dismembering. Cooper was weighing the odds, but it was a good wager this was none other than Chevalier Lafayette, *Champion de France*, brother to the late Captain Lafayette, Solitaire, sixty-four gun and of course distant cousin to Marquis de Lafayette, Lieutenant General, retired. Cooper took pause, contemplating the scales of justice upon which the man now sat. What a wretch. To have let him live had proven no mercy, moreover a fate somewhat worse than death. It had not even been two years and he wondered if there was perhaps anything still left but a vacant husk.

'Good god,' whispered Cooper, unable to hide his distress.

'Do not blame yourself Sir Hayden,' the Marquis generously offered. 'I assure you the prisons of France are much worse. And did not this man commit many a crime grievous against your country? Were not his acts so heinous and god forbid were they not even enacted personally against your king? Come now, he has only himself to blame.'

'Chevalier?' Cooper bade in French, trying to catch the prisoner's attention. There was no response, the host before him a vacant muted creature, perhaps even maddened. Cooper could hardly dismiss the woe beset upon the man, a moral injustice no matter the severity of the transgressions. 'Ah, Chevalier, I have brought your cousin, Marquis de Lafayette.'

The beast roused somewhat, shuffling to discern the hovering figures, eyeing them with more than a little confused disdain. He clawed himself from the darkened corner, a latent brightness partly returning to his open eye.

'Cousin? It is I, Gilbert.'

'You are real?' he finally spluttered, the words dragging in an effort to force the dryness from his mouth. 'I expected it was another delusion. I have had so many over the passing of oh so many years. Has France since won? Have you come to liberate me, what little there remains?'

'Maurice, I am afraid war with England is still yet to commence. It has been maybe only eighteen months since they put you here.'

'What, no! Only eighteen months?' he lamented. 'That cannot be, it cannot be. Please, if you do not come now to free me, you must liberate me from this nightmare. Take your knife, I beg you.'

'Chevalier, calm yourself. With much reluctance would I do as you bid,' Cooper genuinely promised. 'But first, listen to us, for there is a chance, a chance for you to live, to seek vengeance.'

'Vengeance? But it was you who put me here, was it not? Have you now come to offer your head? Alas sir, I have no blade.'

'No Cousin, do not blame Sir Hayden. It is the radicals we must blame, the Jacobins. They have cursed you with their orders, immoral orders, Cousin. Remember, you attempted to kill the son of the King. Who told you to do that? Why would you do that? Is it not an offence before god?'

'Chevalier, your cousin is here because he too has been persecuted by the Jacobins.'

'Cousin, listen to me,' the Marquis pleaded. 'Listen carefully, the Jacobins wish to see our country destroyed, ruled by the mob. They are not interested in the legal assembly of a democratic government. They intend to murder the King and his family. They are dogs. Already has the monarchy been abolished. Madness rules in Paris, terror reigns in the streets. I myself have been branded a traitor. Can this you believe? I chanced an escape through Austria, but was detained and imprisoned. All of France now believes me a royalist and wishes me dead. The rest of Europe believes me a revolutionist and wishes me dead. The Jacobins are to blame. All I have ever wanted was a democratic France, no less than England's democracy. But the monarchy too must prevail, for we are not mutts of the mob. Sir Hayden has saved me from Austrian prison and now we come to save you.'

'They say, what? A traitor? You? Madness, it is madness. You are but a pure son of France. Madness, how have they fallen to such lunacy?'

'It is true. The radicals rule our country, whoring her out no better than a cheap street wench. My ideals of a true democracy have fallen on deaf ears. All my good intentions to preserve the monarchy have undone me.'

'Then, how is it you can save me? You can hardly save yourself?'

'Cousin, Sir Hayden will see you released and you will find yourself again. In France your name amongst the radicals is lauded. They will accept you back with open arms. The entire country will marvel at your survival. They will rally around you as bees to the honey. Only then may your vengeance come. You can undo these radicals from within...'

'Sir Hayden did you say? He is knighted? And hardly can one wonder how this came about. Did he not kill my brother? Did he not take my arm? Why would I do this thing you ask? Are you not mad?'

'You will not do anything, except for yourself. I have spoken to those who were present when your brother fell. Believe me, Sir Hayden afforded him every chance to live. Alas, not only did your brother refuse, but his madness caused the needless deaths of many a good sailor, French sailors. Yet, perhaps we should not blame him. He was told you were dead and he grieved to avenge you. But the Jacobins, they always knew you were not dead. They used your brother for their own gain, just as they have done with all of France. Sir Hayden acted with honour, I assure you. He is not to blame, the Jacobins are. It is they who have misled and abandoned you. But now Cousin, you can return to Paris and I assure you from within, you can truly injure them, if that is your wish?'

'And what of you?'

'Alas, I have been burned in effigy. After the King chanced to escape, the entire country branded me a traitor. It is understandable, no doubt, for it was I who was in charge of his custody and so they assume I assisted his exodus. I did not of course. And France is at war with Austria now, a colossal blunder. In consequence did I publicly denounce the radicals, calling for their removal by force. But I sorely misjudged the climate it seems. Even my National Guard turned on me. I was forced to flee to Austria, tainted a royalist. But upon arriving, it seems Austria feared me as a revolutionist. Such irony, but nonetheless now does France presently believe me to be wasting in an Austrian prison. Thanks to Sir Hayden, I will secretly live in England and from there will I support the overthrow of the radicals with whatever power I possess.'

'Chevalier, if I may?' Cooper softly offered. 'The choice is before you. With the tip of my sword I can send you from this place and may you forever be at peace. Or, you can live. Avenge the wrongs perpetrated against you, albeit as a spy. You once said we could have been brothers? We once shared a moment that should not soon be forgotten, our minds as one. It was a good conversation and for what it is worth I would very much like the opportunity to have another. I have since thought of you, from time to time. Sir, let me now free you.'

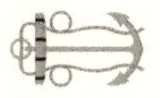

HERE ENDS BOOK ONE OF
BRADLEY JOHN'S
SHIPS OF WAR
TO BE CONTINUED...
IN
"SHADOW OF WAR"

About the Author

Bradley John Tatnell (aka *"Bradley John"*) is an Australian novelist whose ancestry can be traced back to the Norman Conquest in England. His forbears lived mostly in Kent, Hertfordshire and the Isle of Thanet. Some were mariners and some were even of the aristocracy. His direct ancestors arrived in Australia soon after its colonisation in the late 1700's, most of which were proud country folk. James Squire, a notable character in history, who arrived on the first fleet in 1788, was his (sixth) great-grandfather.

He graduated from the Church of England Grammar School at age 16 and the Queensland University of Technology at age 19. His early life was spent mainly in the arena of law.

Bradley John has a love of all things ancient and historical, including golf, to which he plays with ye old hickory shafted clubs including the original heads from pre-1935. He also studies the ancient art of Korean sword, having attained master level. His love of language, in all its forms, now extends to the pursuit of conquering Hangul, the language of the Korean people.

He has been privately writing novels since 2003. *"Ships of War — Murky Waters"*, his first publication, births a series of naval adventure fiction intended to span the length of the French Revolutionary Wars. This of course is the much loved genre which includes the thundering Hornblower series by C.S. Forester, the Aubrey-Maturin series by Patrick O'Brian and the popular *"Master and Commander"* blockbuster by Peter Weir. Owing to Bradley John's English heritage, no guesses are needed to determine which side the book's heroes will sail upon…

Follow the author

www.thehistoricalfictioncompany.com/hp-authors/bradley-john

www.bradleyjohnauthor.com

REVIEWS ARE APPRECIATED

Acknowledgements

Thank you to Historium Press, and to my editor, Dee Marley, as well as the graphics department at The Historical Fiction Company for the stunning book covers.

Image and photo acknowledgements:

Prologue artwork and other artwork within this novel, if not listed below, have been downloaded from Archives.org, Wikipedia Commons, or no viable source found. Used under the 'fair use' law.

"A View of part of the British Fleet at Portsmouth" (1790): a painting by Thomas Elliot depicting the Fleet, dedicated to Sir John Pitt, 2nd Earl of Chatham (1756-1835), First Lord of the Admiralty from 1788 to1794. Part of the Royal Collection. Chapter one artwork.

"Reproduction of a water colour of the Admiralty office in Whitehall, London" (1790): a drawing by an unknown artist depicting the exterior of the Admiralty. Stated to be from the Pennant Collection in the British Museum. Chapter two artwork.

"Boardroom of the Admiralty, Admiralty House, Whitehall, London" (1788), by Thomas Rowlandson (1756–1827) and Augustus Charles Pugin (1762–1832) depicting a boardroom meeting. *"The Board of Admiralty"* engraving was published as Plate 3 of Microcosm of London (1808). Chapter three artwork.

"Broad Quay" (1760): a painting attributed to Philip Vandyke, shows the busy Broad Quay in Bristol. At the time, Bristol was the second most important port in England, after London. Chapter four artwork.

"Trois des vaisseaux francais captures au cap Finesterre en mai 1747": engraved by John Boydell, published by R. Short in 1750, depicting French ships of war taken by the British Fleet 3rd May, 1747. Ruby is shown in this version. Chapter five artwork.

"Crispin and Crispianus": located at 8 London Road, Strood, one of England's oldest establishments. The drawing is depicted in *"The Old Inns of Old England"* (Vol. I of II), by Charles G. Harper. Chapter six artwork.

"Chatham Dockyard" (1790): a painting by Nicholas Pocock (1740–1821) depicting Royal George on the right fitting out in the River

Medway with Queen Charlotte under construction in the centre background. Part of the Royal Collection. *"View of Dockyard at Chatham"*, a later print by B. B. Evans, John Hamilton Mortimer, Pierre Charles Canot and Richard Paton. Chapter seven artwork.

"Chatham Dockyard from Fort Pitt" (1830): an engraving from Ireland's History of Kent, Volume 4, 1831, drawn by G. Sheppard, engraved by R. Roffe depicting a view looking northwards down the River Medway (Chatham Reach) towards the estuary. Chatham Dockyard is on right hand bank of the river. To the right of the dockyard, the elevated area is known as the Great Lines, or Chatham Lines. The built up area sunk between the Lines and the hill from which the view is taken, consists of the town of Chatham on the right, merging into the town of Rochester to the left. The spur of land from the left is Frindsbury. Chapter eight artwork.

"Figures in a Tavern or Coffee House" (1725): a painting by Joseph Highmore (1692–1780) depicting the interior of the House with patrons. Chapter nine artwork.

"A Merchant Ship off the Cliffs of Dover" (1793): a painting by Thomas Luny (1759–1837) depicting ships at sea readying to stand in to port. Chapter ten artwork.

"Alderney" (1757): a map by Jean de Beaurain depicting Alderney and Ortac Islet. Chapter eleven artwork.

"The Gannetry on Ortac": a commissioned illustration — *"The Birds of Alderney"*, Jeremy G. Sanders (2007) — Carmen Ashworth (née) Watson, based in Bournemouth, United Kingdom. Artwork can be viewed at www.coastalimages.org.uk. Carmen studied Natural History Illustration at the Arts Institute Bournemouth and the Royal College of Art London. Chapter eleven artwork.

"Firing of a18-Pound Gun" (c1790): a painting by Louis-Philippe Crépin (1772–1851) depicting the gun crew on the lower deck of a man o' war, a powder monkey on the left. Chapter twelve artwork.

"Chatham Dockyard" (1750): a painting by Joseph Farington (1747–1821) depicting the river banks of the dockyard which includes the Anchor Wharf Storehouses, shipbuilding slips, dry docks, the old smith and some boat houses. St Mary's Island is in the distance on the far left. In the centre, beyond the walls of the Dockyard, is the town of Brompton and, to the right, Chatham Barracks. Chapter thirteen artwork.

"Council of War on board the 'Queen Charlotte', Commanded by Lord Exmouth, prior to the Bombardment of Algiers, 26 August 1816": a painting by Nicolaas Baur (1767–1820) depicting her hove-to in order to conduct a council of war with the fleet's captains. Chapter fourteen artwork.

"A Cutter in a Swell": a painting attributed to Thomas Butterworth (1768–1842) depicting a smaller one-masted craft battling the ocean swell. Chapter fifteen artwork.

"A Danish Yacht Passing": a painting attributed to Christoffer Wilhelm Eckersberg (1783–1853) depicting a smaller one-masted craft. Chapter sixteen artwork.

"Court-Martial on the Officers of H.M.S. Vanguard" (1875): an engraving by an unknown artist, printed by The Illustrated London News, depicting the court martial of the officers of Vanguard, held on board her Majesty's ship Royal Adelaide, the flagship at Devonport. Chapter seventeen artwork.

"36-pounder cannon at the ready": by Antoine Léon Morel-Fatio (1810–1871) depicting a large gun in great detail on the lower decks, most likely, of a ship of the line. Chapter eighteen artwork.

"The Mont-Blanc off Marseille" (1793): by Antoine Roux (1765–1835) depicting her at sea. She was a Téméraire class 74-gun third-rate ship of the line of the French Navy. Pompee, her sister ship, was launched 28 May 1791. Chapter nineteen artwork.

"A Topographical map of the Isle of Wight" (1775): a topographical map by John Andrews (1736-1809), Land Surveyor, of the Isle of Wight in Hampshire on a scale of two inches to a mile from an actual survey in which are expressed all the roads, towns, villages, houses, rivers, woods, hills, noblemen's and gentlemen's seats and everything remarkable in the Island, with the division of Parishes. Chapter twenty artwork.

"Brading Harbour, Isle of Wight" (1836): engraved by E. Finden depicting Brading Harbour. Chapter twenty artwork.

"HMS Amelia Chasing the French Frigate Aréthuse" (1813): a painting by John Christian Schetky (1778–1874) depicting Amelia pursuing the French frigate Aréthuse. She was a 38 gun Hébé class frigate of the French Navy launched in 1785. Sister ship, Vénus, served in Martinique during the American War of Independence. From 1785 to 1788, she undertook a scientific expedition in the Indian Ocean, under Captain de Rossily. She was recorded as wrecked in a storm on her way back to France, on 31 December 1788. Chapter twenty-one artwork.

"La Manche ou le Canal, entre la France et l'Angleterre" (1692): a map of *"The English Channel or Canal, between France and England"* by Alexis-Hubert Jaillot (1632-1712), one of the most important French cartographers of the seventeenth century. Chapter twenty-two artwork.

"Action between H.M.S. Leander of 50 Guns & 282 Men and the French National Ship Le Genereux 74 Guns, 936 Men August 18th 1798. The Leander raking Le Genereux": by Charles Henry Seaforth (1801–1872) depicting action between Leander and Le Genereux, Leander raking Le Genereux. Généreux, a Téméraire-class 74-gun ship

of the line, was the sister ship to Pompee. Chapter twenty-two artwork.

"Espoir and Liguria" (1798): by Nicholas Pocock (1740–1821) depicting the English brig of war, Espoir, engaged with a much larger corvette, Liguria. Published by Bunney & Gold, 1 November 1801. Chapter twenty-three artwork.

"HMS Queen Charlotte anchored in Cadiz Bay" (1790): a painting by Thomas Buttersworth (1768–1842) depicting her at anchor with smaller ships about. She was a 100 gun first-rate ship of the line of the Royal Navy, launched on 15 April 1790 at Chatham. Chapter twenty-four artwork.

"Prison Ship at Deptford" (1826): by Samuel Prout (1783–1852), engraved by George Cooke, published by Longman, Arch & Cooke, depicting a prison hulk in Deptford, Kent. Epilogue artwork.

www.historiumpress.com

Printed in the USA
CPSIA information can be obtained
at www.ICGtesting.com
CBHW031134010924
13775CB00034B/292

9 781962 465564